JULIA JUSTISS

REGENCY
Sisters Of
Scandal

MILLS & BOON

REGENCY SISTERS OF SCANDAL © 2024 by Harlequin Books S.A.

The publisher acknowledges the copyright holders of the individual works as follows:
A MOST UNSUITABLE MATCH
© 2018 by Janet Justiss   First Published 2018
Philippine Copyright 2018   Second Australian Paperback Edition 2024
Australian Copyright 2018   ISBN 978 1 038 91797 3
New Zealand Copyright 2018

THE EARL'S INCONVENIENT WIFE
© 2019 by Janet Justiss   First Published 2019
Philippine Copyright 2019   Second Australian Paperback Edition 2024
Australian Copyright 2019   ISBN 978 1 038 91797 3
New Zealand Copyright 2019

Published by
Harlequin Mills & Boon
An imprint of Harlequin Enterprises (Australia) Pty Limited
(ABN 47 001 180 918), a subsidiary of HarperCollins
Publishers Australia Pty Limited
(ABN 36 009 913 517)
Level 19, 201 Elizabeth Street
SYDNEY NSW 2000 AUSTRALIA

MIX
Paper | Supporting
responsible forestry
FSC
www.fsc.org   FSC® C001695

Printed and bound in Australia by McPherson's Printing Group

CONTENTS

Visit the Author Profile page
at millsandboon.com.au for more titles.

A Most Unsuitable Match

Julia Justiss wrote her first ideas for Nancy Drew stories in her third-grade notebook and has been writing ever since. After publishing poetry in college, she turned to novels. Her Regency historicals have won or placed in contests by the Romance Writers of America, *RT Book Reviews*, National Readers' Choice and Daphne du Maurier. She lives with her husband in Texas. For news and contests, visit juliajustiss.com.

Author Note

Nothing in modern experience can help us fully appreciate how important having an unsullied reputation was for an unmarried Regency lady. Readers of Jane Austen may remember the despair felt by Lizzie in *Pride and Prejudice* after her sister Lydia runs away with Wickham. If a daughter shows herself immoral, society will believe the others in her family must be also.

Prudence Lattimar finds herself in a similar situation. Known as the child of one of her mother's lovers, Pru is considered disreputable before she even takes a step into society. All she wants is to marry a kind man who will settle with her in the countryside and give her the "normal" family she has always craved.

When a fresh scandal makes a debut in London impossible, Pru is taken to Bath. But not only does scandal follow her—the one man she meets who values her for herself is a reckless adventurer intending only a short stay in England.

Lieutenant Johnnie Trethwell finds Prudence to be the most unusual—and beautiful—girl he's met in his many travels, and her unfair treatment by society rouses his fighting spirit. However, friendship with an adventurer won't help her redeem her reputation—and he knows he can't give Pru the settled English home and family she craves.

But sometimes, falling in love makes you realize that what you truly need is completely different from what you thought you wanted.

I hope you'll enjoy Pru and Johnnie's journey!

To Eve and Lenora

Words aren't adequate to express my gratitude
for your love and support since the accident—
especially when finding time to write becomes so
difficult. Every time I've been about to give up in
despair, you've pulled me back from the edge.
I love you guys!

Prologue

London—late March 1833

'She's done it again,' Gregory Lattimar, oldest son and heir of Lord Vraux, said as he ushered his twin sisters, Temperance and Prudence, into the small salon of their Brook Street town house, where their aunt, Lady Stoneway, awaited them.

The vague foreboding she'd felt when her brother pulled Pru from happy contemplation of the latest fashions in *Godfrey's Lady's Magazine* intensified into outright alarm. 'What's happened, Gregory? Whatever it is, surely we won't have to delay our Season yet again!'

That pronouncement was met with a groan from her aunt, who came over to give Prudence a hug. 'I'm so sorry, my dear! I thought for sure we'd be able to launch you girls this spring!'

'So it's no Season for us, eh?' Temperance asked, crossing her arms as she regarded her brother grimly. 'What's the latest event to besmirch our reputations?'

'Your brother heard about it over breakfast at the Club and summoned me for a strategy session straight away.'

'A strategy session about *what*?' Temperance cried.

'Easy, Temper,' Gregory said, putting a hand on her arm. 'I'm about to tell you.'

Though, as usual, she suppressed the emotions her more volatile twin was expressing, Pru could hardly refrain from raising her own voice. 'What happened, Gregory?'

'Farnham. Well, not being officially out, you won't have met him, but he's recently down from Oxford and followed the usual convention of appearing enamoured of our mother. He and another young admirer, Lord Hallsworthy, have been snarling at each other around her like two dogs over a choice bone. Apparently last night, with both of them well in their cups, Farnham claimed Hallsworthy had insulted Mama's virtue and challenged him to a duel. Which Hallsworthy accepted, the two of them dispensing with the usual protocol and going off at once to Hounslow Heath.'

'At night?' Temperance said incredulously. 'Besides, I thought duelling was illegal—and out of fashion.'

'There was a full moon and it is,' Gregory said. 'I don't know what got into them. The upshot was, before anyone realised what was going on, Farnham put a ball into Hallsworthy. The friends who caught up with them took Hallsworthy to a surgeon, but he isn't doing well. Farnham has fled to the Continent and, by now, the news of the duel, and over whom it was fought, is all over London.'

'Well, I say "bravo, Mama!" if she's still bewitching young men at her age,' Temperance said defiantly.

'If she only would consider how much her actions reflect upon us!' Pru cried, beset by the familiar mix of admiration and resentment for her dazzling mother.

'To be fair, it's not her fault, Pru,' Aunt Gussie said. 'Paying court to London's longest-reigning Beauty has been a rite of passage for young men coming down from university since the Season your mama debuted. You know she does nothing to encourage them. Quite the opposite.'

'Which only intensifies their rivalry,' Gregory observed with a sigh.

'Mama *has* been trying to shield us, Pru,' Temperance added. 'Though she's certainly had offers, she hasn't taken any new lovers these last five years.' At her aunt's gasp, she snapped, 'Oh, please, Aunt Gussie, there are no innocent maidens *here*. Not after what we've seen going on in this house.'

Though her sister didn't blush, Pru felt her own cheeks heat at the reminder. They'd barely been out of leading strings when, even relegated to the nursery, they'd started noticing the parade of handsome men paying calls on their mother. They were hardly in their teens when they'd pieced together the whispers among the staff and come to understand exactly why.

'The Vraux Miscellany,' society called them. Knowing that only Gregory was truly the son of her legal father, while her brother Christopher and she and Temperance were acknowledged to be the offspring of other men.

Keenly as she felt this latest scandal, which might well delay once again her chance to find the love and family she yearned for, fairness compelled her to agree with her sister. 'I know Mama has been trying to live less…flamboyantly, just as she promised us. For all the good that's done,' she added bleakly.

'It's not her fault society conveniently forgives a *man* the errors of his past—but never a woman,' Temperance retorted.

'I haven't always agreed with her…wandering tendencies,' Aunt Gussie admitted, 'but married to my brother, I could certainly sympathise. He'd already begun to show passion only for the beautiful objects he collected before I made my come-out. I remember one morning in the breakfast room, I tripped over his latest acquisition, some sort of ceremonial sword. He rushed over when I cried out—it gave me a nasty cut! And completely ignored *me*, all his concern for whether the *sword* had been damaged!'

'If only he hadn't chosen *Mama* to add to his collections,' Temperance muttered.

'Well, that's past lamenting,' Gregory said briskly. 'We need to decide what we shall do now, which is why I asked Aunt Gussie to join us. Do you think the hubbub will die down soon enough for the girls to have their Season this year?'

Aunt Gussie shook her head. 'I received two notes from acquaintances before I'd even arisen from bed this morning, wanting to know what was truth, what rumour. With the Season beginning in just two weeks, Hallsworthy so badly injured he may hover on the cusp between life and death for some time, and Farnworth having quit England, it's likely to remain the *on dit* for months.'

'We could just brazen it out,' Temperance said. 'Really, Aunt Gussie, do you truly think we will ever escape being tainted by Mama's reputation? Since we are her blonde, blue-eyed images, we must naturally possess the same reckless, passionate character. As far as society is concerned, we're the "Scandal Sisters", and always will be.'

'I know it's unfair, child,' Aunt Augusta said, patting Temperance's arm. 'I understand your bitterness, but there's no need—yet—to give up on the goal of seeing both of you well settled—eventually. It's what your mama desires, as much as I do! Not this Season, alas. But soon.'

'That's what you've been saying for the last four years,' Pru said, trying to stave off her desolation over this new delay. 'First, you ended up having to assist at your daughter's lying-in the year we turned eighteen, then you were ill yourself the next year, then Aunt Sophia died, and last year, Christopher married Ellie. An absolute darling, whom I love dearly, but trying to overcome the infamy of your mother's reputation right after your brother marries a notorious former courtesan is clearly impossible. If we have to wait much longer, we will be too old for *any* man to wish to marry us!'

'You should rather pity the girls who did debut and marry,' Temperance told her flippantly. 'Stuck home now with a husband to please and a babe on the way.'

'Perhaps *you* would!' Prudence flung back, raw disappointment goading her out of her customary restraint. 'But having a husband who cares for me and a normal household filled with our children is all *I've* ever wished for.'

Looking contrite, Temperance gave her a hug. 'No female under Heaven is sweeter, lovelier or more deserving of a happy family. I'm sorry for speaking slightingly of your hopes. Forgive me?'

Feeling guilty—for she knew if she didn't keep such a tight control over herself, her reactions might be just as explosive as her sister's, Prudence said gruffly, 'I'm no angel. I know you were teasing. Forgive *me*, for being so tetchy.'

'If squelching the rumours is impossible, what should we do, Aunt Gussie?' Gregory asked.

'I think it would be best if I took the girls out of London for a while.'

'Not to Entremer!' Temperance cried. 'With nothing but

empty moors and coal mines for miles, I'd expire of boredom in a month!'

'I should know, I was raised there,' Aunt Gussie said with a shudder. 'No, I propose taking you somewhere much more pleasant. Granted, with the Season beginning, it will be thinner of company than I'd like, but my dear friend Helena lauds its excellent shopping and the lending libraries. There will be subscription dances and musicales, as well as the activities around the Pump Room—'

'You mean *Bath*?' Temperance interrupted, looking aghast. 'Activities, yes—like assisting septuagenarians to sip the vile waters! That's almost as bad as Northumberland!'

'The city may not be as fashionable as it once was, but anything would be better than rusticating in the country,' Gregory pointed out.

'It's not as large a stage as London, to be sure. But for a lady more interested in a congenial partner than in snagging wealth and a title, it might do. At the very least, you girls would be able to mingle in society and perhaps meet some amiable gentlemen, without whispers of this affair following you everywhere. You'll gain some town bronze and if you find no one to your liking, there's still next year in London.'

'Sounds like an excellent idea,' Gregory said. 'And one that seems more likely to get my spinster sisters off my hands than inviting the censure of the *ton* this Season, as our intemperate Temper proposes.'

'But most of the *ton* hostesses know we were supposed to be presented this year,' Temperance argued. 'I don't want them to think I'm a coward—or that I'm ashamed of Mama! It's not *her* bad behaviour that precipitated this.'

'Do you want to make it *worse* for your mother?' Aunt Gussie asked sharply. 'Then, by all means, confront society and aggravate a scandal not of her making into such infamy that you can never be respectably settled!'

When Temperance looked away, her defiant words subsiding in a dull flush, she continued more gently, 'Your mama would be the first to urge you to be prudent.'

'Dear Aunt Gussie, always offering sound counsel to keep me from doing something rash,' Temperance said with a laugh, her anger disappearing as quickly as it had arisen. 'Very well, I may not attempt to breach the hostile walls of the *ton* this Season. But neither do I intend to languish in Bath. I'll stay in London—*discreetly* showing my support for Mama. Since I have no intention of ever marrying, what difference does it make to me? In the interim, if I promise to send him any treasures I uncover, perhaps I can persuade Papa to release some of the blunt he's put away for the dowry I won't need and let me go adventuring in Europe.'

'But you, darling Sis,' she said, turning back to Prudence, '*should* go to Bath. And I hope with all my heart you will find there what you are seeking.'

'You are adamant about remaining in London?' Aunt Gussie asked Temperance.

'Much as I will miss Pru, yes, I am.'

'I'd prefer if you could get Temper out of my hair, too, until this fracas dies down,' Gregory said to Aunt Gussie, ignoring the face Temperance made at him. 'But if you can at least take Prudence out of harm's way, I'll appreciate it. So the two of you will pack up and leave for Bath as soon as possible?'

'We will. And hope to find her that agreeable gentleman,' Lady Stoneway said, with a fond look at Pru.

The very possibility helping her crushed hopes revive, Prudence said, 'That would be wonderful!'

'Be careful what you wish for, dear Sis,' Temperance warned.

With the family conference ended and their aunt returning to her own home, Prudence and Temperance walked arm in arm back up to their chamber. 'Are you sure I can't coax you to come with us? We've never been apart! I shall feel so lost without you,' Pru said, the reality of being without her twin beginning to sink in with dismaying clarity.

She soothed herself with the thought that, painful as their parting would be, at the end of a sojourn in Bath might be new love and support—from a husband. And unlike the twin, who despite her protests to the contrary, must some day marry and leave her, *he* would love and support her for ever.

'I shall miss your cautious voice warning me against taking some impulsive and usually rash action,' Temper was saying, smiling at her. 'I do think it's a good idea for Aunt Gussie to take you away, though. Leave London, where, after this latest contretemps, we're bound to be pointed out and stared at wherever we go.'

Prudence groaned, the truth of that statement bringing a surge of the resentment and prickly discomfort she always felt when going out into public view. 'Thank you for the reminder. I shall avoid the modiste and finish obtaining any necessary gowns in Bath. It was bad enough last week.'

Temperance laughed caustically. 'Ah, yes, last week, at Madame Emilie's. When that whey-faced little heiress kept staring at us?'

'Very subtle, wasn't she?' Pru said, sarcasm lacing her

voice. 'She could hardly wait for us to disappear behind the curtains for our fitting before asking in a horrified "whisper" that could be heard by every shopper in the establishment, "so *those* are the Scandal Sisters"!'

'If I hadn't been clad only in my chemise at that moment, I would have popped out, bowed like an opera dancer taking an encore and cried, *"Voila, c'est nous!"*'

'Whereas I would rather have left by the back door.'

'Only to sneak into the chit's bedchamber that night and strangle her in her sleep?' Temper suggested with a grin.

Pru laughed. 'The notion does appeal. Oh, Temper, I wish I could face it with humour, like you do. But it just *grates* on me like nails on a slate and all I want is to be *rid* of it! The scandal, the notoriety, the whispers behind the hands whenever we walk into a room. Oh, to become Mrs Somebody Else, wife of a well-respected man and resident of some small estate far, far from London! Where I can stroll through a nearby village whose residents have never heard of "the Scandal Sisters", able to hold my head high and be talked about only for my…my lovely babies and my garden!'

'With a husband who dotes on you, who never tires of hugging you and kissing you and cuddling you on his knee…instead of a father who barely tolerates a handshake.'

Both girls sighed, wordlessly sharing the same bitter memory of years of trying and failing to win the affection of a man who preferred keeping them—and, to be fair, everyone else, including his wife—at a distance. Though Temper persisted in approaching Papa, Pru had given up the attempt.

'I don't expect to find the kind of radiant joy Christopher has with his Ellie,' Pru said softly. 'All I long for is a quiet gentleman who has affection for me, as a woman and his wife, not a...a relic of infamy and scandal. Who wants to create a family that treats each member with tenderness.'

'A family like we've never had,' Temper said wryly.

That observation needing no response, Pru continued, 'To a man like that, I could give all my love and devotion.'

'Then he would be the luckiest man in England!' Opening the chamber door, she waved Pru into the room. 'I shall pray that you discover in Bath the eminently respectable country gentlemen you long for. That he'll ask you to marry him, settle on his remote estate and give you a flock of beautiful children for me to spoil. Now, we'd better look through your wardrobe and see how many more gowns you'll need to commission in Bath so you can dazzle this paragon.'

Chapter One

Three weeks later, Lieutenant Lord John Trethwell, youngest son of the late Marquess of Barkley and recently returned from the 2nd (Queen's Royal) Regiment of Foot in India, limped beside his great-aunt, Lady Woodlings, down a path in Bath's Sidney Gardens. 'Ah,' he said after drawing in a deep breath, 'Bath in the spring!'

'It *is* lovely,' his aunt said as he helped her to a seat on a convenient bench. 'Though it doesn't offer quite the fleshly amusements a jaded adventurer like you might prefer,' she added, punctuating her reproof with a whack of her cane against his knee.

Surprised into a grunt, he rubbed the affected leg. 'How unsporting, to strike an injured man.'

For a moment, his aunt looked concerned. 'I didn't mean to—'

'Just teasing, Aunt Pen,' he reassured her. 'No harm done. But you malign me, assuming I mock the beauty of April in Bath. After blistering tropical heat, and jungle fevers, and pursuit by hostile natives, it is a soothing balm to return to the cool, tranquil beauty of England.'

His aunt studied his face, probably searching for the lines of pain he tried to conceal. '*Are* you recovering, Johnnie? You still have that dashed limp.'

'I'll be rid of it in good time,' he replied, hoping he spoke the truth.

'As you're going to be rid of the army? You know I hope to coax you into remaining in England, don't you?'

Johnnie shrugged, ignoring her last comment to reply, 'I'm done with the army, for sure. After seven years, I've had enough of restrictive rules not to my liking and kow-towing to some jumped-up Cit whose father paid to have him made a Company official.'

'Jumped-up Cits, eh?' His aunt chuckled. 'Blood will tell and yours is the bluest! Much as you've tried to distance yourself from your family! Not that I blame you. Idiots, most of them.'

'I never set out to distance myself,' he corrected, grinning. 'But with all his building projects, trying to make Barkley's Hundred the equal of Blenheim, Papa had virtually bankrupted the estate even before Robert inherited. With dowries for the girls—'

'And the profligate habits of your other three brothers.'

'There was left little enough for the youngest son. I didn't want to be a further drain on Robert's slender resources—then or now. Once I leave the army, I must have another way to earn my bread.'

'You know the best way to do it.'

'You'd have me to find a rich woman to marry. '

'Marrying a rich woman has been the alternative of choice for well-born but indigent younger sons for centuries—and a much safer alternative than trekking off to barter for treasure in foreign lands, as you propose to do! You might not possess a title, but your breeding can't be faulted.'

'The breeding you just disparaged?' he pointed out.

'Nothing wrong with the blood,' she flashed back. 'Just with several recent possessors of it.'

Declining to point out the lack of logic in that statement, he said, 'I happen to believe setting up a trading operation is a better route to wealth than sacrificing myself on the altar of some India nabob hoping to marry his daughter into the aristocracy. Or confirming the whispers already swirling around Bath that I'm a fortune hunter, intent on seducing a rich lady of quality. The "parson's mousetrap", they call marriage. Whereas I'd describe being tied to just one woman as more like...fitting myself for a garrotte,' he teased.

'A garrotte, indeed!' she scolded, whacking him on the arm. 'Those who disparage marrying money never seem to object when someone in their own family manages it. Since you claim to be unable to tolerate wedding an heiress, I suppose you think if you dance attendance on *me*, I'll leave you *my* fortune to invest in that trading empire?' she asked tartly.

Johnnie merely chuckled. 'If I were totty-headed enough to entertain that hope, I'd better be prepared to wait a long time! I expect you'll outlive us all. Besides, I would think your own sons stood in line before me in that regard.'

'They inherited wealth enough from Woodlings not to need mine.'

'Your grandchildren, then.'

'Both *my* boys had sense enough to marry girls with large dowries. Their brats won't need my money either.'

'In any event, I visit you—as you well know—because

you're the most interesting relative I possess. You may leave that fortune to your dog, for all I care.'

'Hmmph!' his aunt said, looking pleased at his response. 'It would serve you right if I left it to some improving school for the instruction of indigent girls.'

As she spoke, the periphery of his gaze caught on a flutter of movement. Turning in that direction, he realised what he'd seen was the ripple of pale fabric against the green verge beyond the path.

Two ladies walked towards them down the central alley. He'd just begun to turn back towards his aunt when his gaze, scanning lazily upwards, landed on the faces of the ladies and stopped dead.

A bolt of pure physical attraction immobilised him, spiking his pulse, suspending breath. He'd bedazzled dark-eyed *maharanis*, beguiled matrons famed as the Diamond of their cantonment, but he didn't think he'd ever beheld a woman more breathtakingly beautiful than the one now approaching them.

Realising, if the walkers continued straight ahead rather than taking the nearby cross-path, they would soon draw too near for him to make any discreet enquiries, he bent to whisper in his aunt's ear. 'Good L—Heavens, Aunt! Who is that divine creature?'

Lady Woodlings peered down the path before straightening with a snort. 'Precisely the sort of female you need to avoid!'

Surprised by her vehemence, he gave the girl another quick glance. 'Avoid—why? I know fashions have changed since I've been away, but she doesn't look like a high flyer to me.'

'She might as well be,' Lady Woodlings retorted scornfully.

'Aunt Pen, I'm only a simple male,' Johnnie said with some exasperation. 'A clearer explanation, please.'

Sadly for a body eager to have the seductive Beauty pass more closely, but fortunately for his compulsion to find out more about her, the lady and her older companion did in fact turn on to the cross-path and proceed away from him. In partial compensation, though, he was able to stare openly at her enticingly rounded figure as she glided away, the gold curls beneath her elaborate bonnet shining brightly in the afternoon sunshine.

'Very well, Aunt Pen,' he said, once he was sure they were out of earshot. 'Who is she and why must I avoid her?'

'One of the Scandal Sisters. The twin daughters of infamous Lady Vraux.'

No more enlightened by that information, he said, 'Meaning, she was embroiled in some scandal in London? Remember, Aunt, I left university straight for the army and haven't been near the city in years.'

With considerable relish, his aunt launched into the tale of a beautiful but immoral, high-born lady who, after presenting her long-suffering husband with a son and heir, proceeded to scandalise the *ton* by blatantly flouting her many lovers, one of whom sired her second son, another giving her twin daughters. 'Why the devil Lord Vraux allowed her to name the chits Prudence and Temperance, I can't imagine! As if transgressing moral boundaries weren't enough—she must mock them, too.'

'So the daughter has shown herself as profligate as her mother?' he probed.

'Not yet. She's not even out, officially, though she must be approaching the age where most young ladies would be at their last prayers! The *on dit* was the girls were to be presented in London this Season—but then, a few weeks ago, two imbeciles just down from Oxford fought a duel over their mother. Of course, a presentation in the face of that would have been impossible. I'm surprised her aunt— that was her father's sister, Lady Stoneway, walking with her—dares to let the creature show her face, even in Bath! Though one must pity the poor woman, trying to find husbands for such a pair. It won't be easy, their fat dowries notwithstanding!'

'But you know nothing to the detriment of the daughter?'

'How could I, when she's not out yet?'

'Precisely my point, Aunt,' Johnnie said drily.

'Never you mind, she'll embroil herself in some scandal soon enough. As I've been saying, blood will tell. And you may get that look out of your eye, Johnnie Trethwell!'

'What look, Aunt?'

'The look of a hound who's just scented a fox! Why is it that, whenever one tries to warn some rascal with more energy than sense to steer clear of danger, he's immediately compelled to charge after it?'

'Probably because he's a rascal,' Johnnie replied with a grin. 'Come along now, Aunt Pen. Introduce me.'

His aunt drew back, a horrified expression on her face. 'I will never! I know I've been urging you to marry an heiress, but the poor looby who marries *that* girl? He may be able to spend her money, but he'll never stop worrying over who he'll find in her bed.'

'A pity. I shall have to contrive some other way to make her acquaintance.'

'Mark my words, John Stewart William Trethwell,' his aunt said indignantly. 'Take up with that creature and you'll never see a penny of *my* money!'

Johnnie leaned down to kiss his aunt's hand. 'There's nothing for it, then,' he said as he straightened. 'You'll have to leave it to the dog.'

With a hint of a limp, he set off down the pathway, determined to wangle an introduction to the divine Miss Lattimar.

Keeping a discreet distance, he trailed the young lady and her aunt as they left the gardens and proceeded towards the Pump Room. Once there, he was able to station himself across the room from her, where he could observe her without his scrutiny being obvious.

Her beauty certainly did not pale upon closer examination. Eyes of the deepest cerulean blue set in an oval face graced with flawless porcelain skin, full, apricot lips, those glorious golden curls and a figure that approached the voluptuous... He'd never seen a lady so breathtaking. But having seen—and possessed—a great number of ladies, as he observed her behaviour, his scepticism about the validity of his great-aunt's claims about her character increased.

It wasn't just the ethereal beauty of her face, which brought to mind the image of angels singing in heavenly chorus. There was a sweet gentleness and deference in her manner towards the lady who'd been identified as her aunt—and a wary caution when they were approached by anyone else. The blush that tinged her cheeks and the slight stiffness in her manner when a gentleman stopped to greet them—even the old retired soldiers there to take the waters—was so at variance to the sort of flagrantly seductive behaviour of which her mother was accused, he couldn't believe she was cut from the same cloth.

Unless she were the best actress in the history of the English stage, he concluded that she was exactly what she appeared to be: a beautiful, well-bred, pretty-behaved virgin.

Not, to be frank, the type of female with whom he had previously had any desire to further an acquaintance. But something about the unfairness of having this woman, who in his observation was exactly the lady she purported to be, accused and convicted virtually sight unseen of being a wanton, even by someone normally as non-judgemental as his great-aunt, roused his fighting spirit. And when a crony of his aunt's, one of the old *beldames* who ruled Bath society, gave her an obvious snub when her chaperon attempted to call the lady over, he found himself on his feet before he knew what he intended.

Limping quickly over, he seized the *beldame's* hand before she could walk away. 'Lady Arbuthnot, what a pleasure to see you again and looking so fine!' he said, bowing. 'That's a charming bonnet!'

Pinking with pleasure, the lady replied, 'I'd heard you were visiting Lady Woodlings, Lieutenant Trethwell! Welcome back to England. What a relief it must be to be home again! I do hope you are making a good recovery from your injury.'

'How could I not, back in the salubrious climate and genteel company of my home country? Speaking of that—' Leaving a hand on her arm, he subtly steered her around. 'Would you do the honour of introducing me to these charming ladies?'

Too late, the woman realised that Johnnie had manoeuvred her into facing the women she'd just attempted to cut. The charm of the smile he fixed on her at odds with the tension in his gut, he waited to see whether the embarrassment of making a scene by refusing his request would outweigh her righteous indignation at having to acknowledge a girl of whom she disapproved.

Deciding to throw his last weapon into the fray, he said *sotto voce*, 'If you could do so at once, ma'am? Standing's not good for my bad leg.'

Apparently, that was enough to tip the balance. 'I suppose I can't refuse the request of one of his Majesty's brave soldiers,' she said with ill grace. 'Lady Stoneway, a pleasure to see you in Bath. May I present to you Lieutenant Lord John Trethwell, the great-nephew of my good friend Lady Woodlings and brother to the new Marquess of Barkley?'

The Beauty was even more beautiful at close range, Johnnie thought, everything masculine in him leaping to the alert. Though *she* stood serenely unmoved while the introductions were made, the flush on Lady Stoneway's cheek and that lady's tremulous smile showed at least her aunt recognised the significance of his intervention. 'Delighted to make the acquaintance of one of our brave soldiers, Lady Arbuthnot,' she replied. 'As is my niece, Miss Lattimar. Aren't you, my dear?'

He'd thought her shy, but the Beauty who dipped him a graceful curtsy was quietly self-contained, he thought, rather than nervous or uncertain. 'Almost past her last prayers,' his aunt had described her. Though a female possessing such youthful beauty could never be considered a spinster, she was no blushing ingénue, even if she hadn't been formally presented. And small wonder she was self-possessed, if ever since she'd budded into womanhood, she'd been facing down innuendo that equated her to her infamous mother.

'A pleasure to meet you, Lieutenant.'

Her voice was as lovely as her face. He'd intended only

to force Lady Arbuthnot to recognise her and then remove
himself—not having, despite his aunt's urging, any interest in trying to entice a wealthy young female to wed him.
But he found he simply couldn't walk away.

Instead, he held out his hand. 'With your permission,
Lady Stoneway, may I make a turn about the room with
your niece?' And before her chaperon had a chance to reply,
he clapped a hand on Miss Lattimar's arm and bore her off.

Chapter Two

Not sure whether to be amused or indignant, Prudence obliquely studied her escort from the corner of her eye as she walked beside him. 'Was that an introduction, or a kidnapping?'

'You really couldn't refuse to stroll with me. Not after the signal service I just performed.'

He had her there. Truly, she wasn't sure what to make of him.

The image of a pirate had flashed through her mind when she'd first observed him in Sidney Gardens, leaning his tall, raw-boned frame down to murmur in his aunt's ear, dark golden hair curling over the collar of his regimentals. And the gaze he'd given her! Admiration and interest shining in grey-green eyes with a look so penetrating, it seemed he was trying to see right into her soul.

She felt another stir of…something, in the pit of her stomach, just recalling it.

Viewed up close, his lean, tanned face was even more

compelling, with its high cheekbones, thin, blunt mouth, purposeful nose and arresting eyes. His regimentals hung rather loosely on him, as if he'd been ill. A fact his slight limp and Aunt Gussie had confirmed, when her aunt, alas, had steered them on to a side path back at the Sidney Gardens, warning Pru she should avoid this youngest son of a notoriously rakehell family.

Rakehell or not, he'd boldly coerced that disapproving matron into recognising her. A move that, had it failed, would have embarrassed him as much as her. Was he compassionate, clever—or just reckless, indifferent whether the gamble would work or not? Uncaring, if it failed, that he had brought humiliating and unwelcome attention to her?

But it *had* worked and would give a definite push to her campaign for acceptance.

'In fairness, I do owe you thanks,' she acknowledged at last. 'Lady Stoneway's credit and that of her friend Mrs Marsden are sufficient that most of Bath society deigns to receive me, but there have been…recalcitrants, Lady Arbuthnot chief among them.' She laughed. 'Now that you've so cleverly manoeuvred her into recognising me, I can breathe a sigh of relief. Although, ungrateful as it may seem, I'm afraid I can't afford to show my thanks by associating with you once this stroll is concluded.'

'What, have you been warned against me?' he asked with a smile. 'Didn't think I'd been in Bath long enough for that.'

'I saw you at Sidney Gardens earlier today with your aunt. I don't mean to be uncivil, but Aunt Gussie said you have the reputation of being a…a reckless adventurer. And with it presumed that you're about to leave the army, it's also said you are…' She hesitated, her own experience with rumour and innuendo making her loath to repeat further ill of him without knowing the truth.

'A fortune hunter?' he supplied, seeming not at all offended. 'Or have you heard the other version, the one in which I'm in Bath trying to turn my aunt up sweet, so she'll settle funds on me? You mustn't feel uncomfortable, repeating the rumours, Miss Lattimar. After all, I've been warned against you, too.'

She stiffened, a feeling almost of…betrayal escaping. So her scepticism had been warranted. He hadn't helped her out of kindness, just on a whim, too devil-may-care to worry about the consequences. 'I wonder then that you bothered to rescue me,' she said, unable to keep the anger from her voice.

He halted, forcing her to look up at him. 'I should think you, of all people, would understand. I dislike seeing someone branded for something only rumour alleges—me, or anyone else. A sentiment I suspect you share. I shall judge you as I find you, not for who your mother was. Everyone in Bath ought to do the same.'

So he *had* acted out of compassion. Anger faded, replaced by chagrin that such a gesture had been necessary—and that she'd initially judged him more harshly than he had her. Following on that was something else more unexpected— a deep sense of…kinship at his empathy. As if they understood each other.

She had no business feeling either chagrin or connection for a penniless soldier of dubious reputation. Calling on years of practice, she suppressed the volatile emotions before they could show on her face.

She'd be wise to escape the company of a man who had, in the space of a few moments, called up feelings strong enough to compromise the tranquil façade she must present to the world. And whose escort would do nothing to further her aim of attracting an eminently respectable man to marry.

Once she was sure her voice wouldn't tremble, she said, 'Much as I honour you for those sentiments, you must realise that with *my* reputation, I can't afford to be seen on easy terms with a man usually regarded as a careless adventurer.' She gave him a deprecating smile. 'The fortune-hunter part is less of a problem, since it's widely believed that only my large dowry would ever induce a man to risk marrying me.'

'Then he would be a very great fool.'

Surprised, she lifted her gaze back up to those grey-green eyes—and was mesmerised. Something flashed between them, some wordless connection accompanied by an attraction as fiery as it was unexpected. Her stomach swooped, her breathing grew unsteady and she could almost feel his arm burning her fingertips through the layers of her gloves and his sleeve. A sudden, inexplicable desire filled her to move closer, feel his arms around her, his lips…

With a start, she looked away, ending the fraught moment. Merciful heavens, what had come over her? *This man is even more dangerous than I thought.*

Jerking her hand free, she said, 'I had best return to my aunt.'

He caught up to her in a step. 'At least, let me walk with you. Otherwise, it will be said that you found my conversation so improper, you felt it necessary to abandon me in the middle of the Pump Room. Which will do *my* reputation no good.'

'Very well,' she said, not looking at him—and very careful not to take his arm. 'But as I already told you, I won't be able to walk with you again.'

'Do you always do what propriety dictates?' he asked.

She looked at him then. 'I haven't a choice,' she said bleakly.

'We always have a choice, Miss Lattimar. I'll say "goodbye", not "farewell",' he murmured as they reached her aunt. 'Lady Stoneway, Miss Lattimar, a pleasure,' he said more loudly, bowing as he turned her over to her chaperon.

And then left them. She couldn't help watching as, his soldier's bearing erect despite his injury, he limped away across the room.

Her aunt's fan tapping at her wrist recalled her attention. 'That was handsomely done,' she said, inclining her head towards the departing soldier. 'I hope you thanked him as you walked with him, because you mustn't do so again. It would do your chances no good for you to become more closely acquainted.' Aunt Gussie sighed. 'A shame, for he is a handsome devil, isn't he?'

'Is he a womaniser? Or is his reputation just rumour?' *As mine is.*

'His reputation is more that of an adventurer. He went out to join the army in India right after university. Not that he had much choice, with the family already done up and no source of income for him here in England. Got himself wounded in some clash with the natives. His oldest brother inherited while he was away—a mountain of debt. With three other brothers who never met a lightskirt they didn't try to seduce, a horse they wouldn't wager on, or a Captain Sharp they didn't try—and fail—to best in a game of chance, it's no wonder he stayed away. Or is considering wedding himself to a fortune, if he's decided his wandering days are done. His pedigree is elevated enough that, despite his lack of funds, he might very well accomplish that—though he hasn't thus far shown any interest in doing so.'

'Has *he* never met a lightskirt he didn't try to seduce, a horse he wouldn't wager on, or a Captain Sharp he didn't want to best?'

'Whether he's as profligate as his brothers, no one knows. As I said, he's been away from England practically since he was a schoolboy. Another rumour claims that he has no wish to marry and is hanging about Lady Woodlings's skirts instead, hoping she'll leave *her* money to him. That one may be more credible, given the tittle-tattle about him cutting a swathe through the faster matrons at the cantonments in India. There are even rumours of a Eurasian paramour—a *maharani*, if I recall correctly.'

With her upbringing, Pru was hardly scandalised. Instead, she realised ruefully, she felt a little *envious*, that a man could go anywhere in the world and do anything he wanted. While she had to watch every word she said and every action she took.

His reputation as an adventurer might make him unsuitable husband material for *her*—but it certainly enhanced his fascination.

'People love to gossip about the strange and foreign.'

Aunt Gussie chuckled. 'When they aren't gossiping about the present and familiar! In any event, I doubt he's lived as a saint—not a man adventurous enough to leave hearth and kin at such an early age with scarcely a penny to his name and make his way in a continent halfway around the world.'

What would it be like to have such adventures? Pru wondered. To boldly go wherever the whim took you, pit your wits and courage against whatever obstacles you encountered?

Something she would never discover, she thought wistfully. She'd count herself fortunate to land a respectable husband and settle in a quiet, conventional village.

Suppressing the envy as she did every other disturbing emotion, she said, 'With his birth and that handsome countenance, I doubt it would take him long to charm some susceptible lady of fortune into marrying him. Charming his aunt, I'm not so sure.'

'I'm sure of neither, despite that handsome face. He'd do better to cozen up to a rich widow. Although, with his lineage, he'd be considered a good catch by most society families, the highest sticklers might not favour having a man with an adventurer's reputation marry their daughter.' Her aunt gave her a look. 'A young lady of...*fragile* reputation should never let an adventurer approach her at all.'

'You needn't preach, Aunt Gussie. I understand my limitations quite well.' Even if she had to squelch a ridiculous little pang of loss at the idea of never speaking again to the intriguing Lieutenant Trethwell. Never being able to coax him to tell her about his adventures in lands she and Temper had only read about in travel journals and memoirs—what a Hindustani village really looked like, what it was like to hunt a tiger, what sort of jewels a *maharani* wore.

Even if her fortune interested him, she couldn't redeem her reputation by marrying a man almost as infamous as she was. Those few heated glances, that unexpected rush of attraction, were all she'd ever have of him.

What they wanted for their futures was completely different.

She tried to picture him in civilian dress in some small

country manor, talking about crops and dandling a baby on his knee, and laughed out loud.

Impossible!

As was any foolish desire for more of his company. She needed to keep her mind fixed on her goal: to marry a man with a reputation impeccable enough to rehabilitate her own, live with him and raise their children in a quiet village, creating a warm, happy family far away from the gossip and casual cruelty of society. She should lose no time scouring Bath for such a man—and then charming him into marrying her.

Feeling somehow dispirited, despite that firm conviction, she said, 'Shall we return to the Circus, Aunt Gussie?'

'Perhaps we shall. I am feeling a bit weary after all our walking.'

But as she took her aunt's arm to lead her to reclaim their cloaks, Lady Stoneway suddenly halted. 'Not quite yet, my dear! There's someone over there I should very much like you to meet.'

The tone of her aunt's voice could only mean the 'someone' was an eligible young man. A spurt of excitement pulling her from her melancholy, hoping the brisk walk in the gardens that had put roses in her cheeks hadn't disordered her curls too much, Pru clutched her aunt's arm more tightly and allowed herself to be led to the opposite side of the floor.

'Lady Wentworth, Mrs Dalwoody! How nice to see you both!'

The two ladies turned...their movement then copied by the tall man who stood beside them and Pru caught her breath.

She needed no introduction to know that this swoonworthy gentleman was as wealthy and nobly born as he was handsome. He wore his exquisitely tailored clothing with the unconscious sense of superiority found only in those with old money and important connections.

Or at least, he *appeared* wealthy. The distinguished family name, she could count on. The two society matrons her aunt had just called out would never have allowed a *nouveau-riche* Cit with social aspirations in their midst. And no man of lesser breeding would emanate such an aura of self-confidence, as if both accustomed to and taking for granted the notice he attracted.

For in truth, she realised, hers weren't the only eyes focused on him. He was the object of the interested gaze of every female in the vicinity—and most of the gentlemen.

'Lady Stoneway, I'd heard you were visiting Bath,' Lady Wentworth said warmly, giving her aunt—a friend of longstanding, Pru knew—a hug. 'With your charming niece, too!'

'Augusta, how good to see you again,' Mrs Dalwoody said. 'And, my dear, how lovely you've grown! Already budding fair to become a Beauty last time I met you, though I'm sure you don't remember. You couldn't have been more than fourteen, that summer I visited dear Augusta at Chemberton Park.'

With an amused smile, the young man cleared his throat. 'Please, ladies, in your enthusiasm for greeting one another, you've quite left me out! Won't you introduce me to these charming newcomers?'

'How impolite of me!' Lady Wentworth exclaimed. 'Lady Stoneway, Miss Lattimar, may I present Lord Halden Fitzroy-Price, youngest son of my good friend, the Duchess of Maidstone? Newly come down from university, and waiting to be appointed to an ecclesiastical post!'

He made them a bow as impeccably tailored as his coat—which was cut in the latest style, tightly nipped in at the waist with flaring tails. 'Ladies, honoured to make your acquaintance.'

The glance he gave them was politely brief—until, to Pru's gratification, it returned to linger on her. 'Miss Lattimar, Mrs Dalwoody is quite right. You are an Incomparable! Why have I not encountered you in London? I believe my friends must have been deliberately keeping you from me, to hoard this treasure for themselves!'

Pru knew her cheeks must be pinking at his gallantry, but she replied calmly, 'You must not think so slightingly of your friends, Lord Halden. I've not yet been presented in London.'

'Ah, that explains it, for I should never have forgotten so enchanting a face. Won't you stroll with me, so we might repair Fortune's lapse?'

Still a little dazed by his magnificence, at her aunt's encouraging nod, Pru placed her hand on his sleeve. 'You are newly come from university, you said. Which one?'

'Cambridge. I'm not the most downy of scholars,' he acknowledged with a deprecating glance designed to be disarming, 'but I did well enough that, as Lady Wentworth said, my cousin, the Earl of Riding, has promised me one of the livings in his gift.'

'Younger sons must make their own way,' she acknowledged, firmly yanking her thoughts away from another more scandalous and all-too-attractive younger son who'd been making his own way in the world. 'You had no taste for the army, I take it.'

He grimaced. 'With the wars ended, there'd be no way to distinguish oneself by bravery, and who would want to be posted in some colonial backwater, enduring the heat of India, or the storms and humidity of the Indies? No, I fear I'm just a solid Englishman, perfectly content to never leave these shores.'

She curbed the impulse to reply that she would love to explore beyond England's shores. And squelched the whisper of scepticism that said he was telling her what he thought she'd prefer to hear.

Why wouldn't he? He'd probably been raised from his nurse's knee to make himself agreeable in company.

Instead, she smiled and said, 'Why would a true Englishman want to be anywhere else?'

'My sentiments exactly.'

'A political career didn't interest you, either?'

He wrinkled his nose in distaste. 'Pandering to a lot of rabble in a clutch of grubby villages to win yourself a seat in Parliament? Decidedly not. And as for the government—well, a career in the diplomatic service is likely to land you at some point in the heat of India or the humidity and storms of the tropics! I'll keep my feet firmly planted in English soil. What about you? Testing your wings in the placid pool of Bath before venturing into the treacherous waters of London?'

'Something like that.' Knowing there could never be any successful union without complete honesty, she added, 'If you know anything of my...family situation, you would know that being in Bath is...more suitable now.'

He frowned and her heart sank. Rather than honestly acknowledging her circumstances, if he truly was unaware of them, had she blundered into making him suspicious that she was not as blameless a young maiden as she appeared before they'd hardly begun to get acquainted?

Then his face cleared and he smiled. 'I suppose we all have skeletons in the cupboard. Let's speak of something more pleasant. I take it from the ladies' greetings that you are only recently arrived. Has your aunt subscribed you to the balls at the Assembly Rooms? Quite refined, although of course nothing to rival London.'

'I believe she has.'

'Excellent. I shall count upon the pleasure of leading you into a dance at the next cotillion ball, then.'

The sound of boisterous voices ahead drew their attention. They both looked over to see a group of soldiers entering, one of whom, scanning the room, spotted them and gave a wave. 'Fitzroy-Price, old fellow,' he cried, leading the group over. 'Just knew there had to be someone among all these octogenarians with red blood in his veins.'

'And the prettiest girl in the room on his arm,' one of his companions observed.

'Well, don't just stand there!' the first one said. 'Introduce us!'

'I'm not sure your chaperon would thank me for making these rascals known to you,' Lord Halden said, looking uncertainly at the newcomers. But after several raised their voices, protesting his unfairness, he capitulated. 'Miss Lattimar, may I present Lieutenant Lord Chalmondy Dawson, a friend from childhood, and Lieutenants Trevor Broadmere and Austen Truro, whom I know from university. One could hardly find a more capital group of fellows—for rousting about. But how do you come to be here?'

While Dawson explained the unit containing the former college mates had set up an encampment to conduct training exercises west of the city, and had come into town in search of some jollity, Pru's eye was caught by a moving flash of scarlet as another soldier entered the Pump Room. He, too, looked around and then beckoned for a uniformed man already in the room to come join him.

Lieutenant Johnnie Trethwell.

After a short exchange, the newcomer plucked Trethwell by the sleeve and led him towards their group.

Pru drew in a sharp breath. Would Trethwell greet her by name—revealing she was already acquainted with just the sort of experienced adventurer society would assume a girl of scandalous reputation would seek out, reinforcing the image she was trying so hard to dispel?

While she waited, almost dizzy with anxiety, looking away as the two men approached, another soldier called out to the approaching men, greetings and genial insults being exchanged after the newcomers arrived. Even though she'd been deliberately ignoring him, the wave of awareness Trethwell generated when he grew near telegraphed his presence.

While she struggled with that, Trethwell's companion said, 'Lord Halden! Heard you'd landed here after bouncing out of Cambridge. *Persona non grata* with the *pater* in London now, are you?' he added with a laugh—which her escort acknowledged with a thin smile.

'Lieutenant Markingham, Miss Lattimar,' Lord Halden said. 'Always did have an acid tongue. And...' He paused, his eyes scanning the Lieutenant.

'You're not acquainted with Trethwell?' Markingham asked.

'Trethwell?' Lord Halden repeated—while the adventurer, whose amused expression, after a glance at her face, faded to a mask of politeness, stood by silently. 'Sounds familiar. Ah, yes! Isn't that the family name of the Marquess of Barkley?'

'It is,' Trethwell replied.

'Then I was at Cambridge with your brother, James. Lord Halden Fitzroy-Price,' he said, according the soldier the slightest of bows. 'You are the scapegrace youngest brother who ended up in the army, I take it?'

Did Pru see or only imagine the flicker of anger in Trethwell's eyes before his lips quirked in amusement? 'At your service,' he drawled, returning a much more elaborate bow.

'I sincerely hope not,' Lord Halden said. 'Miss Lattimar, if I may escort you back to your aunt? I fear she would consider these rowdy comrades less than suitable companions for an innocent young lady.'

Ignoring the boos and laughter his dismissive comment created, the Duke's son clasped her arm and led her off.

'Sorry to be so presumptuous, Miss Lattimar,' he said. 'Most of that group were questionable enough. But your aunt would likely chastise me soundly were she to learn that I'd had the bad judgement to introduce you to a Trethwell. With the Lieutenant's eldest brother holding so elevated a title, the family is still received, even though rumour says their estate is mortgaged to the hilt. But the younger brothers are penniless rakes to a man, with the Lieutenant reputed to be the most infamous of the lot.'

On the one hand, as a member of an infamous family herself, Pru could sympathise with the anger she glimpsed beneath Trethwell's mocking tone and exaggerated bow. She knew all too well what it was like to be tarred with the same brush for a relative's transgressions. On the other, she could hardly fault Lord Halden for trying to protect her reputation.

Would he be so concerned, once he learned about her

circumstances? Or would he conclude that she no longer deserved such consideration?

She hoped he would end up being as fair as Lieutenant Trethwell. She didn't yet know enough about Lord Halden's character to accurately judge whether or not they would suit. But if he should decide to pursue her, she couldn't fail to recognise that he didn't just fulfil, but wildly exceeded, every requirement on her list.

He wasn't only a respectable gentleman, but one of high degree, from an ancient family.

He wasn't going to pursue a career in the rough and tumble of politics, which would require residing for months in the gossip hotbed of London, or interested in the army, which would take him from home for months or years at a time. No, he, like many a younger son, appeared to be destined for the church.

Waiting to receive an appointment, probably in some charming village far removed from the stench and bustle of the capital. Where as part of his living, he'd receive a fine manor house, doubtless with a large garden and enough income from grand and lesser tithes to employ a small staff of servants and live a comfortable life.

What more effective way to polish a tarnished reputation to gleaming brightness than to become a clergyman's wife? Making rounds of the parish, calling on the sick, taking care of the lost and needy, and performing other good works?

Of course, it was a very large leap from a simple introduction and a man's far-too-common admiration for her pretty face to mutual esteem, love and marriage.

But he *had* liked her pretty face. She intended to use that attraction to lure him into getting to know her better.

A vicar's wife, respected, honoured and beloved by the

community, she thought again, a glow warming her heart. For the first time since hearing of her mother's latest scandal, Pru began to hope she might free herself from the shackles of her past after all.

Chapter Three

Two days later, Prudence Lattimar strolled with her aunt through Sidney Gardens in the pleasant morning sunshine. Though a few of the highest sticklers refused to receive her, Lady Stoneway and her friend Mrs Marsden had done their work well. By now, she'd been presented to pretty much everyone currently residing in Bath with any pretentions to gentility.

Unfortunately, her sister's dismissive remark about the calibre of the resident bachelors had been all too correct. Even Aunt Gussie had admitted herself rather disappointed at how thin on the ground eligible bachelors were, comparing the current landscape unfavourably with what the city had been like thirty years ago, when she'd been a single young miss.

'You could find almost as many eligible *partis* walking in the gardens here as you might find strolling in Hyde Park,' Aunt Gussie murmured, shaking her head as they passed yet another old gentleman being wheeled around in a chair. 'There were, to be sure, a contingent of the elderly and infirm come to drink the waters, but a large number of the Upper Ten Thousand also chose to spend the Season here! Well, we shall just have to do the best we can with what's available.'

'Speaking of which,' Pru replied, her voice lowered to a murmur, 'isn't that Lord Halden, walking with the older woman over there?'

'It is indeed!' Aunt Gussie said, her face brightening. 'That's his mother's cousin, Lady Isabelle Dudley. Keeps a house here as well as in London, generally residing at one or the other for most of the year. Apparently she doesn't much like the country, even though her husband's estate, Cliffacres, reputedly rivals Blenheim Palace. An earl's daughter who married a commoner, but one from an old and fabulously wealthy family, it's said she makes all her extended family dance to her tune.'

Pru's hopes in Lord Halden's direction took a plunge. Just what she needed—someone else who would probably dismiss her without a glance because of her mother. 'A high stickler?'

Aunt Gussie chuckled. 'No, just a tyrant. She caused her share of *on dits* in her day! A Beauty who had half the men of the *ton* dangling after her before she settled on Dudley.'

Prudence cut a covert glance towards the woman, noting the high cheekbones and tall, elegant figure that testified to how lovely Lady Isabelle must have been in her prime. She looked exactly as Aunt Gussie had described her: rich, handsome—and reigning regally over her family.

'Reformed sinners are usually more disapproving than most of those they consider to have fallen off the straight and narrow,' Pru observed.

'Perhaps. But it's also said her primary qualification when evaluating possible wives for "her boys" is fortune,' Aunt Gussie said. 'Shall we go greet them, my dear? If Lady Isabelle is determined to blight your chances with the most attractive marriage prospect currently in Bath, better to discover that early rather than late, so we may shift our focus elsewhere.'

The image of a certain tawny-haired lieutenant flashed into her head before she dismissed it. Even with Lord Halden eliminated from consideration, the globe-trekking Johnnie Trethwell wouldn't make her list of desirable prospects. Better to concentrate her efforts on the sort of respectable country gentlemen she sought.

'True enough.' Bracing herself for what might be a humiliating set-down, Pru laid her hand on her aunt's arm, summoned a smile, and prepared to brave the lion.

'Lady Isabelle, Lord Halden, good morning,' Aunt Gussie said as they caught up to the couple. After exchanging bows and curtsies, Aunt Gussie continued, 'Lady Isabelle, may I present to you my niece, Miss Prudence Lattimar?'

After her scanning her so thoroughly, Pru felt like a prize cow whose worth was being assessed by an auctioneer, the older woman gave her a nod. 'Miss Lattimar. My young cousin, Lord Halden, was just telling me how he'd met you in the Pump Room yesterday, and been charmed. Now I see why.'

Pru exhaled a shaky breath. Though Lady Isabelle most assuredly knew her history, evidently she'd passed muster anyway. Even better, Lord Halden's relation would have fully acquainted him with her circumstances. If he knew them, and still found her 'charming', the biggest obstacle to developing a relationship with him had just been hurdled.

For perhaps the first time in her life, she silently thanked her father for being such a careful curator of his vast wealth.

'You've just come from London, haven't you?' Lady Isabelle said. 'Walk with me, Lady Stoneway. You can acquaint me with all the latest happenings while these young people become better acquainted.'

That was so bald, Prudence had a hard time not blushing. The auctioneer, turning the prime merchandise over to the potential buyer. Dutifully taking the arm Lord Halden offered, she tried to settle her nerves.

Once they were a short distance down the pathway, she said, 'I hope you don't feel coerced into escorting me.'

The Duke's son laughed. 'My cousin isn't very subtle, is she? Completely accustomed to getting her own way, too, so there's little use trying to resist her. However, I don't need any coercion to walk with the most beautiful lady in Bath.'

Gratified, she smiled. 'You are very kind. I understand Lady Isabelle has a house here. Are you staying with her?'

'No. Not that she wouldn't have me,' he added. After that curious statement, he continued, 'It would be rather…restricting to live under the roof of someone bound to observe every detail of your comings and goings. A man needs a little freedom, after all.'

Prudence suppressed another pang of envy. If he considered living in his cousin's house chafing, he should try being an unmarried young woman of suspect character, whose every word and movement were scrutinised. Trying to summon up some sympathy, she said, 'Yes, a young man should be able to stay out late playing a hand of cards or finishing a fine ale, without having someone waiting on him, watching a clock.'

'Exactly!' he exclaimed, looking on her with approval.

'I'm so glad you're not one of those missish girls, who thinks I should stay at home with my cousin, holding her yarn while she knits, or something equally rubbishy.'

He stiffened when Pru, after trying to suppress a giggle, finally laughed. 'Sorry, I simply can't envision you dutifully hefting a skein of yarn! Does she knit?'

Relaxing, Lord Halden grinned. 'Heavens, I don't know. If she does, the stitches had better do what she tells them.'

Prudence shook her head. 'Alas, mine never do.'

'Not a needlewoman?'

A potential clergyman's wife would be expected to knit and sew for the unfortunate, she realised in a flash. 'I confess I'm not the most talented, but I am committed to doing better.' She bit her tongue to avoid adding, *Despite the fact that I detest needlework and would much prefer to be outside, riding or mucking about in the garden.*

'What amusements do you favour?' she asked instead, preferring to bring the focus back to him and avoid any potentially damaging questions about her other interests—or her *too* interesting, scandalous family.

'Besides drinking and cards?' he riposted, still smiling. 'I'm quite enthusiastic about horseflesh. There's nothing finer than a prime beast in full gallop, outstripping all the others on some track! Or on the hunting field. I generally spend the entire hunting season following one or another of the best hunts. Lady Isabelle rents a box at Melton Mowbray, and we get to the Belvoir as well.'

'You must be a capital rider, then.'

'Oh, yes. Sat my first pony when I was only three. Evaluate and purchase all my own mounts, too. Wouldn't leave so important a task to some groom!'

'Have you acquired any new horses lately?'

That simple question was enough to set him off on an enthusiastic recital of the merits and fine points of the perfectly matched pair of blacks he'd just purchased for his new high-perch phaeton, several hunters he was currently training for the upcoming season, and the flashy, high-stepping chestnut he kept for riding in Hyde Park.

Her contributions to the conversation limited to an occasional 'Oh, my!' or 'How excellent!' they'd made almost a complete circuit of the main pathway before he paused for breath.

'I dare say, it's capital to discover a young lady who appreciates horseflesh,' he said at last, giving her hand a hearty squeeze.

Before she could think of an appropriate response that wouldn't set him off again, the group of soldiers they'd seen in the Pump Room the day she met him rounded a corner.

'Lord Halden, well met!' Lieutenant Lord Chalmondy cried. 'And Miss Lattimar. How lovely you look.'

After giving Pru an inspection that lingered on her bosom so long she felt her face colouring, he murmured to his companions, 'What a hot little charmer she is, eh, boys?'

A flash of anger deepened the heat. Evidently Lord Chalmondy thought that, in the open air of the park, surrounded by his companions, he could get away with a crude remark he would never have chanced having overheard within the proper confines of the Pump Room.

Either not hearing or not realising how insulting the comment was, Lord Halden said, 'With this pack of half-wits about you, no wonder you were looking for some clever company.'

Lord Chalmondy laughed. 'There is that. But there's also some capital sport going on this afternoon.' He lowered his voice, although not so low that he wasn't perfectly aware she could still hear him. 'A cockfight down at the Mare's Tail and then a sparring match between the local champion and a man from Liverpool. Supposedly he used to work the looms in some factory. A regular bruiser! Should be a prime dust-up.'

'No gentleman with red blood still running in his veins would want to miss it,' Lieutenant Broadmere said.

'Sounds like just the thing for you soldiers to while away a dull afternoon,' Lord Halden said.

'Zounds, man, we're on our way now. Why not come with us?' Lord Chalmondy gave Pru another leering glance. 'You'll have all evening to charm the ladies. Or do you feel you may need a glass of Pump Room water to make it through the day?'

Lord Halden hesitated, obviously drawn by the prospect of sport—and unwilling to be thought less virile than his former university mates. 'Very well,' he conceded after a moment. 'Just let me escort this lady back to her aunt.'

There was a snigger and Pru was certain she heard one of them mutter 'lady?' in a contemptuous undertone.

Giving her another appraising glance that said exactly what he thought about her character, Lord Chalmondy said, 'Good heavens, it's mid-morning in a public park. I think Miss Lattimar is clever enough to find her way back without your help. Aren't you, Miss Lattimar?'

Resisting the strong urge to slap the mocking smile off his face, Pru hesitated. No gentleman, having received permission to take a young lady for a stroll, would go off to do something else until he'd returned her safely to her chaperon. Lord Chalmondy was making it quite clear that, though her fortune might have rendered her acceptable to

Lord Halden's cousin, this duke's son did not consider her deserving of being treated as a gently born maiden should be.

He was obviously fully aware of her reputation, and would treat her—at least where there was no one from society to reprove him—as one of the Scandal Sisters.

Furious, but determined not to let it show, she said, 'Clever enough to need no further encouragement to quit the company of *gentlemen* such as yourself.'

'Excellent,' Lord Chalmondy replied, appearing not at all disturbed by her thinly veiled rebuke. 'You see, Lord Halden, the lady has released you.'

'You are sure you don't mind, Miss Lattimar? I'll see you somewhere later, then. You'll tender my farewells to your aunt and Lady Isabelle, yes?'

At her curt nod, he dropped her arm, left her there on the pathway and set off with the soldiers.

Fuming…and humiliated, for a few long minutes, Prudence simply stood, watching them lope down the path and out of the park, their loud laughter and jesting trailing after them. Lord Halden never gave her a backward glance.

Still angry, worried her debut in Bath might turn out to be as disastrous as a foray in London would have proved, with dragging steps, Prudence turned around and set off to find her aunt.

Meanwhile, Johnnie Trethwell was limping through his second circuit of the paths at Sidney Gardens. He'd been happy to drop his aunt off to visit one of her cronies rather than have her accompany him, which allowed him to walk at a faster pace. Pushing himself and his knee to the limits of its endurance was the only way he was going to regain its full strength—no matter how much he was going to regret that determination come evening, when it would likely pain him in earnest.

He'd just turned the corner of the outer pathway when he spied Miss Lattimar, walking alone a dozen yards in front of him.

Johnnie halted, stifling his immediate impulse to go to her. He'd felt only too keenly the anxiety on her face in the Pump Room when Markingham had pulled him into the group of soldiers conversing with her and her evident escort, Lord Halden. Not that he'd been insulted by her obvious reluctance to have the Duke's son know they were acquainted. Though his attentions had been keenly sought the world over by bored matrons with more lust than morals—an arrangement that suited him perfectly well—he was only too aware that keeping company with a man of his reputation would do nothing to help her efforts to entice a proper suitor. Not burdened as she was with *her* questionable reputation.

He remembered the bleak resignation in her eyes when she stated she had no choice but to adhere to every rule of propriety. For a lady whose extraordinary beauty would normally have given her licence to be as capricious as she chose, that was the saddest comment yet.

He should remain silent and let her go her own way.

But the pathway ahead of her was deserted. There was no one about to see or disapprove. With that treacherous fact to encourage him, he couldn't quite defeat the desire to talk with her.

Still debating, he quickened his pace, closing the distance between them. Then, as he got nearer, he noticed how dawdling her steps were, how her head drooped and her arms trailed loosely at her sides, her reticule dangling by twisted cords, unnoticed. She looked the picture of—dejection?

Concerned in spite of himself, over his bad leg's protest, Johnnie pushed harder, until he was within hailing distance. 'Miss Lattimar!' he called. 'What's this, walking alone? Has a press gang rounded up every man in Bath, or have they all gone blind?'

Under his keenly observing eye, she first stiffened, then straightened, then slowly turned towards him. Hurt and mortification in her expression, she opened her lips to speak, must have thought better of it and forced a smile instead. 'It's such a lovely morning, I thought I'd have a stroll while Aunt Gussie rested on a bench.'

He was fairly certain, according to his vaguely remembered standards of conduct for single young females, that walking alone in a respectable garden in a genteel city like Bath with her chaperon nearby wouldn't be considered precisely *fast*. But he did clearly recall his more adventurous sister being roundly scolded for leaving her maid behind on such a foray, her governess emphasising that 'a well-bred young lady never walks *anywhere* unaccompanied. Never!'

Her troubled expression revealed the same distress he'd read on her face in the Pump Room. As he stood, watching her, something flashed between them, some wordless connection, spurring in him the urge to move closer. He had the absurd wish that he could take her in his arms and somehow ease her burden.

'Is something wrong? How can I help?'

Her eyes widened with alarm before, shaking her head, she said, 'How did you know I was upset? I've worked so hard on the ability to appear serene, regardless of the circumstances!'

That response was so unexpected—and delightful—he

had to laugh. 'Well, I did come upon you from behind, when your guard was down.'

'Then you couldn't have seen my face.' Her exasperation deepened. 'Or did I give myself away when I greeted you? Please, let me know! In my circumstances, I *must* be able to control my demeanour, or the wolves truly will devour me alive.'

That truth was enough to extinguish his amusement. 'I suppose you're right. But don't worry too much. Most people see only what they expect to see. Half the time, they are too occupied with their own needs and desires to notice much of anything around them. If I'm a keener judge, it's because I've had to be. Travelling among various native groups in India, most of them hostile to one another and often to the English, one had to be a keen observer. Able to evaluate a man's stance and expression to fill in the many gaps in my comprehension of the local dialect, so I might accurately assess whether I was being invited to join a hunt—or was the object being hunted.'

As he'd hoped, that teased out a genuine smile—and he had to suck in a breath. The effect was like coming out of a dark cave into brilliant noon sunshine.

Basking in it, he said, 'May I escort you back to your aunt? Perhaps we can scandalise and confound a few disapproving matrons on the way?'

But she hadn't completely recovered, for his joking suggestion brought an immediate, alarmed widening of those enchanting blue eyes. Hastily he added, 'Excuse me, I was just funning. As you can see, the gardens are deserted. I should be able to return you safely to your aunt without endangering your reputation.'

She looked at him, the wry smile on her lovely lips making him wish she *were* as scandalous as society branded her, so he might kiss that luscious mouth, right here in the park.

While he beat back the desire, she said, 'You're right and I apologise. I've been suspicious of you at every turn, while *you've* done nothing but seek to protect me.' She sighed. 'If only my reputation were less…tarnished. I wish it were sterling enough to allow me to associate openly with the only man I've ever met, outside my own family, who hasn't judged—and dismissed—my character without meeting me or having me utter a word. How I wish we could be friends!'

Somewhat to his surprise, Johnnie had to acknowledge he shared that wish. Outside his own sisters, he had next to no experience of gently bred maidens, having left England right after university and having carefully avoided newcomers from the Fishing Fleet during his time in India.

Not that avoiding them required much effort. With the dearth of single English females in India, the ladies venturing out in search of husbands on the yearly voyages from England had no trouble finding partners. Even those with little beauty and few charms had numerous suitors, clearing the field for him to turn his attentions to the more dashing married matrons.

True, he found Prudence Lattimar's beauty arresting. He sensed a fire beneath her carefully controlled façade, no matter how stringently she was trying to mask it, that couldn't help but draw him like the proverbial moth to her flame. He had the tempting suspicion he might be just the man to coax that flame into a very satisfying conflagration.

More surprising, though, he was discovering himself equally captivated by Miss Lattimar's lack of artifice, her directness and honesty—traits he suspected were in short supply among females looking to attract a husband. Not just husband-hunters, he amended. He'd found those qualities lacking in virtually every female he'd ever known.

'I would enjoy your friendship,' he acknowledged—though what he'd do with the friendship of a woman he could neither bed nor wished to marry, he didn't know. Dismissing that qualm, he said, 'We must consider ways to make that happen. But not at this moment. Now, let us just enjoy as much conversation as we can squeeze in before I must surrender you to your aunt. So, how goes it with your Duke's son?'

She tilted her head at him. 'You truly want to know? I got the impression you didn't like him very much.'

'Just because he looked at me in my regimentals as though I were a slug that had just crawled on his shoe, before dismissing me as a nonentity? Excuse me, not just a nonentity, but scapegrace rakehell who shouldn't be allowed within speaking distance of his—or your—pristine person?'

While chuckling at his description, she shook her head. 'He did treat you badly, which was not at all well done of him.'

Johnnie shrugged. 'One can't expect wisdom or discernment from a university dandy—or a bunch of play soldiers who've never been within a musket-sound's distance of a real battle.'

'Unlike you, who are a real soldier?'

Grief and pain twisted in his gut. Fortunately, she could have no idea the cost of being a 'real' soldier, he thought before he shut down the memories and summoned a smile. 'Now you've caught me being as dismissive of them as they were of me! I admit, I have something of a distaste for Fitzroy-Price's ilk. I served under too many colonial officials whose chief qualification for the job was their papa's elevated title or connections. However, though I may have spent most of my adult life outside England, even I am not too dim to recognise that wedding the son of a duke must top even "wealthy", "young" and "charming" on every fond mama's list of the sort of husband she'd choose for her daughter.'

She nodded. 'He would be accounted a prime catch. Especially for someone like me.'

He frowned. 'Someone like you?'

'Yes. He's to receive a living from his uncle, Aunt Gussie tells me. How better to redeem my reputation, than to become the blameless wife of a clergyman?' Her enthusiasm faded a bit. 'Though I would hope he would learn not to be drawn in by rough companions and to treat all people with more respect. But he's young. His solemn role as a spiritual advisor will mature him and endow him with wisdom and compassion, I'm sure.'

With an effort, Johnnie restrained himself from rolling his eyes. In his experience, pampered, wealthy young men went on to become self-important, pompous older men, supremely confident in their superiority and disdainful of the rabble—which included most everyone else in society—beneath them.

But, as young and sheltered from the world as unmarried maidens were, Miss Lattimar had probably not yet learned that lesson. It wasn't really his place to teach her.

While he worked hard to keep from expressing his opinion, Miss Lattimar said, 'Enough of Lord Halden. Might I ask you a question?'

Primed now to expect almost anything, he immediately replied, 'Of course! Although if it deals with society, I can't promise to have the expertise to accurately answer it.'

'You absolutely have expertise about this society! I've

never seen more of the world than our estate in Northumberland, the town house in London and the little I've experienced so far of Bath. I'm so envious of the travels and the
adventures you've had! Please, can you tell me what it was
like, living in India?'

'Tell you about India?' he echoed, surprised. 'Ladies usually beg to hear about storms at sea, or pirates. Generally,
only men ask me about India.' *And then, mostly for tales
about the women.*

'I'm sure you're a marvellous storyteller. And I truly
would like to hear about your life there.'

'Very well, India. Let me see if I can pick out the bits
best suited for a maiden of your tender years.'

She giggled. 'Oh, no! I want to hear all the spicy bits,
too!'

Did she have any idea how irresistible she was? he
thought, totally charmed. 'All right, then. Let me see if I can
find bits spicy enough to titillate you without losing whatever credit I might have with your aunt for protecting you
on your walk back.'

Quickly searching through memory to select a story that
might entertain her without veering into the salacious, he
launched into a description of the grand procession in the
State of the Nawab of Surat in which troops from his regiment had participated. 'After the termination of the fast of
Ramadan, one of the holiest events in the Muslim year, the
Nawab ordered a grand parade from his durbar to the prin-
cipal mosque. A select few of us British regulars marched
after him, followed by elephants and camels carrying ket-
tle-drummers and musicians, local men on horseback, their
mounts as richly dressed as they were, and finally a state
palankeen bearing representatives of the East India Com-

pany, members of the ruling British council, the Governor of the castle and the Admiral of the Mogul's fleet, all in dress uniform. Ah, the noise of the excited crowds calling and hooting, the women ululating, the tramp of boots, hooves and elephant feet! The sound of the drums and the strange melodies of the native lutes, the scent of marigolds, incense, perfume—and dung. And clouds of dust, enveloping us and coating our mouths and uniforms.'

She laughed, her eyes shining. 'You describe it so vividly I can almost hear it—and smell it! You *are* a marvellous storyteller! My twin sister, Temperance, who has a great desire to explore foreign places, has collected all the travel journals and memoirs she can find, but hearing such episodes described by someone who actually lived them is so much more fascinating than merely reading about them. Tell me more!'

So he did, secretly delighted when she begged him to continue his tales through one more circuit around the park before he returned her to her aunt.

When they finally turned down the pathway and saw Lady Stoneway and another matron sitting on a bench, her rapt expression faded. 'I hate it that it isn't wise for me to associate with you. It was so…energising to talk about something truly interesting, rather than having to confine my remarks to innocuous observations on the weather, or monosyllabic murmurs of appreciation for whatever a gentleman is prosing on about!'

'Good heavens! Is that what you have to do to look respectable?' When she nodded, he shook his head. 'How… stifling. And how much I admire you!'

She gave him a sharp look. 'It isn't polite to mock.'

'No, I'm entirely serious! It's fortunate I have no desire

to mingle in polite society, for I probably wouldn't last half an hour before I got thrown out on my ear. I'm far too prone to ignore convention and say exactly what I think, hang the consequences.' He chuckled. 'Which, probably, is why I was never a success at school and the Army in India looked askance on me. I ask too many questions and probe into too many areas they would prefer left unexplored.'

Miss Lattimar smiled—and she really was temptation incarnate when she smiled, he thought. A soldier ought to get a medal for bravery or restraint for resisting the completely understandable urge to kiss her senseless on the spot.

'My governess was for ever warning me and Temperance against doing that,' she was saying. 'Although Temper is so much braver and bolder than I am. She *does* tell people what she thinks. Defies them about casting us in the image of our mother, too, instead of trying to deflect them and please everyone, like I do.'

'It takes self-control and admirable discipline to limit what one says. Particularly when the comment one struggles to suppress is bang on the mark. I'd say that makes *you* the one who is strong and brave.'

She looked startled, as if she'd never thought that of herself. 'How kind of you to say so! I only wish I could believe it. Much as I try to be perfectly behaved, so that society will come to believe I am *not* my mother, I must confess, sometimes I feel like giving up the effort. Abandoning prudence and caution, raising my skirts and running through Sidney Gardens shrieking, just to see the look on some censorious matron's face. Or stripping off my stockings and wading in the fountain—like Temper and I used to wade in the river at home.'

'Probably best to suppress such impulses,' he said—even

as it pained him to think she felt compelled to restrain that bright, exuberant spirit. 'I doubt they would be considered very suitable in a vicar's wife.'

He regretted the words immediately, for they extinguished the merriment on her face in an instant. 'I might be able to wade in a fountain, in the privacy of my own garden, with my children accompanying me,' she said after a moment.

'I hope you will.' Yet, he couldn't help a probably futile wish that somehow, she would avoid a fate that, to him, seemed destined to lock her for ever in a role where her natural charm and zest for life would be straitjacketed.

Just beyond speaking distance from her aunt, she stopped, as if she needed to armour herself to return to the world of rules and subterfuge. Lips parted, she gazed over at him, regret at having to part and longing on her face.

A wave of desire swept through him to carry her away from the propriety-bound world she was about to re-enter, off somewhere they could be alone. Where he might succumb to the urge to kiss her that had dogged him from the moment he saw her again.

From the widening of her eyes and the little intake of breath, he knew she felt that sensual pull as strongly as he did. And he was as helpless to resist it as a cobra hypnotised by a mongoose.

Giving him a tiny negative shake of her head, as if wordlessly acknowledging both the desire and the impossibility of indulging it, she said, 'I have to go back.'

'To the world of society and its rules.'

'Yes. But I can't tell you how much I enjoyed our walk. Maybe…maybe we *can* find a way to walk together again in future. I imagine my aunt will be fatigued and want to return home at once, so I'll say good day to you now, Lieutenant.'

He bowed. 'And to you, Miss Lattimar.'

They had nearly reached the bench on which both women sat before their approach was noticed. 'Prudence—and Lieutenant Trethwell?' Lady Stoneway said, looking both surprised and confused.

'Miss Lattimar!' the other woman exclaimed. 'Where is my cousin?'

'Lord Halden...encountered a group of friends, who pressed him to accompany him immediately on a...a mission of some importance.'

'But—he just *left* you, unaccompanied?' Lady Stoneway cried.

'Fortunately, Lieutenant Trethwell was at hand to make sure I returned safely,' Miss Lattimar said, giving him a quick, silent plea that he not contradict her slight alteration of events.

His lips tightening, he understood all too well. He'd already overheard some salacious remarks made about her by several of the soldiers joking with Fitzroy-Price that day in the Pump Room. Men who spoke of her like that would have no compulsion about insulting her by carrying off her escort and leaving her to fend for herself.

But it didn't say much for her escort that he'd agreed.

No wonder she'd been looking so dejected when he came upon her!

'Well, Lord Halden shouldn't have left me here, without proper escort back to my house!' the other matron said angrily. 'And so I shall tell him, when next I see him. Careless boy!'

Johnnie's cynicism deepened. He had no idea of the identity of the overdressed, self-important woman with Miss Lattimar's aunt, but she conducted herself just like the wives of the high-ranking men he'd known in India. Concerned only with her own consequence and well-being, sparing not a thought for the beautiful young woman her cousin had left alone, vulnerable to attack by any ruffian who might have come upon her. No matter how unlikely it was that a ruffian would be roaming about Sidney Gardens on a sunny morning.

'Shall we all walk together to engage a sedan chair, Lady Isabelle?' Lady Stoneway suggested. 'I'm sure that's what Lord Halden expected we would do.'

The matron visibly brightened. 'You are right, Lady Stoneway. Of course that's what my cousin must have thought. No need of him to keep his friends waiting, when we might escort each other.'

'Before we go, Aunt Gussie, don't you want to thank Lieutenant Trethwell for making sure I came to no harm?' Miss Lattimar said, her voice calm, but something steely in her eyes. 'And present him to Lady Isabelle?'

Lady Stoneway looked uncertain for a moment before nodding assent. 'You are quite right, Prudence. I do thank you for safeguarding my niece, Lieutenant. Lady Isabelle, may I make you acquainted with Lieutenant Lord John Trethwell? His elder brother, as you may know, is now Marquess of Barkley.'

Lady Isabelle's cool expression indicated she knew exactly who he was and, for a moment, Johnnie wondered if she were debating whether or not to give him the cut direct. Which wouldn't bother him in the slightest, except for the embarrassment it would certainly cause Lady Stoneway and Miss Lattimar.

The latter, he noted with no little amusement, despite her self-professed craven submission to society and its dictates, was staring almost defiantly at Lady Isabelle, as if daring her to refuse the introduction.

Not at all to his surprise, the older woman capitulated—barely. 'Lieutenant,' she acknowledged with the slightest incline of her head.

'Lady Isabelle,' he replied, offering a bow considerably more polite than the one he'd given Lord Halden.

'Shall we be off?' Lady Stoneway said, obviously reluctant to press her luck any further with the matron. Her aunt's kindness—and concern for Miss Lattimar's status—were the only reasons Johnnie resisted the urge to further tweak Lady Isabelle by insisting he accompany them.

'I should be going myself,' he said, with an ironic quirk of his lip. 'Good day to you all. Miss Lattimar,' he added, unable to stop himself as they turned. 'Safeguarding you was a pleasure.'

Her eyes lit up and the smile she gave him was pure enchantment. 'I very much appreciated it,' she replied, before taking her aunt's arm and walking off, Lady Isabelle beside them.

Johnnie stood and watched them until her lovely figure disappeared from view.

Reviewing his impressions after their second meeting, Johnnie found Miss Lattimar's appeal had only increased. Along with the physical attraction he would expect her beauty to evoke in any red-blooded male, he'd felt an unexpected and disturbingly powerful connection on some deeper level. Having had a glimpse of the exuberant, uninhibited character she was trying to suppress—he chuckled, envisioning her, skirts held up, wading in the Sidney Garden fountain—he felt a strong urge to prompt her to be herself, without restraint. Even though the woman she became when she did so was not just more natural, she was even more devilishly attractive.

He sighed. He very much wished he could pursue her openly—in spite of the fact that he had never previously pursued, nor had any use for, a well-bred virgin. Following that trail led to marriage, something he had always avoided. Not just because he wasn't sure, with the vast floral garden of the feminine beauty and charm the world had to offer, he'd be able to limit himself for a lifetime to plucking just one bloom.

He also knew his wanderlust nature too well and the chances that he'd ever want to stay for long in one place were slim. A good English wife would probably prefer a settled countryside home with a husband in it to look after her and any children. To offer marriage without being able to pledge that wouldn't be fair to any lady, no matter how much she attracted him.

And when he travelled, he travelled alone. He'd witnessed first-hand the agony of someone who'd lost a beloved. He might sometimes be lonely enough to wish for a heart's companion, but loneliness was an old friend, something he'd grown accustomed to enduring. Better to suffer a quiet flame than to open oneself to an all-consuming conflagration.

How unfortunate the enchanting Miss Lattimar wasn't the worldly-wise *Mrs* Lattimar! Were she a dashing widow, he would have free rein to indulge in the delightful dance of desire. Sadly, seducing and then abandoning a well-born innocent was out of the question.

To experience the charm of Miss Lattimar's intriguing personality, he was pretty sure he could settle for *friendship*—novel as the notion was of being merely a friend to a desirable woman. But if he respected her desire to change society's perception of her from a scandalous young woman to a well-behaved, conventional Beauty, he couldn't lure her into solitary rendezvous. No matter how attractive the prospect of amusing her with further tales of his exploits or exchanging philosophical observations on the world.

For the first time, he regretted spending his adulthood roaming the world, collecting the stories and lovers that made him unsuitable company for a girl trying to redeem her reputation.

Never one to dismiss a desired goal as impossible, he put aside for the moment the problem of how to become her friend without compromising that quest and shifted his focus to the next issue.

What about Lord Halden Fitzroy-Price?

He'd heard that the Duke's son—handsome, well born, and behaving like he knew it—was languishing in Bath, supported by the beneficence of his rich cousin while he awaited a desirable sinecure as a cleric.

Johnnie might not be intimately acquainted with the inside of a church, but based on his few exchanges with the man, Lord Halden appeared to be less well suited than any individual he'd recently met to become a clergyman. Unless a parish wanted as pastor of their flock a self-important, arrogant man faintly contemptuous of those he believed were beneath him.

If that were truly his character, Johnnie wouldn't want to see a lady as lovely, charming, and innocent of the ways of vice as Miss Lattimar wasting herself on him.

He stopped short, surprised at the ferocity of that feeling. Why should he feel so protective of a girl he barely knew?

He might have only met her twice, but her unique personality intrigued him. He genuinely *liked* her. Almost immediately, there had sprung up a sort of...kinship between them.

Maybe he felt so strongly because he understood all too well what it was like to be a member of a disreputable family, to be accused of the same faults and vices by people who knew nothing about one but the family name—Lord Halden's dismissive remarks recurring to irritate him again.

He had no doubt whatsoever about *his* ability to best the Duke's son and any of his toy-soldier compatriots, but a gently born female like Miss Lattimar had few weapons with which to counter their malice. The warrior in him naturally felt compelled to defend someone smaller and weaker.

For all those reasons—admiration, desire, anger on her behalf about how she was treated—he felt linked to Miss Lattimar by the same sort of bonds a soldier develops for his fellows, a loyalty that propels him to watch out for and protect others in battle, even at the risk of his own life.

Dismissing the 'why', his officer's brain shifted to the 'how', mulling over the best strategy for his next move. He had to admit, having suffered slights and insults in the past from men of Fitzroy-Price's rank and birth, the man's position as a duke's son automatically prejudiced Johnnie against him. He really ought to reserve judgement until he had observed him long enough to make a dispassionate assessment of the man's character.

After a bit more reflection, he came up with a plan. It might, he thought with a grin, astonish his aunt, but it would also accomplish both the goal of keeping an eye on Fitzroy-Price and allowing Johnnie to satisfy his pressing desire to see more of the delectable Miss Lattimar, without risk to her reputation.

After all, even his aunt would have to admit that staying near enough to make sure Miss Lattimar came to no harm would be the noble act of a selfless friend.

Chapter Four

Returning to his aunt's town house in Queen Square, Johnnie tracked down Aunt Pen in her private salon, where she was dozing, some needlework abandoned in her lap.

He paused on the threshold, his fond glance tracing over a figure that radiated confidence and independence even in sleep. Penelope Woodlings wasn't just the most interesting of his relations, she was also the one who'd been least interested in society—and the sole encourager of an energetic young boy, youngest of a large brood and left to his own devices. The happiest memories of his childhood had been created while visiting her and her reclusive scholarly husband at their rambling country estate, joining her and her two sons in collecting rocks and bugs, chasing butterflies, climbing up trees after bird nests and crawling into dens to inspect the homes of badgers and foxes.

But it didn't end with the quest. In the evenings, she sent the boys into the library to discover more about the treasures they'd uncovered. Along with finding out facts about rocks, frogs and trees, he'd stumbled across volumes of memoirs and travel journals.

Those accounts had awakened a keen interest in the world around him and a burning desire to explore it, not just England, but beyond her shores.

It had been Lady Woodlings, not his impecunious and uninterested family, who funded his Oxford education, equipped him for the army and continued to write him letters of encouragement that followed him on his adventures to India.

A wave of affection and gratitude washed over him as he watched her dozing. 'Who will care for you, if I do not?' she'd gruffly replied when he'd thanked her for taking him in after he'd dragged his lame and still fever-ridden body back from the subcontinent. In all his turbulent existence, she'd been the one rock he could count on, no matter how stormy the waves and winds of his life became.

Though she'd never been much interested in society, marrying over her family's objections an unfashionable young scholar she'd pronounced the most intelligent of her suitors, she kept abreast of its news, as she followed all the developments in the world.

So of course, she'd known about Miss Lattimar's family background. Being normally the most reasonable and least judgemental of individuals, he knew it was her desire to protect him that made her urge him to court any wealthy lady but *that* one, whose purported propensity for infidelity might break his heart if he were unwise enough to fall in love with her.

But then, Aunt Pen had no idea of the true character of the lady. He would just have to see that she discovered it.

As he cleared his throat loudly, she startled, her eyes flying open.

'Johnnie, you're back. How was your walk? You didn't push that leg too hard, now, did you?'

Probably. 'I don't think so. Did you have a good visit with your friends?'

'Just a comfortable coze with some old acquaintances from my come-out days.' She shook her head, smiling. 'Still occupying their time with society events and gossip, and trying to lure me into doing the same.'

'Maybe you should attend more society events. The Subscription Balls, for example. Some concerts and plays.' He paused. 'I'd be happy to escort you.'

Any lingering drowsiness dissipated in an instant. 'You would be willing to *escort* me? Into society, where you might meet some *eligible* ladies?'

'I did some thinking during my long walk. Perhaps it's time I took more part in respectable society. After all, it's not fair to dismiss it as a boring waste of my time when I left England before I could ever truly become involved in it.' *Though I saw enough of its copy in India to know it doesn't interest me.*

'So you no longer fear that participating will make it look like you *wish* to find a wife? Excellent!' Aunt Pen exclaimed, jumping up to give him a hug. 'I would be happy to go about more! There are some events which aren't *too* dreadful. Balls—I've always enjoyed dancing. But do you think, with your—?'

'I can manage,' he cut her off.

'Balls, then, and supper events at which dancing will follow. Concerts, if the performer is proficient. I promise, no evenings listening to some young female with more elegance than musical talent! And theatre, if the play and the company are good. I wouldn't drag you to some dreary event I wouldn't enjoy myself.'

'Thank you. So...' he paused '...could you apply for Subscription tickets. Today, perhaps?'

'Today? Even better!' Looking delighted, she said, 'You know I hope you may meet some charming, rich young lady who will persuade you to remain in England, although of course you need not do so, unless...' Her enthusiastic speech trailing off, she tilted her head, inspecting him with suspicion. 'Why this sudden anxiety to get started?'

Before he could come up with an innocuous introduction of his intent—for she was sure to balk, if he began by admitting the only reason he was doing this was to be able to encounter Prudence Lattimar—she crossed her arms over her ample bosom and looked accusingly at him.

'This is about *her*, isn't it? That Lattimar chit!'

He might have known she would be downy enough to figure it out. 'Yes,' he confessed. 'I *was* about to explain, Aunt Pen. I know what it is to be condemned on the basis of your family's reputation, before you yourself have uttered a word. Miss Lattimar has scarcely been out in society yet and I've already heard...insulting remarks made about her by gentlemen who've not even met her. Which, I admit, rouses my fighting instincts.'

While she stood, arms crossed, looking dubious, he continued, 'Come now, be fair, Aunt Pen! Shouldn't she have a chance to prove her reputation one way or another, before those who would condemn her ruin her ability to form a connection based on her true character? I'd like to be around to keep the riffraff away and let her have that chance. Since the only way I could do that without making matters worse for her would be under the watchful eye of that censorious society, I'll have to endure it—put up with the silly, petty rules and the boredom.'

'She accomplished a great deal in one little walk around the Pump Room. Aroused your sympathy *and* enlisted your support!'

Not thinking it prudent to mention their recent stroll in Sidney Gardens, he replied, 'No, you're wrong. She made no attempt to recite some sad tale to arouse my sympathy—I simply observed how others treat her. Nor did she ever ask for my support. This campaign is my idea alone and she knows nothing about it. Yet, of course.' He laughed. 'She knows being seen with me anywhere else would serve to confirm, rather than refute, the reputation she is trying to overcome. Only with your approval, and in the full glare of society, would my attempts to help her not end up doing the opposite.'

'I don't care a fig about *her* reputation!' his aunt returned with some heat. 'It's *your* future that concerns me and I'd not favour you doing anything that might end up hurting you—like tying yourself to a known wanton. Any other lady of modest reputation would be fine.'

She fixed a concerned glance on him. 'You must have some source of income and the safest way I know to do that is for you to marry one. I know I'll only be able to coax you to stay with me until your leg has recovered and I really don't want to see you go back to adventuring all over the globe. Trading for treasure! That might take you into areas even more dangerous than the Army would.'

'I am not keen on pitching myself needlessly into danger,' he admitted. 'But neither do I think I could stand to be leg-shackled to a country estate and a town house in London—however bewitching the owner.'

'Marriage doesn't necessarily mean you'd be tied down to England,' she argued. 'It's always possible you might find a girl who'd be willing to go adventuring *with* you. Adventuring which would be a great deal more comfortable if you had adequate funds to fuel the journey!'

'I hope to obtain those funds another way,' he countered. 'But finding a wife who'd go *with* me?' He shook his head dismissively—and then felt a rush of enthusiasm as the image of Miss Lattimar's beautiful face flashed into his head. Now *that* was a travelling companion who would truly excite him.

Too bad her dearest wish was to settle in some quiet English village, raising children and chickens while her husband wrote sermons.

Then again, much safer for her to remain in the peaceful English countryside, far from attack by dacoits and deadly diseases. Safer for him, not to risk finding a travelling partner who might truly capture his heart, promising desolation if he should somehow lose her.

Shaking off that disturbing thought, he said, 'You can't honestly think some sheltered *ton* miss who can hardly abide being stuck in the country, deprived of the shops and entertainments of London for several months a year, would be willing to go adventuring to some primitive hinterland?'

'Well, it's not *im*possible. I would happily have accompanied Everard on a journey to Greece and Egypt, if he'd had an urge to study the antiquities *in situ*.'

'Ah, but you are a most unusual female, Aunt Pen.'

Pinking at the compliment, she opened her lips to speak, then fell silent. His always-honest aunt couldn't refute the fact that she was probably the only female of her acquaintance who would be willing to undertake such a journey.

Before she could marshal her forces for a new attack, he said, 'Won't having me out and about at society events, keeping an eye out for Miss Lattimar, provide me a better chance of finding this rich but adventure-seeking paragon you talk about?'

'Considering you've hardly done more than accompany me to Sidney Gardens and occasionally to the Pump Room, I expect it would,' she allowed.

'Exactly. But I won't put myself to the pains of behaving through a long series of probably uninteresting events unless you will allow, if not support, my intention of talking and dancing with Miss Lattimar. It's all or nothing.'

His aunt sat for some minutes, frowning at him, her desire to bring eligible females to his attention obviously warring with her goal of preventing his further association with the dangerous Miss Lattimar.

As he'd expected, the inducement of having him meet someone more acceptable won out. 'Very well. You may present me to her and I will endeavour to be polite. However, if she displays the slightest sign that she might be embroiling you in a scandal, I'll carry you off to Woodhaven myself!'

Chuckling, he leaned over to kiss her forehead. 'We've a bargain, then?'

'We have. Off with you, now. I need to write notes to some friends who said they'll be holding entertainments, so they know to send us both an invitation.'

Johnnie groaned. 'Evenings of cards and conversation?'

'You'll have your lovely Miss Lattimar to console you,' his aunt said tartly.

'A consolation which I intend to fully *embrace!*' he said, laughing as he walked out at the reproving finger she shook at him.

Several days later, Prudence stood beside her aunt in the ballroom, having just been returned to her chaperon by the elderly gallant who had squired her through a country dance.

'One has to admire General Gaulford's vigour,' Lady Stoneway said.

'Yes, though I did worry he might have a seizure of the heart during some of the livelier movements.' Pru sighed. 'And he's becoming rather difficult to discourage.'

'Having a coterie of admirers about you isn't a bad thing. I just wish more of them were *younger* and eligible.'

Pru laughed. 'I can't make up my mind whether it would be preferable to marry a septuagenarian and spend my days caring for an invalid, or remain a spinster.'

'I hope it won't come to that, my dear,' Aunt Gussie replied. 'Although, sadly, the number of single gentlemen currently in Bath who are both "young" and "eligible" is disappointingly slim.'

Prudence's thoughts immediately flew to one who was young and *in*eligible...for her, at least. Oh, to be a rich widow, who might make a friend of whichever gentleman she chose! A friend, or *more*.

A wave of delicious sensation rippled through her at the thought of taking Johnnie Trethwell as her lover. Despite growing up in a household tinged with scandal, she had virtually no experience with passion. Mama might have been profligate in taking lovers, but her dalliances had always been discreet. Though they'd overheard stories and read about lovemaking—Papa's library contained a copy of Ovid they'd pored over, titillated—neither Pru nor Temper had ever witnessed so much as the exchange of a kiss.

Still, she knew instinctively that what she felt around Johnnie was sensual. That tingle of her nerves, the melting feeling in her belly and the heat and warmth below... It was probably well that she had to watch her behaviour so closely, for if she were able to do what she truly wished, she would be scheming ways to get him alone and have her first taste of kissing—in Johnnie Trethwell's arms.

'Now, there's a gentleman I hadn't expected to see!' Aunt Gussie exclaimed.

Jolted out of her naughty reflections, Pru found her attention immediately drawn to a tall, thin man wearing his scarlet regimentals with flair, several women gathered around him. A shock of recognition and pleasure zinged through her even before he turned, caught her watching him and gave her a little wink.

'Johnnie Trethwell,' Pru murmured. 'I wonder what he is doing here?'

'Lady Woodlings must have finally persuaded him to come out in society. Perhaps he *is* on the hunt for that rich widow. Or perhaps just staying in her good graces by accompanying her to the entertainments she enjoys.'

'He's not having any trouble finding feminine company,' Pru said, irked more than she would have liked by the evident admiration of the two ladies now conversing with him.

And looking thoroughly charmed.

Why shouldn't they be? She knew only too well how beguiling he was.

A little imp of envy came and sat on her shoulder. If Lieutenant Trethwell were going to appear at respectable gatherings, why hadn't he come over to beguile *her*?

'One would expect a rake to be irresistible,' Aunt Gussie observed. 'Though it is good strategy on Lady Woodlings's part to bring him here. If Trethwell can behave himself long enough to win the approval of the matrons who rule Bath society, he'll expand his opportunities to marry into the wealth he needs. Rather than just the willing widows he can encounter elsewhere, he'll be introduced to respectable maiden heiresses, too. I do wish him luck!'

Surprised, Pru looked over at his aunt. 'You do? I thought you warned me against him.'

'So I did, with good reason. While you try to overcome the rumours, it still wouldn't be wise for *you* to associate too much with him. But his kindness in keeping you company in Sidney Gardens the other day says a good deal about his character. He could easily have pressed his attentions on you, were he as profligate as he's been painted. Instead, he protected you—without any attempt to take advantage.'

'More's the pity,' Pru muttered.

'Prudence!' her aunt exclaimed—and then chuckled. 'He is devilishly attractive, isn't he? No wonder he has the ladies fluttering about him like bees around some exotic flower.'

'Bees around an exotic flower?' a low masculine voice repeated. 'That exotic flower would have to be you, Miss Lattimar. How beautiful you look this evening. And you, too, Lady Stoneway.'

Pulled from contemplating the tawny hair creeping over the collar of Johnnie Trethwell's regimentals—while imagining what it might feel like to be wrapped in his arms—Pru turned to see Lord Halden Fitzroy-Price bowing to her and Aunt Gussie.

Conscious of a little pang of…disappointment, she curtsied. 'Lord Halden. You are looking very fine yourself tonight.'

'Can I beg you ladies to accompany me to take some refreshment? That was quite a lively country dance, Miss Lattimar. I'm sure some punch would be welcome.'

'Very kind of you, sir,' Aunt Gussie said. 'I don't care for any myself, but please do escort my niece. I've just seen an old friend I'd like a word with.'

Lord Halden held out his arm. 'You'll do me the honour, Miss Lattimar?'

Surprisingly reluctant, Pru took his immaculate sleeve. Perhaps she was still angrier than she'd thought about his choosing his friends over her at Sidney Gardens.

'I am glad your aunt saw a friend, for I am mortified enough about my behaviour without having another witness to my chagrin,' Fitzroy-Price said as he walked her towards the refreshment room. 'I must apologise for leaving you stranded in Sidney Gardens after our walk the other day, Miss Lattimar. It was thoughtless and careless of me and I most sincerely beg your pardon. You may be sure my cousin roundly abused me for that inexcusable lapse in courtesy.'

His tone held just the right blend of penitence and boyish charm. Heartfelt—or practised? Pru wondered. And how much of that regret was due to the peal Lady Isabelle had evidently rung over him—not, Pru would wager, for abandoning *her*, but for leaving his cousin without a male escort?

'You hesitate so long, I fear you are not going to forgive me,' Lord Halden said.

Though she was finding it more difficult than she'd originally imagined to fit him into the mould of what she wanted in a husband, he was still her best prospect. He'd made a mistake and apologised for it. Wasn't that what she would want an honest man of character to do?

Summoning up a smile, she said, 'Of course I forgive you, Lord Halden. We all get carried away on occasion by the...exuberance of our acquaintances.'

'We do, don't we?' he replied, looking encouraged. 'How delightful to find you understanding, as well as beautiful.'

Ignoring the little voice that noted his acquaintances were insulting as well as exuberant, she pressed on. 'You must be looking forward with great anticipation to beginning a career as inspiring as the ministry. While you were preparing at Cambridge, which of your studies did you find most engaging? '

He gave her a self-deprecating smile. 'I'm afraid, as I already confessed, I wasn't much of a scholar.'

Hopefully he at least knows his Bible, Pru thought. 'The living is in the gift of the Earl of Riding, you said. Where is it located? Is the countryside suitable for hunting? I imagine you would very much like to continue one of your favourite pursuits.'

'It's in Hampshire. I haven't yet visited there, so I don't know much about the location. But your suggestion is an excellent one! I must discover the nearest hunt of repute. If it's not too distant, I might be able to stable horses there.'

At what expense? Pru wondered. *And how diligent would you be, leaving your parish for days at a time to gallop over the fields?*

'But so pretty a lady couldn't be concerned about the mundane details of a country living. Especially not while in a town as charming as Bath. Have you visited many of the sights yet? Surely you'll indulge in some shopping in Milsom Street. The shops are quite superior. After a stroll, one can take tea, or sample some of the famous Sally Lunn cakes at the bakery. You must let me escort you! Then, a drive along Lansdown Hill towards the racetrack is quite refreshing. If I may say so, my team is well matched and beautifully paced. Riding in a high-perch phaeton might appear a bit frightening at first to a lady, but I've such an experienced hand at the ribbons, you need not worry. You must promise to ride out with me, the next fine day we have.'

He certainly was trying hard to redeem himself—though whether from the charms of her person, or his cousin's exhortation that he should redouble his efforts to secure the largest dowry in Bath, she wasn't sure.

'Tea, Miss Lattimar?'

'Yes, thank you, Lord Halden.'

'Where would you prefer to be, then, if not in Bath?' she asked after taking a sip.

'Oh, in London, of course! One could never be bored there! So many sights to visit, the coffee houses and clubs, boxing and fencing and driving in the parks, and then the evenings! Balls, musicales, concerts, the opera, the theatre! Are you fond of the theatre, Miss Lattimar?'

'I confess I have not been much yet. My sister and I used to put on impromptu theatricals for our brothers, so I look forward to seeing more of it. Though I understand, many of those attending are more interested in visiting with friends and commenting on other attendees than watching the play.'

'Well, naturally,' he said, evidently finding ignoring the efforts of the actors on the stage perfectly understandable. 'Always fascinating to see who is attending and with whom. Never a dull moment in London! Nor any danger of being reduced to taking a solitary ramble along some country pathway in search of amusement. Always interesting company about, ready to accompany a man to some frolic or other.'

'Like a sparring match, a cockfight or some late-night cards at a gaming hell?'

Smiling, he shook a finger. 'No talk of that around a lady!'

You may not talk about it...you'll just go off and do it, she thought. His enthusiasm about the metropolis paradoxically dampening her spirits, she said, 'The lending libraries are excellent. Do you like Hatchard's?'

'I seem to recollect picking up a package for my sisters,' he said, shaking his head. 'Not bookish, myself, you'll remember.'

'So you told me.' Somewhat desperately trying another tack, she said, 'There's prime horseflesh to be found at Tattersall's, if my brothers can be believed. I'm very fond of horses myself. I'd love to view the offerings there.'

'Oh, no, that would not do at all, Miss Lattimar!' he said, looking appalled. 'You must know Tattersall's is a *man*'s domain, no ladies permitted.' He softened the stricture with a smile. 'Nor would a lady choose to be present. There are not just gentleman in attendance, but coachmen and grooms as well, with their vulgar talk and coarse ways. Not at all suitable for one of refined sensibilities. Ladies keep their own company during the day, with calls and visiting.'

And shredding reputations over their tea. How difficult it was going to be for someone like her, who would never fit the mould of a society lady, to survive a Season and accomplish her goal! 'No, we females must confine our excursions to shopping for gowns, bonnets, gloves and reticules,' she said with asperity.

'Such a wonderful variety to be found in London,' he agreed, oblivious to her ironic tone. 'Everything in the height of fashion, which one can't always guarantee about establishments outside the metropolis, even here in Bath. I quite enjoy escorting Lady Isabelle to her favourite shops. The haberdashers, bootmakers and tailors do exceptional work, too.'

'As evidenced by the elegance of your attire, Lord Halden.'

'One does one's possible,' he said modestly, flicking a speck of dust off his otherwise immaculate coat sleeve.

At least he wasn't a coxcomb, she thought. He took care with his appearance, but hadn't seized upon her opening to launch off into a monologue about sartorial splendour and how he achieved it—unlike one or two others among the few young men who'd squired her through dances at the last parties she'd attended.

'Perhaps we might ride together some time. I understand the area you mentioned, up Lansdown Hill, offers lovely vistas, while the open down land beyond allows for long, uninterrupted gallops, if one rides early enough.'

'I imagine you ride delightfully. But not early, surely! When one of the points of riding in a public place, rather than someone's private estate, must be to let others admire the handsomeness of your mount and the proficiency with which you control him.'

No, the point is to have a rousing gallop. Realising it was no more politic to express that view than it had been to admit a desire to visit Tattersall's, she stifled the remark.

By this time, they'd finished their tea. Talking of London all the way, Fitzroy-Price returned her to her aunt, Pru promising him a waltz later when Lady Isabelle arrived and bore him off.

To Lady Stoneway's enquiring glance, Prudence gave a sigh. 'I'm beginning to think General Gaulford might be a better option after all.'

'Truly?' Aunt Gussie said, immediately concerned. 'Surely he didn't say or do anything—'

'No, no, he was perfectly proper.' *And with his enthusiasm for London and society, perfectly—dull.* Pushing away that discouraging reflection, Pru said, 'It's just he seems... much more enthusiastic about living in London than in taking up the duties of a country cleric.'

'You mustn't fault him too much, my dear,' Aunt Gussie said. 'Most young gentlemen would prefer to be in town, where there are always friends to see and things to do. I'm sure he'll...settle into his responsibilities quite well. As one grows older, those shiny amusements lose their sparkle.'

That observation cheered her...a little. 'He is a capital horseman, so we can share that enthusiasm. Surely after he discovers the enjoyment offered by riding and driving through the exceptional vistas only the countryside can offer, he will become more enamoured of it.'

'I'm sure he shall. What could be more entertaining for a man than chasing *you* about some meadow on that great black beast you prefer?'

'I'd probably have to let him catch me, though.'

'Yes, you probably would,' Aunt Gussie allowed. 'Few gentleman can tolerate being bested by a lady.'

'At least I'll be in the country while I'm doing it,' she observed, trying to put the most encouraging shine on it.

Aunt Gussie patted her hand. 'You've always loved the countryside, haven't you, my dear? Even that vast stone pile in Northumberland that the rest of us find so dreary!'

'His living will be in Hampshire, he said. That's a lovely

county, isn't it? Rolling hills and meadows, fine woods and quaint villages?'

'So the guidebooks say. I've never visited myself.'

Another of Pru's elderly courtiers arrived then to carry her off for the next quadrille, ending the conversation. As she went through the figures of the dance, Prudence tried to find some encouraging bits in Lord Halden's conversation.

Of course, he was young and would be enthusiastic about indulging in a young man's usual fascination with gambling, dicing, racing…and women? With the expectation that maturity and repetition would diminish the attraction of shallow pursuits, she thought she could tolerate the former.

She wasn't so sure about the latter.

Though aristocratic women since time immemorial had learned to look the other way about a husband's dalliances, with observation of her parents' arrangement to scar her, she didn't know how well she could tolerate having her spouse spending time with another woman. To say nothing of the fact that such behaviour would be highly inappropriate in a clergyman.

Not that she had any real hope of finding the absolute, all-consuming love her brother had discovered with his Ellie.

Christopher was a man. He could marry whomever he chose, even a former courtesan, and still be received by his family and friends, if not by larger society.

Though she wasn't prepared to accept just anyone who wooed her with an eye to her fat dowry, with her restricted prospects, she'd settle for mutual esteem with a kind man who had a settled occupation. Lord Halden's attentiveness to his aunt argued that he was kind—if occasionally thoughtless, she allowed, the incident at Sidney Gardens still grating. They did share a love of horses, surely an enjoyment they could pursue together. And a clergyman's wife took an active part in the business of the parish. Assisting her husband with his tasks and responsibilities would bring them closer.

The greatest point in his favour, though, was that of all the men who had thus far paid her particular notice, he was the only one whose future included an occupation more likely than any other to mould a man into a more perceptive and compassionate individual. And to allow his wife, in turn, to become known as a model of gentility, modesty and virtue.

Despite her misgivings, she wouldn't give up on Lord Halden—yet.

As the evening transpired, he squired her for the waltz she'd promised—and then another. The marked attention he showed her confirmed her impression that he'd decided to court her in earnest.

She ought to be thrilled.

Even if being with him had none of the ease and excitement she felt when walking with Johnnie Trethwell.

But then, how could it? With a rake who wasn't a serious marital prospect, she didn't have to watch everything she said and did, lest some inappropriate observation escape—like that bit about wanting to attend an auction at Tattersall's. And, as Aunt Gussie observed, one would expect a rake to be amusing and full of interesting banter—how else could he attract enough ladies to be considered a rake?

Lieutenant Trethwell certainly hadn't had any difficulty attracting ladies tonight. She couldn't help noticing as she changed partners and chatted with other gentlemen that he'd been surrounded the entire evening by a bevy of laughing, admiring females.

Not that she blamed them. He alone, among all the un-attached younger gentlemen, possessed an air of being completely at ease in his own skin, radiating a calm self-confidence that said this man could handle whatever might happen with aplomb and, yes, a certain swagger. The dashing regimentals didn't hurt either.

He'd even managed to get that old dragon Lady Arbuthnot laughing.

She should be happy that his aunt's campaign—if such it was—to lure him into entering society was working. She tried not to feel bereft and envious that he'd made the rounds of so many other ladies but neglected to approach her.

He was keeping his distance to protect her. It was an act of kindness, she told herself. She should appreciate it.

Maybe, but she didn't have to like it.

So, later in the evening, when she walked back at the end of a dance on the arm of yet another retired gentleman to discover Johnnie Trethwell conversing with her aunt, her heart leapt.

The shiver along Pru's nerves increased and her stomach did a full swoop when he took her hand. 'Miss Lattimar, may I have this dance?'

'I—I'm afraid the next set has already formed,' she stuttered, unable to rip her gaze from that handsome face and those arresting hazel eyes.

'A pity. You'll walk with me, then? With Lady Stoneway's permission, of course.'

Scarcely waiting for her aunt's nod, he took her nerveless hand and bore her off.

Chapter Five

As Johnnie led her away, Prudence felt both fully energised and truly relaxed for the first time in that long evening. It was more than just being freed of the burden of keeping constant watch over her speech and behaviour—being with him seemed to heighten all her senses. The candlelight reflected more brightly off the mirrors, the chandeliers, the ladies' jewels. The music sounded more lively and tuneful, the room seemed warmer and more fragrant with the pleasantly mingled scents of wax, perfume and savouries from the tea room.

The compelling aura of confidence, the sheer *maleness* emanated by the man on whose arm she walked made her feel giddy.

For once, she'd not even try to suppress that alarming reaction. For the next few moments, she'd simply enjoy being with him.

'I must admit, I'm surprised to see you, Lieutenant Trethwell.'

'Surprised? How could you be? We traded glances hours ago, the moment I first entered the ballroom.'

'No, I meant surprised—' At the twinkle in his eyes, she broke off. 'You're teasing me,' she accused.

'Guilty,' he admitted. 'But that confused look is so delightful, Miss Lattimar. How can any man resist trying to provoke it?'

'Wretch,' she reproved, letting herself be charmed. 'As you know very well, I meant "surprised to see you at this gathering".'

He grimaced. 'Aunt Pen, trying to enlarge my acquaintance. She believes, if I only spend some time in it, I will discover that I actually enjoy participating in society.'

She couldn't help smiling. 'So...are you enjoying it?'

'Gad, no! The evening has seemed interminable, waiting and waiting until I could approach you.'

'Waiting? Why, waiting?' she asked. 'Or are you just trying to "confuse" me again?'

'Not this time. First, you see, I had to make the rounds of all the dragons. Ply them with just the right blend of flattery and respectful attention, so they might come to believe that the wild beast they've heard about can be tamed into a polite society lapdog.'

She laughed outright at the image. 'Sounds dreadful!'

'Not really, aside from the fact that it took too much time to visit them all. Making a lady feel attractive and appreciated, regardless of her age and degree of beauty, is a worthwhile endeavour, don't you think?'

You are a kind man, Johnnie Trethwell. 'I never thought of it that way, but I suppose you're right. Most men only flatter a woman when they want something.'

'Well, I'm not a complete altruist. I did need to charm

them into approving me before I dared approach you. You should commend me for endurance and patience, as well as caution, for beginning the process of gilding my reputation just so I might stroll with you without endangering yours.'

She was about to accuse him of teasing her again, until a swift procession of images made her stop. Recalling all the ladies—mostly older, married ones—with whom he'd danced or spoken, she realised he *had* approached every influential matron present at the ball tonight.

Surprise, delight—and gratitude—warmed her. 'You truly have been watching out for me.'

'Of course. After that...episode in Sidney Gardens, I wanted to make sure you get your chance.'

With other men...not with him. Banishing that poignant truth, she said, 'Then I must humbly thank you.'

'As you'll recall, we were both hoping to find a way to spend time together without inviting the censure of society. So, behold me, storming the barricades of the Subscription Room, battering down the walls of disapproval surrounding you so I may claim the prize of true friendship.'

Yes, friends. At least she could hold on to that. 'Like a true medieval knight.'

He chuckled. 'Or something. So, how are you finding your partners tonight?'

She shook her head ruefully. 'Mostly ancient.'

'True, though General Gaulford and Captain McQuery were very attentive, they were a bit...full in years. Mr Pleasance Wellington-Foxe, too, although I understand he's quite rich.'

'He would have to be, to support all those expensive sons. Most of whom are older than I am.'

'There does seem to be an unfortunate dearth of younger

men.' He paused, then added casually, 'I haven't seen any other gentlemen in regimentals—Dawson, Broadmere, Truro or their group.'

'No,' she said shortly, having to quell a flare of anger as she recalled the sniggers, the insultingly disrespectful gazes they'd raked her with in Sidney Gardens. 'I imagine this entertainment is far too tame to tempt them.'

'Fitzroy-Price seemed to find it to his liking.'

She looked up and stared at him. 'You *have* been watching me all evening!'

He shrugged. 'Of course. I told you, being able to meet you was the only reason I came here. I admit, I'd much rather we meet in Sidney Gardens for a stroll, exchanging opinions and views on the world in quiet and privacy, but intimate walks alone would undo all the good work you're been doing, attempting to shore up your reputation. If that means accepting the chafing confines of a ballroom and having to spin a lot of moonshine to soften up a bunch of starched-up old dragons too full of their own power, I'm prepared to do it.'

His exceptional kindness—and his championship of her—brought a burn of tears to her eyes. 'I… I don't know what to say.'

For a moment, he simply gazed at her. She stared up, lost, the world narrowing to encompass only the warm sympathy in his grey-green eyes, the mesmerising spotlight of his close attention. Something tingled in the air, arcing between them, making her catch her breath, setting all those simmering nerves aflame. Oh, how she wished she might kiss him!

Then he grinned, dispelling the sensual hold. 'Take advantage of our limited opportunity and say something interesting. Even after spending a full fifteen minutes soothing the Arbuthnot, who initially cut up stiff over that forced introduction in the Pump Room, I can't risk appearing to find you *too* fascinating. I feel like there's a mantel clock ticking in my head. You love horses, you said? Tell me about your horses.'

And so as they walked, Pru found herself telling him about her first pony. How she and Temper had come to cuffs over which one would get to sneak into the stables at Entremer, the family's Northumberland estate, to steal Papa's favourite hunter for a forbidden dawn gallop. How riding made even being in London, where, not having yet been officially presented, she could hardly go anywhere or do anything, tolerable.

'There's nothing like the rhythm of being in the saddle to help one think, or settle down angry thoughts and restore one's perspective,' Johnnie observed.

'Exactly! Sometimes, in the city, it feels like the only place I can truly be myself.'

'Especially if you're galloping *ventre à terre*,' he guessed.

'Is there any other way to gallop?'

'Of course not. Though it is impossible to do so in Bath. One has to go out of the city to find a suitable place.'

'Perhaps I should start looking for one.' Maybe she should resume riding in the morning. Expecting a full round of social activities—and the business of beguiling a suitor—would occupy her time and, knowing she'd have to go further than the city's parks to ride, she hadn't enquired with a local livery stable for a suitable mount. But having found, with the shortage of eligible *young* gentlemen and the lingering rumours still hanging about her, that transitioning to Bath hadn't significantly improved her prospects, it might be time to look into finding a horse.

'Perhaps you should look for one. I can't tell you how much it brightened my spirits when my leg recovered enough that I could ride again. Now, I just need to get it back into marching form.'

He halted and Pru realised they'd completed a full circuit of the ballroom. 'Regrettably, I should return you to your aunt. Can't risk too long a conversation, lest we set tongues wagging about you.'

She hesitated, everything within her protesting having to part so soon. Stifling the desire to plead for more time, she said instead, 'But I will get to see you again?'

'What entertainments are you to attend this week?'

'There's a musicale given by Lady Standish, a supper and ball hosted by Lady Caston and the Cotillion Ball on Thursday.'

He nodded. 'I'll try to be there.'

'Good. Then I'll have something to look forward to,' she said, the words slipping out before she could prevent them. Realising at once she shouldn't have felt, much less admitted such a thing to him, she felt her face heat.

'As will I.' His smile and the genuine warmth of his regard took the sting out of her embarrassment. Maybe they could be…just friends.

Even though, gazing at those tempting lips, sensing the strength emanating from that lean, whipcord body, she couldn't help wanting *more*.

The following afternoon, Prudence accompanied her aunt back to the Assembly Rooms, where Lady Stoneway had engaged to meet some old friends at the Card Room.

Which was, Prudence reflected, perhaps a better venue for speaking with eligible gentlemen than the Subscription

Ball, since the lure of gambling during daytime hours enticed even the younger set to attend.

Spotting among the group the soldiers who'd insulted her at Sidney Gardens, she initially stiffened. But, under the close scrutiny of Lady Stoneway and two of her friends, Lieutenants Dawson, Broadmere and Truro offered her bows and perfectly respectable greetings.

Relaxing after having passed that hurdle, she was able to enjoy herself, cheerfully greeting the elderly gallants who came at once to pay their addresses and enjoying a light banter with two bachelors her aunt's friend presented to her, whom she'd not previously met.

The only thing to mar her enjoyment was the absence of Lieutenant Trethwell. But since her aunt had not announced her plans for today's meeting until they were on their way home from the ball, and thinking it imprudent to try to send him a note, she'd had no way of letting him know they would be here this afternoon.

As Pru was indifferent to both cards and gambling, before her aunt settled in with her friends for several hands of their favourite piquet, Lady Stoneway sent her off with one of the older gentlemen, advising her to take tea and chat with friends rather than bore herself to flinders playing badly a game she didn't enjoy.

She'd just walked back into the card room after sharing tea with the ever-gallant Sir Reginald, when, rising from one of the gaming tables at the far side of the room where the serious gamblers had gathered, she spotted Lord Halden.

Who, spying her in return, gave her a smile and immediately headed in her direction.

She told herself it was a happy chance that he'd decided to play cards today, affording her another opportunity to get to know the gentleman better and hopefully discover more interests they had in common.

'Miss Lattimar, Sir Reginald,' he cried as he reached her. Making his bow, he continued, 'I had thought to content myself only with winning a few guineas. What a delight to discover the company suddenly grown so much more charming!'

'It's good to see you, too, sir. And good to hear that your efforts were prospering.'

'Indeed. But I was in need of refreshment, which was why I had them deal me out of the next hand. Might I escort you for something?'

'Sir Reginald and I have only just returned from having tea.'

'Then you'll take a turn about the Octagon with me? Sir Reginald, having already claimed the lady for some minutes, it's only fair that you cede her now.'

Apparently realising the Duke's son was not to be denied, the older man bowed. 'Delightful to speak with you, Miss Lattimar. I shall look forward to having a dance at the ball Thursday night.'

As that gentleman walked away, Lord Halden claimed her hand, patted it on to his arm and set off with her.

'Do you often play cards here during the day?' she asked—hoping through discreet enquiry to discover just how much a gamester he was.

'Yes. Lady Isabelle enjoys a round of whist and a chat with her friends. The play is rather tame, but one can usually win a few guineas, enough to make it interesting, before the more serious gaming in the evening. Do you play?'

'I'm afraid I've never been much interested in games of chance.'

'Not interested?' he exclaimed. 'However do you pass the long winter nights? One cannot count on having every evening an entertainment worth the trouble of braving the weather.'

It wouldn't be helpful to admit she preferred to spend such evenings reading—an activity in which she already knew he had little interest. Neither could she prevaricate by stating she occupied herself doing needlework, which she detested, no matter how suitable that pastime might be for a vicar's wife. Instead, she turned the question back to him. 'Do you have any particular favourites among games of chance?'

'Piquet and whist are the usual fall-back, since most older gentlemen can be induced to play when there is no livelier competition about. But I much prefer hazard and faro. Faster paced and usually the stakes run far higher.'

'And it's more exciting to play for high stakes?'

'Of course! Even my old great-aunt gambles for chicken stakes. But ah, there's nothing like testing your skill against other masters of the game when an amount of true substance is riding on the outcome!'

Not if it were going to be her dowry that funded the truly substantive amount, Pru thought, her unease growing.

'What's this, Fitzroy-Price, you've discovered a game where "amounts of true substance" are being wagered in the middle of the day? You must let us know where!'

They turned to see Lieutenants Dawson, Broadmere and Truro approaching.

'If there is such a game, I'm sure Miss Lattimar would excuse you—again,' Lieutenant Lord Chalmondy said.

'Or perhaps she could accompany us to the hell,' Lieutenant Broadmere said with a smirk. 'Joining other…ladies of her ilk. I understand her mother often does.'

Fury and chagrin held Pru speechless. No young lady of quality would dream of setting foot in a gaming hell, which was patronised only by men—and women of the demi-monde. As these Lieutenants knew quite well. To state that truth—or attempt to defend her mother—would probably only result in more snide comments.

She was debating whether she should deliver some blighting set-down—if she could think of one—and walk away when a tingling along the back of her neck and a sense of charged energy alerted her. She knew Johnnie Trethwell was approaching, even before she looked over her shoulder to see him drawing near.

'Why would you believe Miss Lattimar would even consider visiting a gaming hell, Broadmere?' he asked in a pleasant tone at odds with the steely look in his eyes.

'Well, I…um…' the Lieutenant stuttered.

'If you know something detrimental about the young lady's character of which society should be aware, by all means, do reveal it.' Ignoring the look Pru sent him, begging him to desist, Trethwell continued, 'Do you have such information?'

Pinned like an insect to a display board by Johnnie's implacable stare, Lieutenant Broadmere mumbled, 'I have… it's nothing specific. Just…just an idle remark.'

'I would rather call it ungentlemanly, hurtful and censorious. Lady Vraux may have made a name for herself, but Miss Lattimar is not her mother, is she? In my observation, she has been everything that is gently bred and pretty behaved. She's here under the patronage of Lady Stoneway, a matron of impeccable reputation, and since her arrival has conducted herself with the utmost propriety. Has she not, Lieutenant?'

'I...suppose so.'

'Suppose—or know?' Johnnie persisted.

'I... I know that to be true,' the Lieutenant replied, by now red-faced and looking back at Johnnie with undisguised animosity.

Something about the intensity of the exchange must have telegraphed itself around the room, for the assorted groups who'd been conversing near them had at first fallen silent, then edged nearer to better overhear the unfolding drama.

While Pru stood frozen, wishing a sudden earthquake would create a convenient crevasse for her to disappear into, Johnnie said, 'Then I believe you owe the lady an apology—if you wish to continue calling yourself a gentleman.'

For a long silent moment, the two men stared at each other. Finally, Broadmere looked away. Clearing his throat, he said ungraciously, 'I beg your pardon, Miss Lattimar. My remark was...undeserved.'

Hoping her face wasn't as scarlet as the Lieutenant's, Pru gave him a tiny nod.

'We're finished here, don't you think, Broadmere?' Lieutenant Lord Chalmondy said. 'We'll look for you later, Lord Halden.' And with that, the three soldiers sauntered off.

'Nothing shows an individual to be more petty and meanspirited than indulging in unfounded, malicious gossip,' Trethwell announced. Giving a significant look to the group who stood about gawking, he added, 'Do you not agree, good people?' in an ironic tone that, had she not been so mortified, Pru might have appreciated.

Trethwell waited until the group around them had dispersed before turning back to her. 'Miss Lattimar, will you accompany me for some tea?' he asked, holding out his arm. 'I'm feeling devilish thirsty.'

Head held high—she'd take him to task later for prolonging a humiliating interlude she'd have preferred to snip off in the bud—Prudence was about to refuse when Lord Halden, tightening his grip on her arm, said in an angry undertone, 'I imagine the last thing she wants is to take tea with *you*! Whatever possessed you to make such a scene? A woman of sensibility would just have ignored Broadmere. Now you've made the incident the talk of Bath!'

'If you understand that little about human nature, Lord Halden, I wonder at your presuming to think you can guide a flock,' Johnnie replied. 'Surely you know Broadmere's nasty remark would be repeated and sniggered over regardless of how blamelessly Miss Lattimar reacted, reinforcing an image she has been at pains to dispel. Instead, society will now be tittering about how Broadmere was forced to admit his innuendo was false and agree she has conducted herself impeccably, then offer her a very public apology. However grudging.'

He was right, Prudence realised, impressed. Johnnie Trethwell was a keener student of human nature than she'd realised.

'Observers of the scene will also pass along their impressions of Miss Lattimar's response to the attack,' he was continuing. 'Not the defiant pique of an amoral Beauty who believes herself above the rules, but a true lady's distress and embarrassment. Making those who would condemn her on her mother's behalf reconsider their opinions. A far better outcome, I would argue, than having Broadmere's insulting innuendo circulate unrefuted.'

Turning to Pru, he continued, 'I'm sorry to have caused

you additional distress, Miss Lattimar. But since that reprobate's remarks were already distressing you, I thought we might as well use them to best advantage. Now, Lord Halden, if you feel my behaviour had made Miss Lattimar too much an object of speculation to be seen with, I invite you to return to your card game.'

Lord Halden paused, irresolute, obviously enough of that opinion that Pru's humiliation deepened. 'N-no,' he said at last. 'Better that she go with me.'

'Since your consequence is enough to shield hers? But wasn't enough that you were willing to defend her to those louts? I think not. Miss Lattimar?'

Trethwell held out his arm to her again. This time, Prudence didn't hesitate to take it. 'I expect I shall see you later, Lord Halden,' she said coolly and walked off with Johnnie.

Chapter Six

But instead of guiding Prudence to the tea room, Johnnie led her into the mostly deserted ballroom. Angry as he was at Broadmere for his malicious attack, he knew the object of it might be almost as furious with him for dragging out the scene. 'Now you may blister my ears with that reproof for my presumption in intervening, without half of Bath society overhearing you,' he said as he escorted her to an unoccupied bench.

'It was presumptuous!' she replied—but with much less heat than he'd anticipated. 'Do…do you really think it was wiser to make a scene, rather than just let it go?'

'I know it's easier for a man than for a lady to insist on confrontation, but in my experience, it's always a mistake to let your enemies get their punches in unopposed. If the jackals learn that they can attack with impunity, the pack becomes even more vicious. Once word of Broadmere's rout makes the rounds of the gossips, others of his ilk will think twice about attempting to circulate unsubstantiated rumour. Attack is the best defence, I've always found.'

Pru sighed. 'Temper thinks so, too. I've always tried to... avoid and evade.'

'It *is* wiser to avoid a pitched battle—when you can. But when the time comes to make a stand, best to initiate the fight on your own terms, on your own ground.'

She gave him a little smile, still looking unsettled—as well she might. He felt another stirring of rage against the cur who'd casually smeared her name.

'It did feel...satisfying to watch him squirm. To have *his* conduct held up as reprehensible, rather than my own.'

'Attack being best defence,' he repeated, smiling. 'Which is why, after I return you to your aunt, I intend to make the rounds of all the important matrons, giving them the story first-hand, while apologising that a uniformed officer of his Majesty's service would treat a gently born maiden so poorly.'

'Many of the matrons probably believe what he said. They just don't have the temerity to say it to my face.'

'Oh, those are the ones I shall talk with first. Assuring them that I knew *they* would never judge hastily based only on rumour, when their own observations show the contrary to be true. I'll also appeal to them to show extra kindness when next they meet you, as an innocent maid could not help but be cast down by having to endure such an ugly episode.'

She raised her eyebrows. 'Don't empty the butter boat completely, or they will be sure to suspect something.'

He grinned. 'Suspect me? I'm finesse personified.'

In an instant, her reproving look faded. Tears sheening her lashes, she said softly, 'Thank you. For that swift and eloquent defence. For taking the time to explain it to me afterwards. You are a true friend, Johnnie Trethwell.'

His grin faded as he gazed into those big, cerulean-blue

eyes, losing himself in their luminous beauty. As he watched her, gratitude sharpened into something else, something hot and needy that arced like a flame of pure energy from her to him, from him to her. Sucking in a breath, he felt compelled to draw closer.

'Oh, my dear, there you are!'

Lady Stoneway's voice dispelled the tension of the moment. Prudence stepped back, only then making him aware that she, too, had moved closer as she lifted her face to his.

'Yes, I'm here, Aunt Gussie,' she replied a little breathlessly. 'It was so...stifling in the Card Room, Lieutenant Trethwell escorted me here so I might have some...air.'

'After giving you a rousing defence, I hear! Whatever could that Lieutenant Broadmere have been thinking, to have tried to humiliate you so publicly? I have a mind to write to his commanding officer, asking if he's aware what sort of gentleman he's accepted into his company! Thank you, Lieutenant Trethwell, for defending my niece and sending that scapegrace off with his tail between his legs!'

Lady Stoneway halted, touched her hand to his sleeve. 'This is not the first time you've come to Prudence's rescue,' she said softly. 'We are both much in your debt.'

'Not at all, Lady Stoneway. No man with blood in his veins could stand by and let such slander be spread about a wholly blameless young lady. I only hope the story of Broadmere's comeuppance shields her from suffering such unwarranted abuse ever again.'

Lady Stoneway chuckled. 'Now that his ungentlemanly behaviour has been pointed out, the town's matrons will not be understanding. After all, if malicious gossip is going to be spread, *they* want to initiate it.' Looking at Miss Lattimar, she continued, 'I think you've had enough excitement for one afternoon, don't you, my dear? Let's engage a chair and go home.'

Turning back to Johnnie, she held out her hand. 'I'm under obligation to you, Lieutenant. If there is anything I can do to advance any cause of yours, you must be sure to call upon me. I imagine we shall see you at the ball later this week and I'll make sure Prudence saves you a dance or two. Now, come along, my dear.'

Prudence seized a moment to squeeze Johnnie's hand and murmur another 'thank you' while her aunt was making her curtsy.

'Lady Stoneway, Miss Lattimar,' Johnnie said, giving them a bow. 'I shall look forward to the ball on Thursday.'

As her aunt led her away, Prudence gave Johnnie a glance over her shoulder, full of gratitude, longing—and undisguised desire that sent a bolt of heat through him. And then she was gone, disappearing out the door of the ballroom.

His body humming in response, he had to blow out a shaky breath. Heaven forfend, she was both captivating—and provocative.

He'd just have to keep reminding himself that no matter how smoky her glances were, he absolutely could not seduce a virginal innocent.

No matter how much they might both want him to.

Late that evening, Johnnie sat at a table in the small, sparsely furnished rooms in Westgate Buildings occupied by his former army mate, Lieutenant James Markingham. Encountering the man in the Assembly Rooms after Miss Lattimar's departure, he'd been tendered an invitation to join the Lieutenant that evening for a convivial game of cards. Thinking it would be pleasant to revive a friendship that dated back to the first days of their joint service in India—and perhaps gather a bit more useful information—Johnnie had quickly accepted.

'How are you enjoying home leave?' Johnnie asked, throwing down the rest of his losing hand.

'I wish I could get as much time from the army as the Company gives its civil servants—three years, after ten years' service,' Markingham said.

'Perhaps, but you know how turbulent India is, always some nawab or prince scheming or revolting. Your regiment might get wiped out before you returned if you stayed away that long.'

'Or nearly,' Markingham agreed with a laugh. 'Needed time to recover from that fever I couldn't shake last summer, but I suppose it's best not to be gone too long.'

'You might miss out on chances for promotion, too,' Johnnie pointed out. 'As fast as India kills off officers, there are always vacancies—if you're present to claim one.'

'I just have to make sure it doesn't kill *me* off,' Markingham replied. 'Much as I was looking forward to getting away from the blasted heat, I have to admit, after years in India, last winter in Bath chilled me to the bone. But it's cheaper to put up here than in London, with almost as many entertainments available.'

'Seem to be plenty of officers about, with little to do.'

'Ah, yes, there's an encampment outside the city. Some sort of regimental exercise, supposedly, though they seem to be idle more often than they're exercising.' Markingham shrugged. 'Peacetime army in England—what do you expect? Mostly a bunch of quarrelsome younger sons sent by their families into the army to keep them from stirring up so much trouble at home.'

'Yes, you introduced me to some of them,' Johnnie said drily.

Engaged in dealing the next hand, Markingham halted. 'Tore quite a strip off one of them in the Assembly Rooms today, I heard. That's our Johnnie, always valiant in defence of a lady! But…surely you haven't an interest in *this* lady? Not at all your usual type. A noble virgin, isn't she? Whatever can you do with a female like that?'

'Nothing,' Johnnie admitted. 'And definitely not the type of feminine company I usually seek. She's refreshingly different, though, and being unfairly tainted by the reputation of her apparently infamous mother. You know me—can't stand bullies. In fact, satisfying as it was to rout Broadmere verbally, I'd really like to teach the rogue a lesson in a more tangible way. Is there a place hereabouts where the soldiers go to box? I'd love to go a round or two with him.'

'Wasn't brawling one of the reasons you didn't rise in the army as quickly as your merit should have dictated? Along with seducing too many bored officers' wives, of course.'

'If setting straight some ne'er-do-wells who tried to impose their dictatorial will on the weakest amongst us constitutes "brawling", then guilty as charged. As for the other,' he added with a grin, 'if the husbands took better care of their ladies, they would never stray.'

'Returning home at daybreak in a gin-or opium-induced haze isn't conducive to marital satisfaction,' Markingham agreed. 'Still, there was no one like you in all the regiment for gathering intelligence. Done up in your robes and turbans, with your gift for those impenetrable native tongues, you could get yourself in and out of places the rest of us wouldn't dream of trying to enter!'

Johnnie shrugged. 'One does one's possible.'

'Arguing philosophy with half-naked religious mystics in some village?' Markingham asked with a laugh.

'Those half-naked mystics—and the greybeards at the mosques—talk politics as well as philosophy, which was information the army dispatched me to gather.' *While despising me for having the skill required to gather it*, he thought.

'But then, transforming yourself into a travelling pedlar with trinkets to offer also gained you entrée where virtually no other man, Eastern or European, could have gone. I didn't envy you slogging about in your rags, but getting a close-up glimpse of beautiful dark-eyed maidens in the *zenana*? It would almost be worth going about in dust and turbans. The stories you could tell! You ought to publish your journals, like Skinner just did.'

'Not me!' Johnnie protested. 'I'm the soul of discretion.'

'More's the pity,' Markingham said. 'Say now, if you're truly serious about having a mill with Broadmere, you might try the Pheasant & Quail on the west edge of town, closest to the army encampment—the men sometimes get up impromptu matches in the yard behind the inn. Of course, just because you challenge him doesn't mean he'll accept.'

'Probably not. Men who go about insulting defenceless women are unlikely to accept a fair fight with a man who's up to their weight. More's the pity. Do you know anything more about that threesome—Broadmere, Dawson, Truro? Seemed to me too much like limping dandies to be cut out for the army.'

'It's home country service, though. Getting sent on exercises close to cities full of amusement, like Bath? Don't need to be very intrepid for duty like that.'

'Unlike us India boys, eh? Enduring heat, dust, disease, isolation and attacks.'

'Punctuated by months of boredom that can be even more lethal,' Markingham agreed. 'Except for you, of course. Whenever *you* got bored, you just threw on your native duds and went exploring.'

'Surrounded by all that was exotic and unfamiliar, how could anyone with an iota of adventure in their heart not want to explore?' Johnnie said wryly, then held up a hand. 'I know, I know. I was the odd man out there. Most of our countrymen wanted to refashion wherever they were posted into as exact a replica of dear old England as they could manage.'

'The sane ones, anyway,' Markingham retorted. 'Just surviving the hostile climate, strange food and deadly snakes, animals and insects was enough adventure for most of us.'

'What of Fitzroy-Price, who seems to be an old university mate of the soldiers? He wasn't intrepid enough even for a home service army?'

Markingham straightened. 'Ah, now that one is an entirely different breed of animal. First of all, he's a duke's son, so of course his feet don't touch the dust of the ground like us commoners. What need has he of the army?'

'Younger sons require some occupation and he seems to me a poor candidate for the clergy.'

'True. There are already too many men of the cloth who are well connected but ill suited,' Markingham replied with a shake of his head. 'Hardly surprising, when livings are often in the gift of some high-born aristocrat, who can always be counted upon to have a son or nephew or cousin in need of an income. Which is the case with Lord Halden, though I've heard that he'll only take orders if he can't turn up some other alternative.'

'A blessing to whatever parish he ends up not serving,'

Johnnie said acerbically. 'What is he hoping to do instead—marry someone with a fat dowry, like Miss Lattimar?'

'Apparently, he initially intended to try to coax his wealthy cousin, Lady Isabelle, into settling an income on him. But since that lady seems more interested in trying to marry him off so he can spend his wife's money instead, the odds currently favour him wedding Miss Lattimar.' Markingham gave a short laugh. 'After which happy event, he can chuck all this talk of becoming a clergyman, drop the chit off at the country estate she apparently longs for and return to London to live in the style—and dissipations—to which a duke's son is entitled.'

At least the man wouldn't inflict himself on some congregation, Johnnie thought. But that didn't help Miss Lattimar. 'Poor girl. She deserves better.'

Markingham shrugged. 'Better than marrying a duke's son? If you like her enough to defend her, I can see how you might wish for her to avoid that fate—at least, with Lord Halden. Most females would probably be thrilled to land a duke's son—no matter how deficient his character.'

Not this female, Johnnie thought. But how to rescue her from it? For if Lord Halden had set his mind on wooing her, and she believed him destined for the clergy...

'Are you going to play a card, or not?' Markingham's derisive tone interrupted his contemplation. 'It's not chess, you know. The next trick hardly requires that much cogitation.'

'Just strategising on how best to confound you,' Johnnie said, turning his mind back to the game.

But later, he intended to give much more careful consideration to the matter of preventing Prudence Lattimar from wedding a man he was now convinced would make her miserable.

* * *

And so, some hours and a tidy sum won later, Johnnie quietly exited from his friend's rooms and headed back to his aunt's establishment on Queen Square. While keeping a wary eye out—Westgate Buildings, located in the Lower Town, adjoined streets whose poverty, dens of vice and gaming hells meant a man needed to watch out for pickpockets and worse—he continued to mull over what was to be done about Lord Halden.

On the one hand, he despised tale-bearers. Though he trusted Markingham to disclose only what he knew from his own exchanges with the officers who had first-hand knowledge of Fitzroy-Price and his army cronies, the account was second-hand, at best. He'd prefer to hear the man admit his true intentions with his own lips. But he also knew his acquaintance with the Duke's son was neither intimate nor friendly enough that he had much hope of inducing Fitzroy-Price to disclose anything to him.

Perhaps he should just continue to stand by and keep watch. He had been able to do Miss Lattimar a signal service in the Assembly Rooms today, an act which, he thought, smiling at the recollection, seemed to have won over even her suspicious aunt, Lady Stoneway. Though Miss Lattimar was apparently still trying to persuade herself that Lord Halden could turn into the kind of marriage partner she sought, from her tone and her troubled countenance, he could tell that the evidence from her own eyes and the man's own conversation was beginning to make her doubt that fond hope. Sooner or later, she would have to realise what Johnnie already believed: that this Duke's son would make a poor clergyman and an even worse husband.

Crashing sounds and raucous laughter coming from

around the next corner pulled him from his reverie. With the expertise forged by years of creeping through dark alleys, he eased himself back into the shadows, becoming invisibly a part of the building behind him, and crept towards the hubbub.

Illumined by the lamps flanking the entry and in the hall beyond the open door, several rouged and painted bawds lounged, while the burly man who must be the bordello's bouncer was helping a dishevelled gentleman, surrounded by a bevy of guffawing, red-coated soldiers, struggle to his feet.

A gentleman he suddenly recognised as Lord Halden Fitzroy-Price.

'Knew Sadie worked you too hard for you to get another rise,' one of the soldiers called.

'Too weak from your exertions for some dicing at The Golden Fleece?' another asked.

Shaking his head—a motion that momentarily threatened to overcome his shaky balance—Fitzroy-Price said, 'Never. Mebbe have a go at th' bones 'n' come back 'n' visit you ladies ag'n?' Looking over at the laughing bawds, he gave them a salute that sent him lurching sideways.

The soldier Johnnie recognised as Dawson caught and righted him. 'Have to sober up first, or you'll not be able to perform again.'

'Nonsense. Always ready to perform,' the Duke's son said, giving his nether regions a salacious rub. 'Aren't I, ladies?'

'You're a right randy one,' replied the taller tart, her voluptuous bosom almost fully exposed by the extremely low-cut gown. 'Won't have no more time for us, though, once you marry that rich girl you was talking about.'

'Nay, he'll have more time then,' Dawson said with a laugh. 'Send the wife off into the country to breed and dally here—or in London.'

'With more money to spend,' another soldier added.

Fitzroy-Price bobbed his head in assent. 'Lots 'n' lots of money. Rich, beautiful 'n' eager to live in th' country. Best kind of wife.'

'Yes—absent,' Dawson said, to the laughter of all.

Johnnie remained silently in the shadows until the bawds withdrew into the house and the group walked off, Dawson bearing up the inebriated Fitzroy-Price. Thoughtful again, he resumed his stealthy trek to the fashionable side of town.

Well, he had his first-hand knowledge now. He hadn't thought his opinion of the Duke's son could sink much lower, but that episode showed him he'd been wrong.

The very idea of that self-important toad touching the pure loveliness that was Prudence Lattimar made him want to punch something—or someone. But he still didn't fancy turning tale-bearer, even of the damning evidence he'd just witnessed himself.

After a few more minutes of reflection, he decided to stick with his original intentions. He'd keep silent and continue to wait, in the confident expectation that Lord Halden's disreputable behaviour would eventually be brought before Miss Lattimar's eyes or into her hearing. At which time, she would finally allow the doubts she already harboured to convince her to abandon Fitzroy-Price as a lost cause—thereby ensuring she did not mire herself in a disaster of a marriage.

And meanwhile, he'd maintain an even closer watch, to make sure the Duke's son didn't manoeuvre her into an entanglement before she'd got a clear picture of his true character.

Fortunately, the arrogant ass was probably so confident that a young, handsome duke's son far outshone any other competing suitor, he probably wouldn't be in any great hurry to press Miss Lattimar into an engagement.

Chapter Seven

As the warm rays of the sun emerged out of a rosy coral dawn, Prudence reached the summit of Lansdown Hill. Pulling her hired mount to a halt, she paused to admire the magnificent vista down over the city, the pale stone buildings golden and shimmering in the mist rising from the river.

Even better, though, was the prospect offered by open downland that stretched away behind her, wide, flat trails occasionally bordered by small copses of trees that practically begged a horsewoman to indulge in a hard gallop.

Which was just what she needed, Pru thought, a surge of anticipation running through her. Maybe luxuriating in a long ride, a beloved pastime she'd had to forgo since leaving behind the carriage parks of London, would soothe the restlessness that had broken her sleep.

Convinced when she awoke again in pre-dawn blackness that recapturing sleep would prove impossible, she'd abandoned her bed, apologising first to the maid who stumbled in half-awake to help her dress and then to the kitchen staff who scrambled to assemble a meal after she arrived in the breakfast parlour hours before the family normally came down.

The tea, toast and cold ham they'd hastily made ready assuaged her hunger, but did nothing to dispel the ache of unease that sat like a rock in her chest. Knowing only one activity might help, while she finished her coffee, she dispatched a footman to the livery to engage a horse and groom for her.

Of course, no hired hack would be the equal of her fierce black gelding, Fury, she thought, giving the grey livery mare a gentle scratch behind her ears. But even if this little lady turned out to be unevenly paced, a gallop would help clear the cobwebs from her brain and brighten spirits that still hadn't recovered since the ugly incident at the Pump Room yesterday.

Much as she appreciated Johnnie's efforts on her behalf, the very fact that he'd had to make them—and planned to reinforce the gesture by circulating his version of the event to every important society matron in Bath—confirmed the worst fears she'd harboured before leaving London. Aunt Gussie's brave hope that bringing her to the smaller, less fashionable city so she might outdistance the rumours and innuendoes that would have flurried about her, had she attempted a come-out in the capital, had turned out to be futile.

The fact that her behaviour since arriving had been impeccable didn't seem to matter.

If society could only appreciate what an effort it required to always stifle her opinions and reactions, to wear a smile, appear serene and seemingly indifferent to slights! When, outrage suffusing her, she would have loved nothing better than to have slapped the smirk off Lieutenant Broadmere's face, right there in the Assembly Rooms. Repaid the soldiers for their insults during the walk in Sidney Gardens with some scathing replies about their own deficiencies of character. Or pointed out to the snide Lady Arbuthnot how unattractive she looked yesterday in that awful puce bonnet.

But no matter how prettily behaved she forced herself to be, to Bath society she was still just a Scandal Sister, an epithet they might never allow her to outlive.

Not that she intended to give up, she told herself, trying by force of will to raise her sagging spirits. She might be a 'Scandal Sister' to society here or in London, but if she could make a suitable marriage, she might still hope to escape carrying that label for the rest of her life.

She just needed that man of impeccable reputation to wed her and carry her off to some small village that cared little and knew less about London society. A kind, thoughtful man who could see and appreciate her for who she truly was and stand behind his loving, blameless wife in his community.

Wedding a clergyman still seemed the most promising way to accomplish that goal. But yesterday's incident had underlined her doubts that Lord Halden Fitzroy-Price was the right clergyman for the job.

Much as she tried to find common ground between them, aside from a love of horses, they didn't seem to share any interests.

And after yesterday, when he was clearly uneasy about remaining in her company after an incident that was sure to be the first topic of gossip in every drawing room in Bath, she wasn't sure he would continue to court her.

She was even less sure she wanted him to.

But what other prospects did she have? Several elderly retired military gentlemen, like General Gaulford and Colonel McQuery. Mr Wellington-Foxe, with his quiverful of expensive sons to support, or Sir Martin, a portly widower she'd just met who had a rambling household and several young children in need of managing.

And what *choice* did she have, but to marry? There was no other occupation available to a gently bred female. Better to settle for affection, children and a home of her own than to remain her whole life a dependent, living upon the goodwill of her father and, after his death, tolerated as a nursemaid or companion in some other relative's household.

Sadly, none of the eligible gentlemen in Bath appealed to her nearly as much as one handsome, fascinating—and for her, *ineligible*—gentleman. Not the settled, well-respected country gentleman or cleric she needed, but wandering adventurer Johnnie Trethwell.

A flash of fury and aggravation blasted through her, heating her face and making her clench her fists. Damn and blast, she was tired of the endless mental arguments! For the next hour, she'd forget them all and lose herself in the pleasure of the wind in her face and the sound of pounding hoofbeats.

Turning back to address the groom trailing her, she said, 'I'm going to put her through her paces.' Touching her heels to the mare's side, she signalled her forward.

Pushing her mount ever harder, Pru leaned low over the horse's head, urging her onwards with the silent pressure of knees and urgent hands on the reins. To her joy, the little mare responded with a burst of speed.

Wind threatened to pull Pru's hat from her head as the horse flew across the ground, seeming as thrilled as her rider to race to the limits of her endurance. The landscape passed in a blur of trees and shrubbery, her heart exulting with the joyful rhythm of the pounding hooves.

Ah, after the steep-streeted confines of Bath, the endless biting of her lip and stifling of her opinions, to finally be free!

Not until the mare was sweat-slicked and obviously tiring did Pru force herself to ease the horse back to a trot, then a walk, then signalled her to a halt. Laughing with exultation, she slipped down from the saddle, giving the horse another rub behind the ears before taking the bridle to lead the animal forward.

'Let's cool you down while we wait for the groom to catch up,' she said, rubbing the mare's velvet muzzle. 'I wish I'd thought to bring a treat for you, for what a trooper you are, my little grey miss! I ought to buy you from that livery. A girl with such a stout heart should only be ridden by someone who appreciates her.'

For the first time in a long time completely content, at the sound of approaching hooves, Pru smiled. Did she dare tease the groom about being left in the dust? But no, like most men, he'd not appreciate the suggestion that he'd been outridden by a girl.

There was only one man she knew who, she was almost certain, would have the confidence to be amused or appreciative, rather than feel challenged, by a female's abilities.

Dismissing with some difficulty the foolish longing for that unattainable gentleman, she prepared a more innocuous greeting. But as she turned to greet the horseman pulling up behind her, she discovered not the disapproving and probably irritated groom—but a merry-eyed Johnnie Trethwell.

'Bravo!' he exclaimed, giving her a salute. 'That was quite a gallop! Truly *ventre à terre*, just as I'd imagined you would ride!'

Conscious of a soaring delight she made no attempt to suppress, she said, 'As I already said, is there any other way? And oh, how glorious it was, to feel the wind in my face and the strength of a good mount beneath me and to finally *breathe* again! I must do this every day.'

'I don't wonder you felt...stifled. Have you recovered yet?' he asked, raking her face with a concerned look.

Thankful that, with Johnnie, she could for once speak frankly, she admitted, 'I would feel better if I'd been able to give Broadmere the roundhouse punch my brother taught me to deliver. One I *could* deliver, were I a *gentleman* whose reputation he was impugning! But since that is clearly out of the question, I'll have to do with a ride.'

She resisted the strong impulse to give him a full account of her worries. He had shown himself a true friend—hadn't he? But an adventurer who'd explored the bazaars—and if rumour held true, the harems—of the exotic east was unlikely to be very interested in the mundane struggles of an English maiden trying to find a conventional English husband.

'Maybe I can deliver it for you,' he said as she hesitated, debating. 'I have to admit, I'd obtain almost as much enjoyment from giving him a roundhouse punch as you would. A man who attacks a woman?' He shook his head in disgust. 'Beneath contempt. I'm surprised any man in his regiment tolerates him.'

'Probably because they are all of his ilk. If they were

truly manly and adventurous, they would be off somewhere else, not wearing army regimentals in placid old England.'

He grinned. 'My thoughts exactly. Shall I escort you back to that lumbering groom I passed on my way?'

She shuddered. 'Oh, please, not yet! Tell me another story first. Perhaps about hunting tigers.'

'Very well, a story,' he agreed. After swinging down from the saddle, he gathered the reins loosely in one hand and fell in beside her, the two horses nuzzling each other as they trailed their riders.

Having Johnnie so near triggered a familiar, prickling sensory awareness all over her body. Ah, that she might nuzzle *him*, run her lips over his mouth, his chin…

A fiercer heat washed through her. Trying to rein in her thoughts before they galloped any further down that path, Pru forced herself to concentrate on his words.

'Although tigers abounded, tiger hunts were actually less frequent than you might imagine,' he was saying.

'Why—were the beasts too fierce for hunters to want to confront them?'

'Not exactly. It's just that the Hindus have an entirely different view of animals than the English. Believing that humans live through many stages, including in animal form, on the path to enlightenment and perfection, they have a reverence for and desire to protect all forms of life—something I found wholly admirable. In addition to the incredible beauty and diversity of the land! They only hunted when they saw it as absolutely necessary.'

'When did they find it necessary to hunt tigers?'

'Among the mountain tribes in particular, the natives believe a treaty exists between tigers and humans. They never go after one unless a tiger "breaks" the treaty by attacking or killing a villager. Then they send out a hunting party, and after bagging several to "teach the tigers a lesson", they believe the treaty goes back in force, each side ready to co-exist with the other again. They don't even hunt wolves, which are often a nuisance around camps.'

'Why—is there a treaty with them, too?' she asked, fascinated by this glimpse into a foreign land—and the love and enthusiasm for that land that illumined him as he described it.

'No. It's believed that if a hunter slays a wolf, from out of the land where its blood was spilled, several, even fiercer wolves will spring, intent on exacting revenge upon the hunter or his family. I've heard of women or children being carried off at night from within their own houses, with the villagers doing nothing. They're sure that some member of the victim's family must have at one time injured a wolf, who came to invoke a rightful revenge.'

Mesmerised, she shook her head. 'How vividly you make me see it—revenging wolves and treaty-making tigers! What a fascinating land!'

'An exotic and beautiful countryside, populated with an endlessly intriguing variety of cultures and clans. I found it mesmerising.' He shook his head wryly. 'Not, I'm afraid, a view that was much shared by my fellow soldiers. Many of them loathed the place. Though to be fair, the troops have no choice about where their regiments are posted. The East India Company officers were usually more appreciative, since they volunteered to serve there and, as financial and governing agents, had more contact with the population and got to know them better. Though even some of them thought of India service just as a way to make a fortune as quickly as possible so they might return and enjoy it back in England.'

'Were there any who made a fortune and chose to stay in India?'

'A few, and mostly from the early days.' He chuckled. 'I did have the privilege of visiting with Colonel Gardner, an old India hand who actually married into a Hindu family. His sons also married native women and his granddaughter married a Hindu prince. His family was intimate with a famous Marantha princess, Baiza Bai, who, unfortunately, I was *not* able to meet. What a fascinating woman! After her husband's death, she attempted to take over political power in the areas he had controlled. Alas, Indian law was no more supportive of a female's political ambitions than the English.'

'And here I thought all Indian women were cloistered in the *zenana*,' Pru said, impressed. 'How illuminating it would be to speak with such a woman! What stories *she* must have to tell!'

'I'm sure she would,' Johnnie agreed. 'But here comes your groom, looking properly disgruntled. You must charm him out of the mopes.'

'Yes, I must, for having rediscovered the joy of riding, I intend to do so often. Since I must suffer having a groom accompany me, I'd prefer it to be one I can outride!'

'Rascal,' he said, laughing. 'One you can outride, so you may escape scrutiny and go where you wish?'

'That too,' she allowed. 'But I would also just as soon not have someone capable of racing on my flank, urging me to slow down to a more ladylike pace. I do have a care for my mount and would never ride one harder than it could bear. But this little lady seems to enjoy a good gallop as much as I do.'

'Instructive as it might be to watch you perform your magic, I must get back.' He halted, hesitating as the groom approached ever closer. 'Do you intend to ride every morning?'

Outdistancing her groom, so she might escape scrutiny and have a private word with this man who so enchanted her?

As she gazed up at him, the delicious sensual thrill she'd felt the whole time they'd walked together intensified the desire, always shimmering at the edges of consciousness, to be held in his arms, feel his lips on hers.

Meeting him—especially if she contrived to do so after outrunning her groom—was clearly dangerous. Yet, along with the physical temptation he represented, being with him brought her such...*ease* and comfort. Somehow she knew that, for the short time they were alone together, she could safely relax her guard and be herself. Voice her true thoughts, no matter how unexpected, unladylike, or unconventional. A freedom she didn't dare allow herself in any other company in Bath.

Reasoning that, as long as she remained on horseback, the physical distance imposed would keep in check her desire to taste his kisses, she simply couldn't deny herself the pleasure of meeting him again. 'Yes, I shall attempt to ride every morning I can.'

He nodded. 'Then perhaps I'll see you on the trail, as well as at social functions.'

She didn't want to let him go, knowing the next occasion she was sure to meet him wouldn't be until the Subscription Ball, two days hence. 'Would you be available to come to tea today? And Lady Woodlings, of course. Aunt Gussie and I will be at home.'

As he paused, reflecting, she felt a blush tinge her cheeks, that sudden invitation revealing all too clearly how much she wanted to see him. Would her boldness frighten him away?

'I'm not sure about my aunt, but I have no other engagements. Yes, I should be able to stop by.'

Breathing out a sigh of relief, Pru said, 'Very good. I'll look forward to seeing you, then.'

'As I will you. Well met, sir,' he said, turning to the groom who'd just brought his horse to a halt beside them. 'As you can see, the lady is safe and sound. I'll leave her to you, but do have a care. There's an army encampment not far to the west and Miss Lattimar is far too lovely to trot about in that vicinity without a protector. Miss Lattimar.' Giving her a short bow to her curtsy, he swung himself back in the saddle and, with a little wave, rode off.

Pru watched him go, knowing she shouldn't be nearly this excited at the prospect of seeing him again today. They would just be chatting over teacups under the eagle eye of their respective aunts.

But she *was* excited—and energised to start planning more such meetings. As she allowed the groom to give her a leg up back into the saddle, she was already scheming how to persuade this slow-riding chaperon to continue accompanying her on early morning excursions—beginning tomorrow.

Chapter Eight

After bathing, eating and dressing with care, that afternoon Johnnie limped up the stairs of Lady Stoneway's town house at the Circus—alone. He'd been not at all sorry a discreet enquiry revealed his aunt did in fact have a previous engagement, which saved him a possible lecture about the danger of seeking out *more* opportunities to be with Miss Lattimar and perhaps an outright refusal to accompany him. As he handed his hat and cane over to the butler, he had to admit to a feeling of anticipation at seeing the delightfully unconventional Miss Lattimar again.

Furies, but the woman could ride! Watching her gallop down that lane on Lansdown Hill yesterday was like listening to one of Daya's tales about the goddess Durga mounted on her tiger, weapons furled, racing off to defeat the forces of evil. Or to return to Western mythology, the virginal goddess Diana, were she to be mounted for the hunt. Trapped beneath the serene veneer she struggled to maintain was something wild and passionate and, curse him, he was increasingly tempted to try to release it.

The devil of it was, he was almost sure he could. Even as he knew he mustn't. It would be a betrayal of the friendship he'd pledged for him to liberate a wild unconventionality that, combined with the reputation she already carried, would doom for ever any chance she had of contracting the traditional marriage with the proper, upright member of society she claimed to want.

Even though he found it increasingly hard to believe such a future would really make her happy. A proper, upright husband and living a life of pious duty as a vicar's wife in a small village might, after years of sterling conduct, finally put to rest the unfair allegations that she was the moral, as well as physical, image of her profligate mother. But it would also trap her into playing a highly visible role where restrained behaviour and submissive deference would be expected in every aspect of her life. He wasn't so sure barefooted spring-bathing with her own children would escape criticism from the more narrow-minded and censorious parishioners. Could she really be content, if she were forced to suppress that passionate nature for a lifetime?

As much as she was beginning to fascinate him, he was honest enough to admit he could offer her no better alternative. Even if he was warming to the idea of limiting himself to just one woman—to claim a woman like Prudence Lattimar, he might just be able to make that work—at the moment, he was the least likely man to give her what she wanted. Though he had prospects of obtaining on his own the financial backing he needed, he intended to use those funds to launch back out into the unknown—not retire to that estate in the placid English countryside she yearned for.

Such a bright, engaging spirit deserved to find the upright, settled husband she sought—one who not only shared her love of the countryside, but a man who would cherish her for the wonderful woman she truly was. One who appreciated the enchanting, unconventional loveliness of her as much as Johnnie did.

He had to admit, the image of her married to someone else somehow…grated. What delights might he experience, were *he* allowed to free that tempestuous spirit! Had he the least desire to mire himself for a lifetime in the back country of England, he might be tempted to try to win her heart.

Even as the thought formed, he knew it would be the act of a villain to try. Perhaps she could be charmed into quitting her beloved homeland, but for very good reasons, he had always adventured alone. Those reasons were still valid, no matter how intriguing the idea of showing perceptive, receptive Prudence Lattimar the glories and mysteries of the wider world outside England's shores.

Sadly, their planets would not align, he thought as the butler conveyed him to the drawing room. But he could still stand her friend and, within the strict confines of a drawing room, indulge himself in the refreshing novelty of her company, without putting either of them in danger.

Though he wasn't surprised to find other visitors present at Lady Stoneway's at-home, his euphoric mood slipped further when he noted the guest seated beside Miss Lattimar was Lord Halden Fitzroy-Price. Stopping short just inside the room, he hesitated, not sure he could manage to remain politely silent while a man whose true character he knew tried to bamboozle a lovely innocent. Confident in her aunt's ability to keep her safe inside her own drawing room, he'd half-turned to leave again when he caught an urgent look from Miss Lattimar.

Rescue me, it said.

How could any soldier fail to respond?

Telling himself he'd maintain a tight curb over his tongue—and keep his hands, already curled into fists with the desire to plant the scoundrel a facer, close to his sides—he gave her a tiny nod before walking over to greet his hostess, who was seated on the sofa adjoining hers with Mrs Marsden and two other ladies.

'Good afternoon, ladies,' he said, bowing as they nodded. 'Lady Stoneway, so kind of you to include me.'

'Lieutenant Trethwell, you're always welcome! Please, make yourself comfortable,' she said, gesturing to the chair beside the sofa where Prudence and Fitzroy-Price sat. 'Prudence, my dear, offer the Lieutenant some tea.'

'Yes, do join us,' she replied, smiling at him. Nodding a greeting to Lord Halden, who looked frankly surprised to see Johnnie so warmly welcomed into the bosom of the family, he had a hard time suppressing a smile as he took a seat.

Turning his thoughts to a more worthy subject, he paused to admire Miss Lattimar. How lovely she was in an afternoon gown of soft blue that made the gold of her hair sparkle! Yet the hue was only an inferior echo of the magnificent blue of her eyes. She truly was a work of art come to life—though the appeal of the vibrant spirit housed within the beautiful body excited his mind and passion as much as her appearance.

He looked up from appreciating her gracefulness as she went through the ritual of pouring tea to see Fitzroy-Price staring at him.

Having dismissed him as beneath notice at the first, this

cosy interlude must be giving the Duke's son pause. He was looking at Johnnie as if seeing him for the first time and being forced to evaluate whether this nonentity could actually be a threat to his ambitions of securing Miss Lattimar's hand—and dowry.

More of a threat than you imagine, Johnnie thought, meeting the man's eyes with a steely look that had induced many an opponent's face to colour as he turned away. For once, he was glad rumour branded him a charming fortune hunter. The Duke's son might discount his present occupation and prospects, but he would take seriously the unwelcome discovery that another man, apparently approved by her aunt, might be competing with him for the prize of Miss Lattimar's wealth.

Not that he had any designs on that—his wistful but destined-to-be-unfulfilled hopes centred more on capturing her body and spirit. But he was glad Fitzroy-Price now understood that he would not have the free hand to beguile the heiress, unchallenged.

To his credit, the Duke's son held Johnnie's gaze, their wordless confrontation not broken until Miss Lattimar recalled his attention by handing him his cup.

Not offering Johnnie even the courtesy of a greeting, Lord Halden addressed his full attention to Prudence. 'Shall we resume our conversation, Miss Lattimar? I was telling you about the new matched blacks I procured at such a good price from Atley. So many gambling losses, he's had to sell off his stable, poor man!'

Wonder how you'll pay yours when you fail to secure Miss Lattimar's dowry, Johnnie thought.

Still ignoring him—and not pausing long enough for Miss Lattimar to reply—Lord Halden continued, 'Indeed, the afternoon promises to be quite lovely. Won't you ride out in my curricle with me? With my hands on the ribbons, Lady Stoneway,' he added, breaking in on that lady's conversation to address her aunt, 'she will be entirely safe, I assure you.'

Without giving her aunt time to reply, Prudence said, 'Perhaps another time, Lord Halden. Lieutenant, would you relate to my aunt and her friends something more about the treatment of animals in India? As I told my aunt,' she explained to the group, 'I met Lieutenant Trethwell by chance while I was out riding this morning. He very kindly rode with me for a while and regaled me with the most fascinating stories about tigers and wolves!'

'It sounds quite—fierce!' Mrs Marsden said with a little shudder.

'Oh, no! It's just that the Hindus venerate all animals, in such unusual ways,' Miss Lattimar replied. 'Knowing how much you adore animals, especially your darling pug Hero, I thought you'd find it interesting.'

'Venerate? In what way? Please tell us more, Lieutenant,' Lady Stoneway said.

'If you insist,' Johnnie said, trying not to laugh out loud at the shock, succeeded by fury, on Lord Halden's face at having his offer brusquely rebuffed in favour of a story spun about *India*.

'It's true, the Hindus believe all living things possess a soul. For that reason, many of them eat no meat and they try to make sure animals are never harmed. Wild peacocks, partridges and ducks wander through the villages with no more fear of the human inhabitants as if they were domesticated fowl. After harvest, when the corn is threshed by oxen for the villagers to share, peacocks peck at stray kernels, while squirrels dodge around the oxen's hooves to snag a little. Often, monkeys hang about in the trees all around, darting in to claim a considerable handful, without anyone attempting to molest them.'

'Even when they are stealing food the villagers planted, tended and harvested?' Lady Stoneway exclaimed.

'All living things carry within them a part of the divine, the Hindus believe, and as such have a right to sustenance, which should be freely offered. Indeed, travellers going past villages are often brought jugs of water and offerings of bread, grain and fruit. Some villages even maintain thatched huts near the village entrance where travellers may spend the night.'

'How very hospitable!' Mrs Marsden said.

Johnnie chuckled. 'Even when it may not be to their advantage. There were always a plague of stray dogs hanging about the villages, existing on scraps, and sometimes they become rabid. To protect public health, the Company decided to round up the strays. They posted notices that on a certain day, any dogs found wandering unattended would be seized and destroyed. Just before the allotted time, the villagers herded all the strays into their houses, so when the inspectors came by, there were none on the streets to be found.'

'How curious—and fascinating!' Aunt Gussie said. 'You must join us for dinner some evening! I should love to hear more about your travels and experiences. Oh, and we will send you a card, too, of course, Lord Halden.'

'So I might listen to another lecture from the well-travelled Lieutenant? I believe my schedule might be too full,' he said stiffly.

'Yes, I'm sure you are extremely busy,' Miss Lattimar

flashed back, her serene face at odds with the slight edge in her tone. 'Today as well, I expect. We'll understand if you wish to take your leave now, won't we, Aunt?'

'I should be leaving, too,' Mrs Marsden said. 'I promised I'd call on Lady Belk this afternoon. She's not been well of late.'

The company rose. Realising he'd eked out as long a visit as custom permitted—and satisfied to have rattled Lord Halden's arrogant complacency in regard to his hold over Miss Lattimar—Johnnie turned to depart as well when Miss Lattimar caught his sleeve, shaking her head with a silent 'no'.

Halting, he remained beside her as her aunt ushered out the other guests.

'You may be losing your admirer,' he told her *sotto voce*.

'Maybe I should be glad to lose him,' she murmured back, the serenity of her face momentarily breached by a fleeting expression of doubt. 'He was unaccountably rude to you—again.'

'You got back at him, though, inviting me to tell a story about India. I almost felt sorry for him.'

She gave a tight smile. 'He never enjoys a conversation unless he's the centre of it. Oh, my—that sounds unkind! But unfortunately, my experience with him shows it to be true.'

Delighted at this further evidence that the Duke's son's grip on her hopes appeared to be loosening, Johnnie bit his tongue before asking whether this was the kind of man she wanted to spend the rest of her life with.

No need to press. Despite a very strong desire to see her future settled in the manner she hoped, she was gradually coming to see for herself that Lord Halden Fitzroy-Price was not the man to fulfil those dreams.

He wished he were. Shocked by that errant thought, he shut his ears to the whisper before it could utter anything else equally heretical.

'I can't let you linger, unfortunately,' she murmured, recalling him. 'But I wanted to keep you for a moment, to thank you for coming today and sharing another wonderful story. Which I would have asked for, even if I hadn't wanted to rebuke Lord Halden's discourtesy. Will...will you ride again tomorrow?'

'You succeeded in charming the hired groom out of his disgruntlement?'

'No charm required. The promise of a hefty increase in his fee, if he agreed to have the grey mare ready and to accompany me any time I wished to ride, was enough.' She chuckled. 'For the handsome sum I offered, I believe he will let me outride him as often as I like!'

'Perhaps we can test that notion tomorrow.'

'You'll be there, then? Just after the sun is up?'

The ardent appeal on her face lit a little glow in his heart that shouldn't be there. Ignoring the bugle call of warning that fact triggered in his brain, he said, 'I'll be there.'

As the sun warmed the roofs of the buildings in the city below, sending a steam of vapour to mist the morning sky, Johnnie guided his hack on to the trail leading from the heights of Lansdown Hill towards the racetrack. His experience with society ladies, most of whom attended social events until the wee hours and rose correspondingly late in the mornings, made him sceptical that Miss Lattimar would actually make a habit of riding out just past daybreak—a time when generally only tradesmen and servants were up and about. But sure enough, as he rounded the next bend, he spied her on the grey mare she'd ridden the day before, trailed by the stout groom on his bay gelding.

His spirits rose and his body tightened in anticipation. With just the two of them, far from the censorious ears of polite society, what outrageous remarks, what unexpected observations would she gift him with today?

The royal-blue riding habit that hugged her generous curves made him glad they were both mounted. With that brilliant smile she turned on him when she saw him approach drawing him like iron shavings to a magnet, without the impediment of horses between them, he didn't think he could have resisted the urge to kiss her.

'Bravo again, Miss Lattimar. I wasn't sure you would manage to propel yourself from your chamber so early two days in a row.'

'What, you take me for a slug-abed? I've always loved being up early, watching the night recede and the day ride in on its golden chariot. Or wrapped in its mantle of weeping rain clouds, more often.'

'What shall it be first, a walk or a gallop?'

'A gallop, of course! While the road is still deserted. And if your black can match my grey, he's well worth the hire!'

With that, she touched heels to the mare, who leapt forward immediately, displaying the same impressive acceleration he'd admired yesterday.

As it turned out, his black could not keep pace. Some moments later, when he urged his tiring mount past another stand of trees, he found her already pulled up and waiting, sitting easily in the saddle as she retied the strings of her bonnet under her chin.

'Not a slug,' she said with a wave of her hand to his horse, 'but not the equal of my little grey lady.'

'She is exceptional,' he agreed. *Almost as exceptional as her rider.*

'Not that I think your pride is hurt, but I'm sure you'd have made a better showing on a different mount.'

He grinned. 'I think my ego will withstand the blow. However, if I had Stalwart, the horse I rode in India, I believe I could have bested you.'

She pointed her riding crop at him in a challenging gesture. 'And if I had *my* mount of choice, Fury, I am sure you could not! Shall we walk them?'

'Yes, let's cool them down. It will take a while for your groom to catch up. That bay of his didn't seem to want to break a trot.'

'He told me that as long as I don't ride towards the west, in the direction of the soldiers' encampment, he felt confident I could gallop ahead and still be safe for the short time it would take him to reach me. Come, let's walk them while you tell me another story.'

Matching action to her words, she slipped gracefully out of the saddle and gathered her mare's reins in one hand. After giving his valiant black's neck a rub, he followed suit.

'Now,' she said as they strolled forward. 'Since no society matrons are present to disapprove my choice of topic, I want to ask about Indian ladies. Did you take a *maharani* as your mistress, Lieutenant Trethwell?'

Surprised anew, Johnnie threw back his head and laughed. What other English maiden would dare ask him such a question? Even Aunt Pen hadn't been that indiscreet. 'You really don't have any maidenly restraint.'

'Not a jot. I didn't think I needed any, not with you. Given my upbringing, you could hardly expect me to be missish. Temper and I became aware of the significance of Mama's gentlemen callers when we'd barely reached our teens.'

'If we're to chat about something that scandalously intimate, you'd best call me Johnnie.'

'Then you must call me Pru. When no one else is about, of course.'

'Of course.' *Uninhibited, yet still quaintly cautious. Could she be more enchanting?* he thought, entertained by her intriguing mix of innocence and worldliness.

'So, tell me about the ladies of the *zenana*. Is it true that they are always cloistered away from men and cannot go abroad without their faces covered?'

'Yes, most practise *purdah*, a separation from men. But the females of the Mahratta were excellent horsewomen and would ride out unveiled. Peasant women also went to the wells to gather water, which is where soldiers usually encountered them. High-born women were more strictly cloistered, spending their days among other women and their serving girls. Generally a laughing, indolent lot, always exquisitely groomed, eyes accented with kohl, dressed and bejewelled as richly as their circumstances permitted, even in the middle of the day within the walls of the *zenana*.'

She gave him a saucy smile. 'Just how do you know so much about what happens in the *zenana*, if you did not have a liaison with a *maharani*?'

He laughed, recalling it. 'In my information-gathering forays, I sometimes posed as a travelling merchant. Wandering about with a sack full of trinkets, one was nearly invisible in the crowded markets. Then one day, I found myself pulled along by a servant boy into a nearby house. Apparently the mistress had observed me selling my treasures through her shuttered windows and sent the boy to fetch me so she and her ladies could inspect my wares. I must admit, after that fascinating encounter, I sometimes took a break from my intelligence-gathering mission to refresh myself with a vision of feminine loveliness.'

'And the master of the household did not object to this intrusion?'

'Those dark-eyed beauties can have fierce tempers! Once, when one attempted to object, his lady subjected him to such a string of abuse, he gave in.'

'What a shocking rogue you were!' she said, laughing delightedly. 'So, no *maharani*. What of the other native girls? I understand nearly all the British soldiers serving in India took native mistresses.'

Surprised again, he gave her a sharp look. 'What makes you think that?'

'Temper and I read Captain Mundy and Captain Skinner's journals of their sojourns in India.'

'Good heavens!' he exclaimed. 'Your reading material has been as unrestricted as your upbringing!'

'We've always had full access to Papa's library—some of the Greek and Roman translations are quite…sensual. Then, Temper has been obsessed for years by the desire to explore abroad and combs the bookshops for volumes about travel. Naturally, when she saw memoirs about a land as exotic as India, she snapped them up. So, did most soldiers take native mistresses? Did you? I'm sorry, you're not…offended by the question?'

As the bittersweet memories welled up, he shook his head. Having encouraged her to ask outrageous questions, it was hardly fair to object when she did—no matter how painful the nerve they struck. Nor, given her openness, did he feel it right to turn suddenly prim and refuse to answer.

'I'm not…offended, precisely. Many soldiers did take native wives. To some extent, the liaisons can be helpful—mostly for the soldier. He becomes acquainted with the manners and customs of the local people and is able to learn their language. He gains some vestige of a home life, with a kind partner to keep house, cook and tend him when he falls ill.'

'Was that how you learned the language and customs so well, you could pass as a travelling salesman?'

'If that's an indirect way of asking if *I* kept a native mistress, the answer is no. But you're correct, I did learn about language and culture from one such lady. Daya, the consort of my best friend, Tom Alcorn.'

She studied his face. 'It did not end well, this union?'

He'd never repeated the story to any English female—not even Aunt Pen. His regret, anger and grief over Daya's death, his guilty sense of responsibility for Alcorn's, were sores that had never healed. To those who asked about his days in India, he'd always confined himself to relating amusing stories. Why abandon that prudent restraint now?

He looked up to find her compassionate gaze on his face. 'You needn't answer me, if you don't wish to. I have no right to pry into the intimate details of your life.'

Could divulging the tale to this female, whose unusual upbringing had made her more interested in and less judgemental of others than any other English person he'd ever met, help relieve some of that lingering anguish?

Maybe it was having spoken so freely of intimate matters he'd seldom discussed even with the closest friends, but suddenly he felt moved to tell her the whole.

'Daya was a girl from one of the villages near our encampment. "Mercy", her name means, and she certainly exhibited that quality! As I think I told you, usually villagers are very hospitable, bringing water, dates, food, even garlands of flowers to greet visitors. But the towns near the cantonments had become rather wary of soldiers. When we approached the wells, the girls drawing water would usually scatter. Most did, the day Alcorn and I rode up to her village, dusty and thirsty. But not Daya. She walked right up to us, smiling, and offered us the water jug she'd just filled.

'She had a lovely smile and shining dark eyes,' he continued, gazing into the distance as the scene came back to him in all its vivid colour. 'The picture of grace and loveliness in her bejewelled sari. I was struck by her, but Alcorn was completely dazzled. He returned several times to the well, and the last time, he brought her back to camp with him. She was such a shining spirit, so bright, eager to learn English, eager as well to teach us her language and her ways. Her tales about the gods and goddesses, temples, debating scholars and holy beggars, inspired me to begin roaming about on my own.' He laughed. 'She was the one who advised me to dye my exposed skin with betel juice and brought me the native dress that would allow me to stroll about, unnoticed.'

'You were fond of her.'

He tilted his head, assessing. 'Yes, I was. But Alcorn loved her, which thrust him into a dilemma. He couldn't marry her and take her back to England. He knew any children born of their union were destined to be outcasts in both cultures. But he couldn't imagine life without her, either. If things hadn't transpired as they did, I think he would have married her quietly and remained in India, perhaps taking a position with one of the Company's military forces.'

'What did happen?' she asked softly.

'One of the conditions many men made for taking mistresses is that they would not produce children.'

She raised her eyebrows. 'That's not so easy to guarantee.'

'No,' he said shortly. 'Despite the native women's claims of knowing foolproof remedies to prevent conception, they didn't. Daya must have fallen pregnant, but though she had to know Tom would never have abandoned her, she didn't tell Alcorn. Apparently, after the potions failed to work, she went to a woman in the village who promised to take care of it. She bled to death.'

'How awful!' she gasped, reaching out to touch his sleeve. 'I'm so very sorry.'

Finding the gesture strangely comforting, he said, 'Alcorn was never the same after that. I guess we both went a little crazy, he drowning himself in drink, me frequently going off alone to explore. Trying to outrun my fury at inhabiting a world where both societies would allow something like this to happen, I suppose. After being several times reprimanded for it, some higher-up decided if I was going to roam about anyway, I might as well collect useful information while I was at it.'

'They must have found that *wonderfully* useful.'

He grimaced. 'Perhaps. But if I'd been something of a loner already, my expeditions sealed that fate. Although when the British first arrived, outnumbered on tiny outposts, contact between and cordial terms with the local people was tolerated, if not encouraged, but as the Company tightened its grip over the country, there were fewer and fewer exchanges. The English came to see their role as guiding a benighted backward people towards the light, religiously and culturally. All things Indian were disdained and any Englishman who admired their culture or wished to mingle with them was looked upon as peculiar and "un-British".'

She nodded. 'Yes, in our literary explorations of the wider world, Temper and I read Mills's book. He was quite dismissive of the native peoples and their heritage.'

She'd surprised him yet again. 'You've read Mills's *History of British India*? You are an unusual woman!'

'Whether I want to be or not,' she said drily. 'What happened to Alcorn? Did he stay in India after all, or resign and go home?'

Johnnie felt the knife of grief twist again in his chest. 'There were dacoits—outlaws—operating in the area, attacking traders. The army sent us out to investigate. Some of the renegades' scouts must have alerted them, because they had an ambush ready for us. Rather than fall back with us so we could regroup, Alcorn raised his sword and rode straight at them.' He took a shuddering breath. 'When I realised what he was doing, I rode after him...but I was too late. He was slashed to pieces.'

Tears in her eyes, she shook her head. 'Another terrible death.'

'Perhaps. But I think Alcorn wanted to die. Maybe he hoped, in some afterlife between the reincarnation of the Hindus and the heaven of the Christians, he and Daya might be united in death as they could not be in life.'

'You were wounded while going after him.'

He nodded. It haunted him still...realising, to his disbelief, that instead of riding back beside him as he'd expected, Alcorn had wheeled his mount and galloped off alone. He'd turned in the saddle, urging his mount forward again, shouting at his friend to retreat. Watched helplessly as Tom rode into that certain death of slashing sabres, then battled alone for his own life.

'Finally realising what was happening, the rest of the company rode into action behind me. They kept me from suffering the same fate Tom had.'

Their rescue couldn't assuage the terrible guilt he felt over not anticipating Tom's suicidal charge, the agonising doubt over whether there might have been any way he could have saved the closest friend he'd ever had. Nor could any relief over surviving himself mitigate the stark, soul-penetrating grief that came from knowing Tom and Daya had been taken, leaving him once again, as he had been for almost all his life, completely alone.

A devastation he never wished to experience again.

'There wasn't anything you could have done,' she said softly. 'I hope they did find peace together.'

It was only then, as he struggled to pull himself from the past, that he realised she'd somehow known what he'd been thinking—the guilt, if not the devastation. Feeling both warmed by her understanding and dangerously exposed, he pushed the thought away.

'Enough stories from me. What about your past? Your mother and how you deal with her? She must be an incredible beauty, if you are said to be her image.'

'Beautiful, yes. Also witty, well informed and alluring. Men fall for her in droves, even now. To be fair, she no longer looks to attract new lovers. Although her uninterest only seems to spur men on.'

'The lure of the unattainable. Do you admire her?'

She sighed. 'Admire. Resent. I even hated her for a while, when I grew old enough to envision a come-out and realised society would hold her sins against me. Temper was angry with her, too, until she turned sixteen. Then she suddenly decided she would never wed and would attack those who maligned Mama.' Prudence smiled. 'She's going to try to get our father to release her dowry, so she may travel the world, like Lady Hester Stanhope. Though I can't blame her for disdaining marriage. Our parents' union was hardly an advertisement for the estate.'

'My parents', either,' he agreed. 'If he is so indifferent to her activities, why did your father marry your mother?'

'Since his youth, he has collected beautiful things. The only explanation we've been able to come up with is that, having seen her, the most beautiful girl of her debut Season, he simply had to add her to his collection. He was wealthy, and her dowry was small, so her family pushed her into the union. It was only later, after he virtually ignored her, that she began to take lovers. Temper thinks she turned to other men to try to spark Vraux into some reaction. She never got one and, by the time she'd dallied with one or two, she'd acquired that notorious reputation. Defiant as my sister, she embraced it.'

Johnnie could hardly believe a man could possess a wife as beautiful as Prudence Lattimar and be indifferent to having other men seduce her. Were Pru his, he'd gut anyone who tried to touch her.

'Your father was never angry, or jealous?'

She shook her head. 'I've never been able to figure Father out. He seems to have this...horror of touching. When I was a child and tried to embrace him, he would push me away. Gently, but with such a look of...distaste in his eyes,

I soon stopped trying. Once Mama produced an heir, he seemed content to let her go her own way. I'm not supposed to know, but I overheard Aunt Gussie telling my brother Gregory that when Mama was *enceinte* with Christopher, her unmarried lover tried to persuade Father to divorce her, so they might wed and he could claim the child as his own. Father refused. Christopher has…an accommodation with his natural father, who recognises him, and even supported him for his Parliamentary seat.'

'And what of your natural father? Do you have any contact with him?'

'None. Aunt Gussie told Gregory that Christopher's father was the love of Mama's life and, after she lost him, she buried her grief in a string of lovers, one of whom fathered us. But unlike Christopher's father, who only married when he could not have Mama, this gentleman had no wish to acknowledge us.'

As lonely and unappreciated as he'd felt in childhood, how much worse had it been for her? Abandoned by her natural father, pushed away by her legal one.

No wonder she yearned for a man to love and care for her. Compassion welling up, wishing he could do something to ease the pain he read in her tear-bejewelled eyes, he grasped her chin. 'Mine had no time for me, either,' he told her as he lifted her face towards his. 'Too bad you weren't born a man! You could have consigned them all to perdition, as I did, and gone adventuring.'

Gazing into her eyes, he was overcome by the awe and wonder her beauty always evoked in him. But her loveliness was as sensual as it was pure.

The softness of her face burned into his fingers, firing again the passion that always smouldered beneath the surface, stealing his breath, holding him so spellbound he could scarcely move. 'Right now, I am very thankful you're a woman,' he whispered.

The silence of the copse of trees sheltering them hummed with the force of attraction between them. Finally giving in to it, as her eyes fluttered closed and she raised her face, Johnnie bent to kiss her...

And heard the clip-clop of approaching hoofbeats.

Heart racing, he released her chin and stepped away. An instant later, the groom came trotting past the greenery, spotted them and redirected his mount.

Fisting hands that still trembled, half-furious, half-relieved at the interruption, he laughed.

Her eyes startled, her face went pale, then coloured with a blush. 'What?' she demanded, her tone gruff.

Was she as disappointed as he was to have been cheated of that embrace?

'A fortuitous, if infuriating, interruption.'

Apparently, she only then noticed the approaching groom. Jerking her gaze away from Johnnie, she gave a gasp. 'Oh! Stebbins. You're...here.'

'Yes, miss. Sorry it took so long.'

'Just as well,' Johnnie said. 'We've had time to walk the horses and cool them down.'

'Shall I give you a leg up, miss?' the groom asked.

Giving Johnnie a regretful look, Pru said, 'Yes, please. I suppose it's time we were heading back to the city.'

Once remounted, they signalled the horses to a trot side by side, the groom trailing behind.

Knowing the moment for scandalous exchanges was at an end, Johnnie said, 'What would you do, if you could not marry a vicar?'

She sighed. 'Retreat to Entremer, I suppose. Work with the horses. Among other things he collected, Papa acquired some magnificent Arabians and some prime Irish hunters. I'd love to try breeding his prizes.' She laughed ruefully. 'I do love the country. I'm the only one in the family who doesn't see living in Northumberland as punishment and exile.'

'Surely you could go to London next year and have your Season then.'

'What, as long in the tooth as I'll be? I'd be considered past my last prayers by then! Besides, how could I expect to be received more favourably by society there than I have been here? London is even more critical and censorious than Bath.'

'Perhaps. But you can't consider Bath a reasonable test. There are hardly enough eligible young gentlemen to qualify it as a proper Marriage Mart. And while you'd not wish to marry a man who was interested only in your dowry, surely among the many who gather in London, there'll be several wise enough to see the gold of your worth through the dross of gossip surrounding you. Maybe even a clergyman.'

Her eyes had dimmed, but at that, they relit. 'You truly think so?'

In trying to lift spirits that an imminent return to the city had obviously sent tumbling, was he giving her false hope? 'Surely not all young gentleman are as block-headed as the handful you've met here in Bath.'

'Many of them seem to be.' At her suddenly acerbic tone, he turned towards the direction in which she was looking—and spied her three tormentors, Dawson, Broadmere and Truro, riding up Lansdown Hill. Their path back to the city, and the soldiers' towards the encampment, were about to converge and there was no way to avoid them.

Pru stiffened, her expression going blank. Johnnie could almost see the mantle of serene, eminently respectable young lady fall back over her. Raising her chin as they approached, she greeted the soldiers politely.

Perhaps Broadmere had been sufficiently chastened, or perhaps it was Johnnie's glowering presence beside her, but the trio replied with unexceptional greetings of their own. With neither party slowing their pace to allow for conversation, they were soon past them and descending into the city.

Once they were out of sight, Prudence blew out a breath. 'You can rest easy. I resisted the urge to jump out of the saddle, run over and punch Broadmere.'

Surprised again, but delighted by her fierceness, Johnnie laughed. 'A fortunate thing. Once you began pummelling, I'm not sure I could have pulled you off him.'

'They seemed rather subdued. They must have been up early for them to be already returning from making their purchases in town.'

'My poor innocent! They're probably just now returning from their night's revels.'

Obviously embarrassed by her naivety, her cheeks pinked. 'Yes, you're undoubtedly correct.'

There it was again, that flash of innocence in the midst of her worldliness. He felt like gathering her up and running off with her, so she might be his alone.

This will never do, he told himself, trying to cram the potent mix of desire and affection back into whatever crevice of his soul from which it had escaped. Distracted by that struggle, he found himself saying, 'Will I see you again later today?'

'Probably not, unfortunately. I'm accompanying Aunt Gussie to visit a friend who's been ill, after which we'll dine *en famille* with Mrs Marsden.'

'You'll ride tomorrow?'

'In the morning, if the weather holds fair.'

He scanned the sky, frowning. 'With the way the clouds are scudding in, we should look for rain.'

'If it's too wet in the morning, I'll try for the afternoon. We have no other engagements and, having resumed the pleasure of a daily ride, I would hate to miss it.'

By now, they had reached the city, where a bustling transit of pedlars, workmen, maids and footmen running errands, and sedan chairs carrying residents for their morning ablutions at the baths, made conversation more difficult.

Bringing her horse to a halt, Prudence raised her voice. 'I'll head off for the Circus now. Thank you for your company, Lieutenant Trethwell.'

Conscious of a curious little sinking feeling in his chest at the prospect of leaving her, he bowed. 'The pleasure was mine, Miss Lattimar.'

Holding his mount steady, he watched her ride off, trying to resist the ridiculous notion that happiness rode with her.

Turning his mount towards Queen Square, he ignored the urge to ride after Prudence and find some excuse to prolong their encounter. He had no business seeking out additional opportunities to be with her—almost daring himself to fall deeper under her spell. Once his leg had adequately healed, he intended to go to London and approach the men who had indicated interest in sponsoring his work.

While Prudence would doubtless make an observant, curious companion on his travels, as Tom and Daya's deaths had taught him, he'd be wise to stick to his resolve to always travel alone. Leave Bath, before she could engage his emotions any further. Safer for *her* to remain in her beloved England, where, never having truly possessed her, he wouldn't have to worry about how catastrophic it might be to lose her.

And then he had to laugh. Why was he expending all this needless angst? He just needed to remind himself that while he burned to travel the globe, all Prudence yearned for was to settle quietly in the English countryside.

Chapter Nine

Rain coming on as Johnnie had predicted, it wasn't until the afternoon of the following day that the showers eased and Prudence was able to ride up Lansdown Road on to the heights about the city.

Resisting the urge to gallop immediately, she trotted the mare for a time, hoping to hear behind her the welcome approach of Johnnie on his black. But after nearly an hour of proceeding at a sedate pace, restless, she reluctantly concluded that he'd not been able to get away and put spurs to her mare.

Pushing away the questions and worries circling in her head, Pru lost herself in the sound of thundering hoofs, the rush of the wind whipping at her face. Racing around a sharper curve, she had to suddenly veer on to the verge to avoid running down a group of soldiers riding at an easy pace in the direction of the racetrack.

Dawson, Broadmere and Truro among them.

Damnation, did those fellows never go off on military

exercises? she wondered as she guided the mare around that obstacle and back on to the trail. As eager to put them behind her as she was to outrace her dilemma, she urged the mare ever faster. So fast, a sudden gust of strong wind ripped the bonnet from her head.

Unwilling to pull up and retrieve it, she drove the horse onwards until the mare's slowing pace and sweating neck indicated her mount had reached the limits of her endurance. Pulling the grey to a halt, she patted the horse's slick side.

'Sorry to push you so hard, my beauty, but what a game speedster you are!' she murmured. 'This time, I thought to bring you a treat by way of apology. Then we'll fetch my hat.'

Slipping from the saddle, she offered a bit of apple, then gathered up the reins and turned her tired mount back towards the city. After a time, she came upon the small grouping of trees and shrubs where she thought the bonnet had gone flying.

Nothing clung to the branches nearest the road, but there was a gap in the trees leading into a wooded copse beyond. Walking the mare into it, she spied the errant bonnet caught in a tangle of hawthorns on the leeward side of the enclosure. Looping the mare's reins around the closest bush, she set off to retrieve it.

Returning with it to where she'd tethered the mare, she shook off the dust, pulled off the leaves caught in the feather trimming and was retying it on her head when she heard the clop of hoofbeats and a murmur of approaching voices. Realising the riders must be the soldiers she'd bypassed earlier and not wishing to encounter them while alone and unprotected by even the groom, she quickly led her horse deeper into the shrubbery.

True to the adage that one never hears any good when eavesdropping, as the voices grew close enough to be distinguishable, she realised, to her chagrin, that they were discussing *her*.

'Galloping like a circus performer at Astley's, not even a groom in sight!' one voice said derisively.

'Maybe heading to an assignation?' another suggested. 'I wouldn't mind an afternoon interlude at some shepherd's cottage with that little beauty.'

As the voices grew louder, one she recognised as Lord Chalmondy Dawson's remarked, 'An assignation, without doubt. Fast as she was riding, I'll bet she's as hot for it as you would be.'

The voices were now passing the entrance to her hiding place. Incredulous and outraged that they would discuss her so contemptuously, she was torn between running out to confront them—and the wiser course of ensuring she was not discovered. Conflicted, Prudence forced herself to remain immobile, barely breathing. If only there were a way to stop her ears from hearing their degrading remarks!

'Can't you just see it?' Dawson said in mocking tones. 'Our good friend Lord Halden arriving home from his parish church, his virtuous little wife greeting him on the doorstep with open arms extended—to unbutton his trouser flap. Then falling on her knees to pleasure him while he offers a welcome home prayer!'

'Can you imagine anything more ridiculous than that wanton creature thinking to play a vicar's wife?' Truro said scornfully.

'But as he's several times said, once Fitzroy-Price has her money, he won't need a parish,' Dawson reminded. 'He can tether her in the countryside and sample her delights whenever the mood strikes, then leave her there and repair to London.'

'With blunt enough to sample as many other delights as he chooses,' Broadmere said.

Their outburst of raucous laughter gradually faded as the hoofbeats retreated into the distance, their voices reduced to an unintelligible murmur.

Too shocked and horrified to move, Prudence's hands shook as she gripped the reins. Her chest ached with the effort of suppressing the outrage, fury and mortification triggered by the soldiers' crude, humiliating remarks.

She knew that among the privacy of their friends, men probably discussed women in the most base and graphic of terms. But this was *her* they were describing so degradingly. The raging part of her wanted to run after them and abuse them as roundly as they'd just abused her.

But with her face framed by the strands of hair blown out of her coiffure after she'd lost her hat, her bonnet dusty and its once jaunty feather drooping, storming out to confront them would probably only reinforce their view of her as an ill-behaved wanton.

Looping the reins over a bush again, she used her fingertips to comb back under her hat as many errant wisps as she could locate without a looking glass to assist her. She'd remain here another few minutes to make sure the soldiers were too far away to spot her when she emerged. And to master completely the useless rage, burning humiliation and a foolish, juvenile *hurt* she should be far too cynical to feel.

Minutes crawled by while she stood there, taking deep breaths to stave off the stupid urge to weep. As intolerable as it had been to overhear herself discussed in such a disrespectful manner, even more shocking was the casual assertion she'd heard—offered by Lord Chalmondy Dawson, the man who supposedly had known him since childhood—that Lord Halden had no real vocation for the ministry and, if he could gain another source of income, would not take holy orders.

So much for her optimistic hopes that maturity and immersion in the solemn duties and responsibilities of the priesthood would correct the deficiencies of character that had troubled her, turning him into the kind of man she could admire and support.

Instead, he was, in essence, just another fortune hunter, however highly born. Marrying him would gain her, not a respected place in the community as a vicar's wife, but solitary exile in the country—the only safe place to immure a wife with a wanton reputation.

Feeling too heartsick and weary to maintain the cool, calm façade she must present to the world, once she could safely emerge from her hiding place, she would ride back to the sanctuary of her bedchamber as quickly as her mount could carry her. Where, hidden even from Aunt Gussie, she could allow herself to mourn the two bitter truths she could no longer deny. The duplicity of Lord Halden Fitzroy-Price and the death of her dream of attaining respectability by marrying a respectable man.

So upset was she, it wasn't until she led her horse out of the copse a few moments later that she realised the obvious fact that her homeward journey would not be swift. Without a companion and with no convenient log or fence nearby to assist her, she'd be unable to clamber back into the saddle. Until she reached the clearing where the groom should be waiting for her, she could proceed no faster than a walk.

Somehow, that additional delay, a minor irritation she

would normally have shrugged off, seemed the last straw. Though she was able to hold back sobs, she couldn't halt the tears that began sliding down her cheeks, blinding her as she trudged back in the direction of Bath.

Too numb and miserable to even care how she looked, when a horseman approached at a canter, she merely swiped the tears from her face with her sleeve and looked to the side, pretending an absorbing interest in the distant vista of trees and fields.

Until a familiar voice shocked her back to the present.

'Prudence!' Johnnie cried. 'What happened? Did you take a fall? Are you all right?'

To her dismay, the concern in his tone, so at odds with the callous disregard of the soldiers, seemed to make the tears flow faster. Shaking her head in the negative, she tried without success to manufacture a smile while she steadied her voice enough to speak. 'N-no, I… N-nothing happened.'

'Don't be ridiculous! Something happened,' he snapped as he jumped down from the saddle. 'Come, let's get you tidied up.' Snagging her horse's reins with one hand and adding them to his own, he took her elbow, guiding her off the road and behind the partial shelter of a broad oak. 'Your hair's coming down and your bonnet's a disaster. You're sure you didn't fall?'

Looking up at him defiantly, her chin still trembling, she said, 'I never fall. I… I lost my hat while galloping and had to dismount to retrieve it.'

'Oh, truly?' he asked sceptically. 'The disarray of her coiffure and the destruction of her hat was all it took to move the intrepid Miss Lattimar to tears?'

Damn him, that reminder of the cause of her distress increased the flow of tears she was trying so hard to stem. 'Is…is it truly so impossible for me to ever be thought respectable?' she whispered, tears once again blurring her vision.

She heard what sounded like a strangled curse. Then he pulled her directly behind the broad tree trunk and took her in his arms. Where, to her added mortification, she could no longer restrain the sobs.

Feeling again like the lost little girl crying after a fall who'd been passed by, unnoticed, by a mother on the arm of her latest lover, she lay her head on Johnnie's chest and wept out her grief, chagrin and searing disappointment.

The flood finally slowed to trickle, then stopped. She pushed against him and immediately he let her go. Ignoring the sense of being bereft that swept over her once she lost the comfort of his protective arms, she muttered, 'Sorry. I'm not usually prone to waterworks. It's your fault, for being so sympathetic.'

That evoked the wisp of a smile. 'So, seeing you in tears, I should have pulled you up short and slapped some sense into you?'

'It's what my brother Gregory would have done. Or Temper. She says tears are a waste of emotion.' In truth, she felt no better for allowing herself the deluge. 'She's probably right,' she added with a sigh.

'Whatever brought them about had nothing to do with the destruction of your headgear. What did happen? Did you encounter some soldiers? I heard in town there was to be a race this afternoon.' His eyes widening, he grabbed her shoulders. 'You weren't *assaulted*, were you?' he asked roughly. 'You're not protecting…someone, are you?'

'No, you mustn't think that! I didn't precisely *encounter*

soldiers. If I appear in disarray, it's because I galloped past a group of them and lost my hat. I thought it might have blown into a little woodland glade just off the road, so I walked my mount back to look for it. I was retrieving it when I heard the soldiers passing by. And I didn't confront them—I remained hidden, like a coward. Even after I discovered they were discussing me…in all the low, degrading ways you would expect soldiers to talk about a *doxy*,' she ended bitterly.

Johnnie sighed. 'You want them punished?' he asked after a moment. 'I can probably find a reason to challenge them—especially Broadmere. I assume he was among the group?'

'What, you're going to fight them all?' she asked. Despite her scornful reply, the wave of gratitude and warmth at his understanding almost brought on another round of tears. Suppressing it, she continued, 'There are too many of them and boxing their ears wouldn't change their opinion of me. If they figured out the reason for the challenge—and after your previous exchange with Broadmere, they very well might—it would only reinforce their view of me. They would simply believe *you* were the man that they assumed I was galloping to meet at some clandestine rendezvous and be certain you are already enjoying my salacious charms.'

'Ah, would that it were true,' he said with an elaborate sigh as he tapped her nose with a finger, obviously trying to cheer her. '*Chahna*, you mustn't upset yourself over what that worthless bunch of malingerers think. They've most likely shredded the reputations and mentally disrobed every female in Bath handsome enough to catch their eye.'

'I wouldn't concern myself—if their views weren't probably also shared by much of Bath. And if I hadn't learned something else...so very distressing.'

Suddenly alert, his amused smile vanished. 'About Lord Halden?'

Her initial surprise at the accuracy of his guess deepened into dismay as she realised its implications. 'You know about him, too? Am I the only one in Bath who didn't?'

'About his hopes of marrying money, so he need not take orders? Or his women and his gaming?'

'His desire to marry me and conveniently deposit me somewhere in the country so he could go to London and use my money to disport himself?' she asked, hoping to have him confirm or deny that awful conclusion by appearing to be already aware of it. Johnnie might not tell her something he thought would distress her—but she knew he wouldn't lie to her.

Struck anew when he merely shrugged, she made herself press harder. 'Do you know for a fact that he gambles extensively and frequents...houses of ill repute, or is that just rumour?'

'You truly wish to know?'

'Heavens, Johnnie, I've been considering *marrying* the man! Don't you think I need to know the truth about him?'

'Most women wouldn't need—or want—to know more than the fact that they'd be marrying a duke's son.'

'But I'm not "most women", am I?' she tossed back bitterly. And then was totally stopped in her tracks by the penetrating gaze, full of wonder, admiration...and *tenderness* he fixed on her.

'No. You are extraordinary,' he said softly.

Before she had a chance to consider the implications of that look and tone, he continued brusquely, 'I'm not privy to Lord Halden's intentions concerning you, though I've heard his...acquaintances declare that is his plan. I have observed his gambling and...sporting proclivities first-hand, however.' He shook his head. 'In any event, he hasn't given much indication he possesses the character one would hope to find in a man about to take holy orders.'

'Spoken as one who shares his proclivities?' she said sharply, then felt ashamed. 'Excuse me, that was unfair. As an unattached gentleman who has made neither overtures nor promises to any lady, you may enjoy whatever pleasures you wish without censure.'

'I'm not all that much a rogue!' he protested with a laugh. 'I'll admit to enjoying a little gaming among friends, but I've never thought it amusing to play Johnnie Raw to the sharps at the hells and my liaisons have been...discreet. I do see others about, though, when I'm walking out late.'

At her eyebrows raised in enquiry, he made an impatient gesture towards his leg. 'Sometimes, when it won't let me sleep, I try to ease it by walking. Not wishing to wake Aunt Pen and have her fuss over me, I leave the house.'

The reminder of his injured leg made her feel even worse for snapping at him. 'I'm sorry again. It's not my place to criticise your activities, of whatever sort.' She took a deep breath. 'I'm calm now. If you'll give me a leg up, we can ride back.'

Instead of moving to let her walk away, he tipped her chin up, so she had to look directly into his eyes. 'You lose nothing by giving up on Lord Halden. The man's not worthy of you. Switch your efforts to enticing someone who is.'

'And who might that be?' she asked wryly. 'As you've already noted, Bath isn't exactly thick on the ground with likely prospects. Besides, if you knew of Lord Halden's true intentions, every man in Bath, if not ladies, know it too. After being so closely associated with him, it's difficult to think about turning my attention in some other direction, knowing th-that—' the very thought of it brought the anguish back, making her voice hitch '—that everyone in Bath is laughing at me for thinking I might retrieve my reputation by marrying a respectable man, and then fixing my efforts on…on a fortune hunter like Lord Halden.'

He shook his head. 'I doubt the rest of society thinks anything more than that you were trying to entice a duke's son—and isn't that what every society mama trains her daughter to attempt?'

That truth cheered her—at little. 'I hope you're right. That's far more flattering than thinking of myself as a…a laughing stock,' she said, once again choking back tears of anger and humiliation.

'Nonsense!' he said bracingly. 'If you are disdained at all, it's only because the other ladies are jealous of your beauty and wit.'

She sighed, not quite believing him, but grateful for his efforts to bolster her spirits. 'Regardless of what others think, it's humiliating to realise how long I persisted in encouraging Lord Halden, in spite of the doubts about his character that have troubled me almost from beginning. Well, enough! I shall encourage him no more. In truth, I wish I could cut him—or treat him with disdain for deceiving me about his true intentions. But alas, I suppose I shall have to at least be polite.'

'If you don't plan to look for other suitors in Bath, what will you do?'

'I'm not sure yet.' What *would* she do, now that her whole purpose for coming to Bath had been exposed as a ridiculous dream of a foolish, naïve girl? That stark realisation lanced through her again, reviving her anguish so that she could no longer hold back the question that had been hovering on her tongue. 'Is it truly so ridiculous to imagine me as a vicar's wife?'

His expression softening, he gently brushed away the tears from the corners of her eyes. 'Not for someone who truly knows you. You're worthy of a man who answers to the highest calling...and ought to be rewarded by finding exactly the sort of gentleman you seek.'

Then, the concern in his eyes changed to another sort of warmth and his fingers on her chin tightened. Muttering something that sounded like 'damn and blast,' as if he couldn't help himself, he bent down—and kissed her.

Surprise shot through her, but she didn't feel the least urge to pull away. Instead, she marvelled at the never-before-experienced sensation of a man's lips on hers, gentle, soft and comforting. Yet at the same time, the sensual charge always in the air between her and *this* man, momentarily suppressed by her emotional turmoil, surged back to life, overwhelming her with an intense awareness of his heat and closeness.

With a murmur, she leaned into him, instinctively seeking the feel of his body against hers. Sparks seemed to ignite wherever her torso touched his, burning along the length of her, urging her closer still. Awkward, but driven, she reached up to clasp his neck.

Suddenly his arms encircled her again, in possession rather than comfort. Ah, what a glimpse of Heaven, that delicate, wet touch of his tongue, tracing her lips! A wash of heat engulfed her entire body, until she felt like she was melting from inside out. Had he not been holding her so tightly, she might have collapsed, her knees buckling under her. When his tongue probed at her lips, begging entry, she opened to him, allowing him to slip into her mouth and explore its moist softness—until his tongue found hers.

Sensation exploded, rippling out in waves from her mouth all over her body. She felt compelled to match him as he led her in a rapier's dance of tongue on tongue, following as he thrust and parried. Her body overheating, she wanted to rip open the thick confines of her wool jacket, unbutton his tunic coat and yank loose vest and shirt. Slip her hands underneath to touch bare skin...

She was fumbling at his buttons to do just that when he suddenly pulled away, setting her roughly at arm's length. His breathing erratic, he gasped, 'It's my turn...to apologise.'

Bereft, protesting, befuddled, she stared at him. 'Why?'

He gave a strangled laugh. 'For almost leading you down the path to become what the soldiers accused you of being. It was wrong of me, so wrong! You deserve, not rough wooing under an oak tree, but a warm chamber, a soft bed—and most of all, your wedding lines.'

As the heat of passion faded and cold reason elbowed its way back into her consciousness, her instinctive dismay over his sudden retreat faded. He was right—were they discovered, she would be irretrievably ruined. Though it was her supposed wanton character that would be affirmed, he, too, would be censured for dallying with an unmarried maiden of good birth.

While she struggled to recover her disordered senses, he tucked wisps of hair back under her hat, straightened her pelisse and attempted to right the drooping feather on her bonnet. She would have been furious at how calm he appeared while she was still reeling…had not his fingers continued to tremble.

'The feather is beyond hope, but I think the rest of you will do,' he said, his voice almost returned to normal range. 'Let's get you back to the city. Wherever is your groom, by the way? He must be riding the slowest piebald hack in equine history.'

'He's not riding after me, he's waiting for me,' she replied, thankful to find she sounded almost recovered as well. 'There's a stand of trees just at the top of Lansdown Hill—not far away from the Feather & Arrow on the Bath Road. I told him he might nip down there and have himself an ale and I would meet him back at the grove after my gallop.'

'He's as useless as a slug for protection, if he's let this much time elapse before coming to look for you. What if you *had* taken a tumble? I know, I know…' He held up a hand to forestall her reply. 'You never fall. I suppose you assured him of that, too. I think your horse is sufficiently rested. Shall I give you a leg up? I'll escort you back to the grove, so he can get you home.'

Home. Where was her home to be now? Would she ever find one?

Though he'd managed for a moment to lighten her mood, in the cold aftermath of frustrated passion, the disappointment and doubts about her future overtook her once again.

'Yes, I should get back,' she said, her voice as listless as her spirits. 'Aunt Gussie will be wondering what happened to me.'

Seeming to sense she had no more taste for discussion, he rode beside her in silence to where the road began its descent back to Bath. There they found the groom, who was dozing on his placid mount.

'Thank you for your escort, Lieutenant,' she said, nodding to Johnnie.

'Shall I see you at the Subscription Ball tonight?'

'I believe Aunt Gussie plans on attending. Though I'm not sure what good it will do.'

His sympathetic gaze raked her face. 'Never give up, Miss Lattimar. When one advance is blocked, shift your attack in another direction. Often, it proves to be a superior one.'

Numbly she nodded. 'I hope so. Shall we go, Stebbins? Until later, Lieutenant.'

Having restored Prudence to the nominal protection of her groom, Johnnie gave her a wave and watched her ride away…his smile fading the moment she disappeared from view. Frowning, he set his own mount back on the road towards the racetrack.

He hated to see her upset, but he wasn't about to lie to cover for Lord Halden, even to spare her further distress. In fact, aside from his fury at discovering how deeply whatever vulgar comments she'd overheard had hurt her, he couldn't help being relieved she had finally discovered Fitzroy-Price's true character for herself, sparing him the unpleasant task of revealing it to her. Which, revolted by the idea of the lovely Prudence throwing herself away on someone so undeserving of her, he would otherwise have felt compelled to do.

The very idea of that womanising gambler forcing his hands on her—his first suspicion when he'd found her alone and in disarray—made him want to skewer the man on his sabre.

Especially given how much he wanted her himself.

Blowing out a frustrated breath, he urged his mount to a trot. When he'd first come upon her, her golden hair coming down, her bonnet dusty and rumpled, her skirts muddy and her glorious blue eyes swimming in tears, he'd been reminded of the barn kitten he'd once rescued as a boy from the dogs tormenting it—a soft, delicate creature attacked by uncaring beasts much bigger and stronger. He'd taken her in his arms, intending only to protect and comfort.

But Prudence Lattimar was not a helpless kitten. Virtually the moment his arms closed around her, his blood surged and his member, always half-aroused around her, hardened.

He thought he'd managed to control himself rather well—until she looked at him with those tear-rimmed eyes, asking if anyone could believe in her, and he'd just *had* to kiss her. And as he should have known the moment he touched her, one soft brush of her lips was not enough.

Not when she turned to fire beneath his fingers. Her initial awkwardness might have been eloquent of her innocence, but she learned quickly, her instinctive response to his caresses containing all the knowledge of every Eve since the dawn of time. With her tongue seeking his and her lush body pressing against him, when her fingers started scratching at buttons he would have been happy to tear loose, he knew with blinding certainty that if he didn't stop that moment, he would no longer be able to resist taking her where those sultry eyes begged him to go.

Fortunately, he'd been sensible enough to stop…this time. But he must take better care not to risk getting himself into such a position again.

Or so he instructed himself, as the little voice in his

head argued that's exactly where he wanted to be—and go further.

Irritated with himself, he blew out a breath. Perhaps he ought to put an end even to circumspect rides and see her only in company. But how was he to determine what her plans were, if they could not talk freely? And how could he protect her, now that her hopes of Lord Halden had been dashed, if he did not know what she intended to do next?

He'd not worry about that now, he concluded, turning his horse back towards Bath. He'd see her at the ball this evening and try to ascertain how it went with her after she'd had time to recover from the distress of the ride.

And look forward to the glory of touching her hand and guiding her through the movements of a dance, protected by the public forum and the crush of spectators from the fierce desire to kiss her again—and claim her for himself.

Chapter Ten

Still too deeply distressed to want to discuss the appalling truths she'd discovered on her ride, Prudence decided it would be easier to face all of Bath at the Subscription Ball than to field the questions Aunt Gussie would surely pose if she tried to cry off from the engagement. And so she found herself later that evening entering the Assembly Rooms beside her chaperon, determinedly pasting her usual serene expression on her face.

A serenity that nearly faltered when, almost immediately after their entry, a smiling Lord Halden Fitzroy-Price walked across the floor to greet her.

Prudence forced herself to smile politely. But she couldn't keep the edge from her voice as, replying to his greeting with its obligatory compliments on her beauty, she said, 'I'm surprised to see you tonight, Lord Halden. From what some of your military friends said when I passed them on the road while I was riding this afternoon, I expected you would be at the track.'

'Ah, yes. But the races were all over by mid-afternoon.'

'And there were no card games to be had tonight?'

'There are always card games. But none that matched the allure of dancing with the most beautiful girl in Bath.'

Biting down the retort that the richest girl must of course be the most beautiful, at her aunt's nod of permission, she allowed Lord Halden to lead her on to the floor, where the next set was forming. Fortunately for her efforts to remain at least nominally polite, the dance was a pattern piece that afforded them little opportunity for private conversation.

She didn't think she could have endured a waltz in his arms.

Hardly had the music ended when she turned from him to walk off the floor, forcing him to trot after her. 'You left the dance so swiftly, you must be in need of refreshment,' he said, snagging her elbow. 'Allow me to escort you to the tea room. I can describe to you some of the excellent animals I saw at the race today.'

Before he could add anything else—and she lost control of her temper and informed him *she* was no longer horseflesh available for his exalted title's purchase—she made him a short curtsy. 'I don't believe I wish to hear about your horses again tonight. I must return to my aunt. Good evening, Lord Halden.'

With that, she left him standing alone at the edge of the dance floor. Fighting down the swell of emotion that continued to hold her on a knife's edge between tears and an explosion of rage, she had nearly reached Aunt Gussie—who was staring at her in puzzled surprise after her abrupt abandonment of Lord Halden—when a familiar uniformed figure caught her eye.

Johnnie came across the floor towards her, his rangy

stride calm and masterful and his smile both intimate and welcoming. Her volatile emotions veering from rage to delight, Pru had to stifle the urge to run into his arms.

'Lieutenant Trethwell, a pleasure!' she said, holding out her hand to him. 'Did you enjoy the rest of your ride… after you rescued me?' she added *sotto voce* as he tucked her hand on his arm.

'A lonely ride it was, to be sure. And are you…recovered from your wild gallop?'

'And my unstable emotions?' she murmured. 'Thank you again for your…sympathy. You helped me more than you could ever know.'

To her surprise, he sighed, a rueful expression on his face. 'Would that I *could* help you in your quest. But at least, in the nick of time, I avoided doing you harm. You are impossibly tempting, you know.'

The unabashed hunger in his eyes seemed to steady her further. She recognised as clearly as he did the danger in the attraction between them. But it was an *honest* attraction, freely admitted. There were no subterfuges between them, no dissembling about wanting one thing while actually pursuing something quite different. She realised she valued more than ever before the frankness and openness she shared with him and perhaps no one else but her sister.

'You are impossibly tempting, too,' she replied—even as, relaxing in his company, she felt some of the weight of her uncertain future lift from her. Was that what it meant to find a true friend one could count upon? 'And since we do tempt each other so much, perhaps we should retire to the refreshment room and feast upon cakes and tea, an indulgence much less dangerous for us both.'

He laughed and she felt her spirits lift even further. *Ah,*

Johnnie, she thought with an inward sigh. *If I believed there were any chance you might be content to remain in England, spending your life as a simple country gentleman, I might dare tempt you further...*

Alas, everything she knew of him told her that he would not be happy living the quiet, settled existence she longed for. Wanting to retrieve what was left of what had been a day of dismal revelations, she vowed to dismiss any further contemplation of her gloomy future and simply enjoy the delight of his company now, while she still had it.

Who knew where she—or he—would end up next and how soon they might have to part?

While they drank tea and nibbled on cakes, she encouraged him to tell her more stories about India. He soon had her laughing with his tales of snake charmers and *shakirs*, and elephant drivers leaning over the backs of *howdahs* to beat away pursuing tigers.

A touch to her arm made her jerk her gaze around—to discover Lord Halden, standing beside them. How long had he been there, listening, before he'd felt compelled to interrupt them?

'Ah, Miss Lattimar, here you are,' he said, according Johnnie a small, unfriendly nod. 'Your aunt told me you'd gone to have tea. I believe a waltz is forming. Will you do me the honour? No other lady here dances so gracefully.'

Prudence feared she might spit in his eye if he tried to hold her as closely as a waltz required. 'Very kind of you to say so, Lord Halden, but I do not feel inclined to waltz. Lieutenant, if you would return me to my aunt? I dare say she is wondering at my long absence.'

'Of course, Miss Lattimar,' Johnnie said. The gaze he fixed on Lord Halden, as if daring him to interfere, was even less cordial than the one the Duke's son had given him. 'It would be my pleasure.'

To Lord Halden's obvious *dis*pleasure, he led her off. Prudence could practically feel his anger and affront at her second snub in the gaze that followed them as Johnnie led her from the room.

'He should have no doubt now that you don't wish him to pay his addresses to you,' the Lieutenant remarked as he led her towards her aunt. That lady, seeing her still on Johnnie's arm rather than accompanying the Duke's son sent in search of her—the man one would have expected her niece to prefer—was once again staring at her, eyebrows lifted in surprise.

'I would be happy to know Lord Halden has taken that point,' she said, looking back to Johnnie, 'but I don't yet feel up to discussing it with my aunt. Could we…take a few turns about the room?'

'You know I can deny you nothing,' he said with a provocative smile.

'You truly can't?' she flashed back. 'Ah, then what might I dare ask for?'

His hand on her arm tightened, then relaxed. 'Best ask carefully, lest we both get burned.'

Oh, that I might dare let you, Prudence thought as he led her away from her puzzled aunt.

They'd made almost one full circuit of the dance floor before the waltz ended. As the last notes faded, Lord Halden emerged from the tea room with a group of friends. But to her exasperation, as the musicians began to strike up the next dance, Fitzroy-Price set his face determinedly and headed in her direction.

'Heavens, he's slow to take a hint,' she muttered. 'Lead me into this set, won't you?'

'Of course,' Johnnie replied promptly. As they took their places, Lord Halden continuing to glower at them, he said, 'This is almost as satisfying as pummelling him in the ring.'

'Much more civilised,' she said, chuckling.

'Probably. I'd still *prefer* to pummel him, but since that opportunity is unlikely to present itself, this will have to suffice.'

'He looks like a spoiled child denied the treat he was expecting,' Pru observed. 'Why did I not fully comprehend sooner how preoccupied he is with his own desires? As if he believed a woman should be grateful a man of his birth and breeding deigned to court her and not expect more than his escort. Especially one of my reputation,' she added with a sigh.

'Well, you need suffer him no more,' Johnnie said bracingly. 'Even an individual as self-absorbed as Fitzroy-Price will have to recognise the meaning of your continued refusal of his overtures.'

'I certainly hope so! I only hope his anger—for I cannot believe he has invested anything more than self-interest in pursuing me—doesn't get directed at you.'

Johnnie's lip curled in disdain. 'You need have no worries on that score. He may be a duke's son, but he's no match for me in a fair fight and he knows it.' Grinning, he added, 'He's even less a match for me in an unfair one.'

'Know some dirty fighting tricks, do you?' Pru asked. 'Would that you were my brother! I could get you to teach them to me.'

Johnnie uttered a strangled groan. 'I can't decide which would be worse. Becoming your brother and giving up the delicious contemplation of having you as a woman, or re-maining simply a normal man, who burns to possess you.'

The sudden heat in his gaze brought back all the memo-ries of their afternoon interlude and the wave of pleasurable sensations that had swamped her as he kissed her...as she kissed him back. 'You are not the only one who burns,' she admitted. 'Perhaps you should return me to Aunt Gussie. I think I've had enough of discouraging Lord Halden for one evening.'

'Perhaps it's best to let the lesson sink in, without the distasteful prospect of having to confront him again,' John-nie agreed, offering his arm. 'To your aunt, then. Will you ride tomorrow?'

She made a grimace of irritation, unhappy both at having to miss a treasured activity—and the opportunity to spend private time in his company. 'I'm afraid not. You remember my aunt's dear friend, Mrs Marsden? After having rented a property in Bath for many years, she's decided to settle here permanently, and recently bought a town house. She's moving in soon and has asked if Aunt Gussie and I would accompany her tomorrow to a warehouse to look at furnish-ings.' Acting upon sudden inspiration and wistful hope, she said, 'You wouldn't be interested in coming along, would you? To give a masculine opinion?'

Lowering her voice, she added, 'We couldn't converse as freely as we do while riding, but it would be better than at these evening entertainments, where we are always sur-rounded by a crowd of onlookers.'

He hesitated and she assumed he was hunting for polite words to refuse. 'Are you sure your aunt would approve of adding me to the company?' he said instead.

'She would appreciate having a gentleman's point of

view,' Pru replied, delighted he hadn't turned her down and sure she could persuade her aunt to agree.

'Very well, then. I'm afraid my expertise at furnishing a lodging extends only to tents, but it might be interesting.' Giving her a teasing smile, he lowered his voice to murmur. 'Perhaps we'll discover some naughty pictures to furnish Mrs Marsden's private salon. Or some nude sculptures?'

'Wretch!' she scolded, feeling her face heat. 'If we should discover anything of the sort, you will *not* point them out to Mrs Marsden!'

'The best classical Greek and Roman sculptures are nudes,' he observed, grinning at her.

'I shall keep that in mind, should I have a need to redecorate my own rooms,' she shot back.

She might have known she couldn't shock him, for he merely laughed. 'I wager you would.'

Enjoying their sparring, she was about to embellish upon her reply when she spied Lord Halden at the other side of the room. Though she avoided meeting his eyes, a sideways glance showed he was crossing the floor towards her.

'Drat and blast, Lord Halden is coming this way again,' Prudence murmured. 'We had better find Aunt Gussie quickly.'

'At your service, ma'am. Shall we try the tea room?'

Walking across to that chamber, they discovered her aunt chatting with a friend. Just before they reached the lady's side, Johnnie said, 'You need only confide to her what you learned today about Fitzroy-Price's true intentions. That will be more than sufficient to explain your sudden lack of interest in him. No reason to mention…anything else you heard.'

He was right, she realised. Immensely relieved that she would not have to repeat the other, far more distressing words that had been spoken about her, she said, 'Good advice. Thank you. For once again coming to my rescue. Will you call for us at nine tomorrow?'

'It will be a pleasure. Lady Stoneway, may I return your niece to you? She was just mentioning how fatigued she is, so I'll bid you both good evening. Shall I summon chairs for you, ma'am?'

'Well—yes, I suppose so. If you truly wish to leave, Prudence?'

'I do, Aunt Gussie. And, no, I don't feel ill, so you mustn't worry. I'll explain later.'

'Then, yes, Lieutenant, I would be obliged if you would arrange chairs for us. Come then, Prudence, let us fetch our wraps.'

'Thank you, Johnnie Trethwell,' she mouthed as he bowed over her aunt's hand. Giving her a little wink, he walked off to do her aunt's bidding.

Chapter Eleven

Fortunately, the bustle required for her aunt to rise and ready herself to leave the house much earlier than usual kept that lady so occupied, she neither remembered to question Pru about her cool treatment of Lord Halden at the Assembly, nor added more than an absent, 'yes, that would be nice', to her niece's blithe assertion that she'd invited Lieutenant Trethwell to accompany them to the shops to secure a masculine opinion. 'After all,' Pru improvised, 'Mrs Marsden often has her sons to stay with her and she wouldn't want them to feel uneasy, having to tiptoe around furnishings that appeared too fragile or feminine.'

Johnnie appeared promptly at nine, chairs were engaged and soon they were disembarking at the warehouse in the lower part of town near the river where they were to meet Mrs Marsden.

'Gracious!' Lady Stoneway said, putting a handkerchief to her nose after she'd alighted from the chair. 'How...insalubrious it is!'

'Not a place for ladies to linger,' Johnnie agreed. 'Shall we ring the bell? I'm sure your friend awaits you within.'

A clerk soon appeared to usher them inside, where to Lady Stoneway's relief, no hint of the miasma from the river penetrated. They followed the clerk upstairs to a long, open room, lit by large windows at either end of the building, its floor space almost completely taken up by various objects of furniture, many of them under holland covers.

Mrs Marsden, attended by an older gentleman who soon identified himself as the establishment's owner, exchanged hugs with Lady Stoneway. 'Thank you so much for coming to assist me! I've never before made such a costly and important purchase, and I am grateful to have your advice.'

'My niece thought, to ensure that Randall and Thomas feel comfortable in their rooms when they visit, you would find a masculine point of view helpful—didn't you, my dear?' She gave Pru a speaking look, which told her though she might have been distracted earlier when her niece casually mentioned inviting the Lieutenant, Lady Stoneway suspected his presence was intended more to gratify Pru than to assist her dear friend.

Before Pru could reply, Mrs Marsden said, 'What an excellent idea, Miss Lattimar! I hadn't previously considered it, but having a gentleman's opinion truly would be helpful. Thank you, Lieutenant, for agreeing to assist.'

'I shall try to be as useful as I can.'

'If you will follow me, ladies and gentleman, I will show the section that contains the collection I described to you, Mrs Marsden. All the pieces were bought or commissioned by the late Colonel Charles McGreavy. The works are of fine quality and blend harmoniously together. Although some are quite rare and costly, rather than sell the pieces one by one, the colonel's heirs were hopeful a purchaser could be found to take most or all the pieces, so their father's collection might be kept together. Shall we have a look?'

Somewhat to Pru's surprise, Johnnie *was* useful. As they removed holland covers from various pieces, it was soon evident that Mrs Marsden was struck more by each item's ornamentation and style than its practicality.

'That gate-leg table does have fine inlay on the feet,' Johnnie said, rolling his eyes at Pru over the crocodile-like decoration. 'Do you intend it for a piece to decorate your reception room, or as a table for dining? If the latter, I fear the damage your sons' booted feet might do to such delicate carving.'

'I suppose you are right, Lieutenant,' Mrs Marsden said. 'Though it is so very handsome!'

'This other dining table is larger and would do better for company dinners,' Johnnie continued. 'It may be plainer, but it is matched by a fine sideboard. Only think how well it would display your china and crystal!'

In a similar manner, he advised her against a gaming table with legs in the Egyptian style, chairs with overlarge ball-and-claw feet just made for tripping over and side tables with startling stripes of zebrawood, recommending instead a number of elegant but sturdy mahogany pieces with a subtle rosewood inlay.

Following his advice, Mrs Marsden ended up selecting all but the most outlandishly decorated pieces in the colonel's lot. While Lady Stoneway and her friend circled the pieces again, refining the final selection, Pru was at last able to have some private words with Johnnie.

'You must have had quite elaborate furnishing in your tents,' she observed with amusement.

'Actually, the Colonel's accommodation was rather splendid,' Johnnie replied. 'I never developed a taste for those animal-headed or footed furniture items that have become so popular, though.'

'The ones with Egyptian motifs?' Pru asked.

'Yes. Perhaps it comes from having forded rivers inhabited by crocodiles. I never wished to invite them into the house.'

As Pru chuckled, Johnnie stopped short. 'The late Colonel must have been an India-serving officer. The pieces under this cloth appear to be Hindu temple carvings.'

Pulling the cloth aside to reveal several stone figures, he pointed at a four-armed one. 'From the iconography of its decoration, I'd say that is a Vishnu and this one a Shiva. The colonel must have been an *early* India hand. It's no longer fashionable to admire native Hindu art or express any sympathy for the religion.'

'Is it so barbaric?'

'I didn't find it so. The idea of the oneness of creation and the respect for all living things I found admirable. I think barbarism depends more on the character of the individual than the religion.'

After rooting further under the cloth covering, he halted, chuckling. 'Then again, the good colonel might just have had a taste for the prurient. There are some statuettes of goddesses back here and, like the classics of Rome and Greece, they are nude. But their activities would certainly shock Mrs Marsden.'

'Let me see,' Prudence said, not sure whether he was being serious or teasing her.

'Better not,' he advised. 'This bas-relief is likely to surprise even a worldly-wise reader of Ovid.'

'Nonsense,' she said, pulling his hand aside—only to drop the cloth back over it a moment later, so truly shocked she felt momentarily light-headed. Knowing her face must be flushed bright red, she stammered, 'M-my goodness! That is...detailed.'

Looking contrite, Johnnie tucked the cloth securely back in place. 'I shouldn't have let you see it,' he apologised, his own face reddening. 'Though its true purpose isn't to...inflame the desires. The Hindus believed that pleasure between man and woman was a delightful part of normal life. There are Sanskrit texts, parts of which are devoted to advice about perfecting the pursuit of pleasure.'

'Texts you have studied?' she asked tartly, trying to recover her composure.

He laughed. 'Alas, my Sanskrit wasn't good enough. Although one can find carvings like this on the walls of many temples.'

'We shall definitely not point that out to Mrs Marsden,' Pru said, her cheeks still hot. She knew she'd not soon forget the expression of bliss on the face of the figure of the reclining woman, the nipples of her full breasts hard and peaked as a man buried his face between her legs.

'An old India hand indeed!' Johnnie said, his voice distracting her from the heated recollection. Reaching under the cloth on an adjoining table, he pulled out a long, carved sword. 'It's a *talwar*—an Indian cavalry sword.' After giving it a quick inspection, he replaced it on the table. 'There are several other good blades in there.'

'Perhaps the colonel was a collector.'

'Apparently there are quite a few collectors in England, not all of them old India hands. Or so the friend for whom I obtained a similar weapon told me. Now that my leg is mostly healed—or as healed as it's going to get—I've been preparing for what I mean to do next.'

'Not a return to the army, surely.'

'No, I've had my fill of that. But a letter I received this morning from my brother James reinforced my intentions to pursue a different possibility. Not that he suggested it directly—indeed, my entire family will probably have palpitations if I succeed at this venture.'

'What, cause your family further distress? Surely you wouldn't think of it!'

He smiled at her teasing. 'Even a family known for its reprobates will baulk at this. James mentioned a friend of *his* had recently bought some swords, scimitars and *talwars* from a dealer, at a price that made me whistle! I've recently discovered there are a growing number of wealthy men who collect weapons and, with Britain's expanding presence in India, an increasing demand for weapons from that region.'

'I'm not surprised,' Pru said. 'My own father has collected weapons for years.'

He nodded. 'I will soon be meeting with several wealthy men, including the one for whom I brought back the *talwar*, who have expressed interest in advancing me the funds to set up a business acquiring similar articles. Given my familiarity with the area and my contacts in the bazaars—where, I assure you, there are weapons to be had for a fraction of what James reported his friend paid for his—I'm sure I could sell the items back in England at a profit.'

'I imagine you could. And not just weapons. Men with time and money to spare collect all sorts of things. When you meet with your initial investors, you should ask them what other items their fellow collectors are looking for— artwork, gemstones, artefacts.'

'I hadn't thought of that—but you're right!' His face lighting with enthusiasm, Johnnie said, 'I've always wanted to penetrate further into the subcontinent than I was permitted to wander from the cantonment where I was posted. Who knows what other treasures lurk, waiting to be discovered?'

'And how many merchants, *shakirs* and *maharanis* there are to meet, entertain and bewitch?' she added, a pang of sadness going through her that she was not a foreign treasure he was eager to acquire, or a distant land he was drawn to explore.

No, she was only a straightforward, ordinary English Beauty who would never hold the attention of a man fascinated by the exotic.

Pushing away that depressing thought, she said, 'I think Mrs Marsden and my aunt have finished making their selections. Shall we rejoin them—before you give in to the temptation to shock her with those carvings?'

He offered his arm and she took it. 'I never shock ladies,' he said primly. 'Unless they want me to.'

She was saved from replying to that by Mrs Marsden coming over to pat her hand. 'Thank you so much for your help. Both of you! I feel much more confident now about how well the house will turn out. And I'm sure my sons will thank you, Lieutenant, for making sure they will feel comfortable around all the furnishings!'

'It was my pleasure, Mrs Marsden. I'm glad we were able to discover so many…evocative pieces.'

Pru felt her face heat again, certain he was referencing the one work they could not let Mrs Marsden discover.

'I'm not much acquainted with the lower part of Bath, but I believe we are not far from Sally Lunn's teahouse,' Mrs Marsden said. 'Let me invite all of you there for some refreshment.'

The party accepting her invitation, chairs were procured for the short transit—Prudence, briefly alone in hers, trying to keep her mind from dwelling on the erotic carving she'd witnessed. Just what was that man doing between the woman's thighs?

Whatever it was, the lady appeared to very much enjoy it.

Which she didn't doubt. Her whole body tingled with anticipation at the idea of Johnnie Trethwell touching her anywhere, much less in so…intimate a place.

They soon disembarked at the bakery and, after some of the famous cakes and some tea, the party decided to stroll up Milsom Street, Mrs Marsden being eager to acquire some linens and glassware to complement her furniture purchases.

They had turned the corner from Burton Street into Milsom when Pru spotted Lady Isabelle gazing at the window of a bonnet shop, Lord Halden looking bored as he stood beside her.

Before she could turn away, *he* saw *her* and, after a word to Lady Isabelle, headed in her direction. Johnnie must have seen him, too, for he tightened his grip on her arm and muttered a curse that echoed her own feelings.

'Don't worry. I won't let him annoy you,' he murmured.

The next moment, Lord Halden reached them. 'Lady Stoneway, Mrs Marsden and Miss Lattimar,' he said, bowing to the ladies. 'Trethwell,' he added frostily.

'Lord Halden!' Mrs Marsden said, beaming, obviously still believing that the Duke's son was a prime matrimonial prize whose escort Pru would certainly prefer to that of a lowly lieutenant. 'How good to see you! We're about to walk up Milsom Street. Would you like to join us?'

'Mrs Marsden, you must see that Lord Halden is presently occupied by his cousin Lady Isabelle—she's over there, at the milliner's,' Pru broke in before the Duke's son could answer. 'It would be most inconsiderate to rob her of her escort and I'm sure she is much too busy for a dawdling walk up Milsom Street. Another time, perhaps? Good day, Lord Halden.'

Inclining her head, she urged Johnnie to walk her past him. 'Now, Mrs Marsden, which shop was it that carries the linens you wished to see?'

Though Pru didn't look back, she could feel Lord Halden's fulminating gaze on her as they left him behind. But either he was too polite to charge after them and abandon his aunt—or more likely, too arrogant to consider running after any female, for fortunately, he made no attempt to follow.

Her snub of the Duke's son apparently recalled to Lady Stoneway Pru's similarly cold behaviour to him at the Assembly the previous evening, for she gave Pru a searching glance. However, thankfully deciding she would not quiz her niece about her puzzling behaviour on a public street, she bent her efforts instead on distracting Mrs Marsden from her shocked reaction to the cut by posing a series of questions about the colour and finish of the linens she sought.

'Perhaps now he will finally take the hint,' Pru murmured to Johnnie.

'Let us hope so,' he replied. 'A man of his birth and self-importance seldom expends much effort on a female who's made it clear she doesn't desire his attention.'

'Not when there will always be so many others who do. Sadly few in Bath, though, who possess so handsome a dowry.'

'Might be good for his character to be denied now and

then,' Johnnie observed. 'I'm afraid I too must abandon you, though. I'm accompanying Aunt Pen to a concert this afternoon. Will I see you at the Harrison musicale tonight?'

'I'm afraid not. The removers come tomorrow and we promised to help Mrs Marsden choose which of her belongings she wanted to keep after considering the other furnishings she bought today.' Pru laughed ruefully. 'Which may serve to delay Aunt Gussie a bit longer from demanding why I'm suddenly snubbing Lord Halden.'

'Just tell her the truth. I'm sure she'll support your decision.'

Pru sighed. 'I hope so.'

'I'm afraid it must be goodbye, then, after I take my leave of your aunt and Mrs Marsden. Will you ride tomorrow morning?'

'I certainly hope so.'

'Then I'll hope to see you.'

He squeezed her hand, leaving her bereft when he pulled away and turned to bid goodbye to the other ladies. After more profuse thanks from Mrs Marsden, he gave them all a bow and walked off.

His limp *was* less pronounced than it had been, Pru noted as she watched him.

Which meant he would soon be recovered enough to leave Bath and go about setting up his trading company. It was just as well, she supposed, her spirits sagging. Now that she'd dismissed Lord Halden from contention, with few other suitable matrimonial prospects in the city, she wasn't sure it was worth remaining here for the rest of the Season herself.

Chapter Twelve

After a mostly sleepless night during which Prudence found herself repeatedly awakening from a fitful slumber to memories of her humiliating interlude hiding in the shrubbery, she rose early. Knowing only a hard ride would drive away the demons and restore to her enough serenity to finally have that talk with Aunt Gussie—she'd put off revealing her discovery of Lord Halden's true intentions towards her again last night, pleading an all-too-real headache—she resolved not to wait until later in the morning, when she might hope to encounter Johnnie.

He'd rescued her on several occasions now, she thought wistfully as her sleepy maid helped her into her habit. But much as she appreciated his protecting and encouraging her—and as keenly as she longed to be back in his arms—indulging in solitary interludes with him might tempt her to actions that truly would ruin her, should anyone discover them.

A wave of heat rippled through her, and once again, she

had to banish thoughts of the well-pleasured lady in the temple relief. Though she was beginning to doubt she would ever find a suitable partner for a compatible marriage, she didn't want to make herself into such an outcast that marriage to a respectable gentleman at some time in the future would be impossible.

And Johnnie Trethwell, dear as he'd become to her, couldn't be part of that future. The best she could hope was that they might remain friends. Maybe when he went adventuring again, they might exchange letters, his relating more amusing, fascinating and exciting tales like those he'd already shared with her about the India he loved, the foreign lands so inextricably part of the man he'd become.

Surprising the livery groom, who had apparently only just arrived at the stable, she sent him off to saddle her grey mare with more than his normal fee to sweeten his reluctance to leave his steaming cup of coffee. And so, as dawn lightened the low-hanging clouds to the east, she was once again riding through the heavy, swirling mist up the road to the heights of Lansdown Hill.

For once, not even the prospect of a gallop cheered her. Which was just as well, for even when she reached the summit, a thick fog still blanketed the ground. Though her fresh mare strained at the bit, obviously eager for a run, Prudence held her to a trot, her mind going round and round as she tried to determine her best path for the future.

With Lord Halden's duplicity revealed, was there any reason for her to remain in Bath? Even if the Duke's son had deceived the matrons of Bath as effectively about his intentions as he had her, eliminating the added humiliation of being laughed at for encouraging him, it required only a quick run-through of her other would-be suitors to conclude that she felt nothing for any of them stronger than a mild appreciation. None had inspired in her a sense of connection or stirring of affection that hinted it might deepen into the love and admiration she needed to pledge herself to someone for a lifetime.

There was only one man who'd elicited a strong response from her—and Johnnie had no interest in marrying and settling down. Though she felt immensely drawn to him and freely admitted she yearned for his touch, she'd been too scarred by growing up with a scandalous mother to ever be comfortable living as his mistress, *carte blanche* being the only offer he was likely to make her. Worse than earning for herself the notoriety she'd tried all her life to escape would be knowing that, sooner or later, he'd grow bored with her or England or both and move on.

How odd that they'd made such an immediate connection, she thought with a wistful sigh. She, a girl who'd seldom been far from home and he, a man who'd travelled half a world away. But despite the vast differences in their experiences, she couldn't help but contrast the free and easy exchange of ideas they shared, the sense of being accepted and valued for herself Johnnie gave her, with the stiffness and disconnection she felt around every other gentleman.

If she were brutally honest, she was more than a little afraid she'd stupidly fallen in love with Johnnie Trethwell. There was a chance he might reciprocate her affections, though she was not at all sure he felt for her more than an indulgent fondness for a sheltered ingénue.

Perhaps, like Temperance, she was destined to remain a spinster.

And if that were the case, as often as her thoughts seemed to go back to that temple carving, perhaps she should re-

A Most Unsuitable Match

move herself from Bath before her senses outwitted her wit and the potent temptation Johnnie posed lured her into doing something that would disgrace her for the rest of her life.

The sound of hoofbeats approaching through the fog behind her pulled her from her reverie. But the anticipation that leapt in her chest died immediately as the rider emerging from the mist turned out to be not Lieutenant Trethwell—but Lord Halden Fitzroy-Price.

Though he was, as always, impeccably turned out in his dark riding dress and boots polished to a high shine, as he came close, she noticed his eyes looked red-rimmed and weary, and the curve of lips he accorded her when he realised she'd seen him seemed more grimace than smile.

Distaste and resentment bubbled up. Could she not even be allowed the solace of a solitary morning ride? It seemed ironic that, after several weeks of making every attempt to appear where she might encounter him, only now did he seem suddenly bent on making a concerted effort to seek *her* out—despite her pointed discouragement.

He must need her money very badly.

How lovely that she must no longer maintain quite so careful a control over her tongue.

'Lord Halden,' she said, giving him a slight nod, but neither pulling up nor slowing her mare's pace to accommodate his arrival.

'Miss Lattimar. Damn and blast—how can you enjoy riding at such an ungodly hour of the morning?'

'Perhaps because I've not spent my night submerged in brandy and revelry? If you're just returning from those, you're riding in the opposite direction from town, you know.'

'Of course I know!' he spat back, his tone aggrieved. 'As you must realise, I rode out precisely to encounter you.'

'I cannot imagine why. Or how you even knew I was riding, admittedly somewhat earlier than usual. Unless… surely you haven't paid someone to spy on me?' she cried, incredulous, but unable to imagine how else the Duke's son would have known she'd left her aunt's town house.

'I needed to keep track of you and a pretty penny it's costing me,' he replied. 'But since you've suddenly became so persistent about discouraging my escort, I needed to contrive some way to speak with you alone.'

She gave him a sharp glance. 'If you noticed my attempts to discourage you, you must realise there is nothing you need to speak about to me alone.'

'How can you say that, after the very great *encouragement* you've given me these past weeks?'

He had her there, she acknowledged, chagrin heating her face. 'That may be true. But a lady retains the privilege of changing her mind…especially when she discovers compelling reasons to do so,' she added, her tone turning acid. Hoping he wouldn't be arrogant or foolish enough to protest he had no idea what she meant, she kicked her horse into a canter. 'Good day, Lord Halden.'

'Not so fast!' he snarled at her. To her surprise, he rode over and seized the mare's bridle, forcing the horse to a halt. 'How dare you presume to pass judgement on *my* desire to marry wealth? You, daughter of a whore who's shown herself as profligate as her mother, throwing yourself at that shabby-dressed half-pay cripple!'

'Who is ten times the man you'll ever be, despite his limp!' she shot back angrily. 'Release my reins, sir.'

Instead, in one swift movement, he sprang down from

his horse, grabbing her hand and jerking her off her side-saddle as he did so. Flailing to try to prevent herself from falling, she found herself captured in his arms before her feet could touch the ground.

Truly furious now, she struggled to free herself. 'Let me go this instant!' she cried, turning her head away from the brandy fumes that emanated from his person.

'I shall not let you go,' he retorted, allowing her to step away, but tightening his grip on her arm. 'You think I intend to let a dowry as handsome as yours slip through my fingers?'

'When you are probably in debt to every tradesman and brothel in Bath, and have such *fond* plans of spending my blunt in future?'

He uttered a rough laugh. 'Precisely. So you found out about my little...excursions, did you? Your whey-faced soldier carrying tales?'

'I'd like to see you dare call him that to his face. But then, you'd risk getting your arrogant nose broken and your pompous behind tossed in the dirt.'

Apparently not quite self-deluded enough to deny that truth, he ignored it. 'Whatever your suddenly developed distaste for my company, we *will* wed,' he continued, seeming supremely self-confident. 'You've been far too encouraging of my suit for society to consider you anything but a tease and jilt if you don't. Even your papa's guineas wouldn't be enough to buy you a husband then.'

'Better to remain a spinster than marry a man like you.'

'Oh, come now,' he said, his tone turning more beguiling. 'You needn't get your nose in a snit. I've more than enough stamina to keep you satisfied, whatever my other...pursuits. Only remember, you'll spend most of your time running a grand household worthy of a duke's son and maintaining a position in society more elevated than you could otherwise ever hope to attain. And once I've got some brats on you, I won't be too particular about the company you keep.' He laughed. 'You could even entertain your cripple.'

She tugged her hand, trying to break his grip. 'This conversation is over.'

His good humour faded, his face hardening and his eyes turning cold. 'If you're going to be intransigent, we'll resort to persuasion of a different sort.'

With surprising strength, he yanked her towards him and wrapped his arms around her shoulders. Lowering his head, he attempted to kiss her.

Pru ducked away and pushed at him. 'If you don't let me go *this instant*,' she hissed, 'I can't be held responsible for my response.'

'Couldn't help yourself responding, could you, my hot little piece?' Loosening his grip long enough to pluck off her hat, he tore the veil as he tossed it away. In another swift motion, he pulled a handful of pins from her hair, sending a heavy cascade of tresses down her back as he forced her close again. Holding her in an implacable grip, he bent to kiss the bared skin of her neck, sucking hard on the sensitive skin.

Shuddering against the touch of his mouth, she finally understood his intention. 'You—you intend to compromise me!'

'Of course, my sweet,' he murmured against her neck. 'When you return to Bath looking dishevelled, people will be too delighted to confirm what they've always suspected about your wanton nature to refrain from gossiping. And if no one happens to observe you, I shall just drop a little hint about our *excursion* myself. You *will* wed me, or be irretrievably ruined. So why not relax and enjoy what we both know you want?'

'Let me go, you villain!' she cried. Wrestling to try to win enough space to free herself, she managed to elbow him in the side. Grunting, he tightened his hold, his fingernails biting into her arms through the wool of her habit.

'Witch!' he growled. 'Want it rough, do you? Despite your sweet-as-treacle ways, we both know under that bodice is the luscious bosom of a wench who's just as hot for it as her mother. Maybe I won't take you here…but I will have a taste.'

He was too strong for her, she realised. Thinking furiously of some other way to throw him off, she let herself soften a bit, so he was able to force her chin up and kiss her. His insistent tongue probed at her closed lips until, nearly gagging, she let him gain entry into her mouth. As he moaned, his tongue thrusting at hers, she bit down hard.

He cried out and jerked his head away, one hand going to his mouth. Bound to him now only by the one arm, she pulled back as far as she could and used the extra distance to slam her knee up into his tented trouser front, while using her free hand to rake her fingernails across his face.

Howling, he released her, both hands going to cradle his battered anatomy. Hoping she could somehow manage to remount her horse before he recovered enough to come after her—for she had no doubt now that, should he catch her, he'd be furious enough to violate her completely—Pru raced to where the horses had wandered, grazing on the verge.

Her heartbeat pounding in her ears, she grabbed the mare's reins, scrabbling with her other hand to get enough purchase on the horn of the side-saddle that she might be able to get a foot in the stirrup and swing herself up. Struggling with that near-impossible task, she kept a sidelong glance on Fitzroy-Price, still bent over and groaning half-a-dozen paces away.

Oh, how she wished she were free of these clinging, trailing skirts! Back in the meadows at Entremer in a pair of her brother's cast-off breeches, able to grab a horse by the mane and swing herself on to its broad, bare back unaided.

She got her foot up—*almost* into the stirrup before it slipped away. The mare danced nervously at this unusual mounting technique—no doubt further unsettled by the groans coming from the man a few paces away. Panting, Pru crooned to her, trying to soothe the little horse so she could make another attempt.

But, frightened, the mare jerked free, backing away from her. Just as Fitzroy-Price, finally straightening to his full height, headed towards her, murder in his eyes.

Chapter Thirteen

Pru was frantically looking about for a fallen branch, a rock, anything she might fashion into a weapon, when from out of the mist, a rider emerged at a gallop.

So consumed with the urgency of making an escape she'd not even heard its approach, she almost wept with relief when she saw that the man vaulting from the saddle was Johnnie Trethwell.

Before she could utter a word, he'd assessed the situation. Advancing on Lord Halden, he dealt him a tremendous blow to the jaw that sent the Duke's son reeling into the dirt. Following him down, he leaned over to grab Fitzroy-Price by the cravat and lift him up to deliver another blow to his chin. He was raising the booted foot of his good leg, obviously intending to deliver a kick, when Pru ran over to catch his sleeve.

'Enough, Johnnie!' she cried, pulling on him. 'That's enough. Let him go.'

He fixed his gaze on her, his grey-green eyes blazing such

fury she took an involuntary step backwards. And then she realised how she must look to him—her hat gone, her hair half-down, her mouth reddened from the harsh pressure of Lord Halden's kisses, the mark of his mouth on her neck. 'I'm all right,' she said urgently. 'He didn't hurt me. Not really. Let him go. Please.'

She could feel the coiled strength of him radiating to her fingertips as he stared fiercely at her, anger humming through his body. At last, some of the tension eased. 'Very well. For you, I won't kick the life out of him like the cur deserves.'

Pulling from her grasp, he went over to Lord Halden, grabbed the man's hand and dragged him to his feet. 'Not a word, or I'll disregard Miss Lattimar's plea that I stop,' he warned as he pushed the man towards his horse.

After shoving him none too gently into the saddle, Johnnie said, 'Tell your friends you were bested in a friendly boxing match that got out of hand—though I'm not sure how you'll explain those scratches. If you breathe a syllable of what really happened, I'll come after you and there will be no Miss Lattimar to beg for mercy. Now, get out of my sight before I change my mind and finish you here and now.'

Slapping the horse on the rump, Johnnie watched as it leapt forward. A moment later, horse and rider had disappeared into the cloaking mist.

Limping back over, he placed one hand on Pru's shoulder and used the other to raise her face, closely inspecting it. Determined not to give way to tears, she managed a smile. 'As you see, I'm f-fine.'

She almost lost that battle when, with the gentlest whisper of a touch, he ran his thumb over her swollen lips, then traced the livid red mark she knew must stand out sharply against the pale skin beneath her ear. 'Damnation! I should have kicked the hell out of him. Sorry—but other than this, which is more than enough justification for a beating, he didn't…hurt you, did he?'

She shook her head rapidly to displace the few tears that had gathered, despite her best intentions. 'No. Thankfully, you arrived before he could. I… I don't think I could have managed to remount before he caught me.'

He shook his head. 'You can't imagine what went through my head when I heard you crying out, somewhere ahead of me in the mist. You're lucky I didn't kill him where he stood.'

Suddenly struck by an awful thought, her eyes widened. 'You—you can't think that I *asked* him to ride with me! Even to make him understand he must cease his courtship of me, I wouldn't have been so foolish as—'

'No, no, I don't think that. You rode out earlier than usual this morning. Did he meet you by chance on his way back from a night of gaming at the soldiers' camp?'

'It's worse than that,' she said bitterly. 'He paid to have someone watch Aunt Gussie's house and then followed me here. To press his suit. He said since I'd encouraged him so publicly for weeks, if I now refused to marry him, I'd be labelled a flirt and a jilt, and no other respectable man would have me. When I told him I'd rather live out my life as a spinster than marry him, he tried to…force his attentions on me, so that once he revealed what happened here, I would be so thoroughly ruined that no other man but him would wed me. He's certain to spread the word about the incident if I continue to refuse him, "regretfully" admitting he'd been swept away by my charms when I lured him into riding with me this morning, proving me a wanton no sane man would dare to marry. Either way, I end up ruined.'

'You think, with the way his face will look by the time he gets back to town, anyone will believe you submitted to him willingly?'

She shrugged. 'He's a duke's son. Whatever he says will be believed. He might even throw in a faradiddle about nobly sustaining those blows while rescuing me from *you*, after which, overcome by gratitude, I offered him my person.'

'That won't explain away the marks left by your fingernails! Besides, you think he will take my threat so lightly?' Johnnie said hotly.

'Oh, I believe he acknowledges the seriousness of it. But I also think he's arrogant enough to believe, when it comes down to it, I would choose miserable marriage to him over disgrace and spinsterhood. I expect most women would. But I will not.'

'Then if he dares repeat his falsehoods, he will get what he deserves.'

Pru shook her head, a dull resignation seeping through her. 'He'll probably send a note to Aunt Gussie's later, asking one final time if I will accept him—I doubt he'd dare present himself in person. If I persist in refusing him, he's too vain to tolerate such an insult without exacting retribution for having me thwart the easy path to the wealth he feels he deserves. And he's cunning enough to devise a way to ruin me while protecting himself against you. He need only do his damage and disappear into the home of one of his cronies for a while.'

She sighed. 'Johnnie, you of all people know what men of that ilk are like! He will rework this whole scene in his head until he's convinced himself that I am the villainess, he the upright gentleman who offered respectable marriage to a female who didn't deserve it. With his pride and vanity offended, he'll have no compunction about seeing me thoroughly ruined.'

He stood silently beside her, obviously considering her words. 'Damn it!' he burst out a moment later. 'Sorry again, but you're right. A man like that will take self-righteous pleasure in seeing you ruined. And short of tracking him down at his cousin's and putting a ball through him, I don't see how I can prevent it.'

Scorched bare by the emotional firestorm of the last half-hour, shock followed by fury, fear and a near despair, his concern touched her on the raw. 'Dear Johnnie,' she said softly, tracing his face with one finger. 'You've been such a champion for me! At least you know that, whatever Fitz-roy-Price says, you got here in time to prevent him from truly ruining me.'

'His gain. If he'd managed that, he'd be a dead man, no matter where he hid and for however long.'

'Well, fortunately you won't have to delay your future plans to stalk him.'

He released her and walked over to pick up her discarded hat, frowning as he fingered the torn veil. 'Once again, you've managed to destroy your headgear. But if you'll accompany me behind another conveniently broad oak—not that, in this fog, anyone riding in this direction could see ten feet off the road anyway—I'll do my clumsy best to repair your coiffure.'

'Perhaps Temper was right all along,' Pru said as she followed him to the oak. 'Perhaps it's useless to try to play by the rules, when those rules have already condemned me, no matter what I do. A condemnation that will be unanimous and permanent, after Fitzroy-Price does his damage.'

'You…wouldn't consider marrying him?'

She gave him a withering glance. 'Would you consider wedding Lady Arbuthnot to have her additional wealth to fund your venture?'

'Point taken.' Chuckling, he gathered up some of her fallen tresses and attempted to wrap them back around her coiffure. 'Maybe if I coil it tightly, it will stay under your hat.'

'Yes, try that. If you're careful, you can slip out a few of the pins from the front to help secure the back.'

'Keep still while I attempt it.'

As she held herself immobile while Johnnie worked, something from deep within bubbled up, the lethargy of despair and hopelessness slowly overshadowed by a sense almost of…relief. As if a page had been turned, closing off the past and presenting her with a new future, uncharted but clear. A future that offered a freedom she'd never before allowed herself.

'Perhaps being ruined won't be so bad after all.'

He paused to look down at her quizzically. 'What, you're going to take on the whole world?'

'Isn't that what I *have* been doing? Now there's no need any longer. No more pasting an impassive façade on my face, considering every remark before I utter it, every action before I take it. All to meet a censorious society's expectations of how a virtuous young maiden should conduct herself—even as society inspected me like a specimen under glass for every tiny infraction, eager to justify its preconceived opinion that I was *not* a virtuous young maiden.

Doesn't being ruined finally set me free to say what I want? *Do* what I want, without a care for what anyone else thinks?'

Giving her an indulgent smile, he carefully settled her riding hat back over the makeshift coiffure. 'And what do you want, *chahna*?'

With a joyous sense of release, she allowed all the pent-up passion for him she'd been restraining since the moment they met to flood out. 'This,' she whispered.

Reaching up to clasp his neck, she pulled his face down and kissed him.

Like many a soldier, Johnnie knew that being in the grip of some strong emotion—rage, fear, the driving impera-tive to protect one's men—loosened one's hold over all the rest. Like lust. And after rescuing her from being mauled by Fitzroy-Price, his anger was still white-hot.

So the moment Pru's mouth touched his, a little clum-sily, the lack of finesse betraying her inexperience, he went from simmering desire to raging passion in an instant. His craving for her, muted but never subdued, overwhelmed him like that attack of dacoits riding at full cry, snuffing out before it could fully form any thought that this might not be wise, shutting down everything but the compelling need to possess her.

No gentle brush of her lips this time. Wrapping his arms around her and binding her against him, he possessed and ravished them, demanding entry, scouring her tongue with his as he licked and probed, nipped and suckled. Consumed by the fire in his blood, he slid his hands down her back, kneading, caressing, until he could cup her bottom and pull her against an erection so hard it was nearly pain.

She gave him every encouragement to continue, meeting the thrusts of his tongue with bold strokes of her own, her hands clawing at the knot of his cravat, the buttons on his waistcoat.

She broke the kiss, gasping, rubbing her face against his. 'I want you, Johnnie. I understand now why my mother, denied this by Papa, reached out for it with other men. But I don't want anyone else. Only you. Take me. Love me. Show me everything you make me yearn for.'

Her long speech gave sanity time to break through the haze of madness that had possessed him. It would be an unforgivable violation of their friendship for him to take her. But he could kiss and caress her for a while longer before the honourable part of him wrestled free of the grip lust had over him, and forced him to let her go completely.

'Touch me,' she urged. 'I want to feel your hands on me.'

Taking her mouth again, he unbuttoned the jacket of her habit and her blouse to run his hands over breasts so full, so voluptuous, his mouth watered to taste them and suckle the pebbled texture of her nipples. The impenetrable layers of shift and corset making that impossible, he gave her long, drugging kisses, licking her lips in rhythm to the stroke of his fingers over her breasts.

'Too…many garments,' she gasped between kisses.

She worked her fingers under his cravat, prying open his shirt front, sliding her hands down to rub her fingers over his chest. While he shuddered, breaking the kiss, jolted by the fire of her touch, she murmured, 'I want to feel your hands, your mouth, on *my* bare skin.'

Eager to comply, he kissed the tender area under her chin, the velvet expanse of the neck she arched for him. He continued down her throat, his tongue seeking her collarbone, teasing below the edge of her chemise and corset to lave the full rounded tops of her breasts.

Until she shocked him again, leaving him paralysed by sensation as she fumbled open the straining buttons of his trouser flap and touched his rigid member. As he hissed between his teeth, her fingers on him stilled. 'Does that... not please you?' she whispered.

'It's...intoxicating,' he replied, then caught her hand before she could run her fingers down his length. 'But you mustn't.'

'I can't get out of this habit. But here,' she said, drawing up her skirt with one hand, 'I'm bare beneath. And I can bare...this.'

Slowly, tentatively, she stroked down his shaft. Obviously emboldened when, helpless to control his reaction, it leapt under her caressing fingers, she stroked him again.

'I'm not exactly sure how this is contrived between a man and a woman,' she said, nearly driving him to the brink as her even, measured strokes extended further and further, almost reaching the aching tip. 'But you can touch me with this, can't you? And that will bring us both ultimate pleasure?'

He could let her bare him, lay her on his coat, kiss his way up her sweet legs and inner thighs until he reached the throbbing centre of her. Plumb her depths with tongue and fingers until she reached a climax so powerful that, humming with satisfaction, she would probably not feel any pain when he pierced her maidenhood. Having breached that, he could still, letting her adjust to his invasion, kissing her lips, her neck until her body began to respond of its own volition, her hips rocking to invite him deeper. Then he could bury himself in her sweet centre...

And spill his seed, imperilling her with the burden of an illicit child that would complete the ruin of her future.

Sweat dripping from his forehead, he pushed away her exploring fingers and tugged down her skirts. 'A pleasure I have no doubt would be unparalleled. But, *chahna*, the risk is far too great. We have no means of preventing conception. It's madness to count on being lucky enough to avoid that.'

Not trusting himself to touch her, he stepped away, his body still on fire, his arms and hands trembling. 'It's not that I don't want you. I've dreamed of possessing you, almost from the moment I first saw you in Sidney Gardens. But you offered, and I accepted, *friendship*. It would be the act of a villain, not a friend, to steal your innocence and take you so irresponsibly.'

Absently she rubbed at the loose buttons of her jacket. 'Then...you will offer me—nothing?'

From some unfathomable recess of his brain, he heard himself saying, 'Well, I... I suppose you could marry *me*.'

She gasped, her eyes flaring wide...and then slapped him across the face with all her strength.

Reeling a little on his bad leg, he held up both hands. 'I didn't mean to insult you!'

'Bad enough that Lord Halden wanted to marry me for my money!' she raged. 'I'll not have you offer for me out of, of...*pity*! I'll have you know I won't settle for less than loyalty, devotion and *love* from a husband. You can't offer that...can you?'

Could he love her? Did he love her? Before he could put his rattled thoughts in sufficient order to even consider her question, she snapped, 'I thought not. Much as I desire you, I'll not live with you as your mistress.'

Stung, he retorted, 'I would never do you the insult of offering *carte blanche*!'

'Then you would leave me with *nothing* before we part? No taste of passion to warm the rest of my lonely life? Surely there is *some* way to pleasure that doesn't risk conceiving a child.'

Good sense insisted that he deny it and get her back to town. But an insidious little voice was whispering in his ear that he could give her—give them both—that pleasure. There were many paths to a fulfilment he just *knew* would be spectacular, without the threat of her bearing a bastard.

The randy, desperate, foolish part of him urged him to agree, to begin scheming immediately to discover a time and place to make such an assignation happen. The honourable part of him fought back, insisting that taking her innocence without being willing to pledge any commitment to her would be as infamous as making her his mistress.

Fighting that internal battle, he stood silent—until he looked up to see her smiling. 'So there is a way,' she murmured. 'Something sweet and pure and joyous, that will for ever remind me of you.'

Damnation, why couldn't he just lie to her?

Somehow, he couldn't. Clamping his lips shut, he reached over and brusquely began refastening the buttons of her garments. 'Time to make you presentable and get you back to Bath.'

'You said you could deny me nothing. Before you hurry me back to Bath—and the imminent destruction of my reputation at the hands of Lord Halden—I insist on one more kiss.'

When he leaned over to give her a chaste peck on the forehead, she merely laughed. In her dancing eyes, he saw dawning the dangerous realisation of the sensual power she held over him.

Did she have any idea how close she was to breaking him, to cindering all his good intentions in an inferno of passion?

More shaken and unsure of himself than he'd been while facing down charging outlaws bent on his destruction, he finished her last buttons, righted his own dishevelled cravat as best he could with trembling hands and motioned her towards her grazing mount.

As he gave her a leg up into the saddle, she leaned down to touch his sleeve. 'Thank you,' she said softly.

'For what?'

'For not saying "no" to my request.'

Heaven help him, how *was* he going to deny her?

Trying to unstick a mind which seemed to have frozen on an image of pleasuring her, he threw himself back into his own saddle and nodded at her to follow as he led her back to the road and on towards the clearing where the useless groom waited. He shouldn't even consider fulfilling her request—which would be difficult enough to arrange, even if he were convinced it would be wise.

He'd been pursued by bored matrons before, but their invitations to seduction had always been subtle, delivered by passionate glances or in conversations full of innuendo and double entendre. And in the end, he'd been the one who controlled the situation and made the first move.

Then came unique and unparalleled Prudence Lattimar. Who stated her desire plainly and without subterfuge—as she spoke of everything else. Surely, once she regained her equilibrium after the emotional upheaval of nearly being violated by a man she'd trusted, her good sense would tell her such an interlude was impossible.

Saving him from playing the unprecedented role of the seducer trying to avoid seduction.

Chapter Fourteen

Thankful that Aunt Gussie wasn't an early riser, Prudence was able to slip up to her chamber for a quiet interlude after a protective Johnnie insisted on seeing her safely returned to the town house. Using some rice powder to conceal as best she could the mark Lord Halden had left on her neck—and thankful for the discretion of her maid, who asked no questions as she helped her change from her riding habit into a morning gown, then silently offered her a fichu to wrap about her throat—she was able to sit by her window and contemplate what she must do for the immediate future. And decide how to break the news to her long-suffering aunt that the goal that had brought them to Bath would be unattainable.

Despite the traumatic beginning of her day, by the time she walked down to the breakfast room at mid-morning to greet her aunt, she'd regained most of her usual composure. After joining Aunt Gussie for a cup of coffee, she invited that lady to take a turn around the Circus's elegant circle with her after her aunt finished her breakfast.

Though she'd thought her expression serene and her voice normal, upon hearing that request, Aunt Gussie set down her coffee cup, her eyes widening in alarm. 'Something drastic must have happened—I knew I felt something was amiss! And...' she lowered her voice to a murmur '...if you feel it necessary that we stroll in the Circus to tell me about it, it must be drastic indeed!'

There was no point pretending it wasn't. With a sigh, she nodded. 'I don't know how you knew, but it is rather drastic.'

'Fortunately, I've never needed to resort to smelling salts, so I shan't faint dead away on the flagstones,' Lady Stoneway said in a humorous tone, obviously trying to cheer her. Her expression going from amused to concerned, she reached over to squeeze Pru's hand. 'Whatever it is, my dear, we will weather it together.'

Pru swallowed the lump that had risen in her throat. Aunt Gussie had done so much for her, she hated to repay that kind lady with humiliation and scandal, even though it wasn't her fault. Though the unfolding of the upcoming disaster was out of her control, at least she could warn her aunt of the storm about to break over their heads.

'Thank you, and let me say in advance that I'm sorry.'

'No need for apologies. Well, I think I just lost my appetite.' Pushing back her half-empty cup, Lady Stoneway rose. 'It won't take me long to get into my pelisse, bonnet and gloves. I'll meet you downstairs in the drawing room in a trice.'

Pru nodded, then followed her aunt from the room and up the stairs to claim her own outerwear. Walking past the wardrobe where the rest of her clothing was folded, she wondered how soon they would be packing it all up and leaving…for where? Back to London? Or to Entremer?

Once the scandal broke in full force, there wouldn't be much point in remaining in Bath—subjecting her poor aunt to the prospect of being cut by almost everyone in society save her closest friends. At best, Pru might have a few days to settle some scores before most doors in society were closed to her and she shook the dust of Bath from her feet to go into permanent social exile.

A few minutes later, after accepting their cloaks from the butler, Prudence and her aunt exited the town house and began a slow circuit of the Circus's central garden. 'So, my dear, what is this news so alarming that you didn't wish to divulge it within hearing distance of the servants?'

'When you hear it, you may wish you had brought that vinaigrette. I'm afraid it's nothing less than my ruin.'

Omitting the calumnies she'd overheard from the soldiers the previous day, still too painful to repeat, Prudence briefly recounted what she'd learned about Lord Halden Fitzroy-Price's true intentions regarding her and the taking of holy orders.

'So that was why you were so cool to him at the Subscription Ball last night!' Lady Stoneway exclaimed. 'What a wicked man, to lead you on so duplicitously, knowing all along he had no real calling! But I don't see how his subterfuge means your ruination.'

'There's more, and it gets worse,' Pru said grimly, proceeding to give her aunt a carefully edited account of her encounter with the Duke's son during her ride earlier that day. Omitting mention of his threat to ravish her, she described his fury at her categorical refusal to marry him, his tearing of her veil and forcing a kiss on her so that he would

be able to claim she'd been compromised—and would therefore be ruined if they didn't wed.

Though Lady Stoneway snorted with indignation when
Pru revealed how Lord Halden had tracked her down on her
ride, she remained otherwise silent until Pru finished her
account. Then, halting, she took her niece's arm and looked
at her searchingly. 'You are sure he didn't harm you?'

'No, Aunt, other than a punishing kiss, it was just threats.'

'You'll need to tie that fichu higher then, my dear.'

Her hand flying automatically to her neck, Pru flushed.
'I... I expect you are correct.'

'That...that blackguard!' her aunt exploded. 'One has a
mind to call the constable and have him taken up for assault! How dare he try to ruin *your* reputation, when he has
just shown his own character so lacking?'

'You can hardly expect him to admit that. He's probably
been granted his every whim since childhood, so how dare
I stand in the way of what he wants? There's more yet—I'm
afraid. Lieutenant Trethwell heard the altercation and came
riding up to rescue me. He...he dealt Lord Halden some serious blows to the face, which I suspect are going to leave
him looking battered for some time.'

'Heavens! Was Lieutenant Trethwell injured as well?'

Pru laughed drily. 'I think you can guess the answer to
that. Trethwell advised Lord Halden to claim he'd got the
bruises in a boxing match with friends, else he would return to punish him again. Attacking the son of a peer was a
dangerous move, but since I was the only witness—and he
can hardly hope to induce *me* to testify on his behalf—he's
unlikely to take legal action. I can only hope Lord Halden
will take the Lieutenant's threat seriously and not claim he
received the blows from the Lieutenant while trying to pre-

vent *him* from pressing his attentions on me, thereby trying to besmirch the Lieutenant's reputation as well as mine.'

'He'd do better to claim a boxing match gone wrong—else it will be quite obvious, when the curious observe that Lieutenant Trethwell is entirely unmarked, that Lord Halden was thoroughly bested.'

'I hadn't thought of that!' Pru said, feeling better. 'Perhaps you're right. He wouldn't want to bring attention to the fact that he isn't up to Trethwell's weight—a man he sneeringly refers to as a "half-pay cripple".'

'I'm beginning to wish you *had* given Lord Halden the cut direct last night!' Aunt Gussie exclaimed. 'What a thoroughly vile remark! Bravo to Lieutenant Trethwell for once again proving himself your protector. But…' she pinned Pru with her penetrating gaze '…he felt it necessary to mill down Lord Halden merely because the man *kissed* you?'

Prudence felt her blush deepen. 'Lord Halden…might have threatened more,' she admitted in a small voice.

To her shock, her aunt spat out an expletive Pru would never have dreamed might emit from her ladylike lips. 'Then I can only thank Heaven that Lieutenant Trethwell happened along! I suppose it's useless for me to observe that if you hadn't out-galloped the protection of your groom, the encounter might have been avoided.'

Pru shrugged. 'Perhaps, but I doubt it. Lord Halden had only to give the man a charming smile, flip him a coin and suggest he take himself off for some ale at the nearest public house. Stebbins isn't one of our own servants, a long-time retainer who would feel responsible for my protection. He's employed by the livery and would surely think it ill advised to refuse the directions of a duke's son.'

'I don't suppose you could talk Lord Halden out of spreading the story.'

'What, appeal to his honour as a gentleman?' Pru said scornfully. 'Had he any honour, he'd have accepted my refusal with good grace and left me untouched. Besides, he as much as admitted he's deeply in debt. I suspect his family pawned him off on Lady Isabelle to keep him from running up any more bills in London, with the instruction that she find him a rich bride as soon as possible. Hence her willingness to accept even one of the Scandal Sisters.'

'You wouldn't consider giving in and marrying him.'

'Absolutely not! Surely ruin is preferable to the misery of being at the mercy of such a man for a lifetime!'

Lady Stoneway sighed. 'I agree, but it is a brave choice, my dear. No matter that it's the man to blame, the woman is always the one who suffers. With marriages often arranged for the mutual benefit of money and consequence, many would take the easier path. Compared with the prospect of becoming an outcast condemned to remaining single, they would console themselves in the knowledge that, by marrying the villain, they would gain a life of ease and a high position in society.'

'Advantages he himself pointed out, while he was still trying to cajole my acceptance. But I am not such a woman and, thank the Lord, I don't have to be. I'm fortunate that Papa's wealth protects me from having to earn my bread for the rest of my life as an unwanted poor relation—or something worse.'

After that remark, for a long time the two walked in silence. Finally, Lady Stoneway, linking her arm with Pru's, said with a sigh, 'I've racked my brain, but I'm forced to agree that if Lord Halden persists in this scheme to ruin you—and unless you hide yourself away until that mark fades, his accusations will have physical proof—I can't see any way to wiggle out of this. And to think I engineered your introduction to him and encouraged his suit! I am so sorry, my dear!'

'You needn't be, Aunt Gussie. You've done everything you could to try to get me accepted and settled. I admit, I'd begun to have doubts about Lord Halden's suitability before this incident, but even I didn't think him capable of…this.' She touched a finger to her neck.

'I could talk with my friends. Give them a true account of what actually happened.'

'You could try, but it's not likely society would accept my version of events over his. If some *have* heard whispers about his being in debt and amusing himself with ladies of the demi-monde, those are common enough faults many women would be willing to overlook to land a husband of such an elevated degree. Besides, even if some believe my account, they would hesitate to accuse a duke's son of lying and risk offending his powerful family and friends.' She gave a mirthless laugh. 'Especially when his version of events fits so neatly into what society wants to believe about me anyway!'

'Then what shall we do for you, my dear? Retire to London and wait for next year?'

'I don't see any purpose in that. If rumours about my likeness to Mama followed me here, my actual ruination in Bath is sure to become common knowledge in London society, probably before we could pack up and get ourselves back to town. I would spare us both the humiliation of being ignored—or cut—next Season. I think you should bid your friends here goodbye, have your maid pack your things immediately and return to London or Chemberton as soon as possible. I shall remain another few days before I leave for Entremer.'

Lady Stoneway gave her a sharp look. 'You can't think so poorly of me as to believe I would abandon you here alone, without any escort!'

Pru's face hardened. 'Before every door in society closes to me, I intend to set the record straight about the scratches that, along with Trethwell's bruises, now adorn Lord Halden's face. You've already suffered embarrassment enough. I'd not have you get caught up in the ugliness.'

'Then what do you mean to do afterwards?'

'Go to Entremer after I've said my piece.'

'You truly mean to bury yourself at Entremer? How will you ever find a husband there?'

Pru laughed. 'You forget, odd that I am, that alone among the family, I love Entremer. Riding out through the verdant pastures, up on to the ridges, down by the river where the cascades make ferns and frogs flourish… I spent some of my happiest childhood days there, Temper and I trailing after Chris and Gregory and generally making nuisances of ourselves. In any event, after this spectacle in Bath, I expect I shall end up just as notorious as Mama. It's time to admit my naïve dream of finding a husband and family is unattainable. Unless I truly were ready to marry a man more interested in my dowry than my person.'

Lady Stoneway shook her head, tears glittering on her lashes. 'Well, it's not right. I so hoped our sojourn here would end with you engaged, looking forward to having a husband, home and family of your own!'

'Oh, the result may not be so bad. Just think, I'll no longer have to kowtow to ill-intentioned matrons who smile at my face and whisper calumnies behind my back. I shall find something else useful to become. Something where I can be who I truly am, without having to rigidly control every thought and action.'

Lady Stoneway nodded. 'I would like to see you free of artificial fetters, able to be the lovely woman you are.'

Warmed by her aunt's support, Prudence gave her hand a squeeze. 'Shall we return now? You can get your maid started on that packing.'

They walked, once again in silence, back across the garden towards the town house. Pru still felt a weight of sadness at letting go of the dream that had guided every thought and action since she'd first realised what the implications her mother's notoriety would mean for her own future. But the tiny tendril of hope she'd felt earlier had grown and strengthened.

No more struggling to force herself to be someone she was not. With the death of her dream came a quiet acceptance of her fate and that sweet whisper of freedom.

As they reached the town house stairs, Lady Stoneway stopped Pru with a hand on her arm. 'I haven't yet given up all hope of seeing you settled. Surely, somewhere in Bath or England, lives a man who can see past the superficial to the true and beautiful heart of you.'

Pru felt a pang, remembering the man who'd recently told her almost the same thing. 'A lovely thought. Perhaps it will turn out to be true. I think I shall read for a while. Will you go up and begin your packing?'

'What, abandon you because of that scheming weasel? Never. I'd rather like to spit in his face myself! If he does tell his tale and make you infamous, then so be it. I shall stand by you.'

Torn between gratitude and humility at her aunt's support and a desire to spare her any further indignities, Pru said, 'Are you sure? If he does take that step, and I'm almost certain he will, what happens next has to reflect badly upon you.'

Lady Stoneway shrugged. 'Temper insists she will go her own way, my sons are all successfully married and I have no daughters with reputations to protect. What do I care if society spurns me? I know my true friends will not and their company is all that matters to me. Besides,' she added with a chuckle, 'why should your mama have all the fun? It might be quite energising to be thought scandalous—if it induces some charming rogue like Lieutenant Trethwell into pursuing me!'

Trying to imagine her proper aunt slipping off to an assignation with some dashing military gentleman, Pru had to laugh, too. 'I hope it does.'

They walked back inside, but before they could hand their cloaks over to the butler, he held a note out to Pru. 'A footman from Lady Isabelle's brought this for you. From Lord Halden.'

Shooting a look to her aunt, Pru took the missive, unfolded and quickly scanned it.

'Will there be a reply, Miss Lattimar? The footman said he would return after doing another errand for her ladyship.'

'Yes, I'll pen one immediately. Thank you, Soames.'

'It's what I expected,' Pru told her aunt as they mounted the stairs to their respective chambers. 'Ambiguously worded, neither admitting nor threatening anything for which he could be taken to account should anyone other than me chance to read it, but with the meaning quite clear. Accept his offer immediately, or he will see to my ruination.'

Lady Stoneway's lips tightened, her expression turning almost militant. 'Then let the battle lines be drawn. Did you want to go out tonight?'

Pru sighed. 'I think I must—before his story circulates so widely that all doors are closed to me.'

'If you wish to discover immediately whether or not he's made good on his threat, I would suggest attending Lady Arbuthnot's reception rather than the Assembly Ball. She's the most influential—and malicious—gossip in Bath. If he intends to spread a story that will ruin you, he will most likely start with her.'

'Very well. I have a few words to say to that lady anyway. I'll go and write that reply.'

Lady Stoneway reached over to grasp her chin and tilt it up. 'Courage, my dear.'

Prudence laughed, filled with the first genuine amusement she'd felt since the incident this morning that had spun her world out of control. 'No courage needed, Aunt Gussie. Tonight I'm going to shock society and I intend to enjoy every minute of it!'

After pulling out pen and paper in the privacy of her chamber, Pru scanned again Lord Halden's request to call on her that afternoon 'to receive her positive reply to a pre-viously posed question', which, if she were to deny him, 'would have the results we already discussed'.

What a lover-like note, she thought scornfully. Dashing off a reply informing him there was no reason for him to call, as she would not change her answer to that 'previously posed question, whatever the consequences', she summoned her maid to deliver the note for Soames to hand over when Lady Isabelle's footman returned.

Seated at her desk by the window, she watched the maid walk out, knowing with a sense of finality that its receipt would set irreversible events into motion. A moment later, gazing out of the window, she saw Lady Isabelle's footman knock at the town house door, then emerge again, heading back towards the Royal Crescent.

As he paced off, with a sigh, she bid farewell to the sweet image that had energised her for the last month: playing with her children in a flower-filled vicarage garden, her husband watching them indulgently from the garden bench where he was working on his next Sunday's sermon.

Absently she rubbed at the mark on her neck, nostalgia fading as her anger intensified and her intensions hardened. With nothing left to lose, she would inform society just what a scoundrel Lord Halden was before leaving for what, despite Aunt Gussie's fond hopes, was likely to be permanent, solitary exile at Entremer.

Pushing away the image of the contemptible Lord Halden, her thoughts shifted to the man who, though reputed to be a rogue, had shown himself the exact opposite. 'Surely there is in London a man who can see the gold of your worth through the dross of gossip surrounding you,' Johnnie had told her.

What a shame the only man who seemed to value her was a wandering soul whose free spirit would wither, should someone try to box it up in the confines of an English country manor. *If* she could manage to entice him to stay in the first place—by no means a sure thing, despite their attraction and the unexpected offer of marriage compassion had brought to his lips—an offer that seemed to shock him as much as it had her.

Oh, that more than *compassion* had prompted it! But

she'd given him a clear opportunity to confess he'd fallen in love with her—and he'd been unable to take it. Much as it had hurt—enough that, to her shame, she'd actually slapped him—she could only be grateful for his honesty. If he *had* claimed to love her, she might have persuaded herself to believe it and succumbed to the temptation to accept the offer.

Which would have been worse than marrying Lord Halden. At some point, her fat dowry added to the amounts promised by his investors would allow him to finalise the details of setting up his trading venture. Probably sooner rather than later, the siren call to adventure would lure him from her side, leaving her alone in the countryside for months or years. Perhaps for ever.

She didn't know what would be worse. Having him with her, trying to conceal his boredom and restlessness and desire to be elsewhere, or sending him off, not knowing whether some gale at sea or hostile native ashore would snuff out his life. Miring her in permanent anxiety, wondering for ever whether something had happened to him or whether he just wasn't yet ready to return to her. Wondering whether she would ever see him again.

Either prospect was unbearable. Not once she finally accepted the truth her heart had been whispering for some time. Despite cautioning herself to avoid it, she'd fallen in love with Johnnie Trethwell.

Living the rest of her life without him was going to be far more bitter than enduring social exile at Entremer.

Chapter Fifteen

Steeled to her purpose, early that evening, Pru descended to the morning room to find her aunt awaiting her, already dressed for their evening out. 'Are you sure you want to accompany me?' she asked, going over to give that lady a kiss on the cheek. 'I shall always be grateful for everything you've done for me. All your support and l-love,' she added, her voice breaking a little. 'My affection and gratitude will not diminish a jot if you choose to avoid the humiliation of tonight's spectacle.'

Giving her a little hug, Aunt Gussie laughed. 'I wouldn't miss it for the world! I can't wait to see what you've got planned.'

'You'd best brace yourself. Meek, mild, submissive Prudence Lattimar is gone for ever. A defiant, ill-behaved termagant has taken her place.'

'Well, then, my lovely termagant, let me have Soames summon us chairs!'

* * *

Any faint hope that Lord Halden had not followed through on his threat evaporated the moment they entered Lady Arbuthnot's drawing room. Immediately after the butler announced them, every guest within hearing distance turned to stare. While the ladies' eyes registered shock and reproof, the gentlemen, their expressions curious and appraising, gave her the same sort of blatantly disrespectful scrutiny she'd experienced from the soldiers, looks that would have been an unpardonable insult, had they been directed towards any other gently born maiden.

Raising her eyebrows at Lady Stoneway, Pru murmured, 'I had better seek out our hostess immediately, before she learns of my arrival and has the butler toss me out.'

Spotting over the heads of the other guests the nodding plumes in the awful shade of puce Lady Arbuthnot seemed to favour, Pru set off in that direction. As she advanced, the other guests turned their backs on her—rather helpfully, she thought with gallows humour, since it enabled her to cross the room as swiftly as Moses parting the Red Sea. Reaching her hostess, she stood silently, waiting until the lady's conversational partner—or the sudden hush in the room— alerted her to Pru's presence.

Soon enough, the matron talking with Lady Arbuthnot stuttered into silence, her eyes going wide. Lady Arbuthnot turned, recognised her and stiffened.

Before that lady could decide whether to simply cut her, or order her to be ejected, Pru placed a hand on her arm.

Jerking it away, Lady Arbuthnot hissed, 'Hussy! I'm astonished you have the effrontery to enter my house!'

'You did invite me.'

'Well, yes, but that was before—'

'Before you heard Lord Halden's salacious story? From Lady Isabelle, I would imagine, for he himself hasn't shown his face, has he? Probably because he does not wish to appear until the scratches I left there when I fought him off have faded. But I am not ashamed to appear before you, bearing the mark *he* left upon me,' she said, drawing aside the fichu covering her neck.

As those nearby gasped, she continued, 'Perhaps society will forgive his unprovoked attack on a lady whose only fault was refusing to marry him and give him access to the dowry he badly needs. Funds that will allow him to continue his nightly visits to the fleshpots of Corn Street and pay off enough of the debts he's run up to every tailor, bootmaker, haberdasher and wine shop in London, Bath and Oxford that he doesn't have to fear outrunning the magistrate. Didn't his family, no longer wishing to support his dissolute habits, send him here to Lady Isabelle so she might find him a rich bride? Alas, I had no wish to spend my life—and my fortune—on a man who consorts with harlots and throws away thousands on the turn of a card. For that grievous fault, he attacked me, warning that if I didn't relent and marry him, he would see me ruined. Although I suspect that a man so deficient in character cheats at cards as well, at least in this instance, he told the truth.'

'That…that is a monstrous accusation!' Lady Arbuthnot exclaimed when Prudence stopped for breath.

'But true, for all that it is monstrous. In making me his target, he ran little risk, did he not? After all, what other prospects did I have? What true gentleman would risk marrying the scandalous daughter of a scandalous lady? Who, rumour says, was once pursued by your own late husband.'

Her face turning almost as purple as her headdress, before the indignant Lady Arbuthnot could sputter out a response, Pru continued, 'You are probably quite wise to cut me. It's so unpleasant to listen to truths society doesn't wish to acknowledge! Such as the fact that I was certain Lady Isabelle would spread the rumour first to you, since everyone knows you possess the most acid tongue in Bath. I am leaving now, so you needn't summon the butler. Oh, before I go—you really should try gowns and bonnets in a different colour. That puce hue you seem to favour doesn't compliment your complexion at all. Good evening, Lady Arbuthnot.'

After giving the furious woman a graceful curtsy, Pru turned and crossed the silent room to where Lady Stoneway awaited her. Together, heads held high, they walked out as the shocked hush erupted into cacophony.

'A magnificent speech, my dear, and so very effective! I wager I'm not the only person who's wanted for years to confront Lady Arbuthnot—but lacked the courage. No need to drop by any other entertainments—that verbal salvo shall be the talk of the town within the hour!'

Prudence chuckled. 'I'm sure it will. We'd better get back to the Circus before even the chairmen refuse to serve us. You can spend the rest of the evening packing.'

'Not quite yet,' Lady Stoneway replied, her expression merry. 'I shall remain a few more days, visiting my closest friends and hearing all the delicious gossip that is sure to follow.'

'I wish one of the results would be society cutting Lord Halden, but I'm not naïve enough to believe that will happen.'

Her aunt nodded. 'Some will believe you, though even those who do are unlikely to challenge him. At the very least, perhaps the truth may warn off rich widows and the mothers of eligible heiresses he might otherwise have managed to charm.' Lady Stoneway laughed. 'Mentioning the possibility that he cheats at cards was a master stroke! Men might discount your claim that he attacked you—females bring such things upon themselves, they believe—but they absolutely disdain a cheat!'

'Perhaps I maligned him,' Pru retorted. 'If so, I'm not sorry. Let *him* try living with infamy for a change.'

Having reached the side entrance where the chairmen waited, conversation ended as they climbed into the sedan chairs that would bear them back home.

How much longer should she stay in Bath before leaving for Entremer? Pru asked herself as the chairmen set off.

As her aunt noted, she thought her message had been effective. Having followed that lady's good advice by delivering it first to the most notorious gossip in Bath, she could be sure the news would spread swiftly enough that she need not repeat it anywhere else. With no true friends in the city save her aunt in whose company she might wait to assess the results, she had no need to linger.

Only one true friend, she amended. Apparently, Lord Halden had been cognizant enough of the danger to his continued health and safety of trying to extend his revenge to include Trethwell, he'd not implicated the Lieutenant in the affair, for which she was grateful. Since Johnnie's name had not been tarnished by association with the debacle, would he follow the wise path and avoid her? No doubt his aunt would strongly urge such a course.

Perhaps she wouldn't even have a chance to bid him goodbye.

Biting her lip to stave off the tears sparked by that mel-

ancholy thought, she resolved to remain two more days in
Bath. She'd ride out each morning, hoping to see him. If
he hadn't tried to approach her by then, she would know he
had chosen to be prudent and bid him a one-sided goodbye
while riding the trail where she'd spent such happy hours
in his company...falling in love with him.

Which might, after all, be a better outcome. How was
she to bid goodbye for ever to the man who held her heart
without breaking down and confessing her love to him?

Which, because he was kind and felt some fondness for
her, would only distress him and make him uncomfortable
that he was not able to vow his love in return. Not to mention curdling her sweet memories of their rides together by
giving them an unpleasant and awkward finale.

Unless... If he did appear, perhaps she could defer the
heartbreak by luring him into a coming together that would
render her recollection of their parting bittersweet but joyful for all the years to come.

Several streets away at the Assembly Rooms, Johnnie
was biding his time impatiently, exerting his famous charm
conversing with the most influential society matrons present and alert for any hint that Lord Halden had unleashed
the whispering campaign he'd threatened against Miss Lattimar. He was also hoping the lady herself would appear, so
he could offer her his support and protection, should some
ugly confrontation develop.

By the time the hour had advanced to nearly midnight,
when the dancing would end, she had still not arrived, nor
had he heard any rumours. Encouraged, he was beginning
to hope that perhaps Lord Halden had heeded his dire warn-

ing after all. Until, returning to his aunt after dancing with the latest dowager, he noticed a stir of excitement in the ballroom, newcomers plucking friends by the sleeve and leaning close to whisper in their ears.

Which was exactly what Lady Woodlings did as he reached her side. 'Walk with me to the tea room,' she murmured, her face sober as she took his arm.

'What is it? What has happened?' he asked...even as, with a sinking heart, he had a very strong suspicion what news she was about to impart.

'It's about your Miss Lattimar. Apparently she's proved all the sceptics true and gone and ruined herself. She even had the effrontery to confirm it to Lady Arbuthnot's face, confronting that lady in her own drawing room!'

'When? How?'

'Tonight, about an hour ago! Apparently, Lord Halden's cousin, Lady Isabelle, paid a call on Lady Arbuthnot this afternoon, telling her she must banish Miss Lattimar from her company forthwith. Lord Halden had just confided in her—in strictest confidence, of course—that Miss Lattimar had invited him to ride with her, then dismissed her groom and lured him into taking liberties with her person! Such liberties, he became sadly convinced that, though he had hoped the rumours about her character were unfounded, so abandoned did she reveal herself, he had no choice but to regretfully decide he must withdraw his suit. For what gentleman would wish to risk marrying a woman who'd proved herself as dissipated as her mother?'

'"Lured" him into taking liberties, did she?' Johnnie said sarcastically.

'Oh, really, Johnnie! What healthy young buck would have the will to refuse the advances of a woman that beautiful?'

'A gentleman of honour?' he suggested. 'Who then would not "confide" in a woman guaranteed to spread the news as quickly as possible to all the world?'

'I know you have…a fondness for her. But you can hardly continue to defend her character after she has already publicly admitted the lapse!'

'Did she? Just how did *she* describe the incident?'

Lady Woodlings coloured a little. 'Well, she alleged that Lord Halden had attacked *her*, in order to compromise her into marrying him, so he might have access to her dowry, supposedly to settle a large number of debts and to…to support his visits to houses of ill repute. Claiming he told her if she refused to wed him, he would see her ruined.'

'And so he has, hasn't he?' Johnnie said, the slow burn of fury rising up.

'Surely you can't believe her version of events! Not after she defied every principle governing the behaviour of a gently raised young lady! Bad enough to have admitted such a shocking interlude, were she persistently questioned about it. But to go out in public and *proclaim* it to the world? Had such an attack actually happened, a truly virtuous maiden would have been prostrate on her couch with distress and mortification, and done everything in her power to suppress any knowledge of it!'

'Perhaps. But I happen to know her account is true. Because I was there.'

'What?' his aunt gasped. '*You* were present? But—how? Why?'

'I was riding the Lansdown Hill road this morning and heard Miss Lattimar crying out, somewhere in the fog. I galloped up to find her struggling to escape Lord Halden and came to her rescue. Before he could truly ravish her, as he'd threatened.'

Anxious foreboding coloured her expression. 'You…you didn't strike him, did you?

'How well you know me, Aunt. He'll bear the mark of my fists for some time. As well as the marks from the fingernails she used on him, trying to free herself. That is, if he lives long enough. I warned him if he tried to ruin her, I would make him pay for it.'

Seeming to sense the rage in him, she clutched his arm. 'Johnnie, you mustn't do any such thing! Don't you know what would happen, were you arrested for assaulting the son of a duke? At the very least, you'd be imprisoned, if not transported!'

'In truth, I'd rather kill him than assault him, but I suppose ruination isn't a capital offence. Even if it does destroy the life of the woman he maligned.'

'Oh, that you ever insisted on forcing an acquaintance with that woman!' Lady Woodlings cried. 'I was afraid the witch might be the ruin of you!'

'Witch? I'd rather call her courageous and principled. And you probably don't have to worry about having the magistrate invade Queen Square to put me under irons. Miss Lattimar was sure, if Lord Halden did disregard my warning and spread his lies, that he would quit Bath and go into hiding before I found out about it—the cowardly cur. Which I fully expect I'll discover to be the case when I go to Lady Isabelle's town house, after I summon a chair to take you home.'

His aunt took a deep breath of relief. 'I hope to Heaven he has fled! Are you so sure he will have, Johnnie?'

'Nearly certain. If he meant to punish me for attacking

him, I'd have already been taken up by the law. He would also have concocted a way to work my assaulting him into his tawdry little tale. Of course, he would then have to admit he'd been beaten—without landing a finger on me. And he would have known for sure that, sooner or later, I'd come after him. This way, I imagine he's hoping I'll be relieved enough not to have been implicated in this sordid little scene that I will forget about retribution. Either that, or he plans on remaining in hiding until I'm away from England again.'

'Well, I, for one, can only be happy he was too much a coward to involve you.'

'Yes,' Johnnie said bitterly. 'He's only brave enough to involve a *woman*. Whom he can destroy with no more deadly a weapon than false testimony.'

His aunt sighed. 'Sadly, you're correct. Unfair it might be, but Miss Lattimar is thoroughly ruined, whether or not Lord Halden's tale is true.'

With a wry smile, Johnnie shook his head. 'Don't you see how brave she is? Any other woman would have caved in and married the reprobate rather than risk censure and ruin. Or if she could not stomach that, fled the city before the scandal broke over her head. But not intrepid Prudence Lattimar. Not only did she defy Lord Halden, she walked into the house of the most ferocious dragon in all of Bath and boldly told her side of the story—in front of a roomful of guests. What a woman!'

To his surprise, a reluctant smile twitched the corner of his aunt's lips. 'I suppose she *is* brave. Not only did she affirm what any other lady would have died rather than admit, apparently she took Lady Arbuthnot to task for her acid tongue and her wretched taste in gowns.'

Johnnie threw back his head and laughed, warmth and a

fierce pride in Prudence Lattimar filling him. What a soldier and comrade she would have made!

'Devil a bit! I only wish we had witnessed the spectacle. Shall we get you that chair? After all, there will be nothing else happening tonight save heated conjecture over whether or not what she alleged is true. And you know me. If dragged into such a conversation, I might not be able to restrain myself from setting the record straight by giving a personal account.'

Looking thoroughly alarmed, Lady Woodlings seized his arm. 'Let us depart immediately, then. All you would accomplish by revealing your part in it would be to sully your own reputation! There's nothing you can do to salvage hers.'

If only society were a man he could pummel, as he had Lord Halden, Johnnie thought as he let his aunt lead him away. Much as it drove him mad with frustration, Aunt Pen was correct. There was no way he could beat gossip and innuendo into submission.

Rather than elevate the truth, making public his witness of the events would probably further submerge it. News that a second gentleman had been involved would likely lead to colourful additions to the story—speculation about a love triangle, the salacious hint that the assignation had been a *ménage-à-trois*. Scandalous embellishments that would only increase the tale's interest and prolong its life.

It would do nothing to clear Miss Lattimar's name.

Where was she now? he suddenly wondered. 'Did Miss Lattimar leave the reception immediately after her confrontation with Lady Arbuthnot?' he asked his aunt as he assisted her into a chair.

'So I understand. If she knows what's good for her, she'll

be out of Bath by tomorrow.' Lady Woodlings sighed. 'The wolves are going to be merciless.'

With the hour approaching midnight, it was too late now to call on her at Lady Stoneway's. He could only hope she would ride tomorrow morning. So he might assure her of his support and ask what he might do to help her.

But first, he needed to see his aunt home. And check on the whereabouts of Lord Halden Fitzroy-Price.

Chapter Sixteen

Early the next morning, her mood bittersweet, Prudence urged the grey mare up Lansdown Road to the heights above the city on what might well be her last morning in Bath. If the rumours had reached even the hired groom, who wavered over refusing to accept money to accompany her, it was probably time to leave.

'Don't know as I should do this any more, miss,' he'd said, looking torn between offending her and distaste at what he'd obviously heard about her behaviour. 'Might get me turned off, if'n the owner finds out I bin letting ladies go on ren-day-voos.'

'Indeed? If you are taken to task for it, tell him it is more likely to *increase* his business, as every lady in Bath who desires a "ren-day-voo" will hasten to this livery. But don't worry. Should you lose your position, I will compensate you handsomely and make sure you obtain another, better one.'

'Still not sure I want to take yer money,' he replied, daring to raise an insolent gaze to her face. But when she fixed on him the same cold, unflinching stare she'd used on Lady Arbuthnot, he dropped his eyes, colouring, and gave her a little bow, obviously recalling that despite her infamy, she was still a lady and he a hired servant.

She'd probably need to use that expression for the rest of her days. But, fiercely pleased with the effects it had produced in these first two instances, she preferred it to the mask of serenity she'd hidden behind for so long.

Pulling up the restive mare—she had no heart for a gallop this morning—Prudence gazed off to the east, towards the city. Would Johnnie ride out to meet her?

The view over Bath, its dewy rooftops and church spires sparkling in the light of the just-risen sun, was spectacular. She wasn't sure whether it was sympathy with her sadness or mockery at the destruction of her hopes that the morning had dawned so bright, clear and beautiful. Just as she wasn't sure whether she should be relieved or heartbroken if Johnnie did not appear and she left Bath without seeing him again.

It wasn't until after the incident yesterday, when she'd realised she would have to quit the city, that she'd seriously considered what her life would be like in future—and realised how deeply Johnnie Trethwell had penetrated into her heart and mind. What a leap of joy she felt, just seeing his rangy form and winning smile from across the room! How amused and energised she became, listening to colourful tales that gave her a glimpse into the wider world of his travels and experiences, events that had moulded him into the remarkable man he was. How much more invigorated and alive she was when conversing with him, able to freely express her thoughts and reactions.

Despite how small and cold and lonely her own world

would seem without his luminous presence, she would always be grateful for having had him explode into her life like a shooting star. Brief but brilliant, the light he cast had illumined her world and shown her how to free herself from the hopeless role of Perfect Young Lady. He'd demonstrated that, for at least one man, she could be valued for who she truly was.

Whatever friends and associates she made in future would also have to accept her that way.

'I love you, Johnnie Trethwell,' she whispered to the glorious morning. 'I shall pray every day for your safety and happiness as you continue your life of adventure.'

As if her wistful prayer had conjured him, as soon as she'd finished voicing it, she heard the welcome sound of approaching hoofbeats. As her heart gave that now-familiar little leap of joy, Johnnie rode up on his black hack and reined in beside her.

Her emotions still raw and volatile, she'd been afraid she might blurt out her love for him. Instead, she simply gazed at him, mute and humbled and strangely shy. Now that he had made an appearance, would she have the courage to follow through on her tentative plans?

He was staring at her, too, in that intense, completely focused way he had, that sent prickling sensations all over her body and made her feel so intensely alive. The power of their attraction sizzled and sparked in the air between them.

'So, you decided not to abandon me, like the rest of Bath,' she said, at last finding her tongue as she urged her mare to a walk.

'I'd much rather embrace you,' he replied with a laugh, signalling his mount to match the pace of hers. 'What a scene you directed at Lady Arbuthnot's last night! I only wish I had been present to witness it. Although it's probably best that I was not. I wouldn't have been able to keep myself from adding corroborating testimony which, as Aunt Pen pointed out, would probably have only made things worse by adding another fillip of intrigue to titillate the gossips.'

'Yes—well—probably wise,' she stuttered, having difficulty concentrating on his words after he'd said he'd like to embrace her. *Would you truly, Johnnie?* she thought. *We shall soon discover how strong that desire is—if I don't lose my nerve.*

'You were right, by the way,' he continued, recalling her attention.

'R-right? About what?'

'Lord Halden. The cowardly cur must have bolted as soon as he'd whispered his poison into Lady Isabelle's ear. Expecting you and Lady Stoneway would attend the Assembly Ball last night, I'd been biding my time there, tooling various dowagers about the floor, when the news of the contretemps at Lady Arbuthnot's reception reached the hall, probably an hour or so after you'd fired your cannonade. By then, I felt it was probably too late to call at the Circus. But after seeing my aunt into a chair, I did nip up to the Royal Crescent to check on the whereabouts of the intrepid Lord Halden.'

Diverted despite herself, she said, 'What did you do? Bang on the front door and demand to see him?'

'What, and have the servants claim he was "indisposed" or "not at home to visitors"? A waste of time at best, and at worst, the inconvenience of milling down several innocent bystanders before I could reach my real quarry. No, I got in via the mews.'

What a storyteller he was, stringing her along detail by detail! 'And so you entered by through the kitchen?'

'No need to disturb good folk who'd already put in a long and arduous day,' he replied, grinning at her, enjoying as much as she was the game of reveal. 'I took the... *vertical* route.'

That puzzled her for a moment before enlightenment dawned. 'You climbed up the back wall of the town house? But his rooms would have been on the second floor—threatening you with a drop of thirty feet or more, if you lost your grip!'

He made a sweeping motion down his side. 'My dear, you see before you a man who has trekked across bazaars in native dress. Scaled fortress walls and fought off attack by natives brandishing deadly-sharp *talwars*. What to me is a paltry two storeys' worth of smooth Bath stone?'

'Rogue!' she said, laughing. 'What next? Did you break in through an upstairs window?'

'No need to break something that, with a little persuasion, one can open.'

'So you strolled in and...what? Terrified a housemaid by suddenly appearing and asking which was his room?'

'No, no, the household was all asleep by then. It was simple enough to tiptoe through the different bedchambers and discover one—still in quite a state of disarray—that must have been his. Half-emptied drawers standing open, some mismatched gloves and unpolished boots lying about, as if his valet was forced to pack in haste. I knew then he'd left Bath for good.'

'I don't recall the moonlight being bright enough for you to have seen all that in a bedchamber.'

'No need for moonlight. I lit a taper. You can't think I'd

stumble around in the dark. Much too clumsy! If one must housebreak, one should do so with efficiency and grace.'

Beyond amusing her, he'd been trying to distract her from the grim and permanent consequences of yesterday's events. Ruin and exile.

Unfortunately, his clever tale couldn't make her forget for long.

Or mask the fact settling like hot agony in her chest that they would soon part and, most likely, she'd never see him again.

'Thank you for that one last story,' she said. 'I am glad that you did not reveal your part in the events. Not that I worry about an additional layer of scandal being plastered over my already tarnished image, but I would hate to have some of the dirt rub off on yours. Which might…might impede your chances of wedding that rich widow Lady Woodlings hopes to find for you.'

He recoiled, an expression of distaste on his face. 'That might be Aunt Pen's ambition, but as you should know, it has never been mine!'

'Do your…intentions remain the same as they were when you mentioned them at the warehouse? To become a broker for collectors?' she asked softly, her fingers tightening on the reins, trying not to hold her breath as she resisted the faint hope that the traumatic events of yesterday might have led him to the same sort of dramatic revelation about his feelings it had for her.

He was silent a moment before saying, 'I expect so. It's time I turned my efforts to moving on.'

You didn't really expect him to suddenly declare his love, did you? Suffocating what had been only a feeble hope at best, resolutely Pru focused back on her plan. She had one last card to play before this game ended and it would require all her concentration to do it correctly.

And they had almost reached the spot for her to play it—if she didn't lose her nerve.

'How soon do you intend to inform your aunt of your plans?'

'How soon do you expect to leave Bath?'

Only by keeping in mind her intent was she able to ward off a misery that threatened tears. 'As soon as I can make ready. Tomorrow, probably.'

He nodded. 'I'll speak to Aunt Pen today, then.' He chuckled, though the amusement sounded forced. 'Although she might well disown me when she hears what I intend. The horror of it! A Trethwell, becoming virtually a *shopkeeper*! My family would probably prefer I seduce the wives of every man in the Cabinet and die over my ears in debt, surrounded by a bevy of demi-mondaines.'

'You'll be an explorer and adventurer,' she corrected. 'You'll have clerks to handle the actual transactions.'

He smiled. 'A fine distinction. Perhaps it will be enough to mollify Aunt Pen and the family.'

Her heartbeat accelerating as the moment drew near, Pru tried to keep her tone light and teasing. 'Didn't you once tell me that you could deny me nothing?'

The sudden fire in his eyes told her he remembered the conversation exactly.

'I did…within reason.'

They'd reached the little copse by the road where she'd lost her hat—oh, how long ago now it seemed! But it had sheltered her that day. She hoped it would serve that purpose this morning.

Turning the mare into the entrance, she beckoned him

to follow. Once she'd reached the deepest recesses, she dismounted, tethering the mare's reins to a bush where a break at the far side gave on to the meadow behind, full of lush spring grass that would tempt the animal to graze.

Following her lead, Johnnie jumped down from the saddle and tethered his own horse.

Though she made herself step over to him and boldly placed her hands on his shoulders, she had to clear her throat twice to get the words out.

'Remember how you told me that there were ways to experience passion that would not risk my conceiving a child?'

'I never told you that,' he said shortly.

Beneath her fingers, she could sense the tension in his body, almost feel the coiled strength of him, poised to resist—or succumb. Could she persuade him to the latter?

'True. I inferred that…but you didn't deny it. Is that a more correct account?'

'It is,' he admitted, his voice sounding thick.

'Then, Johnnie…won't you please show me? One last gift, before I go into exile at Entremer and you set off on your adventures.'

'I hate it that Lord Halden's infamy has reduced you to exile…and there's nothing I can do to prevent it!'

She shrugged. 'That's past regretting, and perhaps for the best.' She laughed ruefully. 'I probably would have made a wretched vicar's wife. Allowing our children to play in public fountains. Telling off the officious wives of wealthy parishioners.'

Smiling, he shook his head. 'No, you'd be brilliant. At whatever you decided to do.'

'Perhaps. But there's only one thing I want to do now. To fully experience what drives men and women so wild with longing, a man will seduce a woman he cannot keep and a woman will take lovers she cannot hold.'

'Here—where riders pass by not ten yards away?' he asked, a tinge of desperation in his voice.

'You've never taken a woman in a woodland copse?'

When he hesitated, she laughed. 'I thought so. Then… love me, Johnnie Trethwell. Make me forget I'll be infamous for ever, never winning the settled home and husband I've dreamed of. Give me one brief, beautiful, glorious moment of pleasure to warm all the days and nights ahead without you.' Gazing into his blazing eyes, she traced his lips with one gentle finger. 'Please, Johnnie,' she whispered. 'Give us both that gift.'

His breath coming short, he stared at her, the heat emanating from his body firing hope and wild anticipation.

Finally, with a growl, he pulled her closer and tilted her chin up. 'It will be glorious,' he promised roughly. 'But it will not be brief.'

And then he kissed her.

Maybe he shouldn't have given in and granted her request. But as soon as Pru's lips touched his, he knew they had both been made for this. Though he burned to give her *everything*, every last drop of the fulfilment she desired, he would at least give her a taste of the passion she craved— without ruining her for the husband who would surely find her some day, whatever backwater she retreated to.

Not every man in England could be blind and stupid.

That was his last rational thought, before instinct and sensation took over from intellect. Her hands were already plucking open the buttons of his jacket, dragging loose the knot of his cravat and pushing it aside as she insinuated her fingers beneath his shirt to rub at the bare skin of his chest. His hands clenching on her shoulders, he shuddered as her touch set his skin aflame.

'Does that please you?' she murmured against his mouth.

'Yes.'

'And this?' She slid her free hand down his chest to cup his erection. Which surged under her fingers, giving its own answer.

He placed his hand over hers, helping her stroke him. 'More of this later, *chahna*, but not yet.'

'*Chahna?*' she murmured, caressing him.

'It means love. Light. You are both.' Taking her mouth again for another deep kiss, he struggled out of his uniform jacket and tossed it to the ground. Still kissing, he let her finish unknotting his cravat, then pulled it free and dropped it, too. He leaned his head back to let her kiss his neck, down the V of skin exposed by neckline, before she realised there was a better way to bare his chest and began pulling the shirt out of his trousers.

He let her push the fabric up as she slid her hands under, rubbing over the rise of his chest, her fingertips massaging the flat of his nipples, then dipping down to trace the concave abdomen below the rise of his ribs. Before she could descend further and drive him completely beyond control, he seized her hands and kissed them.

'Let me touch you!' she protested, looking up at him, her mouth deliciously kiss-reddened, her eyes heavy-lidded with desire.

'So you shall, my angel. But let me touch you first.'

Placing hands on her shoulders, he urged her down on to the makeshift blanket of his jacket. Easing her back, he kissed her again as he undid the fastenings of her pelisse and tossed the two sides back, then unbuttoned the blouse beneath to expose her undergarments. Working his hands underneath her back, he deftly loosened her stays—she wore only short jumps, thank heaven—and slid them down her torso, below her breasts.

He couldn't free her from the chemise, trapped as it was under the layers of stays and skirt, but was able to push it down enough that his exploring fingers could slide under and reach the dusky, peaked nipples visible beneath the fine linen. As she gasped, he took her mouth again, his tongue teasing and fencing with hers in rhythm with his stroking fingers.

But then he just had to taste her. Releasing her lips, he kissed his way over her chin and down her throat, licking and sucking at the delicate skin in the hollow. He tantalised her, nipping at her collarbones, skimming his lips over the swell of her breasts, his pace slowing as his tongue crept closer to the rigid nipples his thumbs were caressing.

She arched her back, thrusting her breasts up at him, and he drew the cloth-covered buds into his mouth. As the wetted fabric thinned and softened, becoming a barely perceptible barrier, he suckled harder, exulting as her breathing grew shorter and her movements more frantic.

He slid his hand over her riding boot and up under her skirts, his member leaping as his hand left leather for the touch of soft, sweet skin before his fingers met the ankle-length bottom of her drawers. He caressed her linen-clad calves, the skin behind her knee, the long expanse of thigh, nudging her legs wider as he progressed.

Finally he reached the prize he longed for. Finding the slit in her drawers, he pushed his hand within and cupped her mound, as she had cupped him.

She gasped again and bucked. He paused, letting her accustom herself to that intimate invasion. Once she stilled, he began to caress her in time to the long, suckling pulls of his mouth on her nipples. She grew ever more agitated, panting and twisting her torso against him, swinging an arm up to anchor his head against her breasts. As her hips started to thrust upwards, he slid a finger into her cleft—which was as hot and wet as he'd dreamed it would be.

Taking her mouth again, he exulted as she opened herself to him, giving him access to her buried pearl. He rubbed it with his thumb, then moved another finger to penetrate her passage.

She broke the kiss, gasping, her bent arms going rigid as she arched into the pressure of his fingers and thumb. Moments later, he felt the rich moisture as her climax swept through her.

He leaned over her limp, spent torso to gently kiss her lips. Despite the thickness of the copse, this woodland glen was too near the road for him to risk prolonging the interlude as long as he'd have liked. But once she recovered, he was determined to show her at least one more variation on the road to pleasure before he let her go.

He leaned on his elbow by her side, smiling as he silently watched her. How completely she abandoned herself to passion! She seized pleasure freely and without inhibitions, just as she conversed. No subterfuge, no holding back, no concern with doing the right or conventional thing.

Hell's bells, she was a magnificent lover!

A few moments later, she stirred and opened her eyes. 'That was...wonderful,' she whispered, awe in her gaze as she smiled up at him. 'But...not so wonderful for you,' she murmured, reaching over to stroke his still-rigid member.

He groaned, drinking in the feel of her fingers on him.

'It will be,' he promised, leaning over to kiss her finger-tips. 'Just not yet.'

'But I want to pleasure you, too,' she protested, giving him a sultry pout. 'At least, let me touch you.'

Though he wasn't sure how long he'd last if he permitted it, he didn't have the will to refuse her. When he didn't stay her hand, she popped open the buttons on his straining trouser flap—slowly, one by one, as teasingly as he'd uncovered her.

She waited until she'd loosed the last button, drawing a groan from him as cold air hit his overheated flesh, before pulling his mouth down for another kiss. Loving her boldness and enthusiasm, this time he let her take the lead, enjoying her growing expertise as she explored his lips, her tongue touching, testing, tasting...while her fingers explored his erection.

First, she trailed one tentative finger along his length... then used her whole hand to grasp and stroke. Then moved her thumb to massage his moist velvet tip, nearly driving him over the edge.

Knowing his time was short, he broke the kiss and moved away from her exploring fingers. After muting her inarticulate protest with another quick kiss, he tossed back her skirt, petticoats and shift and moved his mouth where his fingers had explored.

This time, he skipped over the drawers to nibble at the hard turn of a hipbone under skin, then kissed and caressed the velvet of her abdomen up to her ribs, as high as he could manage before the stays and chemise blocked his path.

And then he went downwards again, licking and kissing over the sweet rise of her mound until at last, parting the drawers, he slid his tongue to her little bud, revelling in the texture and scent he'd dreamt about and yearned to taste for so long.

She cried out as he sampled her, writhed and gasped and thrust up her hips when he delved his tongue into the honey of her passage. Moving his mouth back to suckle her little pearl, he slid his fingers deep inside, stroking its length until she shattered around him a second time.

She sagged back on to his coat, limp and boneless. Tenderness curled around his heart as he gently smoothed a tendril of hair back from her flushed forehead. When she opened her eyes and smiled up at him, despite the aching need of his unsatisfied member, he had to lean down and kiss her again.

'Now I know why that figurine in the warehouse was smiling.' She ran a finger across his lips when he released her. 'What else can you show me?'

'Greedy girl!' he teased. 'There's so much more, but we dare not risk remaining here much longer.'

'Surely we can remain long enough for…this,' she murmured, reaching through his open trouser flap to stroke him.

He jumped, as needy and sensitive as his member. 'That's not wise, my siren,' he said with a strained laugh. 'Proceeding down that path leads to childbed.'

'Not if I do for you what you just did for me, would it? So won't you…show me? Teach me what you like.'

Once again, temptation paralysed him. He couldn't get his tongue around the words to deny her, or make himself move away from her hand resting on him. Her eyes watching him intently, she stroked his whole length once, twice.

Then, as if she possessed all the knowledge of Venus, she bent her head and licked him. 'You like this?'

He ought to stop her, but he didn't seem to be able to make his mouth work. Arms corded with the effort of holding himself immobile—so that he wouldn't lose his last tentative grip on sanity, push her beneath him, and plunge his aching shaft into the sweet depths of her—he watched as, with a naughty temptress's slowness, she used both hands to explore his shaft. And then—he almost reached completion that instant—took the rigid tip of him into her mouth.

He groaned as she ran her tongue over him. 'Like this?' she asked, licking and releasing him. 'Or more? With me, you went...deeper.'

Following some instinct as primal as it was unerring, she enveloped him. He gasped, then cried out as she took him deeper...and started suckling.

He stood it as long as he could—probably only a few seconds—before he pushed her away, slammed his mouth against hers and hugged her close as a powerful climax roared through him.

Afterward, they lay tangled together on his rumpled coat for some time before he could summon enough energy to lift his head. As he did so, he heard hoofbeats and the murmured voices of a group of riders trotting past.

'We must dress ourselves and return, *chahna*,' he said, giving her a regretful kiss. 'The later the hour grows, the more riders who'll pass this hideaway. All that's needed is for one of our horses to whinny a greeting and we could be discovered.'

He sat up, then chuckled as he looked at her. 'It's a good thing you're already ruined. I don't know how we're going to put you back to rights.'

'We shall do well enough.' Sitting up, she turned to let him slide her stays into place and tighten them, then fasten her blouse and spencer. Readjusting her skirt, she walked over to her mare and extricated some items from the saddlebag. 'I brought these, just in case.'

'So you planned this?'

'I hoped for it,' she admitted. 'After making myself *persona non grata* at Lady Arbuthnot's last night, I... I wasn't sure you'd ride out to meet me again. I imagine your aunt would not be happy you did, if she knew about it.'

Declining to confirm that all-too-accurate observation, he said instead, 'How very prepared you were. I think you'd have made an excellent campaigner.'

She sighed. 'I hope at least to become a proficient breeder of horses.'

She brought the small packet over, opening it to hand him some moistened rags. Using those and the comb she'd included, they were able to make each other presentable enough that a casual observer would never suspect a passionate encounter had taken place within a stone's throw of the roadway.

After returning her supplies to the saddlebag, she stood by the mare's side and looked over at him. 'If you would give me a leg up, we can be on our way back.'

A strange but intense sense of foreboding unlike anything he'd ever before experienced tightened his chest. What was wrong with him? He prided himself on finishing an amorous episode with humour and grace, leaving both partners smiling.

For some reason, he was reluctant to send Prudence Lattimar back to town—to pack up and move out of his life. But what else was he to do? Sweet and intensely pleasurable as his dealings with her had been, he'd known from the beginning that their...friendship, liaison, passion, whatever one wanted to call it, would only be temporary.

Though he hadn't expected it to be terminated so

abruptly, he'd never before had any trouble ending transitory attachments.

Trying to shake off the feeling, he found himself saying, 'Shall I accompany you back to the Circus?'

She hesitated a moment, staring at him, her gaze mirroring the longing he knew must be in his own. Although, except for last time, after she'd been attacked, they'd always discreetly parted before returning to her aunt's house, she said, 'Yes, I'd like that.'

He chastised himself as an idiot for the request on the ride back, for conversation was desultory—she asking where in India he would go to look for artefacts, him answering—but the sparkle had gone from their interaction, leaving an awkward melancholy that had never before been present.

They returned horses and groom to the livery, after which Johnnie walked Pru back to her aunt's house on the Circus. Having reached the address, they both halted.

'It would be better if…if I get started with my preparations, so I won't ask you in,' Prudence said. Her eyes shadowed, her face expressionless, she looked up at him.

'I don't expect I'll see you again, so let me say goodbye, Lieutenant Trethwell. I can't begin to express how much you have enriched my life. I wish you a future full of adventure, excitement and success.'

Feeling strangely bereft, he nodded. 'Goodbye, Miss Lattimar. I wish that you may find a country gentleman worthy of you, who will love you with all the passion and devotion you deserve.'

She gave a sad little shake of her head, as if dismissing such a wish as hopeless. Then, squaring her shoulders, she walked up the stairs and into the town house.

She didn't look back.

Chapter Seventeen

Prudence listlessly mounted the stairs to her chamber, each footstep sounding like the death knell of the happy future she'd come to Bath to find. Entering the room, she glanced at herself in the glass and shuddered. Their attempts at repairing her clothing had been marginally successful, but her coiffure was a disaster.

Sitting at the dressing table, she removed her riding hat and started pulling the pins from her hair, letting the heavy mass fall down her shoulders. After combing it out of her face with her fingers, she picked up her hairbrush, but couldn't summon enough energy or interest to drag it through the tangles.

Staring dully at the hand holding the brush, she told herself she should ring for her maid to help her out of her habit and into a morning gown, so she might go down to breakfast with Aunt Gussie. But she didn't think, in her current turbulent emotional state, that she could endure making polite conversation.

She should begin the tedious process of packing, then. It would be simple; there was no need to take to Entremer the number of morning, afternoon, walking, carriage and evening gowns her aunt had considered necessary for Bath society. She'd pack a few carriage gowns, for when she went into the village for supplies, one or two of the oldest morning and afternoon gowns for when neighbours called, this riding habit—which the maid would definitely need to sponge out before she wore it again—and that would be sufficient.

The other gowns could go back to London for Temper, her twin being able to wear whichever ones appealed to her. She'd have her sister send her other riding habits to Entremer. With the older gowns she'd left in the country and several pairs of Gregory's cast-off trousers she'd secreted away for forbidden gallops riding astride, she would have all she needed.

She mustn't be so glum, she tried to tell herself. The doors to the past would close today and there was nothing she could do about it. She should square her shoulders, start planning her future and make a list of what she must do upon arriving at Entremer so she might move forward as quickly as possible with her goal of beginning a formal breeding operation.

Only by filling her days with so much activity that she fell into bed each night exhausted would she be able to tolerate the anguish of losing Johnnie Trethwell.

Leaving him, she amended sadly. He'd never been hers to lose.

She thought she'd managed her feelings. She thought that, even while admitting she'd fallen in love with him, by knowing all along how slim was the possibility of his falling in love with her, she had armoured herself against the day when she would say goodbye for ever.

She'd been wrong.

The pain that seared her chest was worse than the outrage and humiliation of being ruined by that toad Lord Halden, worse than relinquishing her dream of living a simple, respectable life as a vicar's wife in a small country town. Which probably would not, as Johnnie had predicted, have made her happy.

You would have.

It had taken every bit of will not to try to use the sensual power she now realised she possessed to lure him into fully consummating their union, thereby forcing him into making a declaration. Not even the rogue Johnnie Trethwell would deflower a well-born virgin and then refuse to marry her.

It had then taken every last bit of courage to bid him goodbye before Aunt Gussie's front door, rather than asking him inside. Where, giving up any pretence of pride, she would have broken down and confessed her love, begging him to come with her to Entremer, at least for a while, in whatever guise he preferred—friend, companion, lover.

She knew he cared about her—hadn't he even proposed, when she was in such despair about him leaving her with nothing? Of course, if she hadn't been practical enough to refuse him, when they were both calmer, he would probably have retracted that offer.

He did care for her...just not enough to give up his wandering ways. Nor was there any reason he should. His free-spirited, restless zest for exploration was at the heart of him, what made him uniquely Johnnie. She wouldn't change him if she could.

Even if she had managed to coax him into visiting Entremer, he wouldn't have stayed long. A man who'd known the dark-eyed temptresses of the East, *nautch* dancers, naughty English matrons and females of every stripe in between, wouldn't long be satisfied by a naïve, simple country girl who had only beauty to offer a man who'd tasted so many more exotic dishes at the feminine banquet.

Though, she thought wistfully, a reminiscent heat almost rivalling the pain, the passion they shared had been marvellous. Intense even for him, she was pretty sure, though as inexperienced as she was, she could well be mistaken.

Since she had held herself back and let him go, better to isolate herself at Entremer and stay there. Should she return in the near future to London, every time she went around a Mayfair corner or rode early in the park and saw the flash of a red coat, her spirits would charge upwards on a jolt of excitement and anticipation. Then, an instant later, realising the soldier was not Johnnie, she'd be flayed again by a sabre's slash of loss. Leaving her battered and bleeding, a dull ache of hopelessness thudding in her chest.

Temper had been wiser than she knew when she'd warned Pru to be careful what she wished for. Instead of finding the right gentleman to love her, she'd fallen hopelessly in love with the wrong one.

Dropping the hairbrush, she lay her head on her arms and wept.

For a long time after Prudence Lattimar walked inside her aunt's town house, Johnnie remained frozen to the spot, staring at the door, feeling as if he'd been gut-punched. Finally, his head told his body to stop staring like a looby and get moving. Turning, he headed back towards Queen Square, trying to master the uncomfortable sensations.

His interlude with Prudence had to end some time and, abrupt and unexpected as it had been, now was as good a time as any. He was healed enough that he couldn't justify hanging about much longer, enjoying Aunt Pen's bounty. It was time he focused his efforts on moving towards the future. A future which would lead him and Pru down different paths.

Of course, he regretted that it had happened this soon. He'd admired Pru's beauty and desired her on sight, had his fighting spirits roused by discovering she'd been unfairly tainted by the sins of her family. Coming to value her wit and intelligence, he'd found a kindred spirit in her honest observations and unconventional zest for life. And a perfect partner in passion.

He'd promised himself as an honourable friend he would resist her, but after her pleading—and a temptation impossible to deny—had made him break that promise this morning, he now conceded she'd been right. He was a better friend for giving her a sample of the joy passion could bring her.

And him. What a fiery brilliance burned in her! His first sampling hardly put a dent in the desire she inspired. Ah, to bury himself deep and feel her convulsions all around him! Just the thought of it made him harden again. But he was proud he'd managed to control himself and keep his most important vow, leaving her intact for a bridegroom.

He'd held his emotions in check, too—slipping up only once, when, seeing her so hurt and desolate when she'd accused him of leaving her with nothing, he'd rashly offered marriage. And been justly chided for proposing, though it hadn't been pity that motivated him. More like rage, frustration and pain at witnessing her anguish over the loss of her dream.

Once again, she'd shown herself to be a singular woman. Despite her distress, she'd remained sensible enough to realise that pledging her hand to a wandering adventurer wouldn't gain her what she truly wanted: a respected position in society beside a husband who was a pillar of his local community, who offered her a settled home in the country where she could live in peace with her family and her horses, far away from censorious society.

But then—she hadn't mentioned any of those reasons when she slapped him. Only that she'd not give herself to a man who could not offer her loyalty, devotion and love. Defiantly, she'd dared him to pledge that.

Loyalty would be easy. But shocked, and having never examined his feelings, he hadn't been able to honestly offer love.

Normally, a relationship grew and then withered naturally, without him ever having to consider the nature of his attachment to a lady. This one had been abruptly and prematurely terminated. So what, exactly, *did* he feel for Prudence Lattimar?

He'd admired women before, lusted after them certainly, enjoyed their company. But he'd never felt this…desolate and bereft after ending an attachment. Though he'd always enjoyed a liaison while it lasted, usually he was eager to kiss the current lady goodbye and move on to the next.

Which was what he preferred. After witnessing the agony that had racked Tom Alcorn after he lost Daya, he'd been convinced he never wanted to feel anything stronger for any woman than mild affection.

Still, he was not eager to kiss Prudence goodbye. Was it

because their relationship had never reached the ultimate peak of becoming lovers?

He didn't think so. Novel as it had been to dance attendance on a woman whom he knew from the beginning he could not have, the charm of her person had held frustration at bay and urged him to get to know her better, each interaction sweetened by a delicious undercurrent of desire.

Rather than being impatient to move on to the next adventure, the thought of never seeing her again produced a strange, shockingly deep ache in his chest.

He was going to miss her lovely face and the constant state of pleasant sensual alertness she kept him in. He would miss riding with her, miss hearing her candid thoughts and intelligent observations delivered with no regard to the conventional behaviour expected of a lady. In her zest for life, she appreciated her familiar England, but also, most unusually, the foreign places he described to her. Even for one who'd preferred to explore alone, she'd make a marvellous travelling partner.

When he did finally set off to explore new territories or acquire exotic objects, somehow he *knew* that as he saw them, he would be thinking about how she might respond to those people and places and objects...and regret that she was not with him to share it.

Did that mean...he *loved* her? He had so little experience of the emotion, the only real love from a female he'd received in his life coming from Aunt Pen. What he felt for Prudence was both more, and different.

The love that poets celebrated seemed to require being overcome with a euphoria that took one out of oneself and made one do extraordinary things. He didn't feel like dancing down the middle of Milsom Street or turning cartwheels in the Assembly Rooms or turning up under her bedchamber window to recite bad verse written in her honour.

But he knew what he felt went beyond the physical or superficial. In some way he couldn't describe even to himself, she made him feel more...complete and infinitely happier. As if he were contently trotting his horse along a fine carriage trail through a beautiful woodland in a mist...and she appeared, bringing the sun with her, making what had been merely enjoyable into a sparkling delight.

And in this moment, with his chest feeling like a dacoit's curved dagger had just carved a hole in it, he realised that whatever name he put to what he felt for her, the emotion was far deeper and more intense than he'd ever suspected.

Maybe...maybe despite his intention not to become involved, he had somehow stumbled into love with her. All he knew was he could almost keen with agony at the idea of never seeing her again.

But what could he do to prevent that?

There was no guarantee, intrepid though she was and as enthusiastic as she'd been listening to his adventures, that Pru had any interest whatsoever in leaving her beloved English countryside to embrace the far-more-uncertain future of roaming about the world with him.

As glorious as that possibility appeared to him.

By her own admission, she would have to love and cherish *him* even to consider it. He knew she liked him, that he inspired desire in her...but love?

What did *he* really know about love? He might be completely misreading his feelings, to say nothing of hers.

Putting a hand to that annoying ache in his chest, he tried to convince himself that he felt this pain because their relationship had been cut short, rather than allowed to grow and then atrophy naturally. Or because, although he'd done all he could to help her take her rightful place, it hadn't been enough and he hated to lose a fight. Maybe it was his simmering anger and frustration over that failure that was fuelling these unusually strong feelings of melancholy and loss.

Instinctively, though, he knew it was something far more profound. Something that probably did deserve the name 'love'. Which was why, deep in his gut, it felt so wrong to stand aside and let Prudence leave Bath.

Maybe he should go back to her aunt's town house and demand to see her. Confess how much he'd come to realise he needed her and plead with her to accompany him on his future travels.

As his *wife*. The very word rattled him—a man who'd never before considered the possibility of marriage. But he couldn't contemplate offering Prudence any less than his heart *and* his hand.

If he truly meant to offer marriage, though, he needed to hie off to London and finalise the backing that would move his venture from proposition to reality. To ask her to wed him before he could present himself as the proprietor of a well-funded trading concern would make him appear just as much a fortune hunter as the despicable Lord Halden.

Before he dashed to London, he must break the news of his intentions to Aunt Pen. And then get himself to London and back before Prudence immured herself in the depths of the country.

What if she couldn't be charmed into loving him, or wouldn't consent to travel with him?

His initial excitement cooled as the unwelcome demon in his chest took another bite.

Could he endure a future without her? Of course he

could. Loneliness had been his best friend since childhood. But he knew without her, loneliness would take on a darker, more bitter hue…because, for one shining moment in his life, he'd known what it was to be with someone who lit up his heart and touched his soul.

It would be foolish to let go of that without fighting for her—and Johnnie Trethwell had never walked away from a fight, no matter how slim his chances of prevailing. Forging all his tempestuous emotions into determination, Johnnie set off to find his aunt.

Chapter Eighteen

Fortunately for his impatience, Aunt Pen was in the morning room drinking coffee when he returned. After filling a cup for himself and dropping a kiss on her forehead, he took a seat at the table beside her.

'Riding early, Johnnie?' she asked. 'You look a bit... windblown.'

Happily, he never blushed, so she'd not be able to tell from his countenance just how tempestuous that ride had turned out to be. 'Yes, I went riding. I ended up by deciding it was time to start preparing for my future.' Which was true, even if it did rather drastically edit the events of the morning.

'Ah, yes, your future. You do seem to be managing that leg better now.'

'It's healed, or nearly so. Which makes it time to visit London and start lining up the financing to launch my enterprise. So you see, despite what the gossips say, I don't intend to live on your bounty for ever,' he offered with a grin, trying to soften what he knew would be her disappointment at his announcement.

She sipped her coffee and regarded him thoughtfully. 'Would you remain in England if I settled money on you?'

'Darling Aunt Pen, if I were ready to be roped, saddled and corralled, I could have bedazzled one of those wealthy females you kept wanting to throw at me. Even to please you, I can't see myself remaining in England.'

Sighing, she shook her head. 'My dear Johnnie, you do try the heart of a fond aunt. So I can't talk you out of pursuing that trading venture?'

'I'm truly sorry to disappoint you, but I'm afraid not. I'll start with the arms and armour of the east with which I am familiar, and for which I have known sources, with the intention of moving on to acquire other objects my clients might desire. Silks from China, tapestry and textiles and brass work from India, spices from further east. Calculating the profit the dealer who sold to James's friends must have made, within a few voyages I can probably make enough to purchase my own ship and sail wherever I wish, no longer having to barter for hired transport.'

'If you had additional funds, you would be able to arrange for those things from the start, wouldn't you?'

Surprised, for she had always seemed to oppose this idea so vehemently, he said, 'That would advance the business much faster, yes. You aren't hinting that you might like to become an investor yourself, are you? It's just as risky a venture as you've always warned, Aunt Pen. I could make a great profit—or lose your entire stake, should a ship sink or a cargo be captured by pirates.'

'My dear boy, when have you ever been interested in doing a sure thing? Haven't I gambled on you since you were a child? Taking you in when your family said you were unmanageable? Funding your commission when I was warned you were so ungovernable, you would end up cashiered? And you have always rewarded those gambles. Much more important, you have returned the love I invested with love and loyalty tenfold.'

Johnnie swallowed hard, swamped by a wave of gratitude and love for her. 'Thank you, Aunt Pen. For everything you've done. I promise you, as one of the initial investors, you will stand to profit most if—when—this venture is successful.'

'Oh, *I* don't plan to invest in it.'

He wrinkled his brow, confused. 'But I thought... You said you would gamble—'

'It won't be *me* who gambles. With my own boys settled, nothing is more important to me than your happiness. And if adventuring far from the shores of your native land is the only way to secure that, so be it. I didn't think you should have to wait until I stick my spoon in the wall to take advantage of having a rich aunt who dotes on you.'

'No, Aunt Pen, you don't need to *give* me money!'

'Johnnie Trethwell, since when have I needed to consult you about what I wish to do with my own blunt? Wait right here.' Waving an admonishing finger at him, his aunt rose and walked from the room.

Curious, humbled, impatient, he made himself sit and wait for her, his mind afire with speculation. Had she truly settled money on him? Would it be enough to start his venture immediately, even before he secured backing from his other investors?

She returned a few minutes later, dropping a small book on the table in front of him. 'As you'll see when you look within, I've established an account for you at my bank in London, with funds already transferred into it. Those belong to you and you alone. Go ahead, open it.'

He did as she bid—and then caught his breath, shocked at how large the total was. Jumping up, he came over to wrap her in a hug. 'Thank you, Aunt Pen, for once again believing in my dream.'

Hugging him back, she said tartly, 'All I ask, my dear, is that you write your old aunt—from whatever undiscovered backwater you are adventuring in! But there's one other thing, Johnnie.'

Returning to his seat, he said, 'What's that, Aunt Pen?'

'With wealth of your own, you won't have to wait to finalise arrangements with your potential trading partners in London. You now have sufficient funds of your own to support a wife.'

He stopped short and looked back at her. 'A…a *wife*?'

'Come now, Johnnie, I'm old, but I'm not blind! I've seen how you look at Prudence Lattimar. How a smile lights up your face when she walks into a room. How your whole body nearly hums with excitement and anticipation when she draws near. I know your parents' marriage was a disaster, but don't be a fool and ignore what your heart is trying to tell you. Not all unions are unhappy. Surely you remember how content I was with Woodlings.'

She'd defied her family to marry an obscure baron, given him three boys and lived very happily with him until his death. 'Yes, I remember.'

'I know you've always gone adventuring alone, so you have no experience of what joy it can be to share your life with someone who thinks as you think, appreciates the things you appreciate, who shares your tastes and your interests.' She lifted her brows. 'And your desires.'

Once again, he was glad he didn't blush. Sometimes Aunt Pen was a little *too* knowing. 'I admit, I've only lately come to realise it—' *this very morning 'lately'* '—but I do…understand what you're talking about. I think… I think I've been foolish enough to fall in love with Prudence Lattimar.'

'Well, don't show yourself even more foolish by believing you shouldn't approach her because you can't offer her the usual inducements of a title, an estate to manage and a high position in society. Those things are important to most women—but Prudence Lattimar isn't "most women", is she? If she were, she would have saved face by marrying that scoundrel Lord Halden.'

'Do you think she might consider…adventuring with me?'

'You'll never know unless you ask.' Reading the mix of excitement, joy and trepidation on his face, his aunt laughed. 'Johnnie Trethwell, when have you ever been shy about approaching a woman?'

'I've never been in love before!' he shot back, realising all at once the truth of it. And, now that he had the backing to make his venture possible, he didn't need to go to London first before asking for her hand.

That little demon in his chest took another bite, reminding him how very crucial to his future it was for him to persuade her to accept him and love him back.

His aunt softened. 'Loving her does make a difference, doesn't it? Suddenly, attraction is no longer just a pleasant game, delightful if you win, dismissed with a shrug if you don't. Suddenly, there is nothing more important than being able to spend your life beside the one person in the world who means everything to you.'

'So I woo her with your blessing?'

'You do. I admit, I was wary of your Miss Lattimar at first. But a woman who would turn down a duke's son, face ruin and tell off the most powerful woman in Bath? Who else would make a more splendid match for my unconventional Johnnie?'

Coming around to give her another hug, he said, 'I just hope she agrees with you.'

'Just be your charming self—how could she resist? Now, why are you still hanging about Queen Square, conversing with your old aunt? Off with you! You have adventures to plan—and a lady to win.'

Filled with doubt, wild hope and desperate purpose, Johnnie nearly rushed off to Lady Stoneway's town house that minute. But checking his impatience, he decided that if he meant to bedazzle a lady into being foolish enough to abandon the safety of England and accompany him on his wanderings, he would probably have better luck bathed, dressed in his best coat and not smelling of horse.

How far he'd come in a single day! From unprecedented and troubling distress over the thought of never seeing Prudence again, to allowing himself to consider what she truly meant to him…to being ready to offer marriage.

By the time he'd finished talking with his aunt, the truth of loving her was resonating so deeply within him that he was no longer sure he could exist without her. Somehow, he must win Prudence's hand.

Even if he was lucky enough to have gained her love, it was by no means certain she'd agree to marry him—and trade the safety of England for the wilds of wherever. It was her sister, she'd told him, who wanted to explore beyond her native land. The only fervent desire Pru had ever expressed was to have a conventional husband and a settled home in the English countryside.

She'd been enchanted by his stories...but that didn't mean she'd be equally enchanted at the prospect of living them.

As he tied his cravat and shrugged into his jacket, he let himself consider for the first time what he would do if she could not be persuaded to leave England.

Could he go, without her?

The pain that possibility produced made him realise that, through all his adventuring, he'd been searching for something more, not really knowing what it was. As if he'd put into place nearly all the pieces that made up the puzzle of his life and needed to find just one more to make the picture whole.

Prudence Lattimar was that piece. Without her, he would never be whole or complete.

All he'd ever wanted was to explore new places, new people, new experiences. Could he continue to do that, if Prudence wouldn't go with him?

Could he truly be content remaining in England, breeding horses, if that was the only way he could share his life with hers?

For a long time he sat, gazing into the distance, remembering the joy he'd felt rambling around Aunt Pen's Woodhaven with his cousins, knowing in this one place, with these particular people, he was loved and accepted. He'd never found that anywhere else. He'd always been an outsider, not just with his own family, but at school and in the army.

With Prudence, he would be home again—wherever that home might be. What was more important than that?

To marry Daya, Tom Alcott had been ready to give up his native country and his profession. For the first time, Johnnie fully understood why spending his life with the woman he loved had been more important to Tom than any other tie, any other loyalty. Why claiming that joy had been worth every risk, even the devastation Tom had suffered after losing her.

Johnnie might not have looked to love someone with that sort of all-encompassing tenacity, but now he did. Thinking of how he felt about Pru, the brilliance that life became when he was with her, he was fiercely glad he had fallen for her—whatever happened.

Tom had been right. Claiming such joy *was* worth the risk.

All Johnnie needed to sacrifice to avoid losing the woman he loved was a few journeys for the trading company which, in any event, he could direct from England.

He'd still use all his charm to persuade Pru to travel with him. But if it came down to it, more important than any future explorations would be having Prudence Lattimar beside him for ever.

Decision made, he gave himself one more inspection in the glass and set off.

By early afternoon, Pru had put herself back together, rung for her maid to change her into a plain day dress and given instructions about beginning the packing. Still too battered emotionally to want to face Aunt Gussie or anyone else, she'd asked Soames to inform any callers that she was not at home to visitors and taken refuge in the library. Hunting up her aunt's copy of *Debrett's*, she flipped through, looking for the addresses of several peers she knew who had horses that might make suitable breeding stock for her father's herd and who might be interested in beginning such a project.

She'd completed two letters and was starting a third when Soames's knock at the door interrupted her. 'Lieutenant Trethwell to see you, miss,' he informed her from the doorway. 'I told him you were occupied and not receiving, but he said the matter was most urgent. Knowing that he has been a...particular friend, I thought I should check with you before—'

Johnnie was here? Excitement and trepidation flashed through her. Why would he come, when they'd already said their goodbyes, unless... 'Thank you, Soames,' she interrupted. 'It was good of you not to send him away.'

The normally impassive butler gave her slight smile. 'I rather think that, had I attempted to, he would have simply barged right past me and gone in search of you. I've shown him to the blue parlour. Shall I notify your aunt and send refreshments?'

'Um...yes, that would be good. Thank you, Soames. Tell him I'll be in directly.'

'I expect it will take Lady Stoneway a few minutes to make herself presentable, if you wish to wait for her. Or not.' Giving her a wink, the butler bowed and withdrew.

My goodness! Soames, playing accomplice to an assignation!

Her amusement swallowed by nervousness, Pru jumped up and flew to stand before the mirror over the sideboard. Heavens, why had she chosen to wear this old rag of a gown? She'd told the maid not to bother with her hair, merely brushing it out and plaiting into a long braid that she'd wrapped and pinned around her head. She looked like a down-on-her-luck governess!

No matter. She was far too eager to see Johnnie and discover why he'd sought her out to waste the time it would take to change into a more attractive gown or repair her coiffure.

Feeling like a migrating flock of birds had taken up residence in her stomach, swooping and soaring and beating their wings, she swallowed hard and walked to the blue parlour. Praying his unexpected visit meant what she hoped it did. Knowing she would be so desperately disappointed if he'd merely brought her some book or trifling thing to take with her to Entremer, she might have to flee the room to avoid blurting out her unrequited love and desperate need for him.

She stopped outside the door, taking a deep breath. *Whatever happens, you can bear it*, she told herself. And walked in.

Oh, what a liar she was! Seeing his dear face, smiling at her, it was all she could do not to run over and throw herself in his arms. Wherever the ship carrying him from England went, she was likely to stow aboard. With any luck they'd be halfway to India before he discovered her.

'Miss Lattimar,' he said, rising to his full height as she entered. Recalling how—was it really just this morning?—they had lain together on his coat in the copse beside the Lansdown Road, pleasuring each other, the strict formality of last names and bows and curtsies exchanged seemed ludicrous.

He came to her eagerly, his grey-green eyes ablaze as he handed her a bouquet of flowers. 'Beauties for the beautiful.'

Hope made her heart knock so hard against her ribs she had trouble getting the words out. 'To wish me on my way?'

'In a manner of speaking. May…may we sit?'

Goodness, he seemed so…nervous and uncertain! Nothing like the easy, confident Johnnie she knew.

Suddenly she recalled the butler's words. 'Soames said the matter was urgent. Nothing has happened, has it? No injury to your aunt?'

'No, no, Aunt Pen is fine. She…ah…sends her compliments, by the way.'

'Does she, now? You must be interpreting her words rather loosely! I don't think she's ever approved of me.'

'On the contrary! She thinks very highly of you, I assure you. In fact, it was her regard for…for both of us that propelled me to come.'

He was still so nervous, her hope hadn't died yet, but she was getting more and more confused. 'Your visit has something to do with your aunt?'

'Yes,' he said, looking relieved, as if she understood his purpose—which she did not at all. 'You see, after we parted this morning, I talked with Aunt Pen about the new trading enterprise I want to begin. She not only approved it, she'd already set up a fund for me to begin the venture, even before I secure the additional sponsors in London.'

'Congratulations!' she said, truly happy for him. 'That's wonderful news. When will you depart?'

'That depends. On something else that's even more important.' He paused and looked away, clasping and unclasping his fists.

Pru gazed at him in exasperation. Goodness, her chest might explode from the pressure of ferocious hope and overstrained nerves before she dragged everything out of him!

'It depends upon…what?' she prompted impatiently.

'Well—on you.'

Joy welled up, but she wanted to make sure she wasn't misinterpreting.

'On me? My plans to leave for Entremer?' she probed. 'Which will happen shortly, tomorrow if the packing is complete.'

'But that's just it. I don't want you to go to Entremer. I want you to come with me!'

Joy leapt up and did a few backflips—startling all those birds in her stomach into flight again. 'Johnnie Trethwell… are you asking me to *marry* you?'

'What do you think I've been trying to do?' he cried, his voice rife with exasperation. 'And making just as much a hash of it as I did the first time! My famous address seems to desert me when the matter is vital.'

Everything within her wanted to throw herself at him, shouting 'yes', but this was so important—her very life's heart depended on it—she had to know he was asking her for the right reasons. Not just because he'd decided he'd like a companion on his travels and the passion they shared was incomparable.

'Do you remember my answer the first time you asked?'

'Well, first you slapped me.'

She smiled. 'I'll omit the physical assault this time.'

He smiled back. 'I'd appreciate that. But if you are asking if I remember your conditions, I do. I've discovered a declaration must contain much more than a simple request that you do me the honour of granting me your hand. I know now that I must promise you my loyalty, devotion and love.'

Her heart beat faster. 'And you can now offer that?'

'I can, and so much more. I admit, I hadn't really much

considered how I felt about you until today, when I suddenly faced the prospect of never seeing you again. The thought was...unbearable. So in the course of admittedly very few hours, I've come to realise that, not only do I love you, I cannot tolerate the thought of living without you. Yes, I still wish to travel and have adventures, but they will be so much more satisfying and meaningful, if I can share them with you. Will you let me?'

'Oh, Johnnie,' she whispered, almost not able to speak, so full was her heart.

'Don't give me your answer yet!' he said hastily. 'It's true that I have never wanted anything but to travel and explore. But...but if you think you can't bear leaving England, I think... I know I can give that up, to stay here with you. Thanks to Aunt Pen, I already have the funds necessary to begin my venture, enough to hire agents to carry out the explorations I meant to undertake myself. Enough funds to purchase some property here in England, where we could breed the horses you love, if that would make you happy. I just know that *I* won't be happy, wherever I am... unless you are with me.'

'You would give up adventuring for me?'

'I will. You mean that much to me, *chahna.*'

'Oh, Johnnie,' she whispered again and this time she did fling herself into his arms. 'Of course I will marry you! I've wanted nothing but you for ages!'

'Ages? Until a few days ago, you wanted Lord Halden.'

'That was before I knew his true intentions. But I'm so glad he turned out to be just a fortune hunter! Had he actually been set on entering the clergy, I might never have listened to my heart and discovered what I truly want. The man who led me to discover who I truly *am*. Who loves and values me as I am. Splashing in fountains, insulting dowagers…and sharing passion in a grove ten yards from the Lansdown Road.'

Naturally, after such a declaration, he had to kiss her. When they both stopped to breathe, she said, 'You don't need to give up your life for me. I… I admit, travelling beyond England was always Temper's dream, not mine. I used to think all I wanted was respectability, a home in the English countryside. But the stories you've told have awakened me to how wide, varied and wonderful the world is beyond the borders of our land. I would be thrilled to explore more of it with you.'

His molten gaze sizzled. 'You truly would? It would mean becoming worse than scandalous, you know. In the eyes of many, you'd be nothing more than the wife of a *tradesman*.'

She shook her head. 'I prefer adventurer.'

'I don't care what you call me, as long as we're together.'

'Which is exactly what I want.'

He leaned down to kiss her again. She met him eagerly, revelling in the taste and touch of him, the dance of tongue with tongue. Oh, how she wanted more of him, everything!

Johnnie pushed her away, making her whimper in protest until she heard what he must have—a deep masculine voice clearing its throat loudly. Looking up, she saw Soames standing on the threshold, the tea tray in his hands, smiling at them, before he quickly hid the smile behind his normal impassive countenance.

'Should I assume congratulations are in order?'

'You should!' Johnnie said, laughing. 'Miss Lattimar has just done me the honour of agreeing to become my wife.'

'Excellent! Shall I try to speed up Lady Stoneway and fetch some champagne?'

'Please do,' Pru said—waiting only until the butler had withdrawn before seizing Johnnie by the neck for another deep, passionate kiss.

'So no breeding of horses,' she said a few minutes later. 'What about the raising of children?'

'I think I can promise to follow through on that part,' he assured her, nuzzling her nose.

'Excellent. Might I have an advance on the child-making part...during our ride tomorrow?'

'Certainly not,' he said with mock-seriousness. 'No more trysts, until after we're wed. Besides, I must go to London to secure your father's permission and he might well refuse me.'

'First, I'm of age, so we can wed regardless. Second, he'll be so happy to see me married, he would probably have accepted the loathsome Lord Halden. So don't fear to lose my dowry.'

'We don't need it. Aunt Pen was generous.'

'We can leave it for the children, then. And get some practice at getting them...tomorrow? After all, I have so much more to learn.'

'I shall love teaching you. *After* the wedding,' he said primly.

Pru sighed with exasperation. 'For a former rake and adventurer, you've turned shockingly moral.'

'It must be your previous persona rubbing off on me. But, *chahna*, when I make you completely mine, I want to have a bed and soft sheets and all the time in the world to love you. Not have to worry over some horse's whinny giving us away and being discovered *in flagrante delicto* beside the Lansdown Road.'

'I shall have to wait, I suppose,' she said regretfully,

though that disappointment hardly cast a shadow over the radiance of the happiness filling her. 'Although it might be thrilling to be discovered by the Lansdown Road.'

Laughing, he kissed her forehead. 'Hussy! I think I've loved you since that day in Sidney Gardens. So, you will go adventuring far from home with me, my love?

'With all my heart. Home is where you are—wherever in the world that might be.'

Smiling tenderly, he kissed her nose. 'Then we shall be home, together, my love.'

Throwing her arms around his neck, she laughed, so filled with joy, hope and exuberance she felt she might float off the ground. 'We may end up becoming more infamous than Mama!'

* * * * *

The Earl's Inconvenient Wife

Author Note

There was little scope during the 1830s for women of adventurous spirit who chafed at Society's norms. Although several scientific societies were founded to send out explorers and a growing readership devoured travel journals, exploration was a male domain. Women stayed home and married, traveling abroad only as wives to soldiers or diplomats.

Temperance Lattimar not only longs to explore exotic places, she wants to escape a censorious Society that assumes, based on their close resemblance, that she possesses the same character as her scandalous mother.

But she has a darker reason to break out of the conventional mold. A victim of trauma in her teens, she feels compelled to avoid being trapped into a marriage that would force her to face her worst fears.

Gifford Newell, her brother's best friend, has known Temper most of her life and is one of the few men she trusts. When her father insists that she have a Season, Giff intervenes to find her a sponsor and agrees to watch over her to make sure no unscrupulous men try to take advantage—even though their once easy friendship has recently become complicated by a strong, mutual attraction neither of them wants.

Both believe their partnership will be brief. But when circumstances force them into a marriage of convenience and tragedy strikes, their deepening bonds lead them to discover how friendship can transform into the most enduring love.

I hope you will enjoy Giff and Temper's journey.

To my fellow Zombie Bells, for twenty-odd years of friendship, support and understanding. Along with brainstorming, fixing plot holes, figuring out muddled motivation, clarifying the Black Moment and creating general hilarity. When the text bells start ringing, the muse starts singing!

Chapter One

London—early April, 1833

'You're certain you won't come with me?' Temperance Lattimar's twin sister asked as she looked up from the trunk into which she'd just laid the last tissue-wrapped gown. 'I know Bath isn't the centre of society it used to be, but there will be balls and musicales and soirées to attend. And, with luck, attend without whispers of Mama's latest escapade following us everywhere.'

Temperance jumped up from the window seat overlooking the tiny garden of Lord Vraux's Brook Street town house and walked over to give Prudence a hug. 'Much as I will miss you, darling Pru, I have no intention of leaving London. I won't let the rumour-mongers chase *me* away. But I do very much hope that Bath will treat you kindly—' *though I doubt it, London gossips being sure to keep their Bath counterparts updated about the latest scandal* '—and that you will find that gentleman to love you and give you the normal family you've always wanted.' Letting her sister go, Temper laughed. 'Although, growing up in *this* family, I'm not sure you'll recognise "normal" even if you find it.'

'You mean,' Prudence asked, irony—and anger—in her voice, 'not everyone grows up with a father who won't touch them, a mother with lovers tripping up and down the stairs every day and rumours that only their oldest brother is really the son of their father?'

'Remember when we were little—how much we enjoyed having all those handsome young men bring us hair ribbons and sweets?' Temper said, trying to tease her sister out of her pique.

Pru stopped folding the tissue paper she was inserting to cushion the gowns and sent Temper a look her twin had no trouble interpreting.

'I suppose it's only us, the lucky "Vraux Miscellany", who fit that sorry description,' Temper said, changing tack, torn between sympathy for the distress of her twin and a smouldering anger for the way society had treated their mother. 'Gregory, the anointed heir, then you and me and Christopher, the…add-ons. Heavens, what would Papa have done had Gregory not survived? He might have had to go near Mama again.'

'Maybe if he had, they'd have reconciled, whatever difficulty lay between them, and we would have ended up being a normal family.'

Temper sighed. 'Is there such a thing? Although, to be fair, you have to admit that Mama has fulfilled the promise she made to us on our sixteenth birthday. She's conducted herself with much more restraint these last six years.'

'Maybe so, but by then, the damage was already done,' Pru said bitterly. 'How wonderful, at your first event with your hair up and your skirts down, to walk into the drawing room and hear someone whisper, "There they are—the Scandal Sisters". Besides, as this latest incident shows, Mama's reputation is such that *she* doesn't have to do anything now to create a furore.'

'Not when there are always blockheaded men around to do it for her,' Temper said acidly. 'Well, nothing we can do about that.'

After helping her twin hold down the lid of the trunk and latch it, she gave Pru another hug. 'Done, then! Aunt Gussie collects you this morning, doesn't she? So take yourself off to Bath, find that worthy gentleman and create the warm, happy, *normal* family you so desire. No one could be more deserving of a happy ending than you, my sweet sister!'

'Thank you, Temper,' Pru said as her sister crossed to the door. 'I shall certainly try my hardest to make it so. But… are you still so determined not to marry? I know you've insisted that practically since we were sixteen, but…

Shock, his suffocating weight, searing pain… Sucking in a breath, Temper forced the awful memories away, delaying her reply until she could be sure her voice was steady. 'You really think I would give up my freedom, put myself legally and financially under the thumb of some man who can ignore me or beat me or spend my entire dowry without my being able to do a thing to prevent it?'

'I know we haven't been witness to a…very hopeful example, but not all marriages are disasters. Look at Christopher and Ellie.'

'They are fortunate.'

'Christopher's friends seem to be equally fortunate—Lyndlington with his Maggie, David Smith with his duchess, Ben Tawny with Lady Alyssa,' Pru pointed out.

Temper shifted uncomfortably. If she were truly honest, she had to admit a niggle of envy for the sort of radiant happiness her brother Christopher and his friends had found with the women they'd chosen as wives.

But the *possibility* of finding happiness in marriage wasn't worth the *certainty* of having to face a trauma she'd never been able to master—or the cost of revealing it to anyone else.

'Besides,' Pru pressed her point, 'it's the character of the husband that will determine how fairly and kindly the wife is treated. And we both know there are fair, kind, admirable men in London. Look at Gregory—or Gifford!'

Gifford Newell. Her brother's best friend and carousing buddy, who'd acted as another older brother, tease and friend since she was in leading strings. Although lately, something seemed to have shifted between them…some sort of wordless tension that telegraphed between them when they were together, edgy, exciting…and threatening.

She might be inexperienced, but, with a mother like theirs, Temper knew where that sort of tension led. And she wanted none of it.

'Very well, I grant you that there are some upstanding gentlemen in England, and some of them actually find the happy unions they deserve. I… I just don't think marriage is for me.' Squeezing her sister's hand, she crossed to the doorway. 'Don't forget to come say goodbye before you leave! Now, you'd better find where your maid has disappeared to with the rest of your bonnets before Aunt Gussie arrives. You know she hates to be kept waiting.'

Pru gave her a troubled look, but to Temper's relief did not question her any further. She kept very few secrets from her sister, but this one she simply couldn't share.

Tacitly accepting Temper's change of subject, Pru said, 'Of course I'll bid everyone goodbye. And you're correct, Aunt Gussie will be anxious to get started. Anyway, since you can't be presented this year, what do you mean to do in London?'

'Oh, I don't know,' Temper replied, looking back at her from the doorway. 'Maybe I'll create some scandals of my own!'

Trying to dispel the forlorn feeling caused by the imminent departure of the twin who had been her constant companion and confidante her entire life, Temper closed the door to the chamber they shared, then hesitated.

Maybe she should gather her cloak, find her maid and drag the long-suffering girl with her for a brisk walk in Hyde Park. With it being already mid-morning, it was too late to indulge in riding at a gallop and, as restless and out of sorts as she was this morning, she wouldn't be able to abide confining herself to a decorous trot. While she hesitated, considering, she heard the close of the hall door downstairs and a murmur of voices going into the front parlour.

One voice sounded like Christopher's. Delighted that the younger of her two brothers might be paying them a visit, Temper ran lightly down the stairs and into the room.

'Christopher, it is you!' she cried, spying her brother. 'But you didn't bring Ellie?'

'No, my wife's at her school this morning,' Christopher said, walking over to give her a hug. 'Newell caught me as we were leaving Parliament and, learning I meant to visit you and Gregory, insisted on tagging along.'

Belatedly, Temper turned to curtsy to the gentleman lounging at the mantel beside her older brother Gregory.

'Giff, sorry! I heard Christopher's voice, but not yours. How are you?'

'Very well, Temper. And you are looking beautiful, as always.'

The intensity of the appreciative look in the green eyes of her brother's friend sent a little frisson of...*something* through her. Temper squelched the feeling. What was wrong with her? This was *Giff*, whom she'd known for ever.

'Blonde, blue-eyed and wanton—the very image of Mama, right?' she retorted, hiding, as she often did, vulnerability behind a mask of bravado. 'I suppose you've heard all about the latest contretemps.'

'That was the main reason I came,' Christopher said, motioning her to a seat beside him on the sofa. 'To see if there was anything I could do. And to apologise.'

'Heavens, Christopher, you've nothing to apologise for! Ellie is a darling! We would have disowned you if you hadn't married her.'

Her brother smiled warmly. 'Of course *I* think so. I've been humbled and gratified by the support of my family and closest friends, but there's no hope that society will ever receive us. And wedding a woman who spent ten years as a courtesan wasn't very helpful to the marital prospects of my maiden twin sisters, who already had their mother's reputation to deal with.'

'Society's loss if they refuse to receive Ellie,' Temper said. 'To punish for ever a girl who was virtually sold by her father... Well, that's typical of our world, where gentlemen run everything! Which is why we need to elect women to Parliament!' She gave her brother and Newell a challenging look.

Rather than recoiling, as she rather expected, Christopher laughed. 'That's what Lyndlington's wife, Maggie, says. Since their daughter was born, she's becoming quite the militant.'

'Maybe I can join her efforts,' Temper replied. 'If you and the other Hellions in Parliament are so sincere about reforming society, you could start with the laws that make a married woman the virtual property of her husband.'

'Maybe we should. But the only earth-shaking matter I wanted to address today was to find out what had been decided about you and Pru,' Christopher replied. 'So Aunt Gussie agreed that, in the wake of the scandal, presenting you in London this year wouldn't be wise?'

'Temperance might prefer that you not discuss this with me present,' Newell cautioned, looking over at her. 'It is a family matter.'

'But you're practically family,' Temper replied and had to suppress again that strange sense of tension—as if some current arced in the air between them—when she met Gifford's gaze. If she ignored it, surely it would go away.

'I don't mind discussing "The Great Matter" with you present,' she continued, looking away from him. 'Since you *are* outside the family, you might have a more disinterested perspective.'

'The situation has improved a slight bit since last week,' Gregory said. 'It appears that Hallsworthy is going to recover after all, so Farnham should be able to return from the Continent.'

'Stupid men,' Temper muttered. 'It would have been better if they'd both shot true and put a ball through each of their wooden heads. Honestly, in this day and age, duelling over Mama's virtue! You'd think it was the era of powdered wigs and rouge! It's not as if she's ever spoken more than a few polite words to either of them.'

'Having them both dead would hardly have *reduced* the scandal,' Gregory observed.

'Perhaps not, but the population of London would have been improved by the removal of two knuckleheads who've never done anything more useful in their lives than swill brandy, wager at cards and make fools of themselves over women!'

'Such a dim view you hold of the masculine gender,' Newell protested. 'Come now, you must admit not all men are self-indulgent, expensive fribbles.'

Fairness compelled her to admit he was right. 'Very well,' she conceded, 'I will allow that there still are a few men of honour and character in England, my brothers and you, Giff, included.'

'My point exactly,' he said, levelling those dangerous green eyes at her. 'I could also point out a number of the fairer sex who aren't exactly paragons of perfection.'

'Like the society dragons who won't accept Ellie? Yes, I'll admit that, too. But you, Giff, have to admit that though the ladies and their acid tongues may control who moves in society, it's women who are punished for any infraction of the rules, while men are…mostly exempt from them.'

'We concede,' Giff said. 'Life isn't fair.'

'Shall we move from the philosophical to the practical?' Gregory said briskly. 'As you may know, Christopher, since a presentation in London this Season would be…awkward at best, Aunt Gussie offered to take the girls to Bath. Where at least they could go out a bit in society, maybe even meet some eligible gentlemen.'

'I have no desire to wed some elderly widower and spend the rest of my husband's life feeding him potions and pushing his chair to the Pump Room,' Temper declared.

'And as you might suspect,' Gregory continued after Temper's interruption, 'practical Pru agreed, but intransigent Temper insists on remaining in London and brazening it out. Much as I love you, sis, I really would like to see you out of this house and settled in your own establishment.'

'Since I don't plan to marry, why must I even *have* a Season?' When none of the gentlemen bothered to reply to that, she sighed. 'Very well, but if I must have one, I'd rather have it straight away and not delay yet another year. Most females make their bows at sixteen and, what with one catastrophe or other occurring to forestall a presentation, Pru and I are pushing two-and-twenty, practically on the shelf! The Season will be a disaster, of course, but maybe after that, everyone will leave me alone and allow me to do what I wish.'

'Are you sure you want to press forward this year?' Gifford said. 'If you are cut by most of society, you will have few invitations to balls or entertainments or dinners. Wouldn't it be wiser to wait another year and try then, after this scandal has been buried under a host of new ones?'

'What's to say there won't be a new scandal next year?' Temper objected. 'Paying court to Mama's beauty is practically a…a rite of passage among the idiots coming down from university. Though she doesn't go about in society nearly as much as she used to, she's still as beautiful as ever. And as fascinating to gentlemen.'

'Perhaps even more so, since she doesn't encourage any of them,' Gifford acknowledged with a wry smile. 'The lure of the Beauty Unattainable.'

'The lure of knowing she hasn't always been "unattainable" and the arrogance that makes some man think *he* might be the one to succeed with her,' Temper corrected.

'Let's get back to the point,' Gregory said. 'I'd just as soon not wait to settle your future until next year, either. But if you insist on having your debut here, we shall need some eminently respectable female to sponsor you, since Aunt Gussie will be in Bath with Pru. Obviously, Mama can't do it.'

'Ellie is out, too, for equally obvious reasons,' Christopher said. 'But… I could ask Maggie. As the daughter of a marquess and wife of a viscount, she might have enough influence to manage it.'

'No, Christopher, I wouldn't want to ask her, even though she would probably agree. She's still fully occupied with the baby and, let's be honest, attempting to sponsor one of the "Scandal Sisters" won't enhance the social standing of whoever attempts it. Maggie is too important as a political hostess for Giles, helping him in his efforts to move the Reform bills forward, to risk diminishing her effectiveness, tarnishing her reputation by sponsoring me.'

'But society knows how close we are all, almost as close as family. They will understand the loyalty that would have her stand by you.'

'They might understand her loyalty, but they'd certainly question her judgement. No, if I press forward with this, I shall need a sponsor whose reputation is so unassailable that no one would dare oppose her.'

'How about Lady Sayleford?' Gifford suggested.

'Maggie's great-aunt?' Temper said, frowning. 'That connection is a bit remote, don't you think? I don't doubt that Maggie would take me on, but why should Lady Sayleford bother herself over the likes of me?'

'Maybe because I ask her.' Before Temper could sputter out a response, he grinned. 'She's my godmother. Didn't you know? My mother and her daughter were bosom friends.'

While Christopher and Gregory laughed, Temper shook her head. 'I didn't know, but I'm not surprised. Thick as a den of thieves, the Upper Ten Thousand.'

'You can't deny she has the social standing to carry it off,' Gifford said.

Temper smiled. 'If Lady Sayleford couldn't get her protégée admitted wherever she chose, London society as we know it would cease to exist. But even *she* would have to expend social capital to achieve it. I wouldn't want to ask it of her.'

'Knowing Lady Sayleford, she might see it as a challenge. She's never marched to anyone's tune, knows everything about everyone and has fingers in so many pies, no one dares to cross her.'

'I've never met her, but she sounds like a woman I'd admire,' Temper admitted.

'If you could secure her agreement, Lady Sayleford would be an excellent sponsor,' Gregory said, looking encouraged. 'If anyone can find an eligible *parti* to take this beloved termagant off my hands, it's the Dowager Countess.'

'Need I repeat, I have no intention of ending a Season, even one sponsored by the redoubtable Lady Sayleford, by marrying?'

When the gentleman once again ignored her comment, Christopher agreeing with Gregory that Lady Sayleford would make an excellent sponsor and asking Gifford again if he thought he could coax her into it, Temper slammed her hand on the table.

'Enough! Very well, I admit that Lady Sayleford has a better chance of foisting me on society than any other matron I can think of. But don't go making your plans yet, gentlemen. Let me at least approach Papa and see if I can convince him to release funds from my dowry for me to set up my own establishment—and get out of your house and hair, dear brother.'

The men exchanged dubious glances.

'If I can persuade him to release my dowry,' Temper persisted, 'you'll have no "situation" to discuss.'

'Yes, we would,' Gifford said. 'We'd be figuring out a way to rein you in before you organised an expedition to the Maghreb or India, like Lady Hester Stanhope.'

'Riding camels or wading in the Ganges.' With a beaming smile, Temper nodded. 'I like that prospect far better than wading through the swamp of a Season.'

'Well you might, but don't get your hopes up,' Christopher warned. 'You know Papa.'

Despite her bold assertion, Temper knew as well as Christopher how dim were her chances of success. 'I do,' she acknowledged with a sigh. 'I'll be lucky if he even acknowledges I've entered the room, much less deigns to talk with me. At least he's unlikely to bellow at me or throw things. With all the sabres and cutlasses and daggers he's in the process of cataloguing now, that's reassuring. Well, I'm off to pin him down and try my luck.'

'If I leave before you get finished, let me know what happens,' Christopher said. 'I'll be happy to return for another strategy session.' Planting a kiss on her forehead, he gave her a little push. 'You better go now, so you won't miss saying goodbye to Pru.'

'You're right,' Temper said, glancing at the mantel clock. 'Aunt Gussie could arrive at any minute. Very well—I'm off to the lion's den!' Blowing the others a kiss, she walked out—feeling Gifford Newell's gaze following her as almost like a burn on her shoulders.

Chapter Two

Gifford Myles Newell, younger son of the Earl of Fensworth, watched his best friend's sister walk gracefully out of the room. Just when had she changed from a bubbly, vivacious little girl into this stunning beauty?

A beauty, he had to admit, who raised most unbrotherly feelings in him. Sighing, he fought to suppress the arousal she seemed always to spark in him of late.

Unfortunately, one could not seduce the virginal sister of one's best friend, no matter how much her face and voluptuous figure reminded one of the most irresistible of Cyprians. And though she made an interesting and amusing companion—one never knew what she would say or do next, except one could count on it not being conventional—when he married, he would need a mature, elegant, serene lady to manage his household and preside with tact and diplomacy over the political dinners at which so much of the business of government was conducted. Not a hoyden who blurted out whatever she was thinking, heedless of the consequences.

Sadly, when he did marry, he'd probably have to give up the association that had enlivened his life since the day he'd met her when she was six. He chuckled, remembering the rock she'd tossed and he'd had to duck as he entered the back garden at Brook Street, her explaining as she apologised that she'd thought he was the bad man who'd just made her mama cry.

Her body might be the stuff of a man's erotic dreams, but she was still very much that impulsive, tempestuous child. A mature, elegant, serene wife would be a useful addition to his Parliamentary career, but he would miss the rough-and-tumble exchange of ideas, the sheer delight of talking with Temperance, never knowing where her lively mind or her unexpected reactions would take one next.

He wished the man who did end up wedding her good luck trying to control that fireball of uninhibited energy! Regardless of her childish protests that she never intended to marry, she almost inevitably would. There was no other occupation available for a gently bred female and he sincerely doubted her father, Lord Vraux, would release her dowry so his daughter could go trekking about the world, alone. How would she support herself, if she didn't marry?

She was too outspoken to become anyone's paid companion and no wife with eyes in her head would engage a woman who looked like Temperance Lattimar to instruct her children, unless her sons were very young and her husband a diplomat permanently posted at the back of beyond.

Fortunately, figuring out how to control Temperance Lattimar wouldn't be his problem. Until the day some other poor man assumed that responsibility—or until he bowed to the inevitable, gave in to his mother's ceaseless haranguing and found a wealthy wife to remove the burden of his upkeep from the family finances—he would simply enjoy the novelty of her company.

And keep his attraction to her firmly under control.

He looked up to find both Christopher and Gregory staring at him. Feeling his face heat, he said, 'She's still as much a handful as she was at six, isn't she?'

Gregory and Christopher both sighed. 'Pru will do what she must to fit in, but I'm uneasy about Temper,' Christopher said. 'That's one female who should have been born a man.'

Suppressing his body's instinctive protest at that heresy, Gifford said, 'I would love to see her on the floor of the house, ripping into the Tories who natter on about how disruptive to Caribbean commerce a slavery ban would be.'

'She would be magnificent,' Christopher agreed. 'But since female suffrage is unlikely to occur in her lifetime, we had better be thinking of some other options. I don't think she's going to have much luck squeezing any money out of Vraux.'

Knowing how much tension existed between Christopher and the legal, if not biological, father who had ignored him all his life, Gifford said, 'Probably not. But I'd love to be the parlour maid dusting outside the library door when she tries to talk him into letting her equip a caravan to journey to the pyramids!'

As it turned out, Christopher had left, but Gifford was just striding down the hallway towards the front door when Temper, with an exasperated expression, descended the stairs from the library that was Lord Vraux's private domain.

'I take it the response wasn't positive.'

She let out a frustrated huff. 'As I feared, he barely noticed I'd entered the room. You know how he is when he's in the midst of cataloguing his latest acquisitions! I stationed myself right in front of him and waved my hands until he finally looked at me, with that little frown he has when he's interrupted. In any event, he listened in silence and then motioned me away.'

Gifford knew from Gregory's descriptions how averse the baron was to being touched. Still, it must hurt his children that their father seemed unable to give—or receive—any sign of affection.

'Did he say...anything? Or just go back to cataloguing?'

She shook her head in disgust. 'He said I needed to have a Season so I could "get married and be protected". That women *need* to be protected. I couldn't help myself—I had to ask if that was why he'd married Mama. But he didn't respond, just returned his attention to the display table and picked up the next dagger.' She blew out a breath. 'Rather made me wish *I* could have picked up a dagger!'

Despite the baron's staggering wealth, which meant Gregory had never, as Giff had when they were at school together, gone hungry or had to get his clothes patched instead of ordering new ones, Gifford had always felt sorry for the Lattimar children. Possessed of a mother who, though loving, had made herself such a byword that her daughters' acceptance in society had been compromised, and a father who acted as if they didn't exist.

'I'm glad you didn't grab a dagger,' he said lightly, trying to ease her disappointment. 'The news that you'd stabbed your father, coming on top of the scandal of the duel, would further complicate your debut.'

She gave a wry chuckle. 'Thank you, Giff, for trying to cheer me up. I guess I shall be cursed with a Season after all. But I can't bear thinking about it right now, so please don't summon Gregory and call another strategy session just yet.'

She heaved another sigh. 'I'd rather have a shot of Gregory's brandy, but I'll settle for tea. Won't you take some with me?' she asked, waving him back towards the parlour. 'I haven't had a chance to talk with you since you took up your seat in Parliament.'

When had he ever been able to turn her down? Curiosity over what she might say always lured him in—as it did now, despite his unease over the physical response she sparked in him. 'I suppose I can spare a few more minutes.'

'Giff, a serious, sober parliamentarian,' she said in wondering tones as, after snagging a footman to send for tea, she led him back to the parlour. 'That's a notion that takes some getting used to! Wasn't it just last year that seeing you at this time of the morning would have meant you and Gregory were returning from your night's revels?'

Laughing, she gazed up at him, her glorious eyes teasing, her smiling mouth an invitation to dalliance. Sucking in a quick breath, he slammed his eyes shut. *This is your friend's little sister. You can't let yourself think this way about her.*

Maybe it would help if he didn't look right at her. Or sit close enough to smell the subtle jasmine scent that surrounded her, whispering of sultry climes and sin.

Seating himself a safe distance away, he protested, 'Not last year!'

'Well, maybe the year before. Gregory was just turned five-and-twenty when he inadvertently discovered what a muddle the estate books at Entremer were in and decided the heir must sort things out, since Papa obviously had little interest in doing so.'

'And you must admit, he's done an admirable job.'

'Who would have thought it? His most admirable achievement up to that point had been drinking three bottles of port in a night between entertaining three ladies. While in your company, as I remember, although he didn't divulge *your* totals.'

'How did you—?' Giff sputtered, feeling his face heat.

Temperance chuckled. 'Greg and Giff, what a pair, the two of you! When you staggered into our front hallway at eight in the morning, singing ribald songs, Gregory boasting of his prowess at the top of his lungs… In euphemisms, of course, but Pru and I knew very well what he was referring to.'

'Sometimes you girls are too perceptive,' Giff muttered.

'If we learned at an early age about dealings virginal maidens should have no knowledge of, that wasn't exactly our fault, was it?' she argued, an edge in her voice.

The footman returned with the tea tray and, for a moment, conversation ceased while she poured. Once they both had a cup of the steaming brew, she continued, 'I must say, I was rather surprised when Gregory told us you'd decided to stand for Parliament.'

'Young men must sow their wild oats, I suppose, but eventually one must consider how one intends to make his mark on the world. Especially we younger sons, who can't look forward to having an estate to run.' *Especially younger sons who've been virtually shut out by their family, all the attention of father and mother lavished on the son who would inherit*, he added silently, feeling a familiar slash of pain at that stark reality.

'Joining the Reform politicians is a choice I can admire! Are you finding the workings of Parliament as stimulating as you'd hoped?'

Gratification at her praise distracted him from both his pain and the smouldering anger her unfortunate situation so often sparked in him. Honest, direct and highly intelligent, Temper never flattered, and offered praise sparingly. Despite her youth, of all the females of his acquaintance, she was probably the one whose approval meant the most to him.

'I have to admit, I was dubious when Gregory and Christopher first urged me, but…it *is* stimulating.'

'You've found your calling, then.'

He smiled. 'I think I have. To stand on the floor of the House and realise that what you do there, calling for an end to slavery or for restricting the employment of children in factories, will better the lives of thousands, here and across England's possessions! It's both humbling and thrilling. Even if change doesn't go as far or happen as quickly as we'd like.'

'Yes, Christopher tells me that it will be difficult enough to hammer through the right of all men to vote, that I shouldn't look to see suffrage extended to women any time soon. Unless "women" are added as a class in the bill to end slavery,' she quipped.

He laughed, as he knew she intended him to. 'I'll grant you that married women are…economically disadvantaged. Although their circumstances are not nearly as dire, men with no control over fortune are restricted, too.'

'Your mama has been harassing you about money again?'

Surprised, he forgot his caution and looked at her. Luscious, lovely—and so perceptive. Looking quickly away, before her beauty could wind its seductive tendrils around his susceptible body, he quoted wryly, "'I thought a younger son debauching himself in the capital was expensive enough, but having one in Parliament has turned out to be even more costly".'

'Surely your mama realises you cannot sway the opinions of the brokers of power in a twice-turned coat and cracked boots. And from Christopher's experience, I know even bachelor members of Parliament must sometimes play host to entertainments at the inns or clubs where so many of the compromises are hammered out.'

Damping down his embarrassment that Temper had noticed how shabby his attire had sometimes become, when his quarter-day allowance came late—or not at all—Giff said, 'Quite true. Being a member of Lyndlington's "Hadley's Hellions" group, Christopher had the benefit of being included in the dinners Giles and Maggie gave. Alas, I have no such close connections to a political hostess.'

'Which is why your mama keeps pestering you to marry one. Or at least a girl with money.' His surprise must have shown on his face, for Temper said, 'She's bound to be wanting you to marry wealth—if only to remove the strain of your upkeep from the family purse. Although she may also want some grandchildren to dandle on her knee.'

Gifford tried to imagine such a picture and couldn't. Mama might be interested in the *heir's* children—but never his. 'I doubt that. She'd rather be rid of my expense so she can hang new reticules on her wrist and put more expensive gowns on her back!'

'I may occasionally be angry with Mama, but at least I know, infamous as she is, she loves us.'

Lady Vraux might be a fond mama, but the scandalous behaviour of her earlier years had caused irrevocable harm to her daughters. Gifford had trouble forgiving her for that sin.

'Even if I'm plagued with a Season,' Temper had continued, 'it's unlikely I'll become bosom friends with any pure young maidens. Watchful mamas will probably warn their girls to avoid me like a medieval scourge, lest a daughter's reputation become contaminated by mine. Are there any rich young ladies who have caught your eye?'

'Since, despite Mama's continual urging, I'm not yet ready to make the plunge into matrimony, I avoid gatherings where females of that ilk may be lurking.' He laughed. 'Not that I would be accounted a prime catch by any means.'

'Oh, I don't know! You're handsome, intelligent, well spoken, principled and from an excellent old family. All you lack is fortune and, for a girl with a large dowry, that would hardly be an impediment. If you're not ready to marry, you're probably wise to avoid places where some determined young miss might try to entrap you.' She grinned. 'Besides, though you may not be as…flagrant about your pursuits as in years past, I know for certain that when it comes to feminine company, you and Gregory still prefer ladies of easy virtue.'

'You really do have no maidenly modesty, do you?' he asked, half-amused, half-exasperated by her plain speaking.

'Growing up in this household? I would have to be blind and dumb to have attained my advanced age still retaining any. So, no *gently born* young ladies of interest at the moment. Should you like me to be on the lookout for likely prospects, if I manage to get invited to entertainments where virtuous young maidens gather?'

'Are you going to join my mother in haranguing? Not very sporting, when you profess yourself so opposed to marriage.'

'Not haranguing and our cases are quite different. As long as I can convince Papa to allow me some wealth of my own, marriage offers me no advantages. Whereas, for you, gaining a wealthy bride whose funds would free you from depending on the pittance your family grudgingly doles out would make your job in Parliament easier. Obtaining a hostess like Maggie, who is intelligent, charming and interested in politics, would be even more beneficial.'

The wives of Christopher and his friends were admirable, the couples did seem happy in their unions, and everything she said about ending his money worries and having a capable hostess was true. 'Perhaps,' he admitted. 'But I'm not ready to acquire the advantages of marriage yet.'

'Not ready to give up your ladies, you mean.'

'Let's return to your situation,' he said, having heard enough remarks about his predilection for the muslin company. 'I meant what I said about asking Lady Sayleford if she would sponsor you. She's truly as redoubtable as her reputation claims. If you must have a Season to bring your father around, she would be the best candidate to sponsor you. Anything I can do to help, you know I will, Temper.'

The amusement fled from her face, replaced by a sad little smile that touched his heart. 'I know, Giff. You've been good friend to all of us for as long as I can remember and I do thank you for it,' she said, reaching over to pat his hand.

It was meant to be a casual, friendly gesture. But her light touch resonated through his body with the impact of a passionate kiss. And produced the same result.

He froze, fighting the reaction. Unfortunately, Temper

stilled as well, staring at her hand resting on his, her expression startled and uncertain.

And then, rosy colour suffusing her face, she snatched her hand back. 'Yes, ah, that would be, um, quite... I mean, if I must have a Season, I would appreciate your approaching Lady Sayleford.'

Her voice sounded as odd as her disjointed words. Which must mean that the touch that paralysed him had affected her, too. He wasn't sure whether to be satisfied or alarmed by the fact.

Maybe it was time to leave, before the randy part of him urged him to further explore that intriguing possibility. Setting down his teacup with a clatter, he said, 'I must be off. Shall I call on my godmother and see what I can arrange?'

If the moment *had* been as intense for her, it had passed, for the look she angled up at him was all laughing, mischievous child again. 'Yes, I suppose you must. Imagine— Temperance Lattimar gowned in white, making her debut among the virtuous maidens! That would set the cat among the pigeons, don't you think?'

'It should certainly be...interesting,' he allowed. 'I'll call again later after I've had a chance to chat with her. Thank you for tea and goodbye, Temper.'

'Goodbye, Giff.' She held out her hand to shake goodbye—as they had countless times before—and must have thought better of it, for she hastily retracted it. Not that he would have been foolish enough, after his disturbingly strong reaction to her previous touch, to offer her his hand.

No matter how much he'd like to touch that...and more.

Irritated by the simmer of attraction he was having such a hard time suppressing, Gifford strode out of the room. Trotting down the entry steps of Vraux House after the butler closed the door behind him, he blew out a breath.

He'd been sincere when he assured Temperance that he'd do whatever he could to help her. He truly wanted the best for her. But the attraction she exerted on him seemed to only be growing and doing this service meant he'd likely be seeing her more often than the occasional meeting when he dropped by to visit Gregory.

The prospect of seeing more of Temperance Lattimar was both alluring...and alarming.

Chapter Three

After watching Gifford Newell walk out, Temperance sat back on the sofa and poured herself another cup of tea.

Was she wise to let Giff help her? All she'd done was pat his hand and—oh, my! The bolt of attraction was so strong she'd been immobilised by it. So much that she forgot where she was and what she was doing, her brain wiped free of every thought except the wonder of what it might feel like to kiss him.

She didn't seem to be doing a very good job of ignoring the attraction. Perhaps she ought to regretfully acknowledge that a complication had arisen in what had previously been a carefree, straightforward friendship, and be on guard against it.

The last thing she should do was allow curiosity to lure her into exploring where those impulses might lead.

And then she had to laugh. It was highly unlikely that handsome, commanding, virile Gifford Newell, who probably had never seen her as anything but his best friend's troublesome little sister, would be interested in pursuing such feelings with *her*—even though she was quite certain he had felt the explosive force of that touch. Not when he already had long-standing and mutually satisfactory relations with ladies far more practised and alluring than she was.

Which was just as well. It would be unfair to invite him down a pathway she already knew she could never follow to its ultimate end. The mere thought of what that would entail sent a shudder of distaste through her.

Still, despite the uncomfortable, edgy feelings he roused in her, she enjoyed his company and counted him as one of the few people whose honesty and dependability she could count on. Though in the past he'd often exasperated her with his teasing, as she grew older, he'd begun to listen to her with an appreciation and understanding exceeded only by her sister's. She simply refused to give in and let this... irrational attraction she didn't seem able to suppress spoil a friendship she valued so dearly.

If she were forced to have a Season—and she didn't see how she was going to avoid it, however unpleasant the prospect—she really would prefer to get it over with. She'd vowed, when she turned fifteen and first discovered the implications of her close resemblance to her mother, never to let anyone see how much the censure and unearned criticism hurt. No, she intended to meet society's scorn with a public show of defiance—and weather it privately with fortitude. Though occasionally—if anger got the better of her, which it well might—she might be goaded into doing something truly outrageous, just to live down to society's expectations of her.

The delight of doing that wouldn't make enduring the rest of the ordeal any less unpleasant.

It really would be helpful to have Lady Sayleford guarding her back. Assuming, after meeting her and listening to Temper's frank avowal of how she intended to behave, that lady was willing to take her on.

Doing so, though, would mean having Gifford Newell act as her intermediary.

It wouldn't necessarily mean they'd see each other much more often than they did now, aside from the initial interview with Lady Sayleford, she reasoned. He'd just emphatically reaffirmed what she already knew—that, as he wasn't ready to take a wife, he had no intention of frequenting the sort of Marriage Mart entertainments she would be forced to endure. He would simply turn her over to his godmother and go back to his own pursuits.

She couldn't suppress a little sigh of regret. Despite the recent complication in their relationship, she knew with Gifford nearby, she would be safe—protected from the worst of the insults and scorn of those who disapproved of her and from any men who might seek to take advantage. And she truly would enjoy witnessing his reaction to all the Marriage Mart manoeuvring.

But since it was highly unlikely he would attend any of the entertainments she would be dragged to, she'd better work up the courage to face all those threats alone. After all, when Pru married, as she certainly would—what intelligent man could resist her darling sister?—Temper truly would be alone. Permanently.

For the first time, Temper faced that bleak prospect, not as some distant spectre, but as an event that would likely happen *soon*. She had to put a hand to her stomach to still the wave of bleakness and dismay that swept through her.

Wasn't gaining her independence what she wanted,

though? She tried to rally herself. She'd still have Gregory and Christopher, Gifford's special friendship and could look forward to playing the proud aunt to Pru's eventual children. Doubtless somewhere in her family tree she could find some indigent female relation who would prove both congenial and willing to live with her.

As an independent woman, she'd be able to attend the lectures that interested her, visit the shops and galleries, and—her greatest ambition—work towards equipping herself to travel to the fascinating foreign places she'd read so much about. Foreign places where she could immerse herself in history and culture while she sought out treasures for her father. Where she could be herself, free of the stifling restrictions society imposed over women of her class. And, most important, having escaped the threating spectre of marriage, she might even manage some day to free herself from the dark shadows of her past.

All she need do to attain those goals was make it through one Season.

After ringing for the footman to collect the tea tray, she'd been about to go upstairs when a commotion at the front door announced the arrival of Aunt Gussie.

'Darling Temperance!' Lady Stoneway cried, handing her cloak over to a footman and coming over to hug her. 'How lovely you look!'

'You are looking in fine fettle, too, Aunt Gussie! The prospect of a sojourn in Bath obviously agrees with you.'

'I am looking forward to it,' her aunt allowed, joining Temperance to mount the stairs. 'Are you sure you won't come with us? Pru is going to miss your company—and your support—so very much! And I will, too.'

Dismissing a pang of longing, Temperance said firmly, 'No, I shall stay here. Not that I'm not grateful for your offer, but... I simply won't turn tail and flee, just because some idiots created a scandal that was not in any way Mama's fault.' *Nor am I interested in going where I might encounter a gentleman admirable enough that you and Pru would try to persuade me to marry him.*

Her aunt sighed. 'It is unfair, I admit. To your mama, as well as to you and Pru. But truly, my dear, in Bath we will have a fair chance of avoiding most of the scandal, finally allowing the two of you an opportunity to be courted, find a worthy gentleman to marry and settle down happily in your own households!'

'That's Pru's hope, not mine,' Temper reminded her aunt.

Lady Stoneway shook her head. 'Still dreaming of travel to some faraway place? I thought you would outgrow that foolish wish.'

'I haven't, for all that the wish might be foolish. However, though I couldn't convince Papa to allow me my dowry without having a Season, perhaps after it turns disastrous and he realises marriage to anyone save a fortune-hunting scoundrel is impossible, he will relent.' *For I'm highly unlikely, Papa, to encounter a true gentleman who wants to 'protect' me. Not if he knew the whole truth...*

'I'm not at all convinced it need be disastrous,' Lady Stoneway protested. 'So, you're going to wait for London next year after all?'

'Oh, no. As I told you when the scandal first broke, if I must debut, I intend to do so here, in London, just as we planned.'

Lady Stoneway stopped short, turning to look at Temper in astonishment. 'You intend to attempt a Season *this year*? In London?'

'Yes—if I can find a sponsor. But you mustn't even think of changing *your* plans! Pru is eager to marry and I fully agree her chances of finding a respectable partner will be far better in Bath. Whereas, since I don't wish to marry, it makes no difference to me that having a London Season now will likely produce...disappointing results. In fact, if it's truly bad, I might be able to convince Papa to let me abandon the effort after a month or so. But please, no more talk of that now. I haven't told Pru—she might feel obligated to change her plans and stay here to support me, which is the very last thing I want. She's been waiting so long for the kind husband and happy family she's always dreamed of! I don't want to delay her finding that even a day longer.'

'But who will sponsor you—?' her aunt began, before, at Temper's warning look, she cut the sentence short as Prudence ran out into the hallway to meet them.

'Welcome, Aunt Gussie! I'm all packed, so we may to leave as soon as you've rested and refreshed yourself.'

Giving Temperance a speaking glance, Lady Stoneway said, 'Ring for some tea and after that, I'll be ready. I've already instructed Overton to send some footmen up to collect your trunks. I suppose I should look in on my brother—though if he's in one of his collecting moods, he may not notice I'm in the room.'

'You could stop by, but he just got a new shipment of weapons and is fully engaged in cataloguing them,' Temper warned.

Lady Stoneway shook her head. 'I won't bother, then. Shall we have tea with your mother?'

Her smile fading, Pru shook her head. 'Knowing you

would arrive at any moment, I've already bid her goodbye. Let's have tea in my room.'

'I'll fetch Gregory,' Temper said. 'We can have a pleasant family coze before you two head on your way.'

'I should like that!' Prudence said, coming over to link her arm with Temper's. 'I am going to miss you very much, dear sister.'

'And I, you,' Temper acknowledged with another pang. *Especially since, after your sojourn in Bath, I shall probably lose for ever my best and closest friend.* Shaking off that melancholy thought, she said, 'But how exciting, to send you off into the future! I hope this Season will end with you finding the man of your dreams.'

'I second that happy wish—for you *both*,' Lady Stoneway said, giving Temper a pointed glance as she ushered both girls into their bedchamber.

An hour later, after bidding the travellers goodbye, Temper walked back upstairs. Already the house seemed echoing and empty, now that the serene, optimistic spirit of her sister had left it.

Needing to stave off those unhappy thoughts, she decided to look in on her mama, who, she suspected, might be feeling a bit low. With a loyal maid who kept her appraised of everything happening in the household, she could not help but know that her precious daughter Pru, about to leave her house, most likely never to live in it again, had declined to invite her to her farewell tea.

Temperance could understand her sister's bitterness towards the mother whose profligate behaviour had spilled over to poison their lives. But she also understood how a woman's mere appearance led to assumptions, attack and uninvited abuse.

And knowing her papa, she could completely understand why a woman as vivacious, outgoing and passionate as her mother, denied affection and even basic interaction with her husband, would in desperation have sought it elsewhere.

After knocking lightly on the door, she walked in—to find her mama lounging on her sofa by the window, draped in one of her favourite diaphanous, lace-trimmed negligées. Temper had never seen the inside of a bordello, but she couldn't imagine even the loveliest denizen of such a place looking more beautiful and seductive than her mother.

Smiling at the picture Lady Vraux presented, she walked over to drop a kiss on that artful arrangement of blonde curls.

'Temperance!' her mother said in surprise, delight on her face as she turned from the window and saw her daughter—but not before Temper noticed the bleak expression the smile had chased away. 'I'd call for tea, but I expect by now you're awash in it. The travellers are off, I imagine.'

So she did know she'd been excluded, Temper thought with a wave of sympathy for her mama. Pru's resentment might be justly earned—but that wouldn't make the estrangement any less bitter for a mother who, Temper knew, truly loved her children.

'Gussie couldn't talk you into going with them?' Lady Vraux asked as she patted the sofa, inviting Temper to take a seat beside her.

Temper gave a dramatic shudder. 'To Bath? To drink the vile waters and be ogled by old men? I think not.'

'So what do you intend? I very much doubt Vraux will release your dowry. Christopher, then Gregory, stopped by to visit this morning and told me you intended to approach him.'

'I did and you are right. He won't release it to me.'

Lady Vraux rubbed Temper's hand. 'I'm sorry, my darling. If I had any money of my own, you'd be welcome to it.' She gave a bitter laugh. 'Unfortunately, I never had a feather to fly with, which is how I ended up married to Vraux in the first place.'

Her mother's family had been noble but penniless, Temper knew. The wealthy Lord Vraux's offer to settle the Portmans' debts in exchange for their Incomparable daughter's hand had been a bargain they would not let her refuse. No matter how cold, impersonal and unapproachable the character of the baron who'd made the offer.

'So you'll go forward with a Season?' Concern, regret and sadness succeeded the smile on her face. 'I would advise against it, my sweet. Not this year. Gussie is quite right in assessing your chances of success to be minimal after the Farnham-Hallsworthy fiasco.'

Dropping Temper's hand, she turned away. 'I... I am sorry about that. You do know I did nothing to encourage them! I haven't taken a new lover for more than five years, just as I promised. And I was hopeful that Gussie, with her standing and influence, could smooth a path for the two of you despite...despite your unfortunate parentage.'

Temper gathered her mother's hand again. 'I know, Mama. I don't blame you for the idiocy of men.'

'Pru does, though.'

Temper was trying to find some palliative for that unfortunate truth when her mother continued, 'I've earned whatever infamy I bear, and as Miss Austen's Mary observes,

"the loss of virtue in a female is irretrievable". But I hate
that it continues to reflect upon you.'

'It doesn't matter for me. Unlike Pru, I have no desire
to wed. But if Papa will not allow me to do anything else
until I've had a Season, then I intend to get it over with. I
expect it will be a noteworthy failure—indeed, I hope it is,
the better to convince him a good marriage is impossible
and get him to release my dowry.'

'There's no guarantee he will do so, even if your Season
is unsuccessful,' her mother pointed out.

That was the one great flaw in her plan, she had to admit.
'True. But if I tell him I intend to journey to whatever place
offers the treasure he is currently most interested in acquiring, so I may procure for him exactly what he wants, I might
persuade him. You know he thinks of nothing but obtaining the latest object that catches his fancy.'

'That true enough,' Lady Vraux acknowledged. 'Coming at it from that direction, I suppose there is a *chance* you
might persuade him.' After hesitating a moment, she said,
'Are you so sure you don't want to marry? Not to be indel-
icate, but you're not getting any younger, darling. When I
was your age, Gregory was four, Christopher two, and I was
enceinte with you! I know your father and I have hardly offered an encouraging example of the estate, but Christopher
and Ellie seem happy enough, so you must see that contentment in marriage *is* possible. And marriage would offer you
children. That is a joy I'd hate to see you deny yourself.'

For a moment, Temper was tempted to blurt out the
dreadful truth she'd hidden from everyone for so long. But
since revealing it would probably wound her mother more
than it would bring Temper comfort, she bit back the words.

'I'll have Pru's brats to love,' she said instead. 'You know

I've read every travel journal I could find since I was a girl! Travelling to exotic places—and finding treasures to bring back for Papa—is the only thing I've ever wanted to do. A dream of which a husband is unlikely to approve. And once he got his greedy hands on my dowry, a dream I would no longer have the funds to pursue.'

'That is likely true. A lady with funds of her own to do what she wishes? I can't even imagine it.'

'Well, I can and I like the image very much. So, yes, I'll remain in London, debut if I can find a sponsor and brazen it out.'

'Gregory said that Gifford Newell offered to approach his godmother, Lady Sayleford, on your behalf. A formidable lady!' Lady Vraux shook her head, her eyes sparkling with amusement. 'The Dowager Countess's position is so unassailable, she even invites *me* to her entertainments. Then makes a point of ensuring all the disapproving society matrons see her chatting with me. She just might enjoy sticking her thumb in society's eye by sponsoring you. And under her care, you would be protected from the...disdain which I fear you might otherwise suffer.'

Temper wasn't about to increase her mother's worry by confessing she expected to meet with a lot of disdain, regardless of who sponsored her. She was too angry that, despite six years of impeccable behaviour where gentlemen were concerned, there was neither forgiveness nor tolerance for her mother. Whereas she knew for certain that a number of noble *men* conducted affairs in full view of their wives and suffered no social consequences whatsoever.

'If Newell does secure you her sponsorship,' her mother continued, 'I shall be very pleased to see you immersed in all the activities of the Season. You needn't worry that

I'll feel neglected. I have Ellie and my friends. And who knows what might happen? I will pray for your happiness and success.'

'Then you will be praying for me to journey to exotic places!'

Lady Vraux tapped Temper's cheek, her smile bittersweet. 'There is no journey so exotic and unexpected as a journey of the heart.'

If that journey led to marriage, it was one she could never dare take, Temper thought sadly. But before she could become mired in melancholy, her mama said, 'If you do embark on a Season, let me give you one more piece of advice. Never show fear or weakness, or your enemies will fall on you like rabid dogs. It's better to be scorned than pitied.'

Rising, Temper leaned down to kiss her mama's cheek. 'That's a piece of advice I can embrace wholeheartedly!' After crossing the room, she stopped in the doorway to look back at her mother. 'Whatever society says or thinks, I am *proud* to be your daughter, Mama.'

Lady Vraux took a shuddering breath, tears glistening at the ends of her improbably long lashes. 'Your loyalty is precious, if ill advised. I would wish you to end your Season with more success than I did.'

'If I end it with the prospect of travel to foreign places, I shall be satisfied indeed.' Blowing her mother a kiss, determined to move towards the future *she* wanted, Temper walked out.

Chapter Four

Four days later, Lady Sayleford's butler ushered Gifford Newell and Temperance Lattimar into the Great Parlour of the Dowager Countess's imposing Grosvenor Square mansion. 'I'll tell the Countess you have arrived,' he intoned before bowing himself out.

'What a lovely room,' Temperance said, looking around the chamber, its delicate plaster decoration done up in pastel shades. 'Pure Robert Adams, isn't it?'

Was she remarking about decor to conceal her nervousness? Gifford wondered. He'd discovered an intriguing new side to Temperance Lattimar during their drive here this afternoon—that instead of behaving with her usual blunt exuberance, when she wished to, she could conceal her thoughts and feelings behind an impenetrable façade. Ever since he'd arrived at Vraux House to escort her to this interview, she'd been calm, composed—and for the first time since he'd known her, utterly unreadable.

'It is Adams,' he confirmed. 'Lady Sayleford was one of

his first sponsors, engaging him to redecorate the public rooms of Sayleford House when she was just a young bride.'

'The symmetry, balance and delicacy of the mouldings are beautiful,' Temperance said. 'I'm so glad she didn't decide to change it out for the new Egyptian style.'

'Not a fan of crocodile legs and zebrawood carving?'

'Not unless I'm encountering them on the Nile!'

'Are you truly interested in furnishings and such?' he asked curiously. 'I never knew.'

'Of course I'm interested in furnishings—and architecture and sculpture and painting!' she retorted, giving him a look that questioned his intelligence. 'Why else would I be so interested in travelling to foreign places—or knowledgeable enough to promise Papa I could search out the treasures he seeks? It's not just the changing landscape abroad that fascinates. Just as interesting are the arts and artefacts that reveal so much about culture and character.'

'Little Temper—the scholar?' he teased.

'She certainly will be—once she has the chance,' she shot back. 'Since employment in the Foreign Office or in Parliament is currently denied her.'

Gifford was chuckling at that as she continued, 'Before the Countess arrives, let me thank you once again for arranging the interview. And let me apologise in advance, if my behaviour embarrasses you.'

Puzzled, he tilted his head at her. 'Why would it embarrass me?'

'Because, if I do have a Season, I must warn her I have no intention of behaving like a modest, accommodating young miss eager to attract a husband. I'm more interested in *dis*couraging suitors, so I may get through the Season and go my own way.'

Before he could respond to that, Harris returned to announce the Dowager Countess. Gifford and Temperance rose, the ladies exchanging curtsies while he bowed.

'Gifford, you rascal,' Lady Sayleford said as he came over to kiss her cheek. 'It's a sad thing when it takes an errand on behalf of a chit of a girl to get you to visit your poor godmother.'

'I admit it, I have been remiss,' he said. 'Parliament is busy.'

'I'm sure,' she murmured. 'Leaves only enough time to visit the doxies you favour—in company with this young lady's brother, I understand.'

To his chagrin, Temperance choked back a giggle. 'You are just as well informed as Gifford promised, Countess.'

'So what is it you wish me to do for you, young lady?'

'It's rather what, if anything, *you* wish to do, Lady Sayleford. To be honest, I wouldn't have approached you at all, had Gifford not insisted. Being well informed, I'm sure you know about the latest scandal involving my mother.'

'Farnham and Hallsworthy,' the Countess said. 'Idiots.'

'Exactly,' Temperance agreed, her glorious smile breaking out. 'As you probably also know, my aunt, Lady Stoneway, has chosen not to present my sister and me in London this Season as planned and has taken Prudence to Bath instead.'

'And why you did not wish to accompany them?'

Gifford winced. Trust his godmother to dispense with the standard politenesses and probe directly to the point.

'Unlike my sister, I *don't* wish to marry, so there was no reason to accompany them to a place which would improve my chances of contracting a match. However, since Lord Vraux insists I must have a presentation, I'd rather follow our original plan and debut here, this Season. Once that's over, I hope to persuade him to release some funds so that I may do what I truly want to do.'

'Go exploring foreign places, like Lady Hester Stanhope? You really think you could persuade Vraux to fund that, simply because you fail to marry after your first Season?'

'It will be difficult, I grant. But if I can show him that no respectable gentleman will offer for me and vow to dedicate my explorations to tracking down whatever he's currently seeking, I might succeed. He's only ever been interested in *things*, after all.'

'Too sadly true. So, with Lady Stoneway off to Bath, you need a sponsor. Someone whose standing in society will make up for your mother's lack of it?'

Wincing at the remark, Giff braced himself for the furious defence of Lady Vraux that would likely spell an abrupt end to this interview. Instead, to his surprise, Temperance... smiled.

Granted, the smile was thin and he could almost see her head steaming from the fury she was holding in, but—hold it in she did.

Another revelation! Apparently, Temperance Lattimar could not only mask her feelings, she could withstand being goaded—which he was sure his godmother was doing deliberately, to see what sort of response Miss Lattimar could be prodded into producing.

She was certainly angry, for though her tone remained pleasant, the gaze she fixed on Lady Sayleford was frigid. 'I'm sure I could turn up among my relations a matron more *respectable* than Mama to sponsor me. However, since only a woman of *unbounded* influence could force enough of society to receive a daughter of the infamous Lady Vraux that my father would consider my presentation adequate, I agreed to let Mr Newell approach you. Since sponsoring a daughter of the infamous Lady Vraux is likely to be thought poor judgement on the part of anyone foolish enough to attempt the task, it would be wise of you to steer clear of me. And now, I expect we have taken up enough of your valuable time.'

As Giff drew in a sharp breath, she started to rise—only to check as the Dowager Countess held out a hand. 'Please, sit, my dear,' she said in pleasant tones, as if Temperance's reply hadn't been a defiant rebuttal, however obliquely delivered. 'We haven't yet had our tea.'

As she spoke, the butler walked in with the tray, placing it on the table and pouring for them. Temperance sat in such absolute stillness, then took her cup with such measured precision, Giff had the vision of some wild beast from the Royal Menagerie immobilised by chains. How long could she restrain that anger? And would he be the unlucky victim of that storm when it did break?

After setting down her own cup, Lady Sayleford said, 'So, you think I should "steer clear of you", Miss Lattimar? Do you truly think I am in the habit of being guided by chits of two-and-twenty with no experience of the world and nothing but an outrageous reputation to boast of?'

Temperance's face paled and Giff felt his own anger rise. He'd brought Temper here to ask for help—not to have his imperious godmother subject her to the sort of set-down that had reduced matrons twice her age to tears.

Before Giff could intervene, Temperance set down her cup—and burst out laughing. 'Goodness, no, Countess!' she said when she'd controlled her mirth. 'I sincerely doubt you've ever been guided by anyone.'

Lady Sayleford smiled, as if Temper had passed some sort of test. Which, Giff supposed she just had—neither wilting under the Countess's pointed questioning, nor flying into a tantrum.

'You don't seem inclined to be guided, either,' the Countess observed. 'Certainly not by Lady Stoneway, who you must admit has only your best interests at heart.'

Temperance's amusement vanished as quickly as it had arisen. 'I do know that. But Mama has been treated outrageously for years. By Papa. By society. Lately, for things that are not at all her fault. I don't intend to hide away and act as if I believe they were.'

Lady Sayleford nodded. 'Your loyalty to your mother is admirable and, as you may know, I value family loyalty highly. But you must admit that your mother was very foolish when she was younger and society is not forgiving.'

'Not of a woman,' Temperance said acerbically. 'Especially not one who is beautiful, charming and a magnet for the attention of every gentleman in the room.'

'They are much quicker to exile a Beauty than a wallflower, aren't they?' the Countess replied drily. 'I believe you do have enough backbone to last a Season. So, let me see... Vraux has pots of money. Angela, a niece of my late husband's, is a widow living in straitened circumstances, her son in the Royal Navy, her daughter married to some country nobody. To enjoy a Season in London, she would probably agree to serve as your chaperon. If your father will see her properly clothed and pay her expenses, I shall send for her.'

'Before you offer to help me, I must warn you that, even backed by your approval, I expect to meet with a considerable amount of disapproval. If goaded, I might be...irresistibly tempted to do something outrageous, just to live down to society's expectations. Which, of course, would further my goal of discouraging suitors.'

'It might encourage the unscrupulous, though. You're too intelligent to do anything stupid, I hope—something that might place you in actual danger. Men *can* be dangerous, especially to women they think invite their attentions. Sadly, my dear, with your looks and reputation, it wouldn't take much for them to make that assumption.'

Was it only his imagination, Giff wondered, or did Temperance once again turn pale? But then she shook her head, colour returning to her cheeks.

'I don't intend to encourage *any* man and I certainly wouldn't agree to meet one alone, if that's what you are warning against. If provoked, I might feel compelled to best some smirking gentleman in a race through Hyde Park—in front of a full complement of witnesses. Or I might accept a dare to drive a curricle down St James's Street past the gentlemen's clubs,' she added, chuckling when Giff groaned.

'You are indeed your mama,' Lady Sayleford said, her eyes lighting with amusement. 'But wiser and forewarned. I do hope, though,' she added, sobering, 'that you end up happier than she did.'

After a moment of silence, as if she were weighing whether or not to speak, Temperance said, 'She…she loved Christopher's father, didn't she? Sir Julian Cantrell? I've never asked her, not wanting to dredge up sad memories, and everyone else puts me off. I overheard Aunt Gussie telling Gregory that Sir Julian was the love of her life. That he loved her, too, enough that he was prepared to be shunned by society for marrying a divorced woman, only Papa refused to divorce her. I'm sure you know the truth. Won't you tell me?'

Lady Sayleford remained silent as well, so long that Giff thought she would refuse to answer. Finally, she said, 'I don't agree that it does a girl any good to have the truth withheld from her. It's not as if, growing up a member of the Vraux Miscellany, you have any maidenly innocence to protect!'

'That's true,' Temperance agreed with a wry grimace. 'So—you *will* tell me?'

Lady Sayleford sighed. 'After Vraux refused Felicia the divorce she pleaded for, I half-expected she and Cantrell would run away to America. But she loved Gregory and knew, if she fled, she would never see her firstborn again. She gave up Sir Julian instead. It nearly broke him, especially after he discovered she was carrying his child. By the way, I'm glad he was later able to reconcile with Christopher; a man should have a relationship with his own son, even if he can't claim the boy outright. It was only after Felicia lost Sir Julian that, once very circumspect, she became... careless of her reputation. She *must* have been devastated, else she would never have been taken in by your father.'

'Marsden Hightower?'

'Marsden Hightower,' Lady Sayleford confirmed with a curl of her lip. 'Rich, handsome, charming—and a cad of the highest order. He boasted of his conquest all over town, let slip lurid details of the rendezvous he persuaded her into—meeting him in some hostess's boudoir in the midst of ball, or in the shrubbery at some garden party! Details too deliciously scandalous not to become the talk of society—or to thoroughly offend the hostesses at whose events the purported dalliances had taken place. She was never for-given—not that, being Felicia, she ever expressed remorse.'

'She would have confronted the rumours with her lips sealed and her head held high.'

Lady Sayleford nodded. 'And so she did. Despite the reputation she acquired, she never took a married man for a lover and she had countless opportunities to do so. A dis-tinction I recognise and appreciate, even if many of soci-ety's harpies do not.'

'Is that why you still receive her, when most of the high sticklers will not?'

'I admire honour, as I admire courage. Especially hon-our and courage maintained when one is given no credit for possessing them.'

'Thank you for telling me the whole truth.'

Giff sat in shocked silence. He'd always accepted what rumour said about Lady Vraux, disdaining her as a self-ish Beauty who took lovers to gratify her vanity with no thought to the harm her conduct would do her family. When Temperance told him his godmother invited the scandal-ous Lady Vraux to her home, he'd assumed the Countess did so on a whim, to demonstrate her mastery over society.

After hearing the truth, he realised with some chagrin that he, who prided himself on treating people as he found them rather than believing what rumour whispered, had done exactly that with Lady Vraux. He had to admit a grudging admiration for her courage—and for the cour-age of the daughter who had always believed in and pas-sionately defended her.

Lady Sayleford gave Temperance a regretful look. 'Un-fortunately, knowing the true origin of your mother's repu-tation doesn't change your present circumstances, my child.'

'No. But it does confirm what I've always known—that Mama is not the amoral, self-indulgent voluptuary society accuses her of being. But then, of what value to society is truth? It will believe what it wants, regardless.'

Lady Sayleford nodded. 'If you know that, you are well armed to begin a Season. I shall enjoy hearing about your escapades.'

Giff was smiling—until the meaning of that sentence penetrated. '*Hearing* about them?' he repeated. 'Won't you be *accompanying* her to social events?'

'To every frippery Marriage Mart entertainment that attracts silly young girls and nodcock young gents on the lookout for rich brides? Certainly not! I shall accept only those invitations that interest me, just as I do now. But I will introduce Miss Lattimar before I turn her over to Angela and make sure it's known that I will be watching to see how each member of society receives her.'

'Very well, I'm reassured,' Giff said, relaxing a bit.

'Besides, it's not *me* she needs to watch over her. In order to be truly protected, she'll need a *gentleman* standing guard. You, Gifford.'

Looking as alarmed as he felt, Temperance said, 'Lady Sayleford, is that truly necessary? Surely having a chaperon by my side every minute will afford sufficient protection! I never meant to embroil Giff in a social round he surely doesn't want—'

'Don't be argumentative, child,' Lady Sayleford said, cutting her off. 'It won't hurt Gifford to attend a few society functions. How else is he to find the rich bride a rising politician needs? Cyprians are well and good for pleasuring-seeking, but a career in government requires adequate funds and a suitable hostess.'

Her remarks were, of course, spot on, but that didn't mean Giff appreciated them—especially not in front of Temperance, who had recently preached from the same sermon. Feeling colour warming his face, he said, 'Thank you for the advice. But I'm not prepared to act upon it just yet, so don't be getting any ideas.'

Lady Sayleford smiled. 'What else has an old woman to do, but get ideas? My dear,' she continued, turning back to Temperance, 'do you think your father will agree to have Angela chaperon you?'

'If you approve of her, I don't see why he would object.'

'Just to make sure, I'll pen him a note. Tell him I'm grateful he's sparing my old bones as your sponsor by allowing my great-niece to act in my place. Vraux does like to keep things safe, even if he can't…care for them like normal folk. In any event, I'll sweeten the agreement by sending him a medieval mantelpiece Sayleford once outbid him for.'

'Oh, no, ma'am!' Temperance protested. 'I wouldn't want you to part with one of your husband's treasures!'

'Nonsense! I've been trying to dispose of the hideous thing for years. What better use to make of it than to dispatch it to someone who might actually appreciate it?'

Temperance laughed. 'My mother's reputation might be based on falsehoods, but yours is not. You *are* wise, as well as all-knowing!'

'There must be some benefit to growing old, other than the ability to interfere in other people's lives with impunity. But since I'm so wise, let me offer you one more bit of advice. Don't be blind, fixing yourself so narrowly on a single goal that you fail to see the alternatives that present themselves. As they always will. Now, I shall consult my calendar, but I think next week will do for an introductory tea. That will give me enough time to summon Angela. So drink up, Gifford. You've accomplished your purpose and it is time for me to rest.'

With that, they finished their tea, then stood as his god-mother made her majestic departure.

Standing in the hall while the butler summoned their carriage, Temperance said, 'Lady Sayleford is amazing! I'd like to be her one day.' Then she shook her head, her expression rueful. 'But then, I'd have to be respectable to begin with.'

'You are less of a hoyden than you used to be,' Giff observed. 'I thought you displayed remarkable restraint today. I was initially afraid you might attack with nails and fists when she insulted your mother.'

'She was taking my measure, I think. And I'm not as thoughtless and impulsive as you seem to believe. At least, not all the time. For instance, I intend to keep my chaperon close by whenever there are gentlemen about, so I really don't think you need to attend social events to watch out for me. You'd probably be bored to flinders and hate every minute of it.'

'I hope to sidestep that fate—not because it would bore me, but I would rather avoid eligible young ladies for a while longer, despite my godmother's forceful advice.'

Conversation halted as, his tiger having brought his curricle to the entrance, they exited the house and mounted the carriage.

'If I thought you were going to be compelled to supervise me, I would never have asked for Lady Sayleford's sponsorship,' Temper continued after he'd set the horses moving.

Giff shook his head. 'Too late to withdraw now! If I know my godmother, by the time we reach Vraux House she will already have written to summon her great-niece.'

'I shall be happy enough to proceed, as long as we can convince her not to drag you into the bargain. No point going to market when you aren't ready to buy anything.' She sighed. 'I only wish *I* didn't have to spend time in the Marriage Mart, but since I must, I'll cheer myself with the hope that it might not be for long. With any luck, it will soon be evident that I attract only fortune hunters and fast young men looking to lure the "wanton" into the shrubbery.'

Giff didn't find that prospect very reassuring. Neither type of man was likely to respect Temper—and the latter could, as his godmother had pointed out, actually pose a danger to her.

Maybe he ought to drop by a few of the entertainments she attended, just to make sure she was safe.

'It pains me that society will try to paint you in that light. When we both know that neither you—nor your mother, it turns out—possess such a character.'

'As I told your godmother, people will think what they want, regardless of the truth. But in this instance, I'm glad of it. It should require only a little push to have society confirm that I don't respect its rules, ensuring that no respectable gentleman will pay me his addresses.'

'Just as long as you are not targeted by the truly *dis*reputable.'

'As long as I have a chaperon clinging to my side, I hope I am! Everyone knows *disreputable* gentlemen are the most charming! Except for you, of course, Giff. You're respectable and—alluring.'

The change in her tone—from amusement to warmth of a different sort—pulled his gaze from the road to her. The yearning he read in her eyes fired his always-simmering attraction into full-on arousal.

Fierce, intelligent—and so beautiful. He had an almost overwhelming urge to lean down and kiss her.

The curricle hit a bump, jolting him back to the job of controlling the horses. But his palms were sweating and his breathing uneven when he pulled up his team in front of Vraux House.

'You needn't see me in,' she said as his tiger jumped down and trotted over to help her out of the vehicle. 'I shall try not to be *too* outrageous, so hopefully your kindness in intervening to help me won't come back to haunt you.'

He looked at her full in the face this time, struck anew by her beauty—and the softened lips and molten gaze that confirmed the strong current of desire coursing through him was unmistakably mutual. For a long moment, they simply stared at each other.

She reached a hand out, as if to touch him, then drew it back again. 'Thank you, Giff,' she whispered, then turned away to let his tiger help her down.

Ridiculous, to feel an instant bolt of envy because that skinny, pock-faced boy was touching her—as he wanted to so fiercely and mustn't.

Fists clenched on the reins, Giff watched her walk into Vraux House—both regretting and hopeful that his part in the launching of Miss Temperance Lattimar's Season had just been completed.

Chapter Five

A week later, dressed to attend her introductory tea at Lady Sayleford's, Temper inspected herself in her looking glass. The afternoon gown, one of the new dresses she'd just acquired, was cut with the wide sleeves, narrow waist and belled skirts of the latest style, done up in a deep blue silk that enhanced her eyes. Not the virginal white of a timid debutante, but the colour suited her—both in looks and temperament.

Telling herself she had no need to be nervous, she was walking down the stairs to collect her cloak and have the butler summon her a hackney when the door opened and Gifford Newell walked in. He looked up, saw her—and stopped short.

She froze, transfixed by the intensity of his admiring gaze, for the first time glad that the exaggerated style emphasised the smallness of her waist while the low bodice exposed her neck and shoulders. Then, telling herself not to be ridiculous, she lifted her skirts and continued downwards, ignoring the accelerated beat of her heart and the queer fluttering in the pit of her stomach.

He was, she discovered when she looked up after descending the last step, still gazing at her. 'Exquisite!' he murmured. 'If being the most beautiful lady in the room means society will exile you, your Season will be over before it begins.'

She shouldn't feel such satisfaction at knowing he found her attractive—but she did. 'The colour is lovely, although I can't admire the style. These sleeves and skirts! Impossible to do anything useful wearing something so wide.'

'Of course not. As a society lady, you're supposed to be admired and have everything done for you.'

'In other words, be vacant-headed and decorative.' She sighed. 'Heaven help me survive this Season! You're looking handsome as always, Giff. Come to find Gregory?'

'No, I came to collect you. To escort you to Lady Sayleford's. I'm pleased to find you ready. My godmother detests tardiness.'

'You're escorting me?' she echoed. 'I thought the tea would be a ladies' affair.'

'So did I, but when Lady Sayleford commands, one complies. Unless one is prepared to move to the Outer Hebrides, which would be a rather inconvenient location for a sitting Member of Parliament.'

'I understand carrier pigeons can travel hundreds of miles in just a few hours,' she offered, smiling. 'But I agree, the Outer Hebrides would be inconvenient. Though if it is to be just ladies, I can't imagine why she would require you to escort me. Surely she knows I'm capable of taking a hackney from Vraux House to hers!'

'I long ago learned never to question my godmother's inscrutable ways,' Giff replied. 'Shall we go?'

'Yes. Hopefully once you've delivered me, she will release you back to your duties. As a sitting Member of Parliament.'

To her relief, Newell had brought his curricle, requiring him to keep his attention focused on his driving, rather than on her. With him otherwise occupied, she could sit beside him and enjoy the delicious frisson of attraction that sizzled between them without any chance of being tempted further down a road she had no business travelling.

The afternoon being busy and the traffic noisy, she made no attempt to converse as they made the transit. A short time later, he pulled up his team in front of Lady Sayleford's town house, his tiger springing down to help her out.

They walked in, Harris once again showing them into the Grand Parlour where, this time, Lady Sayleford awaited them.

'Here I am, ma'am, as summoned,' Giff said as he bent to kiss his godmother's cheek after the ladies exchanged curtsies. 'Was that the extent of the service you wished me to render?'

'You think I would require you merely to deliver Miss Lattimar, who is entirely capable of making the arduous journey from Brook Street to Grosvenor Square on her own? No, I have other plans, which will put all your wit and charm to good use.'

Motioning them to a seat, she said, 'As you can see, you've been summoned before the other guests. I want you to meet my great-niece, Mrs Angela Moorsby, and instruct you, Gifford, on the role you must play. That first.'

'What, precisely, would you have me do?'

'I have invited a few of the most important society hostesses. After greeting them all, I wish to speak privately with each one. Your task, Gifford, will be to assist my niece in keeping the other ladies entertained, the conversation flowing brightly, so none are tempted—or able—to eavesdrop on my tête-à-tête.'

'What part am *I* to play?' Temper asked.

'You, my dear, will be sitting by me, so that each lady gets a...proper introduction.'

And with that explanation, which explained nothing, I will have to be satisfied, Temper thought, suppressing a smile. Very well. She was quite prepared to recite her few lines while Lady Sayleford directed the overall action.

'I don't suppose I'm permitted to ask who, what or why?' Giff said, posing what, from the frown Lady Sayleford returned him, Temper knew had been a rhetorical question.

'Ah, here she is! Angela, allow me to present my godson, Gifford Myles Newell, and the young lady you are to chaperon, Miss Temperance Lattimar. Children, this is my great-niece, Mrs Angela Moorsby.'

Sucking in a breath in apprehension, Temper watched a small, plump woman cross the room, her rotund form garbed in a slightly out-of-fashion gown.

'Mr Newell, well met!' she said, curtsying to them, her pleasant face wreathed in a smile. 'And Miss Lattimar! So you are the angel of mercy who is enlivening my dull life by providing me a Season in London. And a complement of lovely new gowns, as well! Thank you! I intend to enjoy myself exceedingly—and, I promise you, to chaperon with a very light hand.'

Temper smiled back at the friendly gaze and open, honest countenance of Angela Moorsby, her fear of having to deal with an incompatible chaperon melting into an instant rapport.

And a sharp stab of guilt, to doom this pleasant, innocent lady to the criticism and censure she expected her presentation would heap on the head of her hapless chaperon. Looking over at Lady Sayleford, she said, 'Have you warned her what my Season will likely entail?'

'Oh, no, my child. I thought it better to allow you to do that.'

So you can listen to me explain one more time before giving final approval? Temper would not be at all surprised, should she express something to incur Lady Sayleford's disapproval, to have the offer of sponsorship revoked on the instant and the great-niece sent back to rural obscurity.

'Are you acquainted with the...circumstances of my family?' she asked Mrs Moorsby.

'Yes, Lady Sayleford related to me the...unusual nature of your upbringing and the reason why you are in need of a chaperon.'

'So you know society expects me to be ill behaved, amoral and capricious. Although I am none of those things, neither am I interested in marriage, so while my behaviour will give no credence to the first two traits, I am perfectly happy to play up the latter. In fact, I may take a few strategic actions to reinforce my reputation as an ungovernable woman no respectable gentleman would have as a wife. Acting as chaperon to such a creature may well be accompanied by...an unpleasantness that may make you wish you had remained in Portsmouth. Are you sure you want to take me on?'

'So that you can fulfil your father's requirement that you have a Season and go on to become a lady explorer? What a marvellous thing! If I hadn't grown so fond of my snug hearth and my comfortable little Portsmouth community, I would almost be tempted to go exploring again myself. I was never the Beauty you are, but I was rather adventuresome myself as a girl, marrying a merchant captain over my family's objections and going to sea with him.'

'How wonderful!' Temper declared, delighted. 'You must tell me about your travels!'

'Some other day, perhaps,' Mrs Moorsby replied.

She looked up to find Lady Sayleford smiling and was struck again by her shrewdness. *You sly old lady*, she thought. *You chose the perfect chaperon for me.*

'I've never held with mealy-mouthed females who haven't the wit to form their own opinion or who constantly look to some man for guidance.' Mrs Moorsby winked at her. 'My aunt warned that you will likely kick over the traces. I shall enjoy watching you.'

Temper smiled wryly. 'I hope it may prove entertaining. However, you may well have your judgement and your competence questioned, or find yourself pitied, when I prove to be…less than conformable.'

Mrs Moorsby shrugged. 'What do I care for the opinions of people I shall never see again, once the Season is over? As long as you enjoy shopping, theatre, concerts and—' she winked at Giff '—the company of handsome gentlemen, I'm sure we shall get on splendidly.'

Harris returned then, intoning, 'Lady Spencer-Woods, Mrs Dalworthy, Lady Wentwith and Mrs Dobbs-Henry.'

'You know what you are to do?' Lady Sayleford murmured as they all rose to greet the newcomers.

'Perfectly,' Mrs Moorsby said with a conspiratorial smile.

'Welcome, ladies,' the Countess said after the exchange

of bows and curtsies. 'I wanted you to be the first to meet my protégée, Miss Temperance Lattimar, who makes her debut this Season. Her chaperon, Mrs Moorsby, and my godson, Mr Newell.'

The pleasant smiles of greeting on the faces of the newcomers froze as Lady Sayleford spoke. Four heads turned as one to fix surprised, then horrified, then offended gazes on Temperance.

Taking a deep breath, she straightened and gazed straight back, a smile fixed to her lips. *Is this how you do it, Mama?*

'Ah, here is Harris with our tea. Won't you be seated?'

Under the Countess's direction, Temper found herself on the sofa next to Lady Sayleford, Lady Spencer-Woods in a chair adjacent to them, while Giff and Mrs Moorsby sat with the other ladies in a grouping of chairs closer to the hearth.

After the initial shocked silence, with a murmur of voices and clink of cups emanating from the group near the fireplace, Lady Sayleford said, 'So, Elizabeth, I expect you will give your usual ball, now that Parliament is in session.' She turned to Temper. 'Lady Spencer-Woods's Opening Ball is the premier entertainment of the Early Season, attended by everyone of importance in society.' Looking back at her guest, she continued, 'You will certainly send Miss Lattimar and Mrs Moorsby a card.'

The guest shifted uncomfortably, shooting Temper a pained, faintly contemptuous glance, 'Really, Emily,' she said in a low voice, leaning forward as if speaking with the Countess alone, 'I know you are somehow…connected to her family, but this is outside of enough! You may amuse yourself, inviting the Vraux woman to your entertainments, but you cannot expect *me* to recognise a daughter of that…creature!'

Temper didn't need the Countess's subtle warning glance to know she must remain silent. *As if I weren't right here, listening to every word,* Temper thought, outrage filling her and the tea turning bitter on her tongue. *You must accustom yourself to hearing this and worse.* Was that what Lady Sayleford meant to teach her, by compelling her to witness this exchange?

'Leaving aside any commentary on Lady Vraux's character, the child is not her mother.'

Lady Spencer-Woods gave a thin smile. 'She might be worse.'

'I'll let that indictment of my judgement pass,' the Countess said mildly, but with a frigid look that saw her visitor's defiance collapse. 'It would please me mightily to have you send Miss Lattimar and her chaperon a card. And see that all your friends do, as well. However, if you wish to be… disobliging, I might suddenly recall a certain incident with a dancing master that happened in our debut Season.'

The matron paled. 'I hardly think society would be interested in…in a silly contretemps from so many years ago.'

'Oh, I don't know. When a lady is one of the premier arbiters of society, whose judgements about the character of young ladies have made or destroyed reputations and Seasons, I expect there might be exceptional interest in the story of a—'

'Never mind,' Lady Spencer-Woods interrupted, bright spots of colour blooming in her cheeks. 'I don't think any further details are necessary.'

Not with a highly interested witness sitting in, Temper thought. *Lady Sayleford, how clever you are indeed.*

'For a woman, "incidents" are never truly past and forgotten, are they? Even when one has lived blamelessly for thirty years.'

'Felicia Lattimar has hardly lived "blamelessly" for thirty years!'

'She might have, had her idiot of a husband paid her any attention. And might have still, had that cad Hightower not spread his malicious stories all over town. In any event, you will invite Miss Lattimar to your ball—won't you? Ladies of power and influence should present a united front.'

Lady Spencer-Woods held her hostess's unflinching stare for a moment, before dropping her gaze. 'I suppose so.'

'Then we understand each other. Excellent.'

Lady Sayleford smiled serenely, as if she hadn't just ma-noeuvred her outraged guest into checkmate. 'You need do nothing more than receive Miss Lattimar. I shall not hold you responsible for her ultimate success, or lack of it. Un-less, of course, I learn you've said or done something dis-paraging to compromise it.'

'I shall not forget this, Emily,' Lady Spencer-Woods said, looking back up at the Countess, her expression a mixture of resentment and reluctant admiration.

'I don't expect you will. Now, I know you'd like to be-come better acquainted with Mrs Moorsby, who will be ac-companying Miss Lattimar to all her entertainments.' She gestured towards the other group, a clear sign of dismissal. 'I shall look forward to seeing you at your ball.'

'I shall be delighted to welcome you. And your lovely protégée,' she added with a resigned glance at Temper. Then, unexpectedly, she laughed. 'Emily, what a trickster you are! One never knows what outrageous thing you will do. Have no fear, I shall play my part.'

'I never doubted it. I know just how...*ingenious* you can

be, Elizabeth,' the Countess replied, amusement in her eyes as her guest's cheeks once again went rosy.

And so it went with each matron in turn. Lady Sayleford immediately demanded support for Temper, countered any objections about her and her mother, then moved in for the kill with a hint about some questionable event in the lady's past the Countess might just happen to recall, should her guest not prove accommodating.

After the guests took their leave, Temper turned to gaze in awe at her sponsor. 'You really do know everything about everyone!'

Lady Sayleford chuckled. 'The benefit of a long life spent building such a reputation for discretion, every bit of scandal finds its way to my ear.'

'Still, I regret that you had to play so many of the trumps you've kept close in hand. I hope giving them up—and the animosity you may have incurred for playing them now—won't come back to harm you.'

'You needn't worry, my dear. I have enough other trumps tucked away to be in no danger of losing whatever game I choose. Now you are privy to some of that knowledge, too.'

'And you made sure all those ladies knew it!'

'I don't intend to go everywhere with you. But they all know their secrets will. Shall we join the others?'

'How well you work your magic!' Mrs Moorsby said to the Countess as she made room for Temperance on the sofa beside her. 'After chatting with you, each lady came back to express her delight in making my acquaintance and her hope that my charge and I would be able to attend the entertainment she intended to give later in the Season. Bravo, Aunt Lilly!'

'One does one's possible,' Lady Sayleford said, a satisfied smile on her lips. 'The two of you did well, too, keeping your group from listening in—though, after each one finished her session, she must have known something similar was being said to the others and been agog to discover what lapse that lady had committed.'

'Have you made out a social schedule for us yet?' Mrs Moorsby asked.

'Not yet. We shall do that together, once the invitations begin to come in.'

'With Mr Newell present, as well? I imagine he has duties in Parliament, and we will want to make sure the entertainments we attend will not conflict.'

'Why would they?' Temper asked. 'Surely with you on hand to provide protection and assistance, Mr Newell's part is finished—and I sincerely thank him for his efforts!'

'Unless I'm mistaken, it's not at all finished,' Mrs Moorsby said. 'I may be your chaperon, but the Countess believes that Mr Newell should act as a sort of...guardian. Don't you, Aunt Lilly?'

The Countess nodded. 'You must admit, Miss Lattimar, that if some...unscrupulous man tried to take advantage, a female chaperon would be of limited assistance. Having everyone know there's a gentleman nearby, watching over you, will ensure that no blackguard makes such an attempt.'

'And while standing guard, Mr Newell shall have a chance to review the field of prospective brides,' Mrs Moorsby added.

'But wouldn't his being in my company compromise his reputation—limiting his chances of meeting eligible young ladies? For their mamas will surely want them to avoid me,' Temper countered.

Lady Sayleford waved a dismissive hand. 'If he were seen as a suitor, perhaps. But as my godson, delegated to look after the young lady I'm sponsoring, society should expect him to be in your company.'

Her chaperon's bright smile indicating how entirely unaware she was of the consternation this alteration in plan had just evoked, Mrs Moorsby stood up. 'I will leave you now to take my rest, but I understand we are to do some shopping later, Miss Lattimar. I shall look forward to it! A pleasure to meet you both.' After dipping them a curtsy, she walked from the room.

'Lady Sayleford, you cannot mean for Giff—Mr Newell to...to dance attendance on me at *every* social event I attend!' Temperance cried as soon as her chaperon exited. 'I would never have consented for him to consult you had I any notion you might require such a thing! You must release him from that obligation, or I shall—'

'What?' Lady Sayleford interrupted. 'Cancel your Season? Kick about the house in Brook Street for another year, or go bury yourself in the country at Entremer? Or do you think making a second attempt to convince your father to fund you will have better success than the first?'

Temper hesitated, torn. As Lady Sayleford was quite aware, none of those options was attractive. But to embroil Giff in a round of social activities he was sure to view as an outrageous imposition? As keenly aware as she was of her vulnerability, she couldn't repay his friendship by saddling him with that!

While she struggled to think of an equally safe and reasonable alternative, Lady Sayleford turned her attention to Giff. 'You did ask me to sponsor Miss Lattimar's Season, didn't you?'

He gave her a pained smile. 'Yes, but I didn't anticipate becoming quite so…involved in every event of it.'

'Gaining Miss Lattimar a sponsor was only part of the job. If you applied half the intelligence I know you possess to considering what will transpire once she actually embarks upon a Season, you must realise she can't be left with just a lone female for protection. You must know she is more vulnerable than an ordinary young miss. So, Gifford, do you truly wish to help Miss Lattimar? Or was your offer to intervene just a casual gesture taken without much thought, something you're prepared to back away from if implementing it will require additional time and effort from you?'

'Of course it wasn't casual or thoughtless,' he retorted, a touch of anger in his tone. 'I may not have anticipated that her having a Season would require additional time on *my* part, but I was—am—entirely committed to making that Season happen.'

'Very well. So, knowing the cost, you are willing to proceed?' With a wry smile, she added, 'Thereby proving the adage that "no good deed goes unpunished"?'

Gifford sighed. 'Let's proceed. I suppose you will instruct me on my additional duties as we move forward.'

'I shall, once our plans are made. But now I, too, must rest before the evening's activities. Manipulation is so wearying! Miss Lattimar, Angela will keep me informed of your progress with shopping and such, and inform you about which activities you are to attend.'

Temper couldn't help feeling that somehow, everything had gone awry. She wanted independence and a future lived on her own terms—but she'd never imagined seeking that goal would embroil Giff in a round of society functions he couldn't possibly wish to attend.

Accurately reading her expression, Lady Sayleford said, 'Don't look so regretful, my dear. Gifford may lose a few evenings with his doxies, but getting a closer look at the females available to become the wife he must *eventually* take will more than make up for it.'

'I only hope he finds it so,' Temper muttered.

'In any event,' she said briskly, 'it's a waste of emotion to regret the necessary. You wanted your chance and now you shall have it. What you do with it is up to you.'

Lady Sayleford stood and perforce Temperance and Gifford stood as well. As conflicted as she still felt, the Countess had made it unmistakably clear that the presentation would be done on her terms, or not at all. If Giff could stomach being part of it, she had little choice but to go along.

'If I cannot promise to appear to your credit,' she said with a sigh, 'at least I can promise to end the Season unharmed.'

Lady Sayleford nodded. 'I'm sure you will. Gifford will see to it.' Giving them a regal nod, she swept from the room.

Temper sank back on to the sofa. 'Giff, I'm so very sorry! You know I never meant to involve you in this escapade, but the Countess seems adamant about having some male to watch over me. I wish I could think of some alternative! And I truly don't want to wait another year. Are you sure you won't be furious if we go forward with this?'

Giff gave her a wry smile. 'I can't pretend to be delighted, either. But neither can I dispute the truth of what she said. Your reputation—however undeserved—does make you more vulnerable than the usual unmarried maiden. Even a respectable man knows he could probably get away with compromising you without having marry you and a borderline scoundrel… Well, *he* might feel free to try with you what he'd never dream of attempting with any other innocent miss. Now that I've thought about it, I have to admit I'd feel…uneasy about you proceeding with only Mrs Moorsby for protection. Since I'm responsible for involving Lady Sayleford—and her rules—in your presentation, it's only right that I see it through.'

'So…you won't resent me for ever?'

'If I'm angry at anyone, it should be at myself, for jumping into this without fully considering all the implications. It won't pain me too much to attend society soirées.' He smiled. 'It might even be amusing—especially if you discover a man who changes your mind about avoiding marriage.'

She shook her head. 'That man doesn't exist! In turn, I will try harder to get to know some of the young ladies. If I'm surrounded by a protective crowd of companions, you will be able to curtail the time you are forced to spend with marriage-minded females.' She grinned. 'Maybe I'll discover among them a lady who will change *your* mind about waiting to marry!'

Despite that teasing comment, Temper discovered as she finished her tea, she wasn't any more enthusiastic about the idea of Giff discovering a woman he'd like to marry than she was about the necessity of dragging him into her Season.

Shaking off that unsettling realisation, she said, 'I suppose I'm allowed to escort myself home now?'

Chuckling, he put down his own cup. 'No, better let me drive you. I wouldn't want to incur the Countess's displeasure before we've even got started.'

They walked out, pausing in the hall as they waited for

the curricle to be brought around. 'I will insist to the Countess that we only attend evening entertainments, so that it doesn't cut into your duties with Parliament,' Temper promised.

'I doubt you'll be able to deflect her from accepting exactly the invitations she pleases, whenever they take place. I'll warn Christopher he may have to take notes for me.'

'Besides,' he added as he escorted her down the steps, 'what worries me more than missing Parliamentary sessions is the unmerciful ribbing I'm going to get from Gregory, once he discovers I managed to trap myself into escorting you for the Season!'

Chapter Six

❧〰〰〰❧

A week later, Gifford Newell rode in the carriage with Lady Sayleford, Mrs Moorsby and Miss Lattimar to the first grand social event of the Season. Shifting uncomfortably on the backward-facing seat, which in the narrow confines of the carriage put him far too close to Temper, he tried to focus on the loquacious Mrs Moorsby.

'You mustn't be nervous about attending your first formal event, Miss Lattimar,' the chaperon was saying. 'I knew you were a Beauty, but the way those creations bring out the gold of your hair and emphasise the blue purity of your eyes? Frankly, I'll be amazed if any man can resist you!'

'She'll certainly create a stir,' Lady Sayleford predicted, giving Temper an approving glance.

'All of you ladies look dazzling tonight,' Giff observed, partly because it was true and mostly to try to distract himself from just how alluring Temper was.

It had been hard enough to control the wave of desire he'd

felt, standing twenty feet away in the hall at Vraux House as she descended the stairway. He'd observed her in day dresses that showed off her narrow waist and voluptuous bosom, but that evening gown! The lacy confection not only bared her shoulders, the neckline swooped so low in front he could see the rising swells of her breasts...

His tongue had stuck to the roof of his suddenly dry mouth, making it impossible for him to return her greeting, while his mind was in turmoil, the body protesting the sacrilege of the evening cape the butler was draping over that glorious form, his brain applauding the masking of a vision that made his heart skip a beat and everything masculine in him leap to the alert.

He'd managed to mumble a few, probably nonsensical, words to her as he followed her out to the carriage, but he couldn't remember a syllable, too unsettled by the thrilling and dreadful knowledge that they would soon be crammed together on that narrow backward-facing seat.

He'd perched as far away from her as he could get. But that still left him sitting so close that she need move her slippered foot only an inch to touch his. Close enough that at any moment, the jouncing of carriage could bounce her hand from the seat on to his wrist...or worse, his thigh. Sat there with her jasmine perfume filling his senses, struggling to rein in an attraction even the knowledge that Lady Sayleford and Mrs Moorsby were both looking on couldn't extinguish.

Feeling sweat trickle down his brow, he looked over to see his godmother watching him, an ironic smile playing at her lips.

The wretch! That smile told him she knew exactly the

agonies he was experiencing—and didn't regret inflicting them on him one little bit.

He wasn't sure whether she'd arranged this to remind him of the costs of involving her in Temper's Season, to test his mettle, or as a silent demonstration of the difficulties he'd brought upon himself by having always spent his time with females for whom there was no need to mask his physical response.

For there was no doubt, had Temper been a Cyprian, he'd have already pulled her close and sampled her lips... in heated anticipation of sampling much more.

When Mrs Moorsby leaned forward, continuing to chat to Temper as she straightened an errant ribbon in her charge's coiffure, Lady Sayleford murmured, 'You should be glad of the current style. Those wide skirts and ridiculous full sleeves give you almost eighteen inches of separation. The straight Empire gowns of former days would have clung right to her figure.'

The vivid image of Temper sliding up against him, clad only in a sliver of silk, burned itself into his brain before he could prevent it. Feeling another wave of heat wash through him, Giff grimaced.

'Well, my dear,' Lady Sayleford said as Temper's chaperon finished her task, 'are you ready for your first foray into the *ton*?'

'As I'll ever be, I suppose. Not...frightened, precisely, Lady Sayleford, though I do thank you for your concern. More like...resigned.'

'You should make up your mind to enjoy these events, not merely endure them,' Lady Sayleford advised. 'There's instruction and amusement to be had in every experience—

no matter how initially difficult.' After a significant glance at Giff, she continued, 'Anticipate the unusual and intriguing, and you will find it.'

'Intriguing people, even among the *ton*?' Temper said sceptically.

'I'm a member of the *ton*, aren't I?' Lady Sayleford replied.

Temper laughed, her sober expression warming into a smile so full of merriment, Giff thought it must lift the spirits of anyone who witnessed it. 'You have me there. I shall just have to look for *other* intriguing and unusual members of the *ton*.'

The carriage began to slow to a halt, indicating they had reached the Portman Square home of Lady Spencer-Woods, for which Giff uttered a silent prayer of thanks. Little as he was looking forward to what he expected to be a boring event, Giff was heartily glad to hop out of the carriage and let the footman hand the ladies down after him.

Though viewing Temper again minus the concealing evening cloak was unlikely to relieve the state of arousal he'd suffered since collecting her, at least he could maintain some distance while he worked on the 'training himself to resist her' wisely suggested by his godmother.

The servants in the hall, busy collecting outer garments and directing guests up to the ballroom, paid them little notice. But as soon as they reached the landing on which guests waited for the butler to announce them, Giff noted the widening of eyes, sharp inhales of breath and inclining of heads to murmur to companions that signalled Miss Lattimar had been recognised.

She noticed it, too, her chin going up and a martial gleam appearing in her eyes. 'Apparently not everyone received the word that I'm to be accepted,' she murmured to Lady Sayleford.

'Those of lesser importance might not know it—yet,' his godmother replied. 'But everyone who matters does. The rest will discover it soon enough.'

'Or incur your wrath?' Temper suggested, a mischievous grin chasing away the militant look.

'Precisely. Newell, if you would?'

Giff offered his arm. Taking it, Lady Sayleford nodded regally to the handful of waiting groups as she bypassed them and proceeded to the head of the line, where the butler snapped to attention.

'Good evening, your ladyship! Who should I announce is in your party?'

'Mr Newell, Member of Parliament for Great Grimsby, Mrs Moorsby and my protégée, Miss Lattimar.'

As the butler announced their names, they walked into the ballroom towards the hostess, who stood at the head of a short receiving line. Looking over her shoulder to Temper, Lady Sayleford said, 'It's as important for the upper servants to become aware of your position as it is for *ton* hostesses.'

'How well I know it,' Temper replied ruefully. 'I've observed Overton keeping callers waiting for ever, if he doesn't think their consequence merits an immediate audience with Gregory.'

The Countess nodded. 'No one is more punctilious—or better informed—about a person's status than those who rule downstairs. Now, shall we greet our hostess?'

Lady Spencer-Woods met them with a wide, knowing smile. 'Lady Sayleford, so good to see you!' she said as the ladies exchanged curtsies. 'Mrs Moorsby, Mr Newell—and Miss Lattimar! How absolutely stunning you look!'

'Almost the image of my mother,' Temper replied sweetly. 'Although I could never hope to be as stunning as she is.'

Their hostess gaped at her, obviously at a loss how to reply, and Giff bit back a grin. Trust Temper to go straight to the attack.

'I'm sure you'll be quite stunning enough,' Lady Sayleford said drily. 'But come along, my dear, we mustn't keep the others in line waiting.'

Lady Sayleford led them into the ballroom, its floor so crowded with laughing, chattering groups that progress would have been slow even if the Countess had not paused every few feet to greet an acquaintance and introduce her niece, Giff and her new protégée. Though some—those 'who mattered', he supposed—returned the Countess's greeting without surprise, there were many who, upon her making the introductions, stood momentarily speechless.

The density of the crowd, the brevity of the introductions and the noise made it impossible for Miss Lattimar to do more than add a nod of greeting. His sense of anticipation growing, Giff wondered how the volatile Temper would weather the evident shock and disbelief her appearance had struck in many.

When they reached the chairs set up along the wall on the far side of the ballroom—Lady Sayleford helpfully giving him some welcome distance by inserting Mrs Moorsby between him and Temper—he was finally able to relax and simply look forward to what she would say or do next.

She didn't disappoint. 'Fortunately, the throng was thick enough that no one was in danger of falling over from the shock of seeing me here.'

'Those who were surprised will recover quickly enough.

We'll let the rest come to us,' Lady Sayleford said as she took her seat.

'Do you think anyone will?' Temper asked.

'Certainly,' his godmother replied. 'I timed our progress to be just long enough that word of our arrival should have percolated through most of the guests. My friends—and the curious—will certainly come by to look you over—'

'Your friends will be wondering what in the world you are doing,' Temper muttered.

'While the gentleman,' his godmother continued, 'once they catch a glimpse of you, will flock to make your acquaintance. Gifford's presence standing by will ensure no true blackguards dare present themselves.'

Almost at once, the influx began. Older gentlemen and ladies whose names he recognised as being particular friends of his godmother came first, their appraising expressions alive with expectation and curiosity as they looked Temper over—an inspection to which she managed to appear impervious. Following them were a select few matrons with marriageable daughters in tow and the society arbiters whom Lady Sayleford had invited to tea.

'What fun I shall have tonight, watching all the gentlemen buzz around Miss Lattimar,' Mrs Dobbs-Henry, last of the four, declared as she greeted them. 'Thank you, Lady Sayleford, for throwing down the gauntlet.'

'I may need a lance and shield to fend off the outraged matrons, once they recover from their shock,' Temper said wryly.

'They'll have to batter their way through the army of admirers first,' the lady responded. 'When the floor clears for dancing and they spy you here, you will be besieged!' Blowing a kiss to Lady Sayleford, she walked off.

As Mrs Dobbs-Henry predicted, once the crowd at the centre of the ballroom thinned, a stir ran around the room, gentlemen's heads coming up and turning in their direction. An ever-increasing stream began to approach them, making their bows to Lady Sayleford and begging her to introduce them to her charming protégée.

All were known to Giff, though some only by reputation. Several older peers he recognised from Parliament, one gentleman he vaguely remembered being a widower and a clutch of former university classmates he knew to be ladies' men who had at one time paid obligatory court to Temper's mother. As they bowed, he noted varying degrees of amazement at her beauty, universal admiration, curiosity—and the feral heat of males within scenting distance of a highly desirable female.

Much as he sympathised with the latter—suffering from the pull of that attraction himself—he also felt an unanticipated degree of hostility. Glad now that Lady Sayleford had detailed him to protect Temper, he had to bite his tongue to keep himself from warning them off—or inviting them outside, where he could punch that leering look off their faces. He might not be able to growl 'mine!', but he could certainly send them off with a ferocious 'not yours!'

Fortunately for his suddenly precarious hold over his temper, Lady Sayleford shooed each of the latter category away, telling them they might return later to claim a dance.

Maybe by then he would have his reactions fully under control.

The receiving line disbanded and the orchestra started tuning up. The guests took up places along the wall, waiting for the dancing to begin and leaving their party, for the moment, alone.

Mrs Moorsby looked around wonderingly, her eyes wide. 'I expected the ball would be impressive, but oh, my, how the reality exceeds my imagination! The sparkle of jewels reflecting the candlelight! The splendour of the ladies' gowns and the men so handsome in their evening attire! Is it not magnificent, Miss Lattimar?'

'Most impressive, even I must admit,' Temper conceded. But her guarded eyes and wary stance told him that though her chaperon might be expecting nothing but unqualified enjoyment, she was armouring herself for challenge and unpleasantness.

A wave of regret and anger shook him. By rights, Miss Temperance Lattimar, well-born daughter of a rich baron, should be gazing around her first ball with the same excitement and anticipation as her chaperon. He hated that air of coiled tension about her, hated even more knowing that she was right to be cautious.

While she replied to another of her chaperon's comments, Lady Sayleford murmured, 'Well done, Newell. From the thundercloud expression you offered every man who greeted her, they will know their conduct must stay in bounds.'

'Was it that obvious?' he replied, disconcerted to think his animosity had been evident.

'Patently, to me. But just enough to others that I'm sure the gentlemen took the point.'

'Protection is my job, isn't it?' he replied, reassured. One didn't wish to look like a jealous guard dog—even if one was performing that function. But as he knew all too well, his godmother noticed a host of things ordinary people never observed.

'Yes. But men willing to brave my presence to get an introduction aren't the ones you need worry about. You must fend off the disreputable.'

'Fend off the disreputable?' Temper echoed, turning back to them. 'Oh, no, it's the *reputable* Newell must send away! I don't want to spend time with any gentlemen who might have honourable intentions! Besides, I predict Newell is going to be too preoccupied by matrons with young ladies in tow to be able to concern himself with *my* admirers.'

The low chuckle from Lady Sayleford alarmed him almost as much as Temper's words. 'I can't think what you mean,' he protested.

Temper grinned. 'Half the eminently respectable matrons at this affair may have nearly swooned at seeing me here, but you will note, a fair number were prepared to brave exposing their innocents to my wicked presence in order that Lady Sayleford might present *you* to their lambs.'

For once, he felt a wave of heat that was not desire. 'I'm sure you exaggerate.'

'Indeed, I do not! Did you not notice how they stationed their persons between me and their sweet innocent girls, offering me a greeting notable for its chilliness, while the tones they used when addressing you were warmly encouraging?'

While he frowned, trying to decide whether or not she was teasing, she laughed ruefully. 'I must apologise in advance! I fear your presence here means you will find yourself targeted by matchmaking mamas, whether or not you are ready for courting. You may be more in need of protection than I am! Unless you decide it's time to find that rich wife after all.'

A rich wife...like Temper? The idea of having a wife like *her* was becoming...less distasteful.

But there was, alas, only one Temper—and she was the little sister of his best friend. 'I'd have to be a great deal more financially pressed to be ready to resort to *that* option,' he retorted.

'I believe the Season shall prove interesting—for both of you,' Lady Sayleford interposed. 'Now, with the dancing about to begin, I'll bid you goodnight.'

'You're *leaving*?' Giff said, aghast.

His godmother gave him a sweet smile in which he could discern no trace of either amusement or irony. 'I turn Miss Lattimar over to you. Well, what are you waiting for? The first set is forming.' She gave his arm a little push. 'Lead her into it before some other gentleman asks her.'

'An excellent idea,' Mrs Moorsby seconded. 'Quickly, now! Several are approaching.'

Well, if his godmother commanded... Besides, leading her into the first dance would underscore to all the men present that he was watching over her—and give himself more time to adjust to the unpleasant notion of having them hover all around her.

'You'll do me the honour?' he asked.

Temper gave him a tiny nod and laid her hand on his arm. Armoured against her as Gifford was trying to be, he still felt the sizzle of contact right through his sleeve. Looking down, he noted her surprise—ah, yes, she felt it, too!—and wariness in her expression. But then she smiled, the delight shining in those magnificent blue eyes warming him down to his toes.

'How pleasant, to open the ball with a friend, a man who will be neither scheming how best to manoeuvre me into the garden or calculating the size of my fortune,' she said as he walked her towards the other couples forming the set. 'Though I do apologise for Lady Sayleford corralling you. As it's hardly likely I'll be attacked in the middle of the ballroom with my chaperon looking on, after this dance you can escape to the card room.'

'Oh, no, standing guard is standing guard,' he said, meaning it—and no longer resenting the task quite so much. 'My godmother and Mrs Moorsby expect it.'

'I have to admit, I feel…easier, knowing you're nearby.'

That statement lit a little glow of satisfaction in his chest, offsetting some of the other, more disturbing emotions. Like fierce protectiveness, an unwarranted sense of possession—and lust.

The numerous patterns of the dance didn't allow for much conversation, other than a mutual exchange of compliments over the excellence of their partner. Easily mastering the movements, Giff was glad his mama had insisted he learn to acquit himself respectably on the dance floor.

The patterns also allowed him to forget about conversing and simply enjoy what a lovely picture Temper made, gracefully going through the movements.

After the music ended, he offered his arm, bracing himself for the now-anticipated shock when she laid her hand on it.

'We'll see how many desert me, now that my champion has departed,' she murmured as he led her off the floor.

'I doubt many of the gentlemen will. Lady Sayleford gave you a very public seal of approval.'

Which meant he would have more than a few men to fend off, he realised, surprised again at the strength of his irritation at the idea of other men courting her, no matter how honourable their intentions.

Indeed, he could already see a fair number waiting beside Mrs Moorsby. And not just gentlemen—a few of the matrons to whom they had been introduced waited, too, their daughters in tow.

Hangers-on, positioning their girls where they might entice one of the throng of gentlemen sure to surround Temper? Giff speculated.

For the first time, Giff felt relieved that Temper espoused the ridiculous notion not to marry. She must, of course, eventually. But hopefully she wouldn't resign herself to that truth any time in the immediate future, which would make his task of fending off fortune hunters and the disreputable easier.

'And as you can see,' he continued, 'it's not just gentleman awaiting you. A few of the chaperons and their daughters want to further the acquaintance, too.'

She looked towards Mrs Moorsby, a surprised expression on her face. 'Perhaps there are some young ladies brave enough to risk my acquaintance after all.' She chuckled. 'I shall have to determine if any of them might make you a good wife.'

He looked down to utter a disparaging remark—and found her smiling up at him. 'Teasing me again, I see. You know I have no interest in being caught in the parson's mousetrap.'

'We shall just have to watch out for each other, then, won't we? Shall we brave the gauntlet?'

At his nod, she tightened her grip on his arm and looked up—giving him a smile and a conspiratorial wink, as if it were just the two of them setting off against the world.

Impossible not to smile back, beguiled by a wholly unexpected feeling of...camaraderie.

Once again, she'd surprised him. Not only had she shown him the little hoyden he'd known was now able to hold her

tongue when necessary, she'd apparently risen to Lady Sayleford's challenge that she view the Season forced on her as
an adventure. One she was inviting him to share. No longer
as watchdog and innocent…but as allies.

Dismissing the contradictory emotions swirling in him,
he told himself to simply enjoy the clever loveliness that
was Temperance Lattimar walking beside him, her hand on
his arm. No longer just his friend's little sister to protect,
but…a comrade.

He resisted the rogue notion that he could become quite
attached to such a partnership.

A moment later they reached Mrs Moorsby, her eyes
merry as she indicated the small crowd surrounding her. 'A
number of other gentlemen have asked that I present them
to you. They were all,' she added in a tone whose irony
would be lost on any but Temper and Giff, 'prevented by…
other obligations from begging that honour of Lady Sayleford before she departed.'

'Unwilling to face the scrutiny of the dragon,' Giff murmured to Temper.

'Before I do so,' Mrs Moorsby continued, 'you'll remember these ladies and their daughters? They would like you
young people to become better acquainted. Lady Arnold
with her nieces, Miss Avery and Miss Mary Avery, the
Countess of Mannerling and her daughter, Lady Constance?'

'Yes, of course,' Temper said as the women once again exchanged curtsies. 'I should love to become better acquainted.
Shall we do so between sets? Now, I believe we should accept the invitations of these kind gentlemen and dance!'

After murmurs of agreement, Mrs Moorsby introduced
the waiting gentleman to all the ladies, after which the

young people paired up, the rakish Lord Theo outmanoeu-vring the other men to claim Temper's hand.

Ignoring a blatantly appealing look from Miss Avery, Giff said, 'As it's impossible to make a choice among so much beauty, I'll cede my place to you other gentlemen and keep Mrs Moorsby company.'

The young ladies and their escorts followed Temper and Lord Theo on to the floor, while several others remained beside Mrs Moorsby, chatting politely while they awaited their chance to squire the Beauty.

Depending on the other men waiting beside her to make polite conversation with Mrs Moorsby, Giff turned his attention to the dancers.

Watching another man claim Temper was even more distasteful than he'd expected, he thought, frowning as Lord Theo pulled her rather closer than the movements of the dance required. Despite knowing she wasn't interested in marrying, she was too alluring, too beguiling—and, despite her upbringing, too innocent—to be trusted to rakes like Lord Theo. He wouldn't want her to be taken in by a dashing charmer—or compromised.

Fortunately, the dance wasn't a waltz. If Lord Theo had tried to hold her as scandalously close as *that* dance allowed, Giff might have found it necessary to intervene.

Just how had he let himself blunder into this aggravating situation?

At least there was one gentleman who had ceased to plague him over it, he thought, thanking Heaven for small favours.

As he'd awaited Temper in the hall of Vraux House tonight, he'd encountered Gregory departing to his evening entertainment at an exclusive establishment where the wine would be excellent, the play deep and the enjoyment afterward far more erotic than the delights available at a respectable society ball. A fact about which his friend had initially bedevilled him unmercifully.

At Giff's irritated response that Gregory ought to be grateful to him for going above and beyond to get his troublesome sister off his hands, his friend sobered.

'I do appreciate it, more than you can imagine,' he responded. 'Had Lady Sayleford not roped you into watching over her, I would have felt compelled to do so myself. I value not just your kindness in stepping in to secure her sponsorship, but also the concern for Temper's safety that prompted you to forgo your own interests to protect her.'

Performing a brother's office, taking care of my baby sister, was the unspoken message.

Recalling it now, Giff sighed. He didn't regret—too much—giving up evenings accompanying Gregory in pursuit of easy, uncomplicated pleasure. He did wish his best friend's 'baby sister' weren't such a beautiful, alluring woman.

It wasn't just blackguards and bounders Giff had to ward off. As Lady Sayleford's trick with the carriage seating tonight had demonstrated with stark clarity, he needed to keep a tight grip over his own behaviour as well. Should Giff succumb to the desire Temper aroused, Gregory would consider it a betrayal of his trust.

He blew out a breath, relieved to be watching her from half a dance floor away, far from the temptation of her soft skin and sinful-thought-inducing scent.

He'd make sure he wasn't tortured by being seated beside her in the coach again. Even so, it was going to be a long Season.

Chapter Seven

While Gifford Newell remained beside Mrs Moorsby, Temper walked off with Lord Theo Collington, a man whom she hadn't needed Giff's warning frown to recognise as a charming rogue. She'd willingly offered Lord Theo her hand, curious to discover whether the Marquess of Childress's younger son would attempt to lure her into indiscretion, or intended to simply toy with her—and annoy Giff—by his attentions.

'At last, you rescue me from the doldrums of this interminable evening by granting me the hand of the most beautiful lady in the room,' he bent close to murmur in her ear.

Sidling away, she replied, 'If you find the evening is so interminable, I wonder that you have remained. Why not seek out more…entertaining company?'

'There may be company elsewhere more…practised, but none so alluring…or delightfully innocent.'

She angled a glance up at him. 'Forgive me for doubting that it is *innocence*, rather than something more…earthy, that appeals to you.'

'Ah, but it is that mix of innocence with the sensual that is truly compelling.'

'An innocence of which you'd be happy to relieve me?'

Surprise—and heat—flared in his eyes. 'You are direct.'

'I have no use for polite subterfuge.'

'Then, yes, I admit I would quite happily tutor your innocence.'

'You being the most expert of instructors?'

He gave her a little bow. 'I do my poor best.'

'For as many as possible, I suspect. But alas, I have no desire to shock the company. Tonight, at any rate. So you might as well seek that "more practised" company elsewhere.'

She turned to walk off the floor, but he stayed her. 'How can I go, when it is so entertaining to banter words with you?'

'And annoy Mr Newell?'

That drew a genuine laugh. 'He does make it appear that, for the least infraction, it would be pistols at dawn.'

'Believe me, Lord Theo, were there to be an...infraction, it would be *my* hand holding the pistol. And without wishing to boast, I must inform you that my aim is true.'

'Is it, now? Is that something in the nature of a threat?'

'Consider it an...advisory. That I am neither the wanton some whisper the daughter of my mother must be, nor a helpless female dependent upon a male for protection.'

The caressing tone and flirtatious look gave way to an expression of genuine interest. 'Beautiful, alluring and ferocious—what a unique combination.'

'You find a dangerous woman alluring?'

'Indeed! What could be more alluring than danger, allied to passion?'

The heat was back in his gaze, yet for all the suggestive-ness of his words, Temper found, surprisingly, that she didn't feel threatened. Just to make sure her instincts were cor-rect, though, she added, 'You would not, of course, dream of using coercion to explore that passion.'

He drew back, a hand going dramatically to his throat. 'Coercion? Certainly not! A man of address need never re-sort to something so vulgar!'

'Since ladies generally fall at your feet most willingly?'

He shrugged. 'No more than you, would I wish to boast.'

Temper laughed, fairly sure now that she had nothing to fear from Lord Theo. 'Perhaps we can continue our as-sociation. Both of us secure in talents of which we don't need to boast.'

He smiled, amusement dancing in his eyes. 'Perhaps we should. Until one or the other of us needs to demonstrate their talent? Passion persuades, but can sometimes lead to regret.'

'Only if it came with wedding lines attached.'

He shuddered. 'That *would* be a frightful outcome.'

'Then you may rest easy. I find that prospect of wedlock even more frightful than you do.'

He gave her a speculative look. 'Indeed? You don't wish to find a husband who would provide…protection for your explorations?'

The notion of falling into a life like her mother's chased away every bit of amusement. 'Certainly not,' she said grimly. 'The last thing I want is to be compelled by an in-different spouse into "explorations" that lead only to loneli-ness, disillusionment and notoriety. So as I told you, I have *no* interest in marriage.'

He chuckled. 'A lady who means what she says? That would truly be an amazing creature.'

'No more singular than a gentleman who tells a lady what *he* truly thinks. Instead of paying compliments to a female he finds unattractive, or whispering words of devotion to a woman he merely wishes to bed.'

Surprise once again widened his eyes. 'You are most astonishingly frank.'

'You may rest easy. The dance will soon end, relieving you of my odd company.'

'On the contrary! I would have more of your "odd" company.'

'Another pretty speech, Lord Theo?'

'Not at all, Miss Lattimar. In this instance, I am following your lead and saying exactly what I mean.'

She turned an assessing gaze on him, which he met steadily. Unable to find a trace of deception in it, she gave a reluctant smile. 'Perhaps you *are* being honest. And if you intend neither to compromise me nor marry me, we might be friends after all.'

'I'll start with "friends".' As he twirled her under his arm in the dance's final figure, he added in a murmur, 'Until a desire for intimacy becomes mutual.'

Another tease—or a challenge for her to try to resist him? Amused, she shook her head at him as she took his arm to return to her chaperon. 'Alas, fond hopes are so often disappointed.'

Lord Theo returned her to Mrs Moorsby, where an earnest young man immediately stepped forward. 'Your chaperon has promised you will grant me the next dance.'

A bit taken aback by his insistence, she raised her brows at Mrs Moorsby, who said, 'Temperance, allow me to pres-

ent Lord Solsworth, who was most persuasive that I recommend him as an agreeable partner for the next dance.'

Ignoring the glowering looks of the other gentlemen waiting around them, Lord Solsworth held out his arm. 'You
will honour me, Miss Lattimar?'

With a little shrug to the others, Temper said, 'With such
a recommendation, what can I do but agree?'

Giving her new partner a rapid inspection as he led her to
the floor, Temper decided he was handsome, determined—
and perhaps even younger than she was. Indifferent about
the success of her Season, unlike most young ladies about
to debut, she hadn't bothered to discover the names and
titles of all the eligible bachelors, but given the deference
shown him by the other gentleman, her partner must be
highly born. 'Are you still at university, Lord Solsworth?'
she asked after they'd taken their places.

'Yes, but I get to town often,' he said. 'I assist my father
in the Lords and hope to stand for a seat in Parliament myself soon. To gain some experience, against the day I must
eventually step into his shoes.'

The heir then, probably with his own courtesy title, who
would take over a place in the Lords after he inherited. 'Is
your father a reformer?'

'Lud, no!' he said with a laugh. 'Almost reactionary!
He don't know it yet, but if I get that seat in the House, we
shall probably cancel each other out. I very much approve
of the goals of the reformers, especially Ashley-Cooper's
to restrict the working hours of children in the mills. But
here I am, prosing on about politics, when what I wish to
say is that you are the most beautiful creature I have ever
beheld! It's a wonder beyond describing to have the privilege of escorting you.'

Indeed, the ardent gaze he fixed on her as she moved away from him, performing the next figure of the dance, supported his claim of dazzled admiration.

'Thank you for your kind words,' she said when she returned to him, 'but any beauty of form I possess owes nothing to me. It is a gift of nature.'

'Such beauty of form could not help but be allied to beauty of character.'

She laughed shortly. 'I think you will find many here to dispute that claim.'

'Because of your mother? I think it monstrously unjust that *you* be judged based on *her* actions!'

'You would be my champion against the malicious?' she asked, thinking him surprisingly naive, but also touched by his gallantry. 'Even knowing nothing of my character? You might find me unworthy of such defence.'

'That, I could never believe.'

Temper ought to say something outrageous to deflect his obvious infatuation, but she found herself reluctant to hurt him—and malign her own character—by uttering some cutting rejoinder. He was obviously the highly eligible son of some peer and, if he was at this gathering, must be at least marginally interested in marriage.

Which made him exactly the sort of gentleman of whom Vraux would approve and therefore one she should discourage, if she meant to end the Season unwed. But how to disillusion him without being cruel?

'I doubt I could live up to the high expectations you seem to have of me,' she said, hoping candour might produce the same result as cruelty. 'It's probably better that we part before I disappoint you.'

'Indeed, not! I am sure knowing you better will only confirm my initial impressions of your excellence.'

Temper wasn't sure how to assess Solsworth's attentions. He seemed too young and idealistic to have ulterior designs on her person and perhaps too young to be seriously considering marriage. Even so, as a highly eligible *parti* of whom her father and society would approve, she should redouble her efforts to discourage him.

She was debating how best to do that when, as the dance ended, a matron in a large turban and an indignant expression stormed over to them.

'Sidney!' she cried. 'I sent you over to dance with Miss Avery! Not with this...*creature*.' Looking down her nose at Temper, the lady continued, 'Mrs Spencer-Woods's standards are certainly slipping, if she's invited the likes of *you*. I may have to cut the connection.'

'Mama, please!' her partner protested, his face going scarlet.

After an initial shock at the suddenness of the attack, Temper schooled her face to a polite mask, inwardly kicking herself for having been caught off guard. After all, wasn't this the sort of reception she had expected tonight?

'I'll pass along your disapproval to my sponsor, Lady Sayleford,' she said in dulcet tones. 'As we haven't been introduced, I can't bid you good evening, Mrs...' She let the phrase trail off, watching the bloom of fury on the woman's cheeks at her insulting neglect to address the mother of a titled man as 'my lady'. 'So I will simply say goodbye. Thank you for the dance, Lord Solsworth.'

Turning her back on them both, she walked back to Mrs Moorsby.

No need for any further worry about how to discourage

Solsworth. His harridan of a mother would make sure in future that her precious son kept well away from the scarlet woman.

More shaken than she'd like to admit by the encounter, as she reached her party, she angled her face away from Giff's searching gaze.

'Was Lady Agremont unpleasant?' he demanded.

'Is that who she was? She didn't bother with an introduction before dragging her son away from my contaminating presence.'

Giff muttered a curse. 'Her husband, the Marquess of Agremont, is one of the highest sticklers in the Lords. I'm surprised her darling only son and heir had the courage to dance with you.'

'Apparently he was so struck by my beauty, he was willing to risk his mother's wrath.' Temper laughed ruefully. 'What an innocent! He seemed convinced my physical loveliness must be accompanied by beauty of character. I'm sure his mother is about to disabuse him of that misconception.'

'She could have been more polite about reclaiming him,' Mrs Moorsby said indignantly. 'Even if she does disapprove of you—most unjustly, as she knows *nothing* about you beyond your name—she could have waited to convey her opinion until after her son escorted you off the floor.'

'I suppose I'm lucky to have suffered only one unpleasant encounter thus far,' Temper said, suddenly tired of the event. 'All I want is to escape the Season with a whole skin and get on with doing what *I* want.'

As the dance floor emptied at the conclusion of the last set, the other ladies and gentleman who had been standing beside Mrs Moorsby began to drift back. After refusing the several gentlemen who petitioned her for the next dance, with Giff and Mrs Moorsby engaged in conversation by several of the bystanders, she glanced behind her. Confirming that the curtained windows created a quiet alcove where she might be alone with her own thoughts for a moment, she was about to slip back there when a hand at her sleeve stayed her retreat.

She recognised the person restraining her to be one of the young ladies she'd met earlier. A young lady who had, she realised, been an onlooker when Lady Agremont verbally assaulted her.

'If you are not going to dance, would you like to chat?' the girl asked.

And dig out all the gritty details about her public dressing-down? Her anger flaring, Temper snapped, 'Miss Henley, isn't it? Didn't you just hear that I'm not a proper person to know? I wonder you dare approach me without your chaperon for protection!'

She immediately regretted her sharpness, for poor Miss Henley had done nothing to deserve her wrath. Before she could apologise, however, the girl laughed.

'Oh, Mama never worries about me,' Miss Henley said, appearing not the least bit upset by Temper's rudeness. 'She could hardly wait to perform all the introductions so she might go off on the arm of one of her gallants.'

Tall, angular, with a long, plain face and nondescript brown hair done in ringlets, Miss Henley had no claims to beauty. But her merry laugh and friendly smile made Temper even more ashamed of her sharpness, while the girl's unexpected comment made her curious to know more.

'Your mama sees no need to protect you?'

'Not really. As she never tires of reminding me, I'm neither pretty enough to tempt a rake, nor rich enough to tempt a fortune hunter.'

Miss Henley's tone was matter of fact, stating the truth as she saw it with no hint of self-pity. Inherently honest herself, Temper wouldn't offer her false protests about her loveliness. But she could admire such a level-headed acceptance of reality.

'How delightful to meet someone who dares to speak the truth, without recourse to flattery or false modesty. Your mama does not value you as she ought.'

Miss Henley chuckled again. 'No, she doesn't. But to be fair, we are chalk and cheese. She's a Beauty, as was my older sister, who thrilled her by making a brilliant match with a duke's youngest son. Whereas she despairs of finding even an acceptable match for me. Although I have to admit, it is amusing, watching the gentlemen try to walk the fine line between being attentive enough to be polite without according me enough attention to raise expectations.'

Easily able to visualise such exchanges, Temper had to smile. 'You are very plain spoken.'

'Yes, one of my many faults. Despite my lack of looks and modest dowry, I'm very choosy, you see, and Papa, though he ignores me most of the time, is not such a bully as to force me into a union I don't want. Since I have a small inheritance from an aunt, he'll not be saddled with my upkeep, should I fail to marry.'

'What a blessing to have independent means! I, too, have enough to live on that I need not marry.'

'But you're so lovely! I'm sure you could have any gentleman you fancied.'

Temper grimaced. 'I don't fancy one. I'd much rather remain single and pursue my own interests.'

'How fascinating! Won't you tell me more? I should love to know how you've acquired a dubious reputation before you were even out. And about your famous mama, of course. Oh, forgive me!' she added, clapping a hand to her mouth. 'My mother would say I am being vulgarly intrusive! If it seems so, I do apologise—but I *am* curious. My life is very dull, you see. I've never been anywhere or done anything interesting.'

'No apologies necessary. You are very forthright—but I like that,' Temper said, her positive first impression of Miss Henley reinforced. 'I'd love to talk at length—but it's far too busy here.' Out of the corner of her eye she could see Giff, having bid goodbye to the lady who'd been occupying him, glancing around for her. Several of her previously dismissed swains were also sidling closer, probably to renew their requests for a dance. 'Do you ride?'

'I do, but tomorrow I promised Mama to wait until the Promenade Hour.' Miss Henley made a face. 'It will mean being restricted to a trot at best, but at least I won't have to sit with her in the barouche. She claims going to the Park is supposed to be for me to display myself to potential beaux, but it's really Mama who loves stopping to chat with friends, or to take some favoured gentlemen up in her carriage. But if you rode with me—and shooed away the gentlemen who would certainly beg to accompany you—we might manage a good coze without anyone interrupting us.'

'Yes, let's do that,' Temper said.

Miss Henley smiled. 'Mama will scold at first, saying that I will show to disadvantage beside an Incomparable like you, but I will counter by telling her that as an Incomparable inevitably gathers an admiring crowd around her, I will have an opportunity to impress the gentlemen waiting to claim your attention. Unlikely, of course, but that view of it will content her.'

'You really are the most complete hand!' Temper said with a laugh. 'Do you manage everyone around you so deftly?'

Miss Henley shrugged. 'As a female, one must learn how to manoeuvre people with subtlety. It's the only way to get to do what you want.'

'Perhaps you can teach me some of your tricks! Until tomorrow, then!'

The girls exchanged curtsies, Miss Henley pressing Temper's hand before slipping past her. As she turned back towards the ballroom, Temper discovered that Giff's progress towards her had been arrested by Miss Avery.

Unaccountably annoyed, Temper absently accepted the offer of the first man to reach her and walked with him on to the dance floor, her gaze straying back to Giff and his persistent admirer.

She was too far away to hear their conversation, but after a few moments' chat, shaking his head and smiling, Giff bowed—an obvious dismissal. Temper saw an expression of pique cross the young lady's face before she smiled as well and gave her hand to a different gentleman.

Though she hadn't any right to be, Temper felt...pleased that Giff had politely turned away the girl's efforts to lure him into a dance. She would want dear Giff to find a companionable wife and there was something about Miss Avery she just couldn't like.

If he were going to do her the favour of watching out for her, she ought to reciprocate by actually evaluating the eligible ladies for him, as she'd flippantly offered, thinning out from those who tried to attach him any she felt would not make him an admirable partner.

Going through the steps with *her* current partner, a callow young man too shy to talk, allowed Temper to look back across the ballroom to where Newell stood beside Mrs Moorsby. She suppressed a little niggle of regret that Giff—who'd turned out to be an excellent partner—hadn't invited her to take the floor with him again this evening.

Of course, he'd been practically coerced into doing so the first time by Lady Sayleford. And it was best that she not put herself so tantalisingly close to him—a fact that unexpectedly disturbing carriage ride had revealed.

Having accompanied her brother and Giff numerous times over the years, she'd taken the seat beside him without a thought—and immediately known it to be a mistake. Unable to think of a way to ask Lady Sayleford to alter the arrangement without the request appearing very odd, she'd suffered through—the sensual tension between them, she thought ruefully, unfortunately mutual.

Dancing with him had been just as fraught, though, thank heavens, the first dance had not been a waltz. It was dizzying enough just walking out on to the floor with her hand on his arm, feeling the tingle of connection all the way up to her shoulder when he clasped her hand to turn her through the figures of the dance. To have his arm around her waist, her hand on his shoulder as the waltz required, so close she could feel the heat emanating from his body, catch the faint scent of his shaving soap… A wave of warmth rippled through her at the thought.

So much for her optimistic hopes that whatever strange effect he was having on her would diminish with time…or become easier to ignore. How, in the space of a few short months, had he changed from her brother's best friend, who'd bedevilled, teased—and encouraged—her since she was in short skirts, into this dynamic individual whose physical presence now seemed to cast some sort of spell over her, making her want to draw close to him?

A spell more difficult to resist because this was *Giff*, a friend she'd known for years, one of the few men she trusted implicitly.

She was beginning to understand why, denied intimacy with her father, her mother had been drawn by another man's physical appeal. But though she might be tempted, she didn't have the protection against misfortune of a married woman, whose child from another liaison might be covered up as long as her spouse, knowingly or not, accepted the child. As Temper's father had.

Nor could she allow herself just a taste of passion with Giff. However willingly she might lure him, if he considered that he'd compromised her, honourable Giff would insist on marriage. With her brother being his best friend, even something as simple as a kiss might be enough to make him feel obligated to offer for her.

And marrying him would mean disaster. As friends, she and Giff had always worked together well, but as a wife, she would destroy him—his career and his peace. She might, given the attraction between them, manage more than just that simple kiss. But even with Giff, attempting something more intimate would risk having the ugly memories surge up and over the barrier she'd constructed to contain them.

Besides, if she were to wed him, she would have to reveal the truth of what had happened that summer afternoon so many years ago. Almost as awful as the event itself would be watching Giff's expression change from shock, to disgust, to revulsion as she confessed it. The idea of telling him the whole, and thereby forfeiting for ever his respect and friendship, was unthinkable.

No, she couldn't risk it.

Acting upon the edgy, unwanted, but impossible-to-ignore attraction between them was simply impossible, she concluded with a sigh. No matter how difficult she was finding it to recapture the uncomplicated friendship they used to share.

Chapter Eight

A few hours later, Gifford escorted his ladies into the carriage for the ride home. Mrs Moorsby, clearly unused to late evenings, soon nodded off in her corner. This time, Temper sat across from him, occupying the seat beside her chaperon left vacant by Lady Sayleford's early departure, leaving Giff mercifully alone on the backward-facing bench.

Inclining her head at her dozing chaperon, Temper said softly, 'Her first *ton* evening might have been a bit too stimulating, but I think she enjoyed it.'

'I'm sure she did. How did you find *your* first ton evening?'

'Not as dull as I feared. And Lady Sayleford did her work well. Aside from that one unpleasant encounter, I was treated kindly.'

'I'm glad.' Recalling the outraged Lady Agremont, he laughed shortly. 'The Marquess's wife is likely to have an unpleasant encounter of her own, once my godmother hears how she treated you.'

Temper smiled ruefully. 'You're probably right. I can almost feel for Lady Agremont.'

Trying to keep his voice casual, he continued, 'You never lacked for partners. Did you meet anyone of particular interest?'

She laughed shortly. 'Most were attentive, but forgettable. Lord Solsworth was the most bedazzled, although I expect his disapproving mother will make short work of that infatuation.'

Giff hesitated. Temper hadn't mentioned the man who was his chief worry. Choosing his words with care, he continued, 'What did you think of Lord Theo? I hope you didn't find him *too* charming, for I have to warn you, he's a rogue through and through. I wouldn't have you...taken in.'

The smile that comment produced was not reassuring. 'Ah, Lord Theo. You need not worry about him, Giff. He's no more interested in marriage than I am. And if it comes to seduction, I've told him I shoot straight.'

Giff stared, not sure at first that he'd heard her correctly, then had to laugh. 'Did you indeed? Did he believe you?'

She chuckled. 'I think so. Or at least, he gave the warning enough credence that I don't think he will put it to the test.'

'That would be a blessing.'

'So might his friendship be—if his continuing attentions solidify my reputation as a "fast" female no prudent man would consider marrying. I'll be spared the attentions of honourable men and, relying on you to chase away the dishonourable, I may be able to convince Papa to end this farce of a Season sooner rather than later. And I find Lord Theo...interesting.'

'That kind of interest could lead to compromise!'

'Oh, I don't think he'd try to take me against my will.'

She grinned. 'I have it on his own authority that he abhors the idea of coercion. Not that I would mind being compromised by him, since neither of us has any desire to marry. A small scandal might help me end this waste of a Season more quickly.'

'That might suit you, but what about a scandal's effect on Lady Sayleford and Mrs Moorsby?'

'Maybe a *very* small one?' She sighed. 'Though I don't want to appear proper and conformable, neither do I wish to repay the kindness of Mrs Moorsby, Lady Sayleford—and your own—by embarrassing all of you. I will *try* to avoid scandal—but I won't be surprised if it finds me.'

'I shall have to work harder at my job, to make sure it does not,' he said emphatically.

'Dear Giff, still trying to protect me,' she said, the warmth of her smile causing a curious tightness in his chest. 'And what a thankless task! I apologise again for catching you up in my battles.'

'I don't mind, truly. I'm as eager as Gregory to see you settled and happy.'

She gave him a grim smile. 'Then you'll have to choose between "settled" and "happy", because I could not be both. Enough! I survived my first evening with only one minor incident and met a potential friend in the engaging Miss Henley, with whom I shall ride tomorrow. During the Promenade Hour, unfortunately, but she has promised to accompany her mother then.'

'Miss... Henley?' he repeated, trying—and failing—to attach a face to the name.

Temper gave him a deprecating glance. 'She's not a Beauty, so men overlook her and her mother doesn't value her. Despite all that, she seems to have turned into an interesting and independent young lady. I'd like to know her better.'

He sighed. 'Tomorrow, during the Promenade Hour? I suppose I can be free to accompany you.'

'I don't mean to ruin your afternoon!' she protested. 'Surely I will be safe enough, riding in the Park amid a throng of the *ton*, with a groom and Mrs Moorsby to accompany me.'

'But Mrs Moorsby doesn't ride,' Giff pointed out.

'Damn—drat and blast!' Temper said, her cheeks reddening. 'I completely forgot. I suppose I could send Miss Henley a note, crying off—'

'No, I promised Godmother I would see the Season through and I mean to do so. Although I would appreciate it if, hereafter, you remember to ride in the morning.'

'Leaving afternoons and a few evenings free for your Parliamentary work.' She sighed. 'Once again, I apologise for embroiling you in the social Season. I shall hope to be discredited sooner rather than later, so that Papa releases *me* from its toils as well!'

The carriage slowed, indicating they had reached the Vraux town house. 'I'll climb down quietly, so as not to disturb Mrs Moorsby,' Temper told him.

'Very well, but I'll see you to the door—and don't even try to tell me it isn't necessary. A gentleman never leaves a lady standing on the kerb like an abandoned parcel!'

She was chuckling at the description as the footman handed her down, Giff resisting the urge to perform that courtesy himself. Better he refrain as much as possible from subjecting himself to the intoxicating effect of her touch, since courtesy required that he offer his arm while she climbed the entry steps.

Ah, and sweet temptation it was, the feel of her hand clasping him. How much more dizzying would it be were she to wrap those slender hands around his shoulders, lean that tempting body against his?

Beating back those thoughts, he pulled his arm away as soon as they reached the landing and summoned up a smile. 'I'm glad you enjoyed your first evening—somewhat. Shall I stop by to collect you tomorrow afternoon?'

She sighed. 'I suppose you must. And I can't even promise you a good gallop as a reward for giving up your afternoon!'

With her head angled up at him, lamplight playing over the gold of her hair, outlining her nose and full, soft lips against the night gloom, his mind jumped to the sort of gallop that would truly be a reward. 'Perhaps another time…for the gallop,' he said disjointedly, trying to rein his thoughts back into line.

'Yes, another time. Until tomorrow, then.' With a smile, she disappeared behind the door the butler had opened for her.

He stood for a moment on the landing, letting his erratic pulse settle. It was too late to back out on his offer to help with her Season. He'd simply have to find a way to better control not just his actions, but his mind as well. He couldn't end every encounter where some act of courtesy required him to touch her by thinking of kissing…and more.

No matter how much he regretted it, kissing her was forbidden.

The following afternoon, Temper rode to the park with Giff, her groom trailing behind. 'I'm rather glad we are not going to gallop,' she told him, glad also that she was meeting Miss Henley and would send him off. The disturbing effect he'd had on her dressed in evening clothes hadn't abated a jot now that he was dressed for riding. And her foolish pulse had sped, making her light-headed for a moment as he handed her up into the saddle before they set out.

'Glad you can't gallop?' he repeated. 'Are you ill? Should I summon a physician?'

She made a face at him. 'I won't mind so much riding a job horse if we're to be limited to a decorous trot. Although this beast seems acceptable, there's no way he could match my Arion at the gallop and I would be sure to miss him.'

Giff tilted his head, seeming to have just noticed she wasn't riding her usual gelding. Was he as distracted by her presence as she was by his?

'Where is Arion?'

'He picked up a stone in his shoe yesterday. Nothing serious, Huggins said, but he thought it best that the bruised hoof be rested for a time.'

'Probably also knowing you'd be hard-pressed to refrain from a gallop if you rode Arion,' Giff observed with a grin.

'You slander me!' she protested. 'I would never do anything to put Arion at risk.'

'And for your safety, too,' Giff continued, his face a careful blank. 'With a sore hoof, he might suddenly stumble or rear up, and land you on your ear.'

'Me, land on my ear?' she echoed indignantly. 'You know I'm never unseated! Surely you've seen me ride often enough…' She let the sentence trail off as he burst out laughing. 'Wretch! You deserve some vile punishment for maligning me so!'

'I beg pardon!' he said, holding up his hand. 'But I couldn't resist. Your eyes blaze such blue fire when you're angry.'

She grinned back, her irritation evaporating in the welcome warmth of their familiar camaraderie. This was the Giff she knew—teasing, cajoling and amusing.

'I concede,' he continued. 'I *have* seen you ride often enough to know you maintain perfect control of your mount, even one as spirited as Arion, and even dressed in the ridiculous full skirts fashion now decrees.'

'I should hope so. Though I admit, I would much prefer a gallop in the open countryside in a pair of Greg's old breeches.'

His face tensed and he swallowed hard. 'I'd rather not envision that.'

With her limbs fully outlined by the worn, clinging calfskin and thin linen shirt? The idea of Giff watching her in such revealing attire flooded her with warmth of a different sort, reviving the strong undercurrent of sensual tension his teasing had momentarily suppressed.

She dared a quick glance at him at him, but could read nothing from his inscrutable expression. Did he feel the same odd mix of ease and discomfort, attraction and the need to repress it? And sadness, for the loss of what had once been such a simple, straightforward friendship?

But she had to be encouraged that they'd managed to recapture their old ease, even if briefly. She'd just have to figure out more ways to make that happen—and keep the disturbing sensual connection buried.

For once, she welcomed the concealment of voluminous skirts and wide sleeves. And knowing that she would soon be meeting her friend in the park and distancing herself from his both engaging and disturbing company.

'Once we find Miss Henley, you can safely take yourself off—else you might be corralled into talking with Lady

Henley. Apparently she is usually accompanied by a cote-rie of gallants. You'll want to escape before she adds you to their number.'

'Thank you for the warning! I shall take myself off swiftly—but remain in the vicinity, in case you have need of me.'

'I should be able to handle cuts and slights on my own, but it does give me more...confidence to know that you are nearby. Able to come to my rescue if I *should* be assaulted in Hyde Park in broad daylight.'

If he had been nearby to rescue her that day long ago... would she still be as set upon living her life unwed?

A street urchin darted out in front of her, pulling her attention back to controlling her horse. The increasingly crowded streets then demanded that they ride single file, Giff leading the way to clear a path, the groom bringing up the rear.

Passing through the entry gates, they found the carriage-way already crowded with riders and vehicles. Though they could once again ride side by side, progress was dawdling and they'd made almost a complete transit down Rotten Row before Temper spotted her new friend, mounted on a grey hack beside a smart black landau.

'That's Miss Henley and her mama over there!'

Giff gazed in the direction of her pointing finger and nodded. 'I'm to stay for the introductions and then take my leave?'

'I'd appreciate it if you remain nearby, as offered, and waylay anyone who seems bent on interrupting us. I can't ask any truly intrusive questions with a crowd around to overhear.'

He chuckled. 'Are you sure you wish to ask intrusive

questions? You might frighten Miss Henley into nipping this potential friendship in the bud.'

'I've already discovered that she prizes plain speaking. If I can say what I truly mean and *don't* frighten her off, she might become a true friend.' Feeling a wave of sadness as she voiced the words, she added, 'With Pru off getting herself married, soon I shall need a friend to talk with.'

'I know you must miss her. It wouldn't be like confiding in the sister you grew up with, but remember, you'll always have me.'

She looked up at him sharply, some nameless something passing in their gazes. 'I hope so,' she said softly before forcing herself to look away.

She'd have him as a friend—until he married. Which he must do, probably sooner rather than later, given his Parliamentary ambitions and slender purse. She mustn't let herself rely on him too much. Better that she concentrate on planning the travels that would take her beyond the restrictions of England, out into the wider world.

A prospect that seemed suddenly a little lonelier and less appealing than it had in all the dreams she'd spun growing up.

Suppressing that disturbing notion, she spurred her mount and rode over to intercept her friend.

Chapter Nine

After greetings all around and introductions to the two older gentlemen who were accompanying Lady Henley, Temper gave Giff a significant nod.

Returning a quick wink, he said, 'I'll just let the young ladies chat, while I catch up with some friends. If you'll excuse me, ladies and gentlemen?'

As he rode away, Temper turned to her companion. 'Shall we try a trot, Miss Henley? With your permission, of course, Lady Henley.'

'Go on, girls, enjoy yourselves,' she said with an indulgent look.

Smiling at Temper, Miss Henley signalled her mount forward. 'I doubt we can manage a trot in this throng, but we can try!'

'Only until we're far enough away to speak without being overheard,' Temper added in an undertone.

'Let us be off, then!'

It truly being difficult to ride with any speed through the

crowd of horses, carriages and pedestrians, the two girls soon slowed their mounts to a walk.

'Now we may ask each other as many "vulgarly intrusive" questions as we please before the world catches up with us again,' Temper said.

'Excellent! I should ask first, for there is truly nothing interesting about me. I've spent most of my life buried in Hampshire and possess no talents other than an aptitude for riding and a penchant for reading. Despite the fact that you could have any man you wanted, you told me you would rather go adventuring than marry?'

'I don't know that I could have any man I chose—assuming I wished to choose one.'

'Ah, yes. Your curious reputation. You exactly resemble your mother, I've heard.'

'I'm nearly her twin. So of course, in the eyes of society, I must share her profligate tendencies. Thereby making me a female no responsible man would dare to marry,' Temper said, trying to keep the bitterness from her tone. 'Then there's my brother Christopher, who married a former courtesan last year, putting the family further beyond the pale. So it's fortunate that I have no desire to wed.'

'Have *you* actually done anything…profligate?' Miss Henley asked.

'Not yet,' Temper replied with a laugh. 'But society is just waiting for me to do something scandalous. Which is so annoying, I may lose my temper, and find a way to behave very badly, just to live down to their expectations.'

Instead of looking alarmed by that prospect, Miss Henley laughed. 'What nonsense, that you are being judged before you've done anything at all! Another example of how ridiculous society is. If you do decide to do something scandalous, may I join you? I'm not pretty enough to catch the attention of a scoundrel, but a whiff of scandal might make me more interesting to the gentlemen.'

'You wouldn't want to be compromised into having to marry a scoundrel!' Temper protested.

'No. But it might be deliciously wicked to ride or dance with one. Until he finds out I'm not daring at all. I suppose I shall end my days living in some little London town house, with an elderly relation to give me consequence and a pug dog at my feet.'

'You mustn't settle for anything so dreary! Come adventuring with me! I've wanted to explore foreign lands since I was a girl and have read every travel journal I could find by individuals who have travelled to India, Russia, the Far East. My father collects weapons and antiquities. I hope to travel with his commission, acquiring things for him.'

'It sounds marvellously exciting, though I'm not sure I'm brave enough to accompany you! I should very much like you to call me your friend, though. Know that you can count on me to be yours, whatever shocking thing you might do!'

In Miss Henley's avowal Temper could find no trace of insincerity. A wave of warmth and gratitude swept over her. Perhaps she *had* found a friend who could partially fill the void left by Pru's departure. Miss Henley seemed to possess the same sunny, optimistic disposition that made her twin so lovable.

'Thank you,' Temper said at last. 'I should like very much to call *you* my friend as well.'

'Good! I'm glad we settled it, for I fear we're about to be overtaken by some of your admirers. See the ones, over there, waving at you?'

'Drat,' Temper muttered, noting that there were indeed

some gentlemen picking their way through the riders and carriages, headed towards them. 'I shall be lucky to recall any names.'

Miss Henley gave her a surprised look. 'Do you not know them all?'

'I actually know almost none of the men who were presented to me last night,' Temper said. 'My mother, you remember, isn't received by many in society and I'm acquainted only with the handful of gentlemen who are my brothers' closest friends. I'm ashamed to admit that I had so little interest in society, I never even thought to discover the identity of its occupants. Lady Sayleford would know everything about everyone, of course, but I'd rather not ask her.'

Miss Henley shuddered. 'I should think not! My mother wouldn't let me step near a drawing room until I could recite from memory the names of every society hostess, every aristocrat of note and every unmarried gentleman in London. I can coach you, if you like.'

'Thank you, that would be most helpful!' And a perfect opportunity to obtain an honest assessment of any member of society she needed to know more about—without having to ask Giff or Lady Sayleford.

'Are there any particular beaux you had in mind?'

'Lord Theo?'

'Ah, a charmer, but one who prefers the amusement of married ladies with indulgent spouses. A younger son who receives a generous allowance from his family, he has no pressing need to marry. Which means, although everyone who is anyone attends Lady Spencer-Woods's Opening Ball, you're unlikely to see him at any of the Marriage Mart events. He's not dangerous, though—I've never heard of him trying to seduce an innocent and Mama would surely have warned me against him if he had.' She smiled, her eyes merry. 'He would make an excellent flirt, though, if you wish to keep fast company.'

'I just might. Your account confirms my impressions of him. Now, what about Lord Solsworth?'

'You mean the biggest catch in London?' she said and laughed when Temper groaned. 'Despite the fact that Lady Agremont would be a horror of a mother-in-law, I can't tell you how many ladies have set their caps for him! But he's young yet to marry, nor has he ever shown a particle of interest in any lady. Which made the rapt attention he showered on you last night so notable.' She giggled. 'The spectacle of her son bedazzled by a lady of questionable reputation must have given his mama palpitations! Which is probably why she dressed you down so rudely.'

'Perhaps that will put an end to his interest—I hope. I don't want to be pursued by anyone my father might expect me to marry!'

Temper was on the point of asking about her tongue-tied dance partner of the previous evening when they rounded the corner to see Giff, who'd ridden ahead of them, drawn up by Lady Henley's carriage—with the Misses Avery on horseback beside him. Temper couldn't prevent an instinctive recoil of distaste.

'Do you know the Avery girls?' she asked, trying to keep her voice neutral. 'Isn't it unusual to have two sisters presented at once?'

'Yes, that's another story. The girls are being sponsored by their mother's sister, their own mother having passed away two years ago. And presented together, rather than one at a time, Mama said, because their father, Viscount

Chilford, plans to remarry and they don't wish to still be at home after he does.'

'I can understand that. It would be hard, watching someone else take your mother's place.' Temper frowned, suddenly making the connection. 'Viscount Chilford?' she repeated. 'He's Ben Tawny's father, isn't he?'

'Why, yes. You know the Viscount?'

'No, but his son Ben is one of my brother Christopher's closest friends! They were at Oxford together. Ben virtually lived at Vraux House after he and Christopher were elected to Parliament, until he married Lady Alyssa.'

'Oh, yes, now I remember Papa mentioning them—Hadley's Hellions, your brother's political group is called, isn't it? Lady Alyssa is an artist?'

'Yes. She's off on one of her sketching expeditions at the moment, but I'd be delighted to present you to her when she returns. And to the other wives of Christopher's close friends. All are unusual—Lady Maggie's been a political hostess for years, assisting her father before she married Lyndlington, and though Faith is a Dowager Duchess, she prefers to be known simply as "Mrs David Smith".'

'The whole group made marriages that were…out of the ordinary. I would love to make their acquaintances—ladies who are actually *doing* something! And I must make you known to my closest school friends, too. Not that we are exceptional in any way, except that we are all fortunate to possess a large enough competence that we will not be forced to wed.' She grinned. 'We call ourselves "the Splendid Spinsters".'

'I should like to meet them. If none of you is desperate to marry, in our world, that makes you exceptional,' Temper retorted.

Just then one of the pursuing riders caught up with them. Though sorry to have her informative tête-à-tête with Miss Henley brought to an end, Temper was relieved to recognise the gentlemen, without requiring any prompting.

'Lord Theo, good afternoon,' she said, nodding. 'Miss Henley, I believe you have met this gentleman. I've been delighted to discover, Lord Theo, that Miss Henley is another of those singular females who says what she thinks and does not hold with flattery.'

'Another forthright lady who disdains flattery and says what she thinks?' Lord Theo said with a smile. 'I must add you with Miss Lattimar to the list of females whom I shall seek out to dance and converse with.'

'And what a very long list that must be,' said a coquettish voice from the direction of the Henley carriage, which they had nearly overtaken. Temper looked over to discover the speaker was Miss Avery, who had turned in the saddle to give the Marquess's son a flirtatious glance as Temper's group approached.

Temper felt herself stiffen again. Had the girl eyes in the back of her head—or just an ear tuned to pick up the sound of any gentleman's voice? Must she claim the attention of every man who came within speaking distance?

'You mustn't credit anything Lord Theo tells you, Miss Henley,' Miss Avery continued in a playful tone that grated on Temper's nerves. 'He is the most shameless flirt!'

'I protest, Miss Avery, you are unfair,' Lord Theo replied—giving no sign, Temper was pleased to note, that he felt inclined to respond to the girl's overtures, despite the fact that even Temper had to admit Miss Avery was quite pretty. 'How could one not wish to make himself agreeable to charming females? But I'm afraid another appointment claims my attention and I must go. Ladies.' Giving them a short bow, he turned his mount and rode off.

After casting another smile in the direction of Lord Theo's retreating figure, Miss Avery turned to Miss Henley. 'If you would allow me to offer a word of advice? Though he is exceedingly charming, Lord Theo has quite a sad reputation as a rogue. As you do not possess the…ah… *striking* form and great fortune Miss Lattimar does, your behaviour—and your choice of companions—must be more circumspect.'

Furious, Temper had no trouble interpreting the veiled innuendo. 'You mean she would be wiser to avoid his company—and mine.'

'Your large dowry and acknowledged beauty may continue to make you acceptable—to some gentlemen—regardless of your conduct, Miss Lattimar,' Miss Avery replied coolly. 'But I should hate to see poor Miss Henley pulled along by you into some…indiscretion.'

Though Temper could have cheerfully throttled the Avery chit for her demeaning attitude towards Miss Henley, her new friend seemed neither upset nor cowed. 'I thank you for your concern, Miss Avery. However, my lacklustre reputation might be *enhanced* by a bit of scandal.'

'Oh!' Miss Avery replied. 'I meant no offence. Only to protect you, as your mama—' she cast a significant glance at the carriage, where Lady Henley was laughing at some sally made by one of her escorts '—seems to frequently be too…preoccupied to offer guidance.'

'And just what would you consider "scandalous", Miss Avery?' Temper asked though clenched teeth.

'With you, Miss Lattimar, I can hardly dare imagine! I don't expect you would go as far as to actually…*consort* with gentlemen, as your mother does. But being such an excellent rider, you might decide to show off your form and figure—riding past the gentlemen's clubs on St James's Street, perhaps?'

Though Temper admitted she'd taken a dislike to the girl the moment they'd met, having limited herself to exchanging only innocuous comments with Miss Avery, she wasn't sure why the girl was being so unpleasant.

With a minute shake of the head to silence Miss Henley, who by the annoyed expression on her face was about to intervene with some plain speaking, Temper said, 'I must make sure to add riding down St James's Street to the list of enjoyments I wish to experience before I quit London. Miss Henley, thank you for the ride. Mr Newell,' she called to Giff, interrupting the conversation of the group around Lady Henley, 'are you not due back at Parliament soon for a meeting?'

Giff took one look at what Temper could feel was the heightened colour on her cheeks and made a show of checking his pocket watch. 'Goodness, you are right! I must hurry to escort you home, else I shall be late. Lady Henley, gentlemen, young ladies, you must excuse us. You are ready, Miss Lattimar?'

'More than ready,' she snapped, barely waiting for him to make his farewells before signalling her mount to a trot.

Giff had to spur his horse to catch up. 'Why the hurry?' he asked as he drew even with her. 'And what happened to put you in such a fury?'

Temper had to damp down her anger to reply in an level tone. 'Miss Avery—whose offensive remarks irritated me so much, I feared I would not be able to remain civil if I had to suffer her presence a moment longer! I certainly hope you haven't taken a liking to her, for I find her to be the most annoying, wasp-tongued female I've yet encountered! I could understand, even forgive, her animosity to me—perhaps, with my large dowry, she sees me as a rival for gentlemen's attention. But she has no reason to be so dismissive of Miss Henley!'

Giff looked surprised. 'Miss Avery, wasp-tongued? She seemed pleasant enough to me—if putting herself forward a bit too much for my taste. She's very pretty, I'll allow, but a gentleman likes to think *he's* the one making the overtures—no matter how cleverly the lady manoeuvres him into it.'

'I hope you won't be making any overtures to her!'

'Believe me, I have no plans to.'

Feeling better now that she'd vented her anger—and discovered Giff had no liking for the girl—Temper said, 'I'm sorry to have pulled you away so abruptly. Though I wager you are not all that disappointed to end a meaningless social encounter and return to Parliament, where you can turn your hand to something important.'

'There actually is a meeting this afternoon. With any luck, I shall catch the last part of it.'

'Concerning one of your reform bills? Christopher told me two of great interest may come to a vote this session. One banning slavery, the other looking to limit the hours children can work in factories.'

'Yes, and both are dear to my heart,' Giff said, his eyes lighting with enthusiasm. 'Especially the factory bill. I took part in some of the inspections done by the committee gathering information for the proposed bill and the plight of some of those children is dreadful!'

'Those poor babes. Bravo to you and the reformers for being determined to help them.'

Giff nodded. 'We try to do what's right. Englishmen may need cloth—but they don't need to obtain it over the exhausted bodies of innocent children.'

Listening to the passion of his words, Temper felt a surge of pride in the work he and other reformers were doing. Lady Sayleford—and her sister, Pru—were right. There *were* gentlemen in London who were both honourable and compelling.

In fact, she felt a renewed pang of guilt for getting Giff tangled up in her Season, forcing him to dance attendance on her and taking him away from business that truly mattered. Though she would sorely miss his company, if he were to suspend his escort, Temper realised. She was enjoying even more than she'd anticipated having the companionship they'd experienced off and on through the years become an almost daily event.

Still, conscience prompted her to ask, 'Are you sure you don't want to dispense with this escort nonsense and concentrate on Parliament? I feel I'm wasting your time, dragging you to meaningless society events.'

'You are an important work, too,' he said, smiling.

She felt a ridiculous little spurt of pleasure that he would think her important and quickly squelched it. 'I have a sponsor and a chaperon to guide me through something whose greatest threat to my security is probably boredom. Those factory children have just a few visionaries like you trying to provide them far more essential protections. I really ought to insist that you give up on my Season.'

'What, you'd urge me to jump ship and have Lady Sayleford hunt me down, like a press gang searching out deserters? It's more than worth missing a few meetings to avoid incurring her wrath. Besides, we don't expect either bill to be ready for a vote before summer. And there's a special treat for tonight—one you will actually be enthusiastic about.'

'A social event I'll be enthusiastic about?' she asked dubiously.

'Lady Sayleford sent me a note, informing me we're to attend the theatre tonight.'

'Truly?' Temper cried, the promised treat wiping away the last vestiges of her irritation. 'I've been so looking forward to attending! Finally, something about this obligatory Season I can actually enjoy.'

'I thought you'd be excited. Well, here we are, back at Vraux House. Go select your prettiest evening dress. I'll join the ladies in Grosvenor Square and pick you up this evening.'

'Thank you, Giff, for sending me off with something you knew would brighten my day,' Temper said as she jumped down from the saddle and turned her horse over to the groom. 'It's daylight and Overton has already opened the door for me, you needn't dismount. This stray package can complete her delivery unaccompanied.'

'Just this once,' he said, chuckling. 'I'll see you tonight.'

The theatre! she thought with delight as she climbed the stairs. She didn't even care which play they were to see. She'd always loved amateur theatricals and couldn't wait to attend her first professional London production.

Not that most of theatregoers would be there to watch the performance. Haymarket, Convent Garden and Drury Lane were second only to the Promenade Hour in Hyde

Park as the place the members of the *ton* frequented to see, be seen and gossip.

She only hoped Miss Avery wouldn't appear there, too, to mar her enjoyment.

Chapter Ten

As he ushered the ladies to their box later that evening, Giff had to smile. Temper had certainly followed his advice. Wearing a gown of deep gold silk embroidered with little silver stars that sparkled like the diamonds at her ears and throat, her face vibrant with excitement in the bright gaslight, she was magnificent.

She'd been enveloped in her satin evening cloak when he'd called for her at Vraux House. But even he, armoured as he tried to be against her beauty, had caught his breath when she removed her cloak and he beheld her in that gown.

Good thing he was going to stand guard tonight. Sitting on display beside Lady Sayleford and Mrs Moorsby in their box, Temper was going to draw male eyes like shavings to a magnet. They would be thronged with gentlemen wanting to meet her.

Despite Temper's scepticism, he thought it likely that some lucky man among all those competing for her attention this Season would succeed in piquing her interest—

and earning her affection. Though she was still Temper, impulsive, difficult to manage, quick to say exactly what she thought, she had matured, he noted. She'd shown an ability to control her volatile temper and could even sometimes mask her feelings. He also appreciated her genuine concern for his Parliamentary work.

But though she hadn't created any fireworks among the *ton* yet, he didn't expect that period of tranquillity to last. She'd never be a conventional lady, an obedient, conformable wife—or the serene, diplomatic hostess a politician needed at his dinner table.

Still, he had to fight the possessive feeling that assailed him whenever another gentleman claimed her as a partner for a dance—or a ride, he thought, remembering her laughing with Lord Theo in the park this afternoon.

Of course he felt...protective. He was her brother's best friend, had watched her grow up. It would be hard to let her go to someone else, but eventually he must steel himself to watch that happen. He swallowed hard against the sinking feeling that thought evoked.

As for the passion she stirred so readily—well, the little girl he had watched grow up was now a desirable woman and he wouldn't be male if he didn't find her alluring. As long as he didn't act on the passion she inspired, the attraction he couldn't suppress wouldn't be a betrayal of her trust—or Gregory's.

He heard the ripple of murmurs moving like a wave though the audience as the ladies took their seats, saw a hundred pairs of eyes turn towards their box. Yes, he would play the watchdog, keep the ne'er-do-wells away and make sure, when she did give her hand and heart, they went to a man worthy of her.

Bleak as that prospect appeared.

'Well, child, is it everything you had imagined?' Lady Sayleford's voice broke into his thoughts.

'Yes, ma'am, it's wonderful!' Temper said, her voice awed as she gazed around the theatre. 'The beautiful domed ceiling, the rich red velvet of the curtains, the vast array of gaslights! Thank you so much for bringing me tonight. I can't wait for the performance to begin.'

'The melodrama to follow may be a bit silly, but I think you'll enjoy the play. The present actors don't rival Kean, Kemble or Siddons in their day, but are competent enough.'

Although the murmur of voices scarcely lessened, actors took the stage and the play began. 'Don't let anyone into the box until intermission,' Lady Sayleford told Giff. 'I want Miss Lattimar to be able to enjoy the performance before she is pestered by gentlemen's attentions.'

And so, one eye on the stage and one on the door to the box, Giff alternated between glimpsing the action onstage, warding off strolling gentlemen who mimed their request to enter—and watching Temper. He couldn't help but smile at her rapt expression as she followed the action of the play, her eyes shining, her lips curved in a half-smile of delight. No feigned boredom for her, or indulging in gossip with her chaperon about the notables in the boxes around them—just complete, enthusiastic enjoyment, displayed as openly as the child she'd once been.

No, she'd never be moulded into displaying fashionable manners. And he was glad of it.

At length, the interval arrived and Giff could no longer refuse the press of visitors demanding entrance. First to push his way inside was Lord Theo. Despite an instinctive resistance to him, Giff had no good reason to bar the man from entering.

'You may put away the dagger, Newell,' Lord Theo said sotto voce. 'I mean her no harm.'

'See that you do not,' Giff said curtly, further aggravated by the man's amused chuckle as he passed by him, a uniformed gentleman in tow.

'Ladies, how magnificent you look! You are enjoying the performance? Lady Sayleford, would you allow me to present this officer?' At her nod, he continued, 'Let me make known to you Lieutenant James Masters, of the Queen's Royal Second Foot, presently back from India on leave. Lieutenant, Lady Sayleford, Miss Lattimar and Mrs Moorsby.'

After bows and nods were exchanged, Lord Theo turned to Temper. 'Having heard you have a desire to travel to foreign places, I thought you would find Lieutenant Masters's conversation of interest.'

'Indeed, I would!' Temper said, her eyes lighting with enthusiasm. 'How kind of you to bring him by.'

'Lady Sayleford, would you tell me and Mrs Moorsby about other versions of this play you have seen performed... perhaps by the great Kemble himself? While those two chat about overseas adventures.'

'Certainly. Miss Lattimar, you may use this opportunity to ask the Lieutenant all the question you like.'

Giving Temper a wink, Lord Theo helped rearrange the chairs, taking a seat beside the Dowager Countess while Lieutenant Masters claimed one beside Temper. Giff, moving his chair to the rear of the box, settled back to keep watch. Though officers in his Majesty's army were usually gentlemen, he'd make sure this newcomer knew how to behave around a lady.

A necessary caution. Because he couldn't count on Temper, enthralled to speak with someone who'd actually been to one of the foreign lands she dreamed of exploring, to display any reserve at all.

'Welcome back to England, Lieutenant! I'm sure you must be pleased to be home among family and friends,' she was saying.

'Indeed, ma'am. A welcome break from the heat and dust!'

'Would you be so kind as to tell me more about your life in India? I would so much like to visit the country! My brother found me a copy of Godfrey Charles Mundy's *Pen and Pencil Sketches*, made during his time as ADC to Lord Combermere. Such enthralling scenery, and such charming glimpses into the life—"*Dak* travelling" and "Tiger's attack on the Elephant".'

'Mundy published his journal? I hadn't heard of it.' He gave her a wry smile. 'If it's an accurate picture of the place, it should tell of monsoons, vipers and attacks by dacoits. Not something, I think, to interest such a beautiful lady. Lord Theo warned me you were enchanting, but the reality far exceeds his description. How delighted I am to make your acquaintance! I hope I shall see more of you while I'm home on leave.'

Giff read the disappointment in Temper's eyes and suppressed a grin. He needn't worry about the lieutenant or his intentions. Most females would have asked about the lieutenant's service out of politeness and been delighted to move on to expressions of gallantry. But by turning aside the subject of her real interest, the man had just squandered his opportunity to make a favourable impression on Temper.

With a wry grimace that seemed to say she'd resigned herself to not receiving the first-hand account of India she'd hoped for, Temper nodded. 'I'm sure all the London ladies will try to make a returning hero feel welcome,' she said politely, her voice, to Giff's practised ear, markedly devoid of the enthusiasm she'd shown earlier.

'I shall not care about the others—as long as *you* are welcoming,' the lieutenant replied, his admiring gaze fixed on Temper.

He couldn't blame the soldier for being awestruck. He still caught his breath each time he saw Temper in one of her new gowns. But if the fellow let his eyes wander from her face down to her bosom, Giff would consider it cause to intervene.

'I'm sure we will all do our best,' Temper said coolly. 'On another matter, I've recently had a letter from my sister in Bath, who tells me she has also met a soldier invalided home from India duty. A Captain Johnnie Trethwell. I know the area in which the troops serve is vast, but do you happen to know him?'

'As a matter of fact, I do. He served, like Mundy, in the Queen's Second Foot. I don't know him personally, having never actually met him, but I have heard of him. He was something of an...oddity.'

'Oh? In what way?'

Giff stiffened, sharing the concern he could hear in Temper's voice. If her beloved sister had been enticed by a bounder, despite the fact that her aunt and friends were chaperoning her, he knew Temper would alert Gregory and have them on the road to Bath by morning.

'He seemed to take to India almost as though he'd been born there. Oh, he amused the ladies at the cantonments, but he never quite fit in among the regiment. Learned to speak the language like a local, liked going off exploring in native dress.'

'But he *is*...a gentleman.'

'I don't think he'd do your sister any harm, if that's what is worrying you. Indeed, always very gallant with the ladies, was Johnnie.'

From the tone of his voice, Giff inferred that Johnnie Trethwell had a rake's reputation, but didn't trifle with innocents.

Looking reassured, Temper said, 'I'm glad to hear it. My sister says he is quite the charmer. However...with India such an exotic and fascinating land, I wonder that you did not also wish to go exploring.'

Lieutenant Masters laughed. 'It is exotic! What with the poisonous critters, dangerous animals, deadly diseases and the heat, life in the cantonments was hard enough. I never had any desire to explore beyond where my duties took me.'

'I do envy you, though. I should love to visit foreign places,' Temper said wistfully.

'You must come out to India, miss. A lovely lady like you—there'd be a hundred officers waiting to snap you up like sugar candy.'

'Oh, I don't want to marry! I'd just like to visit and explore the countryside.'

Lieutenant Masters looked as if to speak, then hesitated. After a forced laugh, he said, 'India contains dangers far beyond what you could ever imagine, miss. It would be a deadly mistake to go adventuring on your own. If you don't wish to live in a cantonment with a husband, you'd be safer to remain in England.'

A shadow fell over Giff, making him turn towards the doorway. A man he didn't recognise loitered there, swaying, his glazed eyes fixed on Temper.

'Damme, you are 's beautiful as y'mama, jes like Lord Theo said,' he slurred. 'Collington, pr'sent me to thish charmer.'

Before Giff could rise to shoo the gentleman off, Lady Sayleford said in a commanding voice, 'Certainly not. You are inebriated, sir. You will quit this box at once.'

The man shifted his gaze to peer at Lady Sayleford. 'Ol' beldame,' he muttered. 'Wanna meet the Beauty. You, Theo—' He waved a hand, almost oversetting himself. 'C'mon, intr'duce me.'

Murmuring an apology to Lady Sayleford, Lord Theo jumped up and moved past Giff to take the man's arm. 'Wendemere, old chap, you're in no condition to meet a lady. Come along, Lieutenant, let us escort this gentleman to…more suitable entertainment.'

The man pulled at his captive arm. 'A'right, I'll go.' Looking back at Temper with a leer, he said, 'Meet you later, Beauty. Wanna get t'know you *very* well.'

He was gazing blatantly down her bosom as Lord Theo and Lieutenant Masters each took an arm and pulled him out, Giff closing the door behind them, ignoring the other gentlemen trying to gain entry. They could hear Wendemere's drunken protests fading as the two men walked him away.

Temper shuddered. 'I feel that I should go home and bathe immediately. Lady Sayleford, who is Wendemere?'

'No one who need concern you,' the Countess said. 'A

younger son with no expectations, Lord Alfred Wendemere is a gamester, drunkard, womaniser and general embarrassment to his noble family. Indeed, if it weren't for his impressive lineage, he wouldn't be received anywhere. Not a man I would trust to escort you around a dance floor, much less on a stroll through the park.'

'He behaved worse than a randy ensign after six months at sea,' Mrs Moorsby said indignantly. 'Can't she just refuse to know him?'

Lady Sayleford sighed. 'He's the Duke of Maidstone's middle son, so his presence in society is tolerated. But even his family understands why matrons with innocent daughters do not invite him to their events. He usually confines himself to women of the demi-monde—or the more reckless married ladies.'

'So he targeted me because of Mama's reputation,' Temper said flatly.

After a short silence, Lady Sayleford said, 'I'm afraid that's likely. You will have to accept the acquaintance, if he turns up in a sober condition at some respectable entertainment, but nothing more.' She smiled. 'By now, I'm sure you're adept at gracefully turning away invitations to dance or dine from persons you don't wish to know better.'

Temper laughed. 'I'm not sure about graceful, but I can certainly be forceful!'

'And I'll be nearby to make sure he accepts his dismissal,' Giff said, having taken an instant dislike to any man who would approach Temper in such a disgraceful state—to say nothing of staring at her as if she were a harlot! If Lord Theo and the lieutenant hadn't dragged him off, Giff would have been tempted to remove him, not just from the box, but out to the street, where he could administer a quick lesson in what happens to boors who insulted ladies under his escort.

'The play's about to resume, so please, Giff, don't open the door again,' Temper said, interrupting his belligerent thoughts. 'I'd prefer that it remain closed for the intervals as well. I came to enjoy the theatre, not to exchange idle remarks!'

'With Lady Sayleford's leave, I can certainly do that. I should not like to exclude any of her friends, though.'

'My friends all know I dislike chatting during the performance and are unlikely to seek me out. A drawing room is the proper place for conversation, not a theatre box! Besides, we achieve all we need to simply by being present, where Temperance can be seen and admired. Making gentlemen who wish to speak with her wait until later is not a bad thing.'

'The unattainable lady thereby becoming even more fascinating,' Mrs Moorsby said.

'Exactly,' Lady Sayleford replied.

'A closed door it shall be, then,' Giff said, pleased that Lady Sayleford had acquiesced. Though he didn't think Temper needed to become any *more* fascinating, now he wouldn't have to endure watching a steady stream of gentlemen try to impress her. Freed from playing the guard dog, he could relax and simply enjoy the performance—and the simple pleasure of watching an enthralled Temper enjoy it.

Late the following afternoon, Giff made an unannounced stop at Vraux House, hoping to find Temperance. Fortunately, Overton informed him that Miss Lattimar was indeed at home and escorted him into the small parlour.

'Giff, what a pleasant surprise,' she said as she entered.

'Were you expecting to see Gregory? He's paying a visit to the solicitor, as I imagine Overton told you, but should return shortly.'

'Actually, it was you I came to see—thinking I might catch you between calls and shopping excursions,' Giff said, rising as she entered.

'Mrs Moorsby and I made another contribution to the profits of the linen drapers, modistes and bonnet-makers this morning,' Temper said, her smile as warming as sunshine and bright as the yellow gown she wore.

He took a moment to bask in it while she continued, 'One ride at the Promenade Hour was enough for a while and we haven't a large enough acquaintance yet that we do much calling, so you find me here this afternoon. But is something amiss? I didn't think I'd see you again until the Randalls' ball.'

'Nothing amiss, but by chance at my meeting today I learned of something I thought might interest you. Perhaps,' he added with a grin, 'it will make up for your disappointment with the unforthcoming Lieutenant Masters.'

Temper sighed. 'How…selfish of him, to have so vast a knowledge of India and yet be unwilling to share it!'

'To be fair, most ladies probably wouldn't be interested. He likely thought you were just being polite.'

She raised her eyebrows. 'That may be true about "most ladies", but I asked him to share his observations quite pointedly. Several times. If he wasn't able to tell I truly wished to hear them, that doesn't say much for his intelligence.' She sighed. 'More likely, he didn't know what to say to a female with such odd, unmaidenly interests. The stories he normally tells are probably tailored for the ribald enjoy-

ment of an officers' mess. Poor Lieutenant! But you said
you had something to make up for that disappointment?'

'Are you familiar with the Travellers Club?'

Her eyes lit. 'Oh, yes! Founded by Castlereagh in 1819,
after the opening of Europe at the end of the Napoleonic
Wars. A place where gentlemen who have travelled abroad
might meet for discussion and to entertain foreign dignitar-
ies. How I wish I might listen in on some of those conversations—or attend the lectures of the Royal Geographical
Society. But, alas, they both are open only to men. Who
seem, like Lieutenant Masters, to want to keep all the fascinating details to themselves! What about the Travellers
Club?'

'Lord Lansdowne—he's currently Lord President of the
Council, you know, the man through whom my committee works to funnel information about our reform efforts
to the Privy Council—is a long-time member. He's currently hosting a Lieutenant Williamson from the army of
the East India Company. Williamson accompanied Alex-
ander Burnes and Henry Pottinger on their surveys up the
Indus River, and was initially supposed to speak to the
Travellers Club here in London. But after he suffered a re-
lapse of tropical fever, Lansdowne moved him to Trenton
Manor, the country property he rents in Highgate Village.
Williamson isn't yet recovered enough to return to London
and deliver a formal lecture, but he has improved enough to
receive company. Lansdowne is hosting a small reception
at Trenton Manor tomorrow afternoon, where members of
the Travellers Club and other interested persons may meet
and chat with Williamson. Lady Lansdowne will offer tea
for any ladies who accompany the gentlemen. Would you
like to go with me? When I told him of your special inter-

est, Lansdowne confirmed that you would be welcome to listen in on the conversations with Lieutenant Williams.'

'Oh, Giff!' Temper cried, leaping up. He thought for a moment she might fling herself at him and, sucking in a breath in mingled alarm and anticipation, braced himself to resist the wave of sensation an embrace would generate.

But at the last moment she skidded to a halt, her cheeks colouring. Dropping her arms back to her sides, she said, 'As my enthusiasm in jumping out of my chair indicates, yes, I would love to go! Lansdowne will let me listen in? Imagine, being able to speak to someone who has actually travelled by *dak* and elephant, seen tigers and leopards, dusty villages and a maharaja's palace! Thank you so much for thinking of me.'

He smiled, delighted to have been able to bring such a look of joy to her face. He found himself wishing he could offer something every day that would make her so dazzlingly happy.

'Mrs Moorsby will accompany us, of course—she can enjoy tea with the other ladies while I attend Williamson's discussion. Might I ask Miss Henley, too? I think she would enjoy the talk—or at the very least, a chance to ride out of London.'

'I believe Lady Henley and Lady Lansdowne are friends, so she may already be planning to attend. The park at Trenton Manor is said to be very fine, with lovely views down towards London. If the weather is pleasant, I imagine the ladies will stroll around the park while the gentleman talk with Lieutenant Williamson.'

'Can you stay for tea now and tell me more?'

'Regrettably, I must return to the House. More meetings.

But I wanted to let you know about the opportunity, so you would have time to prepare.'

'Then I mustn't keep you,' she said, rising from her chair. 'I cannot wait until tomorrow! I'll send Miss Henley a note, inviting her to ride with us, if her mother is not attending. And let Mrs Moorsby know, of course. What time will you call for me?'

'It's not far to Highgate. Leaving Vraux House at noon should be sufficient.'

'I'll be ready,' she promised as she walked with him to the door. 'Thank you again, Giff. It…it means a great deal to me that you take my plans and dreams seriously. Everyone else seems to think them just foolish, childish fantasies.'

He might not think voyaging the world wise and suspected that, in the end, marriage would win out over exploration, but he didn't question her passion for her dream or her commitment to achieving it. 'I've always taken your plans seriously.'

She grinned. 'Perhaps by the time I meet the requirement of having voyaged at least five hundred miles from London and back, the Travellers Club will be ready to admit lady members!'

Laughing, he let Overton show him out.

Chapter Eleven

But as it happened, Temper's maid came to inform her Giff waited below, not at noon, but just after ten the next morning. Horrified that she must have mistaken the time for their excursion, she rushed down to the parlour.

'I'm so sorry, Giff!' she cried, halting just inside the threshold as Newell turned from where he'd been pacing in front of the mantel. 'I can change my gown in a trice. I must have truly been in alt, to have got the hour so wrong!'

'No, you didn't mistake it. We weren't to leave until noon, but I just found out there will be a preliminary hearing on the anti-slavery bill this afternoon. Apparently the drafting team completed a revision last night and want the other members to read it and comment. It's not imperative that I be there—this isn't a final vote, but...'

'Of course you must be there,' Temper said at once, recognising the pull of conflicting loyalties in him—the duty he'd pledged to protect her and his responsibilities to his committee. 'Our coachman will have no trouble finding

Trenton Manor and, in the middle of the day, we don't need a gentleman to escort us. Miss Henley will be travelling with her mother, but Mrs Moorsby and I will be perfectly safe going on our own.'

He looked at her anxiously. 'Are you sure? I shall regret missing the reception, but I could on no account let *you* miss it. Not after having offered you so perfect a treat! Truly, if you do not feel comfortable driving to Highgate alone, I will accompany you as planned.'

'I'm sorry you will miss the reception, too—' more disappointed than she would let him know that she wouldn't be able to share the experience with him '—but your presence at the committee meeting is far more important. With several footmen and the coachman to watch over us, we shall be fine. You tend to your important work.'

He studied her face. 'You are sure?'

She smiled at him. 'Absolutely. And I promise to take careful mental notes, so I may regale you with wonderful stories of the Hindu Kush!'

'Thank you for understanding,' he said quietly. 'Most ladies would be put out at having a gentleman cancel on them at the last minute. My mother would have a fit of the vapours.'

'You clearly don't know the right ladies,' she teased, wanting to bring the smile back to his face. 'Besides, I intend to sail the Indus myself, some day. Compared with that, an afternoon jaunt to a village barely outside London is no more hazardous than a walk in our back garden.'

To her delight, he seized her hand and kissed it. He probably knew as well as she it wasn't wise, but she revelled in the thrill of it just the same. 'Thank you, Temper,' he said again, releasing her fingers. 'I shall hold you to your promise of giving me a full account. Perhaps tonight?'

'Go on to your committee,' she told him. 'I need to go decide which of my gowns makes me look most like a lady explorer!'

Late that afternoon, her mind afire with Lieutenant Williamson's captivating descriptions of his India travels, Temperance walked with Miss Henley towards the outer edge of the garden surrounding Trenton Manor. The impromptu event had attracted a larger number of guests than she'd anticipated, both gentlemen interested in listening to the Lieutenant—to her surprise, Lord Theo among their number—and ladies and gentlemen who gathered on the terrace to take tea and stroll through the garden. Too enthused after the end of the Lieutenant's presentation to want to descend from the plane of high adventure into the mundane world of London society, she'd slipped her arm through her friend's and marched her off.

'Sorry to steal you away from returning to your mama,' she said when, after traversing several circuitous paths, they'd reached the outermost walk.

'No need for apologies,' Miss Henley said. 'I could tell you were bursting to discuss Lieutenant Williamson's stories and wouldn't be able to abide chatting about everyday society events with Mama's friends.'

Temper smiled. 'Although I shall have to be careful. Lady Henley allows me your company because you've led her to believe I will attract potential suitors for you to impress. Bad enough that I just refused all offers to have any gentlemen escort us. If she discovers that I've dragged you beyond where we might expect to encounter any, she will probably curtail our friendship forthwith.'

Miss Henley laughed. 'We'll return and you may begin attracting that entourage, soon enough. I, too, wanted some time to talk about what we just heard. What a fascinating land India is and how vividly Lieutenant Williamson describes it! Though I appreciate the beauties of our own country, too. This view, for instance.' She pointed towards the vista of London, spread below them in the far distance beyond the broad swathe of meadow to the south.

'Beautiful, yes,' Temper agreed. 'But oh, do you not long to view for yourself the forests he described bordering the Ganges River? Imagine, banyan trees, their crowns wide as a town house, supported by not just a thick trunk, but by aerial roots anchored into the soil, or dangling like chains? Or stands of bamboo, the trunks narrow and straight as fishing poles, growing so thickly together that a man cannot walk through them?'

'Exotic indeed!' Miss Henley agreed. 'And his description of the Himalayan country—the vast, huge mountains, wild, lonely, almost mystical glens full of rising mist!'

For the next half-hour, they strolled along the outer pathway, both recalling parts of the Lieutenant's stories and descriptions they'd found particularly compelling. Turning back towards the house, Temper said, 'I suppose I must make myself stop contemplating the thrills of foreign lands and rejoin the company. But before we return, tell me this— was the Lieutenant's account fascinating enough to tempt you into travelling with me?'

Miss Henley laughed. 'I'm still not sure I'm that brave. Hearing about exotic places and visiting them in person are two different matters! I was quite enthralled to listen and thought it very kind of Lord Lansdowne to arrange for us to be seated in the alcove adjacent to the library, where we could hear the discussion, but still be apart from the gentlemen.'

Temper smiled wryly. 'Though Lord Lansdowne didn't say so directly, I rather suspect that it was only because Mr Newell had intervened in advance that seats were arranged for us where the ladies might listen to the talk. I owe Giff a good deal of thanks. Otherwise, I would have made the drive here to be afforded nothing more exciting than the opportunity to curtsy to the Lieutenant when Lansdowne presented him to the ladies.'

'And had instead to suffer through conversation about society people and events—while surrounded by an entourage of eager gentlemen,' Miss Henley said, a twinkle in her eye.

'An entourage of eager gentlemen? Let me be the first to join their ranks.'

Temper and Miss Henley turned towards the sound of the masculine voice, to see Lord Theo striding towards them. 'Ladies,' he said, bowing as he reached them. 'I've spent the last ten minutes trying to find you! This garden is like a maze! When Lady Henley decided to stroll and did not see you, she became worried that you might have been lost. I was fortunate enough to have been given the task of bringing you back to her. If I might offer each of you an arm?'

'How kind of you.' Blushing, Miss Henley laid her hand on his sleeve.

Temper sighed. 'Much as I'd prefer to continue discussing the fine points of Lieutenant Williamson's talk, I suppose it is time to return.' With regret, she, too, laid her hand on Lord Theo's arm.

Listening with half an ear to his banter with Miss Henley, as they turned the corner to start down the next pathway, Temper spied a sculptured stone that made her start with delight.

'Is something wrong, Miss Lattimar?' Lord Theo asked.

Dropping his arm, she hurried forward. 'Oh, it *is* what I suspected!' Turning back to them, she said, 'It's a temple carving—in Sanskrit, I believe. Papa has several that are similar.'

'Yes, I believe Landsdowne is a collector,' Lord Theo said.

Temper ran her fingers reverently over the rows of symbols. 'Ah, that I knew enough to read the stories you could tell,' she murmured.

Realising her companions were waiting for her, she reluctantly pulled herself away—only to exclaim again when they came upon another stone a few moments later.

And so it continued as they proceeded down the pathway, along which their host had displayed a number of carved stones, some containing simply symbols, others adorned with bas-reliefs of plants and animals. Her companions slowed their pace, Temper grateful for their indulgence, but wishing she had far longer to inspect them.

After passing by several far too quickly, arrested by a stone with particularly interesting carving, Temper couldn't resist the desire to linger. She trailed her fingers over the vivid rendering of birds and foliage, thrilled to have this tangible glimpse of the world she longed to explore.

In similar fashion, the Lieutenant's words had given her a tantalising glimpse of her cherished goal, fulfilled. His account fired from dream back to pressing desire the longing she'd felt since her early teens to experience the excitement, and, yes, even danger, of travelling somewhere wholly unfamiliar, where every day brought unusual sights and new revelations.

Bless Giff, who not only appreciated her desire to seek out the exotic, but had gone to some trouble to give her this opportunity to vicariously experience it.

The Lieutenant had mentioned that the wealthy of the Punjab decorated themselves and their ladies with finely worked gold jewellery inset with gemstones, often in fanciful shapes and patterns. Might her papa be interested in collecting something like that?

More likely he'd prefer to acquire weapons from the area, swords and daggers being a particular interest. The wild tribesmen of the north-western frontier were armed with intricately engraved daggers and large, curved swords—*salwars*, Williamson said they were called. She was almost certain that Papa would be interested in obtaining some fine examples of those.

Still musing about which articles he'd prefer, she glanced up from the stone to discover herself alone. Realising the others must have turned on to the next pathway, she hurried to catch up.

As she rounded the corner, she almost collided with an approaching figure. About to apologise, she recognised the newcomer as Lord Alfred Wendemere and the regrets she'd meant to offer died on her lips.

'Well, well, look who I ran into,' he said—looking indeed, as, after a quick glance at her face, his gaze came back to linger at her bosom. 'Returning from a tryst, were you? Collington told me you were attending this gathering—to listen to some rubbishing lecture, he said, though I'm sure he was joking me.'

With the proximity of their near-collision, she could smell the brandy on him. Craning her neck, she could see no one else on this section of pathway. She must have drifted further behind Lord Theo and Miss Henley than she'd realised.

A ripple of dismay going through her, she took a step backwards, fighting the onset of panic.

But she didn't mean to let Wendemere sense her unease. 'Lord Alfred,' she said, giving him a cool nod. 'I did indeed attend the lecture and took a stroll to ponder some of the speaker's points. But now, if you'll excuse me, I must return to my friends.'

'Oh, but I won't excuse you,' he said, giving her an insolent grin and stepping forward, so they once again stood only a foot apart. 'If you were *pondering*, it must have been to decide which man you'd meet with in the shrubbery next. Why not me?'

Mind racing, Temper considered her options. Lord Theo and Miss Henley were out of sight, the voices from the terrace still a distant hum. If she cried out, she wasn't sure they would hear her—or be near enough to intervene.

'I'll consider letting you go—after you give me a kiss as a forfeit,' he continued. 'I bet you're giving that watchdog Newell a good deal more. Stringing him along with tastes of your person, just as your mother does all those men sniffing around her, like hounds following a bitch in heat!'

'If you choose to be crude and insulting, I have nothing further to say to you. Remove yourself from my path, please.'

'And what if I don't please?' He reached, grabbing her wrist. 'What if what pleases me is to have a little taste of what you're giving Newell?'

Despite her vow to remain unmoved, she felt her pulse

accelerate as his look, his tone, jerked at the bonds impris-
oning memories of that other time and place. *The sour scent
of spirits, his arms forcing her down, his body following to
pin her to the ground...*

A sudden wave of panic filled her, flooding her with an
urgent desire to pick up her skirts and flee. Wendemere
tightened his grip and pulled her towards him.

'Struggle if you like. Pretend you don't want it, when we
both know you do. A prime little piece like you, the exact
image of your slut of a mother. Resisting me will make the
taking all the sweeter.'

In his hot, greedy gaze she read lust, excitement—and
the need to dominate. He *wanted* her to struggle and cry
out. To be afraid.

Desperately she tried to beat back that fear. Struggle and
he might immediately try to subdue her. Though she was
no longer an unprepared, innocent fifteen-year-old girl, her
brothers having taught her how to defend herself, she didn't
think she was strong enough to overpower him with a single punch—or fast enough, hampered by her ridiculously
full skirts, to outrun him.

What could she do, then? *Never show fear or weakness*,
her mother's words echoed in her head. Surely, with her
reputation, Mama had faced foxed and threatening men before. What would she do, confronted now by Wendemere?

Temper had no doubt Mama would act as if she were entirely nonplussed by the situation. As if she'd faced threatening, demanding men before—and used their lust to bend
them to her will. So that she, not they, were in control, the
man inevitably ending up doing *her* bidding.

Could Temper manage that? She wasn't sure, but better
to attempt it than to give in to panic and cede control to

Wendemere. No matter how this ended, it would happen as *she* directed.

Sudden fury coursed through her, bolstering her courage and hardening her resolve. How dare he presume to dismiss her—and her mother—as mere toys for his amusement? Designed only for the physical uses he had for them, bound to submit to his lusts?

Instead of whimpering or struggling, as he clearly expected, she relaxed her arm in his grip. 'Really?' she said, infusing her voice with irritation and faint disdain. 'You want to show yourself a "man" by manhandling me? How very *tedious* of you!'

Whatever reaction he'd expected, that wasn't it. He looked surprised for a moment before retightening his grip. 'Don't try to distract me. Whores always want it and you're just a whore like your mother!'

'Perhaps, but I don't want it now. Not if you're going to be boorish as well as boring, wanting me to *struggle*, as if dalliance were some sort of wrestling match! And hardly a *match*—you must outweigh me by several stone! What sort of equal contest is that? If this were a schoolyard, the boys would laugh you out of it.'

She'd thrown him off his script. Before he could recover, she gave an exasperated sigh. 'If you are so uncertain of your prowess that you don't believe you can win a kiss without *forcing* it on me, go ahead, but honestly, I had hoped for better from you. Or—' she paused, giving him a seductive look from under her lashes '—you could *rise* to a challenge to prove your manliness.'

Still fighting the urge to flee, she held his gaze, using every ounce of will to remain looking bored, faintly disdainful—and in command.

She could see the indecision in him, his confusion. His need to cow and overmaster her compromised by her impatient, slightly contemptuous attitude and absence of fear.

'What challenge?' he said after a moment.

'As I said, a wrestling match would be unequal. Why not a contest to test your mettle, in which we are more evenly matched?'

'What sort of contest?'

She batted her eyes at him and laughed. 'Not *that* sort—yet. First, you need to prove to me you have the...stamina I require. Race me. In the park, tomorrow morning. You on your favourite mount—of the equine variety—and me on mine. If you win, you get your kiss—and whatever else you desire. Wherever you desire it—though I trust it will be a place where we can fully enjoy the encounter, not—' she wrinkled her nose in distaste 'some rubbishing *bench* in a windy park. And if you lose, you will never approach me again without my express leave.'

'You propose a *horse* race?'

'I do. It's so similar to what you want, isn't it? The building excitement, the speed, your heart pounding, the rush of breath. The ultimate fulfilment.'

He laughed and licked his lips. 'Trying to increase my anticipation?'

'Anticipation always increases desire, does it not?'

'And all I need do is beat you in a horse race?'

'But fairly. No tricks. So the race will be in Hyde Park and there will be witnesses. Accept the more *manly* challenge—' she forced herself to lean closer and use her free hand to touch his lips 'and you may gain...everything you wish.'

Deliberately, with neither speed nor haste, she withdrew

her arm from his slackened grip. 'Tomorrow morning, eight of the clock,' she said and turned to walk away. Feeling the pulse pound in her head, still having to resist the instinct to take to her heels, she forced herself to move at a decorous pace.

Behind her, she heard him laugh. 'Tomorrow, then.'

Her relief, when it appeared he wasn't going to follow and try to force her into submission here and now, sent such a rush of sensation through her that she felt faint. She knew she was not equal, yet, to returning to the terrace and chatting as if nothing had happened, nor did she wish to appear before the other guests while she was still so dizzy and depleted, still fighting down the vestiges of panic. As the voices from the terrace grew louder, she switched pathways to skirt around its outside edge and walked instead towards the house, until she came to a side entry door.

With a footman's help, she found the lady's retiring room—mercifully deserted—where, in blessed solitude, she was violently ill. Some time later, after recovering herself, she rinsed her mouth, washed her face and straightened her gown. Giving her mama a silent thanks, she waited until her hands no longer trembled, then headed back to the terrace.

She would collect Mrs Moorsby and, after a quiet word to Miss Henley and Lord Theo, pay her respects to her host and hostess, and return to London.

She had a race to prepare for—and, hopefully, a mount with a sore hoof that was now fully healed.

Chapter Twelve

The next morning, Giff sat in his office in the committee room at Parliament, the draft of the anti-slavery bill lying unseen on the table before him, while he read for a second time the letter he'd just received from his mother.

Dropping it, he wiped a hand across his face, his stomach churning with a familiar mix of resentment, the slow burn of anger, an ache of hurt—and a touch of guilt. Damn it, the work he was doing in Parliament *was* important and required all of his attention, especially now, when they were at a crucial point in pressing forward the passage of two major reform bills. Why did his mother have to choose this moment to increase the urgency of her harangues?

Before he could decide what to reply, if he replied, one of his fellow members walked into the room.

'Jolly fine morning,' Thomas Thetford said, giving Giff a slap on the back, entirely insensitive to the cloud of irritation enveloping him. 'My, that chit you've been squiring about for your godmother—she's as much a hoyden as you've said. Going to race in the park! And with Lord Al-fred Wendemere!' He chuckled. 'Looking magnificent, of course, but you allow the girl a looser rein than I would.'

It took a moment for the words to penetrate Giff's ab-straction—and once they did, he couldn't believe he'd heard correctly. 'What did you say?'

Thetford peered down at him. 'Lost in perusing the draft, were you? Brilliant piece of writing.'

'Yes, yes,' he returned impatiently, 'but what was it you said about racing this morning?'

'In Hyde Park,' Thetford returned. 'Not me. I was in Pen-dergrew's tilbury. Meant to walk here this morning—lovely day—but he saw me and took me up.'

'About Miss Lattimar!'

'Ah, yes. Saw the Lattimar girl by Hyde Park Corner, challenging Wendemere. Impromptu match, I suppose, since I doubt you'd have encouraged it.'

'Certainly not!' Giff returned, indignant. 'One would rather shoot Wendemere than permit him to ride with an innocent maid.'

'Won't comment on the "innocent" part. Looked like she was leading him on, to me. But they were about to race for certain.' Thetford shook his head. 'In high fettle, she was. Looked like one of the Furies, about to deliver vengeance!'

'It'll be nothing to what I'll deliver, if she's come to any harm,' Giff muttered, rising. 'Just for the record,' he told Thetford as he shrugged into his coat, 'I didn't know and I don't approve.'

Nearly at a run, he left the buildings, fetched his mount from the stables and set off to Hyde Park as quickly as the throng of handcarts, barrows, wagons and pedestrians going about their morning errands allowed, curbing his fury and anxiety with difficulty as he went.

Heedless, careless, unthinking! he fumed. Not just of her reputation—teasing Wendemere, for the devil's sake!—but of her very safety! And here he'd thought she'd finally matured beyond her childhood wildness.

Granted, she was an accomplished rider, but if that reprobate caught her alone, especially as he'd believe she had encouraged him...

He bit down an oath and urged his mount faster.

Once through the gates of Hyde Park, he spurred the horse to a gallop, heading down Rotten Row, the most likely venue for a race. Sure enough, as he neared Kensington Gardens, he saw Temper, mounted on her gelding Arion. At least, he thought, blowing out a breath of relief, she was surrounded by a small entourage—not alone with Wendemere. Who, he noted as he slowed his mount to a walk to approach them, was nowhere to be seen.

'I knew you rode well, but that was magnificent,' a female he recognised as Miss Henley was saying.

The gentleman nodding at her words was Lord Theo. 'Indeed it was,' he said and laughed. 'Wendemere looked as shocked as he was disgruntled to have been bested—though it was a near-run thing. If your mount hadn't summoned that last burst of speed, I believe he would have beaten you.'

'Had Arion not been recovering from a sore hoof, it wouldn't have even been close,' Temper said, smiling—until she noticed Giff approaching and her whole body stiffened.

'How neatly you dispensed with the annoyance of dealing with him,' Miss Henley said.

'Masterful,' Lord Theo seconded. 'Having agreed before all of us that, should he lose, he would never approach you again, he'll not be able to go back on his word—not if he wants to hang on to the precarious foothold that remains to him in the *ton*.'

'Even his friends would snub him if he cheated on a wager,' Miss Henley said.

Just before he reached them, two riders on side-saddle halted beside the group, trailed by a groom. The Misses Avery, Giff saw—and, despite his pique, he nearly had to smile at the expression of distaste that crossed Temper's face before she schooled her countenance into a polite smile.

'What's this—a wager?' Miss Avery said. 'Not with Lord Alfred, whom we just passed, looking to be in a tearing rage!'

'Miss Avery, Miss Mary,' Lord Theo said, 'good morning to you.'

'And to you, Lord Theo. How pleasant to encounter you this morning!' She gave the Marquess's son a charming smile before offering a tiny nod to Temper and Miss Henley. 'And you, too, ladies.

'But you must tell me, Miss Lattimar,' she persisted, turning to address Temper. 'Did you truly make a wager with Lord Alfred? How...shocking! You are even more outrageous than I thought.'

'Indeed,' Temper replied coolly—but the militant spark in her eye told Giff she was working hard to curb her annoyance. 'I expect I can be far more outrageous than you thought.'

'So what were the terms? Come, you must tell me.'

'Really, Jane,' Miss Mary protested, looking embarrassed by her sister's persistence.

'She might as well, Mary,' she replied, brushing off her

sister. 'After all, Lord Alfred will surely bandy them abroad. The news will be all over the *ton* by this afternoon.'

'I'm sure it will,' Miss Henley said, irony in her voice. 'But I doubt Lord Alfred will be telling the story.'

Just then, the rest of party noticed his approach—or rather, Miss Avery did. 'Mr Newell,' she trilled, giving him the same coquettish smile she'd turned on Collington. 'Come to collect your naughty charge? I don't envy you, trying to keep a lady as…spirited as Miss Lattimar in line!'

'I'm sure curbing a spirit—or a tongue—would be impossible for you,' Temper said sweetly. 'Come to hurry me home, Mr Newell?' she said, her guarded tone telling him she was preparing for a confrontation.

His momentary humour over her riposte to the Avery girl evaporated as he recalled the very real confrontation that must come. 'Yes. Mrs Moorsby is waiting for you.'

Miss Avery laughed. 'I imagine her poor chaperon is *always* awaiting her return from some scrape or other! We will leave you to your task, Mr Newell. Miss Lattimar.'

With a dismissive nod to Temper, she turned back to Collington. 'Would you care to join my sister and I for another turn around Rotten Row, Lord Theo? It's such a lovely morning!'

Lord Theo looked less than enthusiastic about accompanying the sisters, Giff thought, but there was hardly any way he could refuse Miss Avery without being rude. 'I'd be delighted.'

'Shall we go, then?' Miss Avery said, signalling her horse to start.

'Thank you for meeting me,' Temper said to Miss Henley as the others trotted off. 'Newell, have you time for me to see Miss Henley home?'

Seeming to perceive the tension between the two of them, Miss Henley shook her head. 'No need for an escort, Miss Lattimar. I have my groom. Shall I see you at the Witherspoons' dinner and musicale tomorrow?'

'Mrs Moorsby hasn't informed me of our plans, but probably.'

'Good day to both of you, then,' Miss Henley said. 'And bravo, well done, Miss Lattimar!' With a mischievous smile that rendered her plain face almost pretty, she signalled her groom and set off.

As soon as they were out of earshot, Giff dropped his cheerful demeanour. 'Merciful Heavens, Temper, what in the world were you about?'

Before he could launch into full rhetorical flow, Temper held up a hand. 'Enough, Giff! I know you want to ring a peal over me, but wait until we get back to Vraux House. I'd rather the whole of London didn't hear you abusing me.'

He pressed his lips together for a moment, her calm paradoxically increasing his fury and annoyance. 'Until Vraux House, then.'

In any event, the streets were now so crowded that riding side by side to carry on a conversation would have been impossible. With difficulty, Giff contained the anger and the questions, biding his time until they reached the privacy of Vraux House.

Some ten minutes later, they arrived and turned their horses over to the groom. Once they were in the house, Giff could restrain himself no more.

'Good Heavens, Temper, what were you thinking?' he demanded as soon as they'd crossed the threshold into the front parlour. 'I know you don't care about, indeed want to *encourage*, the image of yourself as fast and unreliable—but Wendemere? You can be sure that by this afternoon, the Avery chit will have spread the news throughout London that you wagered with the most amoral, dissolute man in the entire *ton*! Whatever possessed you to do such a crack-brained thing?'

She recoiled a little under his vehemence, then raised her chin. 'If you must know, he caught me in the shrubbery at Trenton Manor yesterday. He wanted... Well, I suppose you know what he wanted. I...put him off by challenging him to the race. The terms, as you heard, being that, if he lost, he would leave me alone. And lose he did. So why are you taking me to task? Having the snide Miss Avery spread whispers confirming the image the *ton* has of me anyway, thereby scaring off any true gentleman, should help me accomplish my goal of ending this unwanted Season more speedily. I'll not apologise for either of those achievements!'

Though Giff heard her, he was having a hard time getting past the appalling image of Temper all alone, trapped in the garden in the grip of a doubtless drunken Wendemere—whose only moral principle was gratifying his own desires. 'You were caught alone in the garden with him? How did you get him to agree to a race—instead of taking what he wanted then and there?'

'By telling him if he insisted, I'd comply, but think the worse of him. And by implying, if he won on *my* terms, he'd get more than a kiss. One can always count on a man to be ruled more by lust than logic. And to feel himself superior to a woman in any pursuit he considers "manly". Like horsemanship.'

'But you took a ridiculous chance! With Arion ailing, how could you be so sure of beating him?'

'I concede, it was hardly a perfect scheme, but it was the best I could come up with in the heat of the…situation. And I admit, I was more than a little uncertain of the outcome. Under normal circumstances, I trust Arion to fly like the west wind he's named for, but after his recent injury, there was a chance I'd have to fulfil the challenge on a job horse—and count on superior riding skill to make up for whatever the mount lacked. Huggins confirmed that racing wouldn't hurt the hoof, but warned Arion might favour it and lack his normal speed. Fortunately, even less than his normal speed was good enough.'

'Still, you took a ridiculous risk. And where was Mrs Moorsby? How *could* you have been foolish enough to walk alone with Wendemere in the garden to begin with?' he demanded, anger over what she might have brought down on herself swamping the relief that she'd survived it, safe and unharmed.

'I didn't go off with him alone,' she snapped back impatiently. 'Miss Henley and I were walking together, discussing Lieutenant Williamson's talk—and how wonderful that was, Giff, you can only imagine! Lady Henley sent Lord Theo to fetch us, but we passed by some marvellous carved Sanskrit stones on the way back, and I…lingered to study them. How was I to know Wendemere would turn up?'

'If it hadn't been Wendemere, it could have been someone else. Good L— heavens, Temperance, with your reputation, you should know better than to let yourself be caught alone anywhere! What were you thinking?'

'Actually, at the moment he accosted me,' she said, her voice gruff, 'I was thinking how much I needed to thank you for giving me such a treat. If I'd known you were going to rake me over the coals so…unhandsomely, I might have had s-second thoughts…'

Her voice breaking a little, with one quick, impatient gesture she swiped at the tears beginning to track down her cheeks.

His anger evaporated. Negligent she'd been, perhaps—but also brave and fierce. Instead of dissolving in tears, or offering what would have probably been a futile resistance at being restrained and threatened, she'd devised an ingenious plan to escape and had implemented it, knowing her tools to win the wager were compromised. All without any assistance.

He couldn't remember ever seeing fierce, rebellious Temper in tears. Unable to stop himself, he reached over and drew her into his arms. 'I'm so sorry,' he said softly into her hair. 'It must have been terrifying.'

He heard the muffled sob she suppressed, sensed the trembling she could not and felt even worse for having harangued her. He was grateful that she'd accepted the comfort he'd felt compelled to offer her.

Fortunately, she pushed him away before desire could reassert itself.

'It was…daunting,' she admitted. 'I think this time it shall be Gregory's brandy instead of tea.'

Ah, Temper—frightened, desperately seeking escape—but ever defiant. As she went to the sideboard and poured them both a glass, he said, 'I expect you've earned a portion of spirits. And you are right—I shouldn't have scolded you. If anyone deserves blame, it's me, for abandoning you. Had I accompanied you to Trenton Manor, you wouldn't have ended up walking in that garden alone—and Wendemere wouldn't have dared accost you. I failed you and Lady Sayleford, not providing the protection I promised.'

'Nonsense, Giff, you mustn't blame yourself! Heavens, you can't dog my every step! I won't apologise for the race, for I think that disposed of the problem of Wendemere quite tidily. He won't dare approach me in public with his disgusting innuendoes, lest he lose face even among his dissolute friends. But you are right—I shouldn't walk alone anywhere, in London or the countryside. I shall take great care never to forget that again, for though he might be compelled to avoid me in public, I doubt Wendemere would pass up an opportunity to take his revenge should he catch me alone. And I can't count on tricking him again.'

'Thank heaven for that! My apologies, too, for being so churlish, a mood for which—' he gave her a wry grin '—you aren't *entirely* responsible.' He accepted the glass and took a deep drink. 'I've been needing this all morning.'

'Indeed?' she said, tilting her head at him enquiringly. 'Something incited your wrath *before* you discovered me playing the hoyden? Did the draft bill not go well?'

He heaved a sigh. 'No, the wording of the bill is excellent and we're moving forward with it.'

'Bad news from Fensworth, then?' She looked up at him, concern and sympathy in her face. Drat, did she have to be perceptive as well as fierce and brave?

'Just another letter from Mama.' He shrugged, trying to mitigate his anger, unease and the impending doom of duty. 'More of the usual haranguing about funds, only more so. Maybe…maybe I ought to take you up on your offer to review the eligible females and recommend one you think might suit. I may not like everyone pressing me to find a rich bride, but even I admit Mama is right. I've been a man

grown for some time, and ought to curtail my "private pleasures"—' he grimaced at his mother's dismissive description of not just his personal enjoyments, but of the work he
was trying to do '—and assume responsibility for assuring
my own finances. As she pointed out, I will not inherit the
estate and the drain of my "increasingly expensive upkeep"
robs my father and brother Robert of funds they need to invest in repairs, improvements and supplies.'

She was silent a moment. 'That's a rather harsh assessment. Does your mama have no conception of how important the work you do in Parliament is?'

He shook his head, not able to conceal all the hurt. 'I
don't think she knows—or cares. Her focus is, as always,
on Robert, the heir.'

'As it always has been?' Temper said softly.

He shrugged. 'He has an important task. Working with
Papa to manage the estate and keep it as profitable as possible. Dropping prices for grain since the end of the wars
has affected producers as well as workers. It's been several
years since Papa has been able to afford to let Mama rent a
house here for the Season. I know she resents my living in
town, when the estate lacks the funds for her even to come
to London to acquire the gowns and bonnets she loves. To
her great chagrin, she's forced to make do with garments
made up by the village seamstress from the fashion plates
she supplies.'

'An unforgivable offence,' Temper said drily.

Giff grinned wryly, Temper's understanding pouring
a soothing balm over his anger and irritation. 'It is, to
her. Here I am, surrounded by theatres, shops, friends and
entertainments, to say nothing of the pleasures of flesh,
while she is stuck in the middle of marsh and fenland, with

hardly enough funds to purchase new gowns to impress the neighbourhood.'

Temper shook her head and, after a brief hesitation, reached out to press his hand. Her turn to offer sympathy and, grateful, he squeezed her fingers in return. And held on, his chest swelling with a mix of affection and the delicious sensual pleasure evoked by the feel of her hand in his.

With her seated near him, her understanding gaze fixed on him, the sweet satin softness of her palm against his heightening all his senses, he felt more energised and fully alive than he had in weeks.

But then desire flamed hotter, firing him with the urge to lean down and kiss her. As if scalded, he sat back and jerked his hand free.

She rubbed at hers, as if she'd felt that sudden heat, too. It was a moment before she said, her voice a little unsteady, 'Sounds like your mama has two admirable sons. It's a shame she doesn't seem to recognise it.'

Had his mother ever appreciated him? Giff couldn't remember a time when he wasn't the second choice, the afterthought walking behind her, tugging at her skirts, while she showered all her attention on Robert. Pushing away the painful memories, he shrugged. 'One gets used to it.'

'Does one ever get used to being ignored? Undervalued?' she asked softly.

She was thinking of her relationship with her father—and how she was treated by the *ton*, Giff knew. Whatever sense of being overlooked he'd felt with his mother was nothing compared to the void between her and Lord Vraux. He, at least, had society's respect and a sense of doing important work as a standing Member of Parliament. Whereas she'd been labelled a wanton by many in the *ton* who'd never even met her. *Looked like she was leading him on to me*, Thetford had said.

Before he could think how to respond, she shook her head, as if dismissing the unhappy reflections. 'So, you think you might be ready to yield to your mama's promptings and find a rich wife? Though we must find you one who has more qualities than just a fat purse. A thrifty household manager, a gifted conversationalist and skilled hostess would be on the list, I think. At least a modicum of beauty and a good dose of common sense.'

Even discussing the matter grated on him. 'According to Mama, the financial situation is dire enough that I don't have time to look for a paragon. A female with a fat dowry and no qualms about accepting a marriage of convenience is all I require.'

After a moment's hesitation, she said, 'You don't want a wife who's fallen in love with you?'

He grimaced. 'Since it's highly unlikely I'm going to fall in love with Miss Fat Purse, no. It would be…awkward, dealing with the excess of emotion, tears and tantrums that would ensue. I've had my fill of those, dealing with my mother all these years. Fortunately, I'm not in need of an heir, though I suppose, if she really wants them, I would be willing to give my wife children.'

'So, someone who is rich—and would be happy enough to allow you to continue your pleasant association with the muslin company?'

Hearing it stated so baldly, he had to laugh. 'Ah, Temper, trust you to reduce matters to their essentials.'

She smiled back. 'It's easier to proceed if one goes to the nub of the matter. If you require so little of a wife, Giff, why not marry me? I'm certainly rich enough, you could continue your exploits among the demi-monde with my blessing and, as long as you promise to set aside enough of my dowry to allow me to travel, I'd call it a fair bargain.'

A brilliant smile broke out on her face. 'In fact, the more I think about it, the more perfect the idea becomes! We've known each other for ever, so there wouldn't be the awkwardness of dealing with a near-stranger. We both understand what we each want and need. It could be a perfect partnership, Giff! What do you say?'

Chapter Thirteen

Marry Temper? Desire her as he did, Giff had never given the notion more than a passing thought, believing she saw him—until recently, anyway—only as her older brother's friend. She possessed few of the characteristics she'd just mentioned as desirable in a politician's wife. But then, he'd stated only two requirements for a wife—that she have money and no inclination to hang about him, demanding attention. Temper certainly met both of those qualifications.

But...*marry* Temper? Could he really take her as his wife...and keep his distance? Permission to dally among the muslin company wasn't a very attractive proposition when he considered the pleasure he might enjoy at home—with Temper in his bed.

In fact, between being preoccupied with squiring Temper and his duties in Parliament, he hadn't visited the ladies in weeks.

'You would marry me if I let you go your own way?' he asked, probing at the matter tentatively, like poking a nest you think, but are not quite sure, the wasps have abandoned. 'And what of…intimate matters?'

Her face colouring, she looked away, not meeting his eyes. 'A *marriage blanc* would be a requirement.'

Giff stared at her, perplexed and, he admitted, the male in him a little affronted. He knew she was attracted to him. The air fairly buzzed with sensual tension when they were near each other, and he knew he hadn't imagined the zing of contact when he touched her of late. So…why this reluctance to take the attraction further?

Maybe a lifetime of watching the disdain with which her mother had been treated for indulging *her* desires made Temper determined to repress her own. Or the distaste for the undeserved comments—like those of Thetford—and unsolicited advances—like those of Wendemere—to which her unjustified reputation subjected her made her want to deny the passionate nature he, and any man with breath in his body, sensed in her.

Whatever the reason, despite the fact that he was her brother's best friend, if he actually had a husband's rights to her body, he couldn't think of anything *less* convenient and more designed to drive a man crazy than being married to Temper, having promised not to touch her.

And then there were the exploits she'd probably embroil herself in, here and abroad. He could hardly devote the necessary time and energy to his responsibilities in Parliament if he had to keep one eye always on Temper, rescuing her from her impulsive starts and protecting her from men seeking to take advantage. Lord help the hapless man permanently saddled with the task of controlling *her*!

Still, she'd made him a generous offer and he didn't want to hurt her feelings. Choosing his words with care, he said,

'That's a tempting proposal, Temper, and I do appreciate it. But—'

'—you'd rather not saddle yourself with a handful like me?' she said gruffly, still not meeting his eyes. 'I understand. You really do deserve a better wife, Giff. Someone with those talents and attributes I just mentioned. A woman you would be eager, rather than resigned, to marry. I suppose you'll just have to put your mama off a while longer while I help you look for this paragon. I just thought for a moment the bargain might work—fulfilling your need for funds and mine for freedom. We're friends who respect and trust each other. At least, I hope you feel that way about me.'

'You know I do,' he said, conflicted. It would be madness to accept her proposal under the terms she'd set, but he knew his refusal must hurt. And foolish as it was, the idea of claiming Temper as his wife, once broached, had an insidious appeal…

She gave him a swift, strained smile. 'You were probably my best hope of attaining my desires speedily. Once Miss Avery finishes spreading the word of my exploit with Wendemere, I shouldn't have much trouble discouraging respectable gentleman. Doubtless, I'll be able to end the Season unwed—but I will still have to endure the whole Season. And even after that, there's no guarantee Papa will release any funds to me. Whereas, if I married someone who sympathised with my hopes and was willing to let me to pursue my dreams, I might not have to spend the rest of my life in England, alone and…miserable.'

She looked so woebegone, Giff felt even worse. But before he could commit the idiocy of reconsidering, she shook her head again. 'Heavens, listen to what a poor, pathetic creature I sound! No, Giff, you're right to hold out for a

proper wife, not saddle yourself with a hoyden whose chequered reputation—and impulsive behaviour—would make
her a millstone around the neck of a rising politician. We
won't speak of it again.'

He agreed completely with her assessment—so why did
the conclusion make him feel so…unsatisfied? 'Very well,
we'll speak of it no more,' he said at last.

'I've taken you away from your duties long enough,' she
said briskly, gathering up their glasses and rising to take
them back to the sideboard. 'Thank you for riding to my
rescue—even though it proved unnecessary. I shall *try* to
be more circumspect and avoid situations that require your
intervention.'

'I'd appreciate that,' he said, rising as well, 'since I'm
likely to be called on the carpet by my godmother for this
event. Though the *ton* may only learn about the race through
Hyde Park, being Lady Sayleford, she's sure to discover the
whole story. And then chastise me for not being present at
Trenton Manor to have averted the situation—even while
she applauds your ingenuity.'

She brightened at the compliment, making him feel better about having just disappointed her. 'I would be gratified if she considered the solution "ingenious" rather than
"madcap".'

She walked him to the door. 'Goodbye, Giff. I hope your
committee meetings go well.'

Giving her a bow, he walked out, heading to the hackney stand to engage a jarvey to return to Parliament. Relieved to be returning with their relationship unchanged,
but still…unsettled.

Would she really end up alone and miserable?

He'd always thought she would eventually find some

compatible gentleman and yield to the practicality of marriage. Based on her last comments, she was nowhere close to reaching that conclusion.

Still, his major concern was making sure she ended the Season unharmed, whether or not she ended it engaged. It wasn't his responsibility to see that she ended up happy.

But she was such a fierce, bright, compelling spirit, he couldn't help wanting her to be.

The next evening, Gifford looked down the length of the dinner table and suppressed a groan. Apparently Lady Witherspoon was a friend of the late Lady Chilford—and had heard the tale about Temperance that the woman's daughter, Miss Avery, had doubtless whispered to every of member of society she'd encountered since that ill-fated race the previous morning.

Temperance and Mrs Moorsby had been seated in the middle of the long table, surrounded by dowagers who must be the hostess's friends or relations and two elderly gentlemen. No young or single men sat within three chairs of them.

Temper herself had given him an ironic lift of her brow as they took their places, indicating she was well aware of the significance of her placement.

Glancing down at her now, he had to suppress a grin. From the relish with which she was bedazzling the elderly gentleman beside her, she was amused by their hostess's manoeuvre. After all, her desire not to marry was so singular, the woman couldn't be blamed for failing to recognise that she'd delighted, rather than slighted, Temper by placing her far away from eligible gentlemen.

Delighted, however, he was not. To his great annoyance, he had ended up with Miss Avery for a dinner partner.

As dinner progressed, matters only worsened. With society's richest matrimonial prize, Lord Solsworth, seated on Miss Avery's other side, he'd hoped to avoid becoming the sole focus of her attention. But, impervious to the glare the Countess of Agremont kept directing towards her son, Solsworth sidestepped Miss Avery's every conversational opening and devoted himself to the married lady on his other side.

Leaving Giff the only eligible gentleman on whom Miss Avery could work her charms.

In the few moments when Miss Avery turned from him to accord the bare minimum of polite comments to the gentleman on her other side, Giff watched Solsworth. The duke's heir hadn't seen Temper since the race, Giff knew, but he'd undoubtedly heard all the salacious stories. Giff couldn't tell from the glances the man occasionally directed towards Temper whether he'd been intrigued, or disgusted, by the accounts.

As soon as the ladies left them to their brandy, however, Solsworth turned to him. 'I understand Miss Lattimar bested Wendemere in a race in Hyde Park?'

He stiffened, waiting for the criticism to come. 'She did.'

'And you knew of this race beforehand?'

'Most assuredly not! Else I would have put a stop to it— though I would have had no doubts she would win. She's an excellent horsewoman.'

Solsworth nodded. 'I'm relieved to hear it. I would otherwise have to re-evaluate my good opinion of you. No true gentleman would have allowed a lady to meet that reprobate Wendemere unaccompanied! I've heard he's been pressing his lewd attentions on her. Can't say I'm happy she decided to take matters in her own hands to dispense with him, but the results were certainly impressive. If the scum dares approach her now, he'll lose the few remaining friends he has.'

Giff sighed. 'You'll hardly be the only member of society to disapprove her methods.'

Solsworth laughed shortly. 'Every beldame in London I've encountered since yesterday has condemned her. Including, of course, my mother.' He grimaced. '*She* would pair me up with the eldest Avery girl who, for all that she is lovely and well dowered, makes me feel like the last mouse fleeing the larder, running smack into the cat.'

'She does…press too hard,' Giff agreed. 'Although no thanks to you for giving me any help during dinner.'

'Sorry, old man,' Solsworth replied, his grin unrepentant. 'But when one is touted as the richest matrimonial prize in London—' he rolled his eyes '—one must protect oneself.'

'Understood,' Giff said. Having apparently discovered what he needed to, Solsworth turned to address their host, leaving Giff alone with his thoughts.

As he'd suspected, the duke's heir didn't intend to be swayed by the disapproval of his formidable mother. Did he mean to court Temper openly, or simply remain an admirer?

Solsworth was a bit young to think of marriage—but a woman like Temper didn't come along very often. He appeared to be strong-willed and confident enough to earn her respect, and intelligent enough to try diplomacy to dissuade her from rash actions, rather than incite her rebellion by forbidding them. If he did pursue her, it wouldn't be for her fortune, of which he had no need, but only because he couldn't resist the beautiful, unconventional essence of her.

If he succeeded in winning her affection, it would be accounted a brilliant match for her.

Why could Giff not feel more enthusiastic about it?

Perhaps because he doubted the wife of a duke's heir would be permitted to roam the world, collecting treasures and having adventures. Could Temper be satisfied with being mistress over a vast ducal empire in England?

Giff didn't think so. And chided himself for feeling relieved.

But then, who *would* make a better husband for the uniqueness that was Temper? Giff wasn't sure. He just knew he hadn't yet met a man he thought would be equal to the job.

Giff's respite ended when the gentlemen rejoined the ladies. While Solsworth, to his mingled relief and unease, made a beeline for Temper, Miss Avery sought him out, first bringing him tea and then asking if he would take a turn about the room with her.

As there was no polite way to refuse, he suppressed a sigh and offered his arm. Somehow this evening, he needed to diplomatically convey that she was wasting her time, attempting to attach him.

Once they were beyond hearing distance of the several groups enjoying their tea, Miss Avery said, 'Have you recovered from the shock of rescuing Miss Lattimar from her latest start?'

Determined not to be drawn into comments that could be construed as either criticism or support, he said blandly, 'She rather rescued herself, I think.'

Miss Avery shook her head. 'She is so bold and beautiful, it's a shame she suffers under the burden of such an impulsive nature. Our situations being somewhat similar, I had hoped we might be friends.'

Biting back the observation that disparaging another female in the presence of other gentlemen was not a tactic likely to win friendship, he'd intended to utter a polite murmur. Then, curious how she could consider their backgrounds anything at all alike, he found himself asking, 'How, similar?'

'She already has a reputation to live down, compromising her ability to make a good match. Whereas, if I do not marry quickly, I may be thrust into a situation of such embarrassing notoriety that my ability to marry at all will be threatened.'

'Indeed? In what way?'

'I probably ought not to say anything...but then, I'm sure I can count on your discretion. As well as, I hope, your sympathy over a poor innocent female finding herself in so difficult a situation.'

Was she trying to elicit his chivalry? Regretting now that he'd invited a confidence, he replied carefully, 'Of course, you can rely on my discretion.' There being no way he was going to guarantee sympathy.

She sighed. 'I imagine you know that my *father*—' she almost spat out the word '—is Viscount Chilford. He's informed the family—in confidence, so I trust you will not repeat this information—that he intends soon to remarry. Which, as it has been two years since we lost my dear mama, I could forgive, even if I cannot understand how he could bring himself to put someone else in her place! I know men have *needs*, but the woman he means to marry is his former mistress, who bore him a child out of wedlock! A low-born former *governess*! The fact that, should he actually commit such a…travesty, my sister and I will be made laughing stocks—'

'Please, Miss Avery, you must say no more,' Giff interrupted, needing to stop her before she uttered anything else to offend him—or embarrass her, once he revealed his connections to the woman she was savaging. 'Viscount Chilford's natural son, Mr Tawny, is a member of my party in Parliament, and a talented gentleman whom I highly respect. Since he also happens to be a close friend of Miss Lattimar's brothers, Christopher and Gregory, I am well aware of your father's plans to marry Mr Tawny's mother. A charming woman I have met on several occasions. I really can't allow you to abuse either of them.'

Her face going white, then red, Miss Avery was rendered, for once, speechless. After a moment, she said, 'Then I will say no more.'

'Perhaps I'd better return you to our hostess,' Giff said, finally sensing an opening where he might politely but permanently escape the girl's clutches. 'Miss Avery, you are a lovely, highly respected lady who will undoubtedly make a fine match, regardless of who your father marries. But given your desire to wed quickly and with me being too occupied by my Parliamentary duties to consider marriage any time soon, you might do better to bestow the privilege of your attention upon…other gentlemen.'

It took a full moment for the implications of that speech, as diplomatic as he'd been able to make it while still conveying his point, to fully register. Giff could tell when it did, as Miss Avery's already pink cheeks darkened to cherry.

'I see. I had heard that you were in dire need of a rich wife—' She halted, pressing her lips together for a moment before continuing, with a forced smile. 'But I see the rumours were in error—as they so often are. How very awkward! I do apologise.' Though her cheeks remained red, she continued smoothly, 'I hope you won't hold my…unfortunate candour against me, that we can remain friends.'

Her brittle smile didn't reassure him that the feelings she would have towards him in future, after that embarrassing faux pas, would be at all friendly. But happy to grasp any olive branch, he said, 'Of course. It would be my privilege.'

He'd turned to walk her back to the group around her aunt when suddenly she halted. 'Is…is *Miss Lattimar* also aware of my father's intentions?'

'I'm sure she must be. As I mentioned, her brother Christopher is a close friend of Mr Tawny.'

Miss Avery sucked in a deep breath. Giff watched with dismay as the mortification of her expression turned to anger. 'So…she has been *laughing* at me all this time! Pretending to be polite, all the while sniggering behind her hand, knowing of the humiliation that awaits me!'

Alarmed, Giff quickly replied, 'Not at all, Miss Avery! Though she reveres Mr Tawny, given her own…difficult circumstances, I'm sure she would have nothing but understanding for how…distressing the situation has to be for you. I assure you, mockery, or delighting in the misfortune of others, is not in her character.'

'She is female, isn't she?'

Giff was trying to think of some placating response when she shook her head, seeming to master some of the anger and chagrin. 'But then, Miss Lattimar is a most unusual female, isn't she? Are you sure you don't have ambitions in that direction?'

The last thing he wanted was for Miss Avery to circulate *that* rumour. 'Certainly not! Miss Lattimar is my best friend's little sister, which is why I was asked to look after her. Somewhat of a hoyden, I have to admit,' he added, silently begging Temper's pardon for disparaging her to this girl who'd already gone to some lengths to present Temper in the worst possible light. 'And most decidedly *not* the sort of wife a politician would seek, even if he were ready to marry.'

'I don't doubt she would lead you a merry chase,' Miss Avery agreed sweetly. 'Although I've heard she, too, claims to have no interest in marrying.'

Hoping that reinforcing that truth might make a girl who was desperate to marry less inclined to see Temper as a rival—or a target for her malice—Giff replied, 'Unusual as that is, I can confirm the truth of *that* rumour. Miss Lattimar has always had a desire to travel the world—a dream she believes a husband might not view kindly.'

'I expect not. He'd be more likely to relegate her to the country, where she could cause him no embarrassment. And use her dowry to fund portions for their children and improve his estate.'

'Probably,' Giff agreed. 'Though I imagine she will eventually end up wedded, for those reasons and more, she's hoping to delay matrimony—at least until after she's had a chance to travel.'

'I wish her well in her ambitions, then,' Miss Avery said as they approached the tea table. 'I'll let you return to your... unusual charge. And thank you for a most...illuminating conversation.'

'A pleasure, as always, Miss Avery,' Giff said, relinquishing her arm. *A blatant falsehood, that compliment*, he thought as he walked away, conscious of a deep relief at having, he hoped, permanently escaped Miss Avery's matrimonial manoeuvrings.

However, he couldn't help worrying that, despite her fine words, his revelations had deepened Miss Avery's jealous dislike of Temperance Lattimar.

Chapter Fourteen

Three nights later, Temper sat reluctantly in the carriage being driven to a ball being given by Lady Arnold, aunt of the snide Miss Avery. When informed of the invitation, she'd initially protested to Mrs Moorsby that she'd rather not attend an event honouring a female she actively disliked, only to discover that not only she and her chaperon, but Lady Sayleford herself, were to attend.

If her imperious sponsor intended to grace the ball with her presence, Temper knew there was no way she could avoid it.

With Lady Sayleford settled in the carriage beside her, Mrs Moorsby on the backward-facing seat beside Giff, her sponsor turned to Temper.

'I realise you are not happy about attending Lady Arnold's ball—and, no, Angela didn't convey your feelings to me. I've heard that Miss Avery has been unpleasant to you on several occasions. However, Lady Arnold is a friend of long standing and I could not slight her by failing to ap-

pear—or failing to bring along the young lady I am sponsoring. I understand Miss Avery has made overtures to you,
too, Gifford, although I expect a gentleman of your address
can sidestep them handily enough, if you choose.'

To Temper's amusement, Giff first looked as surprised
as Temper had been—honestly, Lady Sayleford and her
sources of information were uncanny!—then grimaced. 'I
did choose, and I hope I have "sidestepped" as diplomatically as possible. However, I would not have avoided the
ball. Despite her obvious chagrin at my making my, um,
lack of interest known, Miss Avery said she hoped we could
remain friends.'

'With friends like that, I'd watch my back,' Temper murmured.

Giff smiled wryly. 'I intend to, being no more trusting
of her good will than you are. But I encountered her coming out of Hatchard's yesterday and she pressed me to agree
that I would be attending tonight's affair. Though most of
the time, she grates on my nerves, I have to admit having
a little sympathy.'

'Because her father is to remarry?' Temper said. 'I suppose I can sympathise with her desire to be wed and gone
before that happens—if she weren't so *blatant* about her
need to attach someone. After all, it would be hard for anyone to watch her mother displaced.'

Giff gave a short laugh. 'Impossible, for her. It was all
I could do to remain polite, after she began ranting about
what an *embarrassment* it will be for Ben's father to marry
the "low-born governess" who was his former mistress.'

'She dared to criticise Mrs Tawny?' Temper said indignantly.

'Miss Avery is rather…intemperate,' Lady Sayleford said.

'But she's correct that, on the face of it, the Viscount *is* making a mésalliance. Though Miss Avery may neither know—nor would she probably care—Angelica Tawny was the woman Chilford intended to marry. Only a sudden reversal in the fortunes of the estate he was to inherit and severe pressure from his family to marry an heiress forced him to marry Miss Avery's mother. Nor did he know at the time of his wedding that the woman he loved was carrying their child.'

Temper shook her head. 'You really do know everything about everyone. I think it's marvellous that, after loving each other for so long and so faithfully, they will finally be able to claim the joy they deserve.'

Lady Sayleford nodded. 'As do I—and that is one wedding I shall be delighted to attend. Robert Avery did his duty, but a chilly business it was. There was no pretence of love; I don't think they'd met more than a handful of times before wedding. His family got a much-needed influx of cash for the estate and his bride the guarantee that she would one day become a viscountess.'

'A cold bargain indeed,' Temper said. 'Although I bet it's one her daughter would jump to accept.'

Lady Sayleford nodded. 'I'm afraid the elder daughter possesses the same cold, self-interested viewpoint her mother had. So I would second Miss Lattimar's advice that, if you have…disappointed her, Newell, deal cautiously with Miss Avery.'

'Don't worry, Godmother, I shall be on my guard,' Giff assured her.

Just then the carriage arrived at Lady Arnold's town house, an imposing edifice in Berkeley Square quite as elegant as Lady Sayleford's home. 'Certainly looks as though she comes equipped with a dowry large enough to tempt someone,' Temper remarked as the ladies exited the carriage.

'What a shame she would come with it,' Giff murmured in her ear as they walked in.

After greeting their hostess and her protégées—Miss Avery's brittle smile in response to her curtsy sending a little frisson up her spine—Temper put thoughts of the unpleasant young woman behind her. Freed by Lady Sayleford, who told them that, having put in the obligatory appearance, she intended to leave within the half-hour, her party went off to find more amenable company.

She was delighted to discover Miss Henley and her mother along with Lord Theo and some of his more dissolute friends. As the dancing began, though she never lacked for partners, Temper did notice that some of the more respectable young men who had flocked to her at other social events kept their distance.

Miss Avery had spread her tales well. Once she caught the girl's gaze resting on her—gloating, perhaps?—but as the tale-bearing served Temper's purposes, she was happy to allow Miss Avery her triumph.

Besides, if her satisfaction over diminishing the number of Temper's admirers distracted her from taking retribution against Giff for rebuffing her, it was more than worth it.

Having sent Miss Henley off with Lord Theo, Temper had chosen not to dance this particular set so she might watch Giff take the floor with Lady Constance. Intelligent, lovely, a keen horsewoman, with her father's political connections, she would make Giff an admirable bride.

A notion Temper ought to embrace with more enthusiasm, she'd been telling herself when she noticed Solsworth approaching.

Was the young man as brave as she'd thought? Or just rebelling against his mama's attempt at control?

'So good to see you this evening, Miss Lattimar,' he said, bowing at he reached her side. 'How is it that you seem to be more beautiful every time I see you?'

'It must be the healthy benefits of racing in the park,' Temper replied drily.

Laughing, Solsworth said, 'I only wish I could have seen it! A nasty piece of work, Lord Alfred. How clever of you to have found a way to exile him.'

'I hope he remains exiled,' Temper said. 'In any event, I shall take care to be well chaperoned everywhere I go.'

Perhaps by mutual design, she'd had no trouble avoiding Miss Avery all evening. But not unexpectedly, with the 'catch of the *ton*' conversing with her, as the set ended and the dancers moved off the floor, Temper saw the girl walking towards them. And automatically stiffened.

'I hope you are all enjoying the evening,' Miss Avery said, addressing herself to the group of dancers now congregated near Temper. 'My aunt has just informed me that the musicians will be taking a short break. With lanterns lit along all the garden paths, it's quite lovely. She recommends that the guests go out and enjoy a bit of fresh air. Mr Newell, perhaps you would escort Lady Constance? And, Lord Theo, why don't you continue to squire Miss Henley?'

With some amusement, Temper waited to see if Miss Avery's good will would extend to pairing *her* off with Solsworth—and wasn't at all surprised to discover it wouldn't.

'I'm afraid your mother has delegated me to ask that you

attend her, Lord Solsworth,' Miss Avery said to him with an apologetic smile. 'May I escort you back to her?'

There wasn't much Solsworth could do to refuse, short of calling Miss Avery a liar. Bowing to the inevitable, he gave her a short nod. 'Of course, Miss Avery. I imagine my mother is in dire need. As usual.'

'Miss Lattimar, I'm sure one of the other gentlemen will offer you their escort. You are enjoying the party, too, I trust?'

'Very much, Miss Avery,' Temperance said, having to work to keep the irony from her voice.

'Not as much yet as I hope you will,' Miss Avery answered, with an enigmatic smile. 'Shall we be off, my lord?'

Accepting one of the several offers made after Miss Avery's departure, Temper walked out to the garden, trailed by Mrs Moorsby and a small party of friends. The cool air and the scent of night flowers' bloom *were* refreshing after the closeness and heat of the ball. It wasn't until they heard the musicians begin to tune up did the guests begin to trickle back into the ballroom.

The gardens being extensive and the light thrown by the torches limited, Temper had seen neither Miss Henley nor Giff with their partners during her own walk. Back in the ballroom, she looked about for them, hoping Miss Henley had enjoyed Lord Theo's amusing attentions—and wondering if Giff had found Lady Constance's company as appealing as her credentials to become his wife were impressive.

She ought to be happy for him if he had, she thought without enthusiasm.

Before she could locate either him or Miss Henley, Miss Avery came rushing up. 'Oh, Miss Lattimar, there you are! I'm afraid there's been an accident—nothing serious, but

Miss Henley twisted her ankle while walking down one of the garden pathways. I've had her conveyed to a bedchamber, but she refused to let me summon her mama, saying Lady Henley would make too much of a fuss. She asked if you might attend her? If it's not too much of a bother, of course.'

How like Emma Henley to not wish to be a 'bother', Temper thought. 'Of course I'll go up to her. If you'll excuse me, Mrs Moorsby?'

'How kind of you!' Miss Avery said. 'I'd escort you up myself, but—'

'No, you mustn't abandon your guests,' Temper said.

'Thank you for being so understanding! I'll just have a footman show you the way.' After summoning one of the liveried servants hovering at the edge of the ballroom, Miss Avery hurried off.

'I'll go check Miss Henley's ankle,' Temper said to Mrs Moorsby. 'If it is too painful for her to be able to return to the party, I'll come fetch you, so we may find her mother to have her taken home. Tell Mr Newell what happened, when he returns.'

'I certainly will inform him. Poor Miss Henley!'

With a nod to her chaperon, Temper walked off with the footman.

Meanwhile, as he escorted Lady Constance up the garden stairs into the house, a footman stopped and bowed to Giff. 'Mr Newell?'

After his nod, the servant continued, 'I'm to inform you that one of the guests, Miss Henley, has injured her ankle. Miss Lattimar has gone up to attend her and asked that you come assist.'

'Of course! Poor Miss Henley. If you would excuse me, Lady Constance?'

'Naturally. I hope Miss Henley isn't seriously hurt! Do send for me if I can be of any help.'

'Thank you, I will.'

Lady Constance could be a help—in so many ways, Giff thought with a sigh as he followed the footman down the hallway and up the stairs. She had every requirement a rising Member of Parliament could ask for in a wife—beauty, breeding, impressive family connections and a large dowry. In addition, she was well spoken, intelligent and, though she was by no means as blatant as Miss Avery about indicating it, he could tell she found him appealing.

Unfortunately, he felt not a particle of inclination to pursue her. After Temper, she seemed so...placid.

Probably any woman would seem less dynamic in comparison with the erratic blaze of energy that was Temper. But when he married, he needed a wife who was serene, well behaved and diplomatic—not given to the impulsive, potentially disastrous schemes of his best friend's little sister.

Such as that race in the park with Wendemere.

A few minutes later, he reached the upper floor where the bedchambers were located. Indicating the correct door, the footman bowed and walked away.

After rapping softly, Giff walked in. 'Temper? How can I help?'

From somewhere on the far side of the room, he heard Temper answer, 'That's a good question.'

Peering in the dimness of the darkened chamber, he could just make her out, walking back from the adjacent sitting room, carrying a candle. He went over to meet her, glancing around as her approaching light illumined the bed and the armchair by the hearth.

Neither of which was occupied by a young lady with an ailing ankle.

'Where is Miss Henley?'

'I don't know,' Temper said, walking over to place the candlestick on the nightstand beside the bed. 'Mrs Moorsby told you she'd been injured?'

'No, a footman informed me as I was leaving the garden. Has Miss Henley recovered?'

'Since I haven't yet located her, I don't know that, either. Miss Avery had a footman direct *me* here, explaining that Miss Henley had asked for my assistance. Not finding her in the bedchamber, I thought maybe she'd been carried into the sitting room, but she's not there, either. The footman must have been mistaken about which bedchamber she was taken to.'

'Both footmen?'

'Apparently,' Temper said drily. 'I suppose we shall have to go search for her.'

'I suppose. Although it will look a bit strange, should any of the servants discover us creeping about the bedchambers like housebreakers.'

'Better that than leaving poor Emma sitting all alone in some *other* bedchamber, believing I didn't care enough about her welfare to come help her.'

Then, as if she'd suddenly realised where they were— alone, at night, in the intimacy of a bedchamber, a mere step away from the bed, Temper froze. 'We should probably go in search...now,' she murmured, her voice unsteady.

Her jasmine scent filled his nostrils and he could feel the heat of her nearness. The light from the candle outlined her profile, the round of her bare shoulder above the full sleeves of the gown, the voluptuous curve of her breast.

Desire, thick, hot, fierce, rose in his body, clogging his throat so he couldn't croak out an answer. All he could think was how close she was, how beautiful…how much he wanted to pull her down on to that bed and kiss her.

But to do so would be a betrayal—of her trust and their friendship. Forcing his hands to remain at his sides, he cleared his throat. 'Y-yes,' he stuttered. 'We'd better go rescue Miss Henley.'

With a nod, Temper walked past him to the door and turned the handle—only to discover the door would not open. She pulled harder, but to no avail.

'What's wrong?' Giff asked.

She turned to him, her expression gone blank. 'I believe it's locked.'

'Locked!' he echoed. 'Why would anyone…?'

His voice trailed off as the events flashed through his mind. Miss Avery requesting that Temper assist an injured Miss Henley—a request she knew Temper wouldn't refuse. Two different footmen, each conveying them to the same— wrong—bedchamber.

Miss Avery, who believed Temper had been mocking her. She must be furious that Temper still captured the masculine attention she craved for herself, despite Miss Avery's attempts to disparage her.

Miss Avery who, despite his attempt at diplomacy, probably felt unpardonably insulted by his failure to respond to her advances.

'It must have been locked behind me as I crossed the chamber towards you,' Giff said, his anger rising at Miss

Avery's duplicity. 'However it was managed, we need to find another way out—*now*.'

Temper's grim expression said she understood exactly what was at stake. 'Agreed.'

But before either of them could take a step, they heard the soft snick of a bolt turning in the lock. The door opened— to reveal Lady Arnold, staring at them.

'Mr Newell...and Miss Lattimar!' Lady Arnold cried, her cheeks going crimson. 'Despite your reputation, when Jane whispered that she'd seen you sneaking up the stairs, I couldn't believe you would be so brazen as to indulge your- self with...with a *clandestine rendezvous* in *my* house! How could you abuse my hospitality so?'

'We did not come upstairs "to indulge in a clandestine rendezvous",' Giff interjected, trying to contain his fury. 'Your niece summoned both of us separately to come at- tend to Miss Henley, whom she said had injured her ankle.'

'And if that is so, where is Miss Henley?'

'A good question,' Temper muttered, her face an inscru- table mask.

Before Giff could answer that, a hubbub of voices ap- proached from the stairway. A bevy of guests hurried over to stand behind Lady Arnold, their expressions ranging from shock to outrage to blatant prurient interest.

'You see how I found them,' Lady Arnold said, turning to address the group. 'Virtually *embracing* in the seclusion of this chamber, behaviour so licentious I should not have believed it had I not seen it with my own eyes. Never have I been so deceived and humiliated!'

Turning back to Giff and Temper, she made an imperi- ous gesture. 'You will both leave my house *this instant*!'

A figure wriggled through the goggling spectators to halt by the doorway. 'Miss Lattimar!' Mrs Moorsby cried. 'Are you quite all right?'

'Very well pleasured, probably,' someone in the crowd muttered, eliciting an outburst of laughter.

'This is all a terrible mistake,' Giff felt compelled to say, although he knew explanations would likely prove useless. He and Temper had been found alone together in a bed-chamber. No one in society would care how or why they had ended up there.

Temper was completely and irretrievably ruined. And there was only one thing to be done about it.

'I am not interested in excuses, young man,' Lady Arnold snapped. '*You* should be ashamed of yourself, too. Such rakish behaviour! Now, I believe I ordered you both to leave.'

'We're finished here, Giff,' Temper murmured. Stepping past him to the doorway, she scanned the crowd, meeting the expressions of curiosity, horror and condemnation with a defiant gaze before addressing herself to her chaperon, her voice level and controlled.

'I'm quite ready to leave, Mrs Moorsby. Mr Newell, it's probably best that Mrs Moorsby and I return without you. Thank you for your escort and we will see you later.'

'None the less, I'll see you both to your carriage.'

Though he was almost spitting with fury, he had to admire the magnificence that was Temper. Facing the censorious crowd like an imperious goddess, refusing to offer any explanation, daring with splendid indifference for them to think the worst of her. She let nothing of the chagrin and outrage she must be feeling show on her face or in her manner.

If he could have found Miss Avery—conspicuously absent from the onlookers—he'd have been hard pressed not to seize her by the throat and throttle the life out of her devious body.

Moving into the hallway, she halted to make Lady Arnold a curtsy. 'Thank you for your hospitality, Lady Arnold. What a shame you possess so despicable a niece.'

'You haven't even the decency to look embarrassed,' Lady Arnold cried after her as the crowd parted to let them through.

Chapter Fifteen

Two days later, Giff paced the parlour in Vraux House, having just asked, and received, Lord Vraux's permission to ask for Temper's hand. Resigned to the necessity of proposing to her, though angry and regretful that he'd been manoeuvred into it, he was still conscious that repressed deep within was a wild stir of excitement at the notion of marrying Temper.

His nervousness increased as the door opened and Temper walked in—looking beautiful, defiant and as nervous as he was.

'Well, Jane Avery's spite has landed us in a fine pickle,' she said gruffly. 'I am so sorry, Giff.'

'None of your doing. Unfortunately, she's as damnably clever as she is malicious.'

'You shouldn't feel obligated to offer for me,' she said, looking up at him earnestly. 'There are many who would consider you prudent rather than irresponsible for refusing to marry a lady of my chequered reputation. Especially after we've both tried so hard to circulate a more accurate version of the events.'

Giff laughed shortly. 'Telling everyone we'd been summoned to Miss Henley's aide, with the footmen mistaking the chamber? It was kind of Miss Henley to offer to play along with that fiction.'

'Yes, after discovering Miss Avery had kept her chatting in the ballroom until she was sure her scheme achieved its result, Emma was happy to try to help. Granted, few in society want to believe the truth, not when Lady Arnold's version is so much more salacious.'

For a moment, Temper's sombre face cleared, and she laughed. 'Although it is almost worth dealing with this imbroglio, to have witnessed the horrified expression on her face when she opened that door.'

'"Indulging in behaviour so licentious she wouldn't have believed it, had she not seen it with her own eyes,"' Giff quoted, not nearly so amused.

'Despite her distraught niece having warned her what was taking place,' Temper added drily.

'Oh, yes, her niece. Who later said, Lady Sayleford reported to me, that she knew you were capable of such wickedness—' *damn the witch, getting in that last jab* '—but was shocked and appalled that she'd been so mistaken about my character.'

'She did manage to smear both of us quite effectively,' Temper agreed. 'Once again, knowing that most of society *also* believe I'm "capable of such wickedness" removes any obligation a gentleman might normally feel to propose.'

'I don't much care what *society* thinks. But what of Geoffrey, or Christopher? How could I look your brothers in the eye, knowing the *ton* believes I compromised you and that

I'd evaded responsibility for my actions? To say nothing of my colleagues in the House. No matter how wild your reputation, you are still gently born. It's unthinkable for anyone who calls himself a gentleman to compromise such a lady and refuse to marry her.'

'You feel that your personal honour is at stake.'

'Exactly.'

She sighed. 'I was afraid of that. Miss Avery chose her revenge well, thinking to punish us both by trapping us in a marriage neither of us wanted. You're *sure* I cannot persuade you not to let yourself be trapped?'

For a moment, he felt a brief flare of hope that he might avoid a union about which he had such wildly conflicted feelings—resentment, anger, trepidation, resignation and that sneaky little flare of excitement.

But about one thing he felt no conflict at all. Regardless of what either of them wanted, marriage was the only way to salvage her honour—and his.

He shook his head. 'No, Temper, I cannot. Having obtained your father's approval,' he said, slipping to one knee before her, 'I must ask if you would do me the honour of becoming my wife.'

She gave him a wry smile. 'I suppose I should be gratified that you are doing the asking this time. After you turned me down so definitely. I have to admit, that did sting a little.'

Regret needled him. 'I'm sorry. I didn't mean to slight you, but—'

She waved him to silence. 'I know you didn't. Although a marriage of convenience would serve us both, I'm hardly the sort of wife you'd have chosen.'

'Perhaps not in everything, but I couldn't find a stronger, braver lady.'

'Because I didn't crumble under society's disapproval? Why should I? I've lived with it most of my life.' She sighed. 'Do get up. If you simply can't persuade yourself not to offer for me, we can at least turn our union into a fitting counterstrike to Jane Avery's triumph. She thinks she's forcing us into a marriage neither of us want, having no idea I've already proposed to you once.'

'The best way to thwart someone who wishes you ill is to appear delighted by the situation they engineered to confound you?'

'Exactly. I imagine she thinks my husband will take over my fortune and try to force me to become a conventional, obedient wife. And that you will be vexed and bedevilled for ever by wedding the one woman in London least likely to become the skilful political hostess you need. Well, I do apologise for that! But…if you can agree to the terms I offered when I proposed to you earlier, we might both end up with most of what we want.'

'For you, control over part of your fortune so you may travel the world as you wish?'

'Yes. With you welcome to use the rest to support your efforts in Parliament. While you are also free to…pursue pleasure wherever you please.'

Since the infuriating moment when he realised how Jane Avery had tricked them, he had thought of little else but the terms Temper had offered before—and still hadn't been able to decide one way or the other how he felt about them.

'I can't deny that having an influx of funds to finally put an end to my financial difficulties will be welcome. I also know you've always dreamed of travelling. But, much as I'd like you to be happy, I... I'm not comfortable with the idea of you journeying to the wilds of India and the Orient with only hired guides and a small entourage to protect you. I suppose I could give up my work in Parliament to accompany you, but I know I'd resent—'

'Goodness, no, Giff, you can't even *think* of doing such a thing!' she exclaimed, looking appalled. 'You've found your calling and a vital and important one it is! I could never allow you to abandon Parliament to chase after me to foreign lands, places you've never had any interest in visiting.'

'Could you agree to not go running off until more extensive preparations can be made? So we may equip a support party large and well armed enough that I won't have to lie awake every night, worrying that you've been attacked by bandits or worse?' He heaved a sigh. 'I suppose there's no way to guarantee against shipwreck or disease.'

Her expression softened. 'Dear Giff. I can't think of any other man who would trouble himself about my happiness, especially as what I must do to secure it is so outlandish. If you promise to let me travel, eventually, then I agree to wait until we can arrange the "extensive" preparations you think necessary.'

'Thank you.' That concession would relieve some of his worries. About the rest—

Before he could decide how to word the more delicate part of his concern, Temper, being Temper, came straight to the point. 'You aren't particularly interested in...having heirs, are you? When you talked of marriage earlier, you said you'd give a wife children if *she* wanted them. Meaning, you are...indifferent to the idea?'

'I don't *need* heirs, having no property or estate to pass

down,' he confirmed. 'Are you saying that you'd want the marriage to be…in name only?'

'I don't want to deny you pleasure,' she said quickly, not meeting his gaze. 'I know how much you enjoy the ladies and would be perfectly happy to allow you to continue amusing yourself with them as you please.'

For a man being forced into a marriage he didn't want, having his prospective wife offer him free rein to pursue other women would normally be a welcome concession—he supposed. But would being able to experience passion with other women make him any more able to resist the desire he felt for Temper?

He wasn't at all sure it would. And if he were honest, the prospect of luring Temper into making their marriage complete excited him far more than the idea of pursuing mindless pleasure. And if he couldn't convince her…maybe he'd better equip her to travel as speedy as possible so he might send the temptation she represented far, far away.

Though life would seem much…duller without the zest of wondering what outrageous thing she would do next.

As if reading his thoughts, she said, 'You'll have your work in Parliament to occupy you—meetings and consultations and persuading the recalcitrant to your point of view. It will be so time-consuming and exhausting, you'll have no time to miss your undutiful, wandering wife.'

'Will my undutiful wife miss me?'

Pinking a little, she looked away. 'I shall always miss the friend who gave up so much to give me my heart's desire. The first man ever to treat my dream as a serious intent, rather than a little girl's foolish imaginings.'

'I hardly think of you as a little girl. Nor have I for some time.'

She looked at him and that potent, wordless sensual connection hummed between them again. He still couldn't understand her reluctance to act on it—on an attraction he knew, with *absolute* certainty, to be mutual.

If he'd pulled her down on to the bed that night at Lady Arnold's, she wouldn't have resisted him. He was almost sure she would have responded with all the passion he could wish for.

Almost sure.

When he focused from those thoughts to look back at her, the fraught moment had passed. She was once again tense, guarded, as if poised to flee.

Maybe not quite so sure.

'Would you accept my proposal if I want more than a *marriage blanc*?'

She shook her head. 'I… I don't think I could.'

As puzzled as he was frustrated by that affirmation, Giff wanted to demand some further explanation. But her averted gaze and wary stance made it patently clear she had no wish to discuss the matter. Indeed, she looked so unexpectedly… fragile, he couldn't press her.

In time, he hoped, she would trust him enough to reveal the reasons for her reluctance to embrace the passion between them. Maybe then he'd get the chance to persuade her into changing her mind.

Time they would have, for marry they must. And if swearing not to touch her was the price for winning her acceptance, he had no choice but to pay it.

Gently, he took her chin, raising her face so she had to look into his eyes. 'Then a *marriage blanc* it shall be. Never doubt that I want you, Temper. But never worry that I will ask of you anything you are not willing to give.'

She gave him a little nod, a fine glaze of tears sheening her eyes. 'Thank you for being so...understanding, Giff. Though I apologise again that you're not getting the skilled political wife you deserve, if you can accept those terms for our marriage, then, yes, I accept your proposal.'

A bargain of wedlock meant to last a lifetime should be sealed with a kiss—even if it had to be a chaste one. Never breaking her gaze, he slowly lowered his head. Looking at the same time both wary—and wanting—she didn't try to avoid his lips.

Ah, how soft hers were! Restraining the immediate surge of desire that demanded he press harder, deeper, probe with his tongue to explore the taste of her, he made himself remain motionless, his hands the barest touch at her shoulders, his lips brushing hers in the lightest of caresses.

With a little sigh, she let his mouth linger.

Fortunately for his rapidly unravelling self-control, after a few moments of sweet torture, she broke the kiss and stepped away. But the fact that she had permitted that touch—that he could sense she was holding herself under as strict a control as he was not to respond any further—gave him hope.

Maybe he just needed to convince her that passion could uplift and delight as well as shame and degrade.

And he'd have a lifetime to persuade her of that.

'Shall we go announce the engagement to your family?'

She nodded, her cheeks still a little pink—and the pulse at her throat still beating erratically. 'Before we do, I have one other request. I received a letter from Pru this morning. It seems she has met the gentleman she wants to marry! That soldier I told you about.'

Giff searched his memory. 'Captain Johnnie Trethwell—

late of Her Majesty's Second Foot, invalided home from India?' At her nod, he continued, 'Gregory mentioned she's written him about the man, as well. Not exactly the landed gentleman I thought she was seeking.'

Temper laughed wryly. 'It seems neither of us will end up as we envisioned. Me, who never intended to wed, getting married, while instead of a sober country squire, Pru's giving her hand to the scapegrace youngest son of the late Marquess of Barkeley. Though she did say in her letter that his aunt, Lady Woodlings, intends to settle some money on him, so he won't be coming to her completely pockets-to-let. In any event, they're on their way to London now with Aunt Gussie, to secure Papa's permission and to arrange for a special licence, so they may be wed as quickly as possible. Would...would you be willing to obtain a special licence, too, that we might be wed at the same time?'

He hadn't expected she would want the marriage being forced on them celebrated with a calling of banns followed by a public wedding at St George's, Hanover Square. 'You'd prefer a small private ceremony, with just immediate family and friends?'

'Wouldn't you?'

'Yes. I'll write to inform my father of our intentions— not that I need his permission to marry, though he'd have no reason to withhold it. I doubt he'll wish to leave Fensworth long enough to attend the wedding. Though Mama may celebrate the loss of my expense by arranging a trip here so she may use that quarterly allowance I'll no longer need to have new gowns made up,' he added, trying to keep his voice light and disguise with humour the bitter truth that his parents had only ever seen him as a drain on their resources. 'Enough of that. I can't think of anything more appropriate, than having two sisters who have rarely been apart stand up together on their wedding day.'

She smiled and pressed his hand. 'Thank you, Giff. I will so appreciate having her beside me when I take...take this step into the unknown.'

He brought her fingers to his lips for a brief kiss before releasing them. 'Remember, you may be losing Pru as friend and confidante, but you will always have me.'

She nodded quickly. 'Yes. I'll always have you...as my greatest friend. If you'll wait here, I'll go find Mama and Gregory.'

At that, she walked out, leaving him staring after her.

Her greatest friend. Much as he wanted to protect her and let her be happy, could he marry her and live with being only that?

Chapter Sixteen

'Goodness!' Johnnie Trethwell exclaimed, looking from Temperance to her mother back to a beaming Prudence, whom he had just ushered into the parlour at Vraux House on a sunny afternoon two days later. 'One of you alone is dazzling, but the three of you together is almost more than a man can take in!'

He was certainly charming, this rogue who was to be her brother-in-law, Temperance thought as she and her mother made their curtsies, while Captain Trethwell went on to shake Gregory's hand.

'We're trying not to overwhelm you, Captain,' Temperance said. 'It's just the three of us now, but Christopher and Ellie will be joining us for dinner, along with Gifford Newell.'

'And Papa...?' Pru asked.

'I wouldn't count on Vraux making an appearance,' their mother said drily. She hesitated, an uncertain look crossing her face before she walked over to give her newly returned daughter a hug.

Which, Temper was pleased to note, Pru not only tolerated, but returned with equal warmth. Perhaps her sister's time away had given her a new understanding and tolerance for their mother.

But then, radiant happiness did have the splendid effect of expanding to encompass everything around one.

Once her mother stepped back, Temper took her place. 'My turn! Welcome home, sister dear! How I've missed you!'

'And I, you,' Pru said, hugging her back fiercely.

'Oh, I don't know,' Temper said, stepping away. 'I think you've found a more than adequate replacement.'

She thought she'd accepted when she sent her sister off to Bath that the person who'd been closest to her in all the world would never fill that role again. But the ache in her chest at voicing that truth aloud told her that, though her head might have recognised the fact, her heart was only now beginning to face it.

You'll always have me, Giff had told her. The memory both comforted…and disturbed her.

'I must go hunt down Lord Vraux,' Captain Trethwell was saying. 'As I mean to become a member of this family with all possible speed, I'll want his consent at once, so I may head off to Doctors' Commons and go about obtaining a special licence.'

'I'll take you up,' Gregory said. 'He's in his library, cataloguing. As usual.'

'Excellent,' the captain replied. 'I have a number of questions to ask him about his collections.'

Gregory shrugged. 'You may ask. I can't guarantee you'll get any answers.'

'While your fiancé confronts the dragon,' Temper said to her sister, 'why don't we have some tea? You can tell us all about your sojourn in Bath—before Aunt Gussie joins us and you have to censor your account.'

'Mama, shall we have tea sent to your sitting room?' Pru asked, looking at her mother with an affection Temper hadn't seen her display in years.

Nor had that lady either. Pru's request prompted a brilliant smile from Lady Vraux, tears glittering in the corners of her eyes as she nodded her assent.

'I should like that very much. Welcome home, my precious daughter.'

And so the three women walked up to Lady Vraux's boudoir, Pru still radiant with a happiness that caused a deep pang of melancholy—and foreboding—in Temper's breast. Not that she resented her sister's joy—indeed, she was thrilled that Pru had found the man, and the life, she wanted.

While Temper had no misgivings about the character of the man she was to marry, she wasn't sure what she was getting herself into.

'Isn't he wonderful?' Pru said as they took their seats around their mother's divan.

'Certainly a handsome devil,' Lady Vraux said, giving her daughter a knowing smile. 'I shall have no worries about you sleeping well at night in your nuptial bed. At least, not for the part of it you sleep.'

'I am so looking forward to that,' Pru confirmed, a naughty twinkle in her eye. 'Stolen kisses on a riding trail are one thing—but to have the luxury of time and the comfort of a bed!'

Laughing, Temper covered her ears. 'No licentious details, please! But do tell us *everything* about your captain and how he convinced you he would be much better for you than that gentleman farmer you always said you wanted.'

And so, over tea, Pru explained how her attempts to be the perfect society maiden, undercut by the reputation that followed her to Bath, were eventually abandoned in the face of society's hypocrisy—and the realisation that her highborn, titled suitor was a much lesser man than the untitled adventurer who had freed her to be who she truly was. 'I even managed to create a scandal—and insult the most highly placed social arbiter in Bath!' she said with a laugh as she finished her tale. 'I discovered that I am much more like you than I imagined, Mama.'

Her humour fading, she took her mother's hand. 'Will you forgive me? I've been…awful to you, the last year or so.'

Lady Vraux shook her head. 'Nothing to forgive. Without having the least intention of doing so, I made the path difficult—for you and Temper. That you both will marry well and be happy is the best present each of you could ever give me.'

Pru's eyes widened. '*Both* marry well?' Whirling to face Temper, she said, 'What have you been keeping from me?'

'Nothing! The matter was only settled two days ago.' Temper forced a smile. 'You'll recall that before you left, I threatened to create a little scandal of my own? You weren't the only sister who managed it. Only I inadvertently dragged Giff into mine. As it…appeared he'd compromised me, he, of course, insisted on doing the honourable thing.'

'Now you must give *me* all the details,' her twin said.

Once she'd finished, though her sister exclaimed angrily over the duplicity of Miss Avery, she ended by saying, 'You know, Temper, I think Giff will make you an excellent husband. You know and trust him, and what's even more important, he knows and trusts you. He won't be expecting marriage to change you into a conventional, biddable wife who will be content with just managing his house and raising his children.'

Temper shifted uncomfortably, aware of her mother's thoughtful gaze fixed on her. 'He knows what he's getting, that's for certain. Though if it hadn't been for the scandal, I doubt he'd have offered for me. Aside from wealth, I'm hardly the sort of wife a rising politician would choose.'

'Why not?' Pru replied. 'You are lovely, intelligent and far more knowledgeable about what is going on in the country—and the world at large—than most of the women in society!'

'Thank you, loyal twin. But we both know I am also impatient with fools, far too apt to say whatever I'm thinking, and…and far too restless to remain in England. Though I won't make Giff much of a wife, he *is* probably the best husband for me—if I must have a husband. He's willing to let me travel, so I don't expect we'll spend a great deal of time together after the wedding. In fact,' she ended, brightening at the prospect, 'once I can work out the details of an entourage large enough to satisfy him about my safety, I can drag out of Papa the sort of objects and artefacts he wishes to acquire next and head off in search of them!'

Pru's smile dimmed. 'Oh. About that. I… I haven't yet told you what Johnnie means to do, now that he will be leaving the army.'

'And what will that be?' Lady Vraux asked. 'Use some of your dowry to buy you that horse farm in the country?'

'No. His aunt, Lady Woodlings, and some other backers have invested their funds in a trading company he will own and manage. Using the extensive contacts he's developed after his years in India, he plans to travel there and throughout the Orient and the Magreb, acquiring weapons, objets d'art and artefacts to sell to collectors like Papa. He planned to query Papa today about what he'd like him to look for.' She took a deep breath. 'And I intend to accompany him on his travels.'

While Temper sat frozen, trying to mask her shock and dismay, Lady Vraux laughed and clapped her hands. 'My little Prudence, who has always wanted to settle in some quiet English backwater, will travel the world? How wonderful!'

Prudence gave Temper a searching look, to which Temper hoped she returned a convincing smile. 'Amazing! How oddly our destinies have changed. You, the girl who never thought to leave England's shores, setting off with an adventurer, while I...marry a politician tied to London and Parliament.'

'I'm sorry, Temper,' Pru said softly. 'You'll still be able to travel, won't you? If you want to.'

'Of course I shall travel! Our match is a simple marriage of convenience—not a grand passion, like yours.'

Her mother reached over to touch her hand. 'I would wish a grand passion for you, too, my darling.'

'Oh, Mama, you know me. All the passion I possess is a quick temper,' she replied, trying to ignore the sick feeling in her belly. She'd planned now for years on exploring to fill her father's treasure chests. What would be her purpose now? And where would she go?

'You can always travel with us,' Pru offered.

Temper laughed. 'Not even the most charming and toler-
ant of gentlemen would be amenable to dragging his new
sister-in-law along on his honeymoon! Never fear, I shall
come up with…alternate plans. Now, shall we switch to
the most important topic? What we shall all wear to the
wedding!'

Though her mother gave her another searching glance,
Temper was easily able to distract Prudence, whose thoughts
never wandered far from her Johnnie, into a lengthy discussion of which styles, colours and fabrics would make
her look most beautiful when he claimed her as his bride.

While distracting herself from her misgivings over what,
exactly, her own future was going to be.

Less than a week later, Temper stood beside her sister
outside the formal drawing room at Vraux House, where
the clergyman, the two bridegrooms and a small company
of guests awaited them.

To the surprise of both sisters, their father had announced
he would not only attend the nuptials, he intended to give
the girls away. And to their amazement, as he met them
outside the parlour, immaculately dressed in the formal
dress coat he rarely wore, he looked both of them in the
eye, murmured, 'As beautiful as your mama', and *kissed*
each of them on the cheek.

If she hadn't already been so nervous about what she'd
committed herself to do that she was scarcely aware of
anything else, Temper might have fainted from the shock.

'You do look beautiful,' Pru murmured.

'We both do,' Temper replied, desperately anxious to get

through the next few minutes, when she would be the focus of all eyes and must play the happy bride.

She was hoping her sister's obvious glow of joy, as shimmering as the golden gown she wore, would attract most of the guests' attention. Her own gown, in a style that matched her sister's, with its low, off-the-shoulder neckline, full, gathered sleeves and tiny waist, was in a turquoise-blue silk Mama said matched her eyes.

Then her father gave the footman a nod, he opened the door and they walked into the parlour.

Catching the besotted glance of giddy delight that passed between Pru and Johnnie as she approached her bridegroom, Temper felt a stab of pure envy. Such bliss, such perfect contentment—and such promise of sensual fulfilment—would never be hers.

But at least she need not fear her bridegroom and could enter this marriage assured that Giff would abide by the terms they'd set. Even if the reality of a marriage of convenience hadn't turned out to be nearly as simple and straightforward as she'd blithely assumed when she'd first suggested one to Giff—was it only a few weeks ago?

In the interim, that inescapable, edgy attraction between them had intensified. She didn't worry that Giff would try to trick or force her into abandoning the restrictions of the *marriage blanc* she'd insisted upon.

But would she?

She sneaked a glance at him now, so tall, solemn—and handsome—as he stood beside the priest. Despite her nervousness, a ripple of desire eddied in her belly as she recalled the tenderness with which he'd kissed her after she'd accepted his proposal.

As the swirl of heated sensation rushed through her at

the velvet-soft touch of his lips brushing hers, she'd had to force herself to remain immobile…lest she press herself against his heat and hardness, or pull his head down to extend the kiss.

Each time he touched her, arousing those volatile sensations, she was tempted to let down her guard and allow him to take her into a deeper intimacy—an intimacy she wasn't at all sure she could tolerate. Each time, once away from his disturbing presence, when she thought about allowing attraction to progress towards its natural end, the cold revulsion she kept locked away threatened to break through. No, she didn't dare risk it.

Then she was at Giff's side, his warm hand covering her cold one, sending another of those sensual shocks through her. The soft air, heated by the amassed candles and guest-filled room, wafted to her the scent of shaving soap and virile male.

She tried to ignore it, needing to muster all her scattered wits to focus on making the correct answers to the questions being posed by the priest, lest the guests notice how completely panic-stricken she was beneath an outward mask of calm. Or realise what a shocking contrast the two couples presented—one ecstatic, the other coolly reserved.

In another few minutes, she would become what she'd never expected to be—a wife. And now, too late, she wasn't at all sure that had been a wise idea.

Standing before the priest and the assembled guests, Giff envied his prospective new brother-in-law the sense of eager anticipation about his upcoming nuptials he'd displayed since the moment they'd been introduced at the welcome dinner at Vraux House a week ago.

Gazing now at the man's expression, his delight in the bride he was about to acquire patently obvious, Giff felt, like a cold rock in his stomach, the contrast between Trethwell's exuberant happiness and his own misgivings—which he could only hope he'd buried deep enough to conceal.

He'd tried to respond with appropriate enthusiasm when Trethwell had congratulated him at that dinner on winning the hand of Pru's sister. 'They are astoundingly similar, at least in looks,' he'd said. 'My Prudence is a bit softer and sweeter. Your Temperance, she tells me, is a firebrand!' Giving him a wink, he added, 'I hope you've been conserving your strength. If the twins are alike in every way, you're going to need every bit of your endurance for the honeymoon.'

He'd need to conserve his strength for the honeymoon, all right, he thought, suppressing a sigh. Enough strength to keep desire under tight control, once the beautiful woman now standing beside him, repeating the ancient words of the wedding ceremony, belonged to him completely, his to take with the full permission of the law and the church.

Just not with hers.

Before he knew it, the vows were completed, the clergyman put away his prayer book and led the two couples off to an anteroom to sign the parish register.

He was married now. To Temperance Lattimar. The beguiling, bewitching, exasperating, unpredictable woman he desired, respected and never, except in some quickly repressed erotic daydream, ever expected to wed.

Once out of sight of the assembled guests, the smile she'd fixed on her face faltered, giving him a glimpse of anxiety, confusion—and surely it wasn't *fear* he read there!

His own misgivings instantly submerged by concern for

her, once they'd affixed their signatures—Temper writing in a firm, quiet hand despite the turmoil he'd glimpsed in her eyes—he caught her arm, retaining her before she could follow the others back into the parlour.

'Let's take a moment before we rejoin the assembly,' he murmured.

She exhaled a shaky breath. 'Yes, let's. I need to…muster my composure.'

Tenderness, laced with a bit of amusement, tempered his concern. 'Temperance Lattimar, *dis*composed? I would never have believed it.'

'Well, I've never been married before, either,' she snapped back with more of her usual zest.

He lifted her chin so she had to look into her eyes. 'I may be your…husband now—and it takes me aback to say the word, too—but I'm still Giff, the man you've known since you pitched a rock at my head when you were six. You can still count on me to watch out for you. You can trust me to keep my promises.'

She stared into his eyes for a long moment before nodding. 'I know,' she whispered. 'But can I trust myself?'

Before Giff could wonder what she meant by that enigmatic utterance, Overton entered the anteroom. 'Mr Newell, a rider has just arrived with an urgent message for you. I've allowed him into the parlour with the guests, so he might deliver it immediately.'

'Of course. Temperance?'

As she took his arm to walk back to the parlour, Giff wondered what could have prompted someone to dispatch a rider to him with an urgent message. Not from Parliament— a runner on foot would have been sufficient for that. So it must be from Fensworth. Sent with speed and urgency, it couldn't be good news.

Though all his family had been in good health last he heard from them, disease could strike—and kill—with speed and suddenness. Setting his lips in a grim line, Giff approached the mud-spattered rider.

'You have a message for me?'

Engaged in gulping down a glass of punch, the dispatch rider choked to a stop. 'Yes, sir,' he said, holding out the folded paper.

Breaking the seal, Giff scanned the document. The noise of the room, the conversation of the guests, even the concerned presence of Temper beside him, faded into the background as he read it through a second time.

'What is it, Giff?' Gregory asked, coming over to halt beside him. 'You've gone as white as that parchment!'

Giff looked up at his friend, the news so unbelievable, he still couldn't take it in. 'There's been an accident. My father and Robert have put every penny they could scrounge into building more steam engines to drain water from the lowest areas around the fens. Two— No,' he corrected, looking at the date on the letter, 'three days ago, Robert was driving them in his gig to inspect the latest project when one of the carriage wheels caught in the mud under the standing water from the previous day's rains. The horse panicked and bolted. The gig slammed through the railing at the top of a wooden bridge and went over, ending upside down in the stream below. Trapping Father and Robert.' He swallowed hard. 'They drowned. Both of them.'

'Oh, Giff, I'm so sorry,' Temper murmured, pressing his hand.

'This way, Gifford.' Through the roaring in his ears, the

eerie sense of unreality that suffused him, he heard Lady Sayleford's voice. 'Give them some room, please, ladies and gentlemen,' she continued, her hand on his arm as she led him out of the parlour.

'Brandy,' she ordered the butler who followed after them, before pushing Giff towards a sofa in a room he vaguely noted was the family's private back parlour. 'Sit here, catch your breath.'

'Admit the Lattimar brothers,' she told Overton as he returned from the sideboard with a brimming glass, 'but no one else. Temperance, help him with that.'

Temper put her hand up to reinforce Giff's trembling one, until the hot burn of the brandy down his throat steadied him.

Temper's brothers entered, their faces grave. 'Gregory told me what happened, Giff,' Christopher said. 'I'm so very sorry.'

'What can we do to help?' Temper asked, cradling his fingers around the whisky glass. 'You'll want to go to Fensworth as soon as possible.'

'Yes. I must prepare to leave at once. My mother...the solicitor says she was so distraught when they broke the news, they had to dose her with laudanum. She'll be devastated. She doted on Robert.'

'She has another, equally capable son,' Temper said stoutly.

He managed a grim smile. 'Not that she ever seemed aware of it.'

'She will be now,' Lady Sayleford said gently. 'You'll want your new wife to accompany you. Plan on taking my carriage for the first stage; you can arrange for post chaises for the rest.'

He nodded distractedly. 'Yes, I'll have Temper and her maid travel later, but I must ride now, so I can reach Fensworth as quickly as possible.' Turning to Christopher, he said, 'I'll send you my notes on the factory bill. Can you take over attending the hearings for me?'

'Of course. I'll send you reports, since we don't know how long you'll need to be…away.'

Gregory froze, his eyes widening. 'Hell and damnation—excuse me, ladies! Giff won't be coming back to Parliament, Christopher. At least, not to the House. Behold, before you, the new Earl—and Countess—of Fensworth!'

Chapter Seventeen

Returning late the next morning from a flurry of shopping for appropriate garments—the last time she'd lost a relation close enough to require the wearing of mourning having occurred when she was thirteen—Temper began directing her maid to organise and pack the few articles of clothing she currently possessed that were suitable to wear on the trip into Lincolnshire.

While she was engaged at that task, Overton came in to inform her that Lady Sayleford was awaiting her in the downstairs parlour.

Curious what Giff's godmother might require of her—and surprised the Dowager Countess had called on *her*, rather than sending her a note requesting that she present herself in Grosvenor Square—she quickly tucked back the stray strands of hair that had escaped her careless coiffure and hurried down to the parlour.

'Lady Sayleford,' she said, curtsying as she entered. 'What can I do for you? Would you like tea?'

'No tea, thank you. I came to see if there was anything I could do to assist your departure,' the Countess said, rising to return Temper's curtsy. 'Although you know,' she said as she resumed her seat, 'I should now curtsy first. You outrank me, the Fensworth Earldom predating the Sayleford honours by a century.'

Temper laughed ruefully. 'I'm afraid it's going to take some adjusting. Within a space of twenty-four hours, I've gone from being "Miss Lattimar" to "Mrs Newell" to "Countess of Fensworth". When the shopkeepers "miladyed" me this morning, I kept looking around to see which titled female had arrived.'

'How is Gifford doing?'

'Honestly, I don't know. I haven't seen much of him. After the guests left the reception yesterday, he went off with Gregory to expedite the transfer of my dowry funds to his bank, then back to his lodgings to pack up the rest of his things. Our decision to marry having been...accelerated by events, we'd not yet had time to decide where to set up our own household. Giff intended to stay here at Vraux House in the interim.'

'Not much of a wedding night,' Lady Sayleford observed.

'No,' Temper answered shortly, not about to reveal that the doors between their adjoining bedchambers had remained closed.

'I'm glad that he'll be able to tap some funds immediately.' The Countess shook her head. 'Poor Gifford has been coping on a pittance for years. Now, suddenly, he'll have all the expense of managing an estate.'

'If the transition from commoner to countess was—disorienting—for me, it has to be so much worse for him. Saddled now with the responsibility for the care and upkeep of an inheritance he knows hardly anything about.'

'I never approved of how his parents focused all their attention on his brother, virtually ignoring my godson. He should have been taught about the estate from childhood. After all, with his brother having not yet married and produced another heir, Gifford was next in line. His father shouldn't have left him in ignorance about how things stood.'

'It never seemed to me that either parent valued him as they ought.'

'No. It's going to be a difficult adjustment for him, taking up duties for which he has been given no adequate preparation. Having those new duties compel him to leave London at such a crucial moment, with the factory bill he's been working so hard for soon to come to a vote. Then, once he can return, having to find his place among an entirely different set of political associates in the Lords.' She paused. 'He will need help and support, my dear. Which makes me thankful that he managed to wed you before this happened.'

Temper gave a rueful laugh. 'I shall do everything I can to lighten his burden, certainly. But I can't help thinking that if he had become the Earl of Fensworth before the…contretemps with Miss Avery…he would have been so besieged by matchmaking mamas and eager maidens of quality, he would have ended up marrying a woman much better suited to becoming a politician's wife and a countess than I am.'

'I'm not so sure about that, my dear,' Lady Sayleford said with a smile. 'Gifford would look for more than just "suitable" qualities in a wife. So I hope you will be…gentle with him. He's in love with you, you know.'

'In love with—!' Temper echoed, astounded. 'Lady Sayleford, I am certain you are mistaken! He still sees me as the troublesome little sister of his best friend. A madcap whose disreputable exploits dragged him into a situation that, according to his overly fine sense of honour, could only be resolved by marriage.'

'You are a bit too prone to act or speak before you think,' Lady Sayleford acknowledged. 'But you also possess courage, intelligence, compassion and a fierce independence, traits that will endure and will make you a valuable wife and a worthy countess. And I assure you, though of course he hasn't realised it yet, Gifford does, in fact, love you. Why else would he have gone to so much trouble to ensure you had a Season? Or have kept so close a watch over you? Or so quickly decided that the only answer to Miss Avery's treachery was to marry you at once?'

Chuckling softly, she shook her head. 'So I repeat, be gentle with Gifford. He is worthy of your loyalty and your deepest consideration. Now,' she said, rising, 'I'll return you to your packing. My coachman is prepared to leave as soon as you are ready.'

Still flabbergasted, Temper rose as well. 'Remember,' Lady Sayleford said, pressing her hand as she walked out. 'The key to your happiness—and his—lies in your own hands. And I must say, I've never sponsored a more entertaining debut.'

Scarcely knowing what to reply to those parting words, Temper merely curtsied as the Countess made her departure. Sinking back on to the sofa, she stared into the distance, trying to wrap her mind around what she'd just been told.

Gifford Newell—no, the Earl of Fensworth—was *in love* with her? She simply couldn't credit it. She knew he desired her. She was pretty sure he *liked* her and she was certain that she amused and entertained him. But…love her?

If anyone other than Lady Sayleford had uttered such nonsense, she would have laughed in her face. But…the omnipotent *Lady Sayleford*, who knew everything about everyone?

Still, Gifford Newell was her godson. Perhaps her fondness for him had skewed her perceptions.

But what if she was right…if Giff truly had fallen in love with her…? Even though he didn't know it yet?

Putting her hands to her aching temples, Temper shook her head. She wouldn't, couldn't think about that possibility now. She was still struggling to comprehend all the implications of going in a few short hours from a maid to a politician's wife to the wife of a peer.

Whatever else he was or might be, Gifford had been first and foremost her friend. A friend who had been saddled with a heavy burden he'd not been trained to handle, had had the new calling he'd come to love snatched away from him and was dealing with the shock of losing almost his entire family in one blow.

Her first task, as both wife and friend, was to help him weather those catastrophes.

The question of love, and what she was going to do about the ever-increasing pull of passion between them, would have to wait.

A week later, after several days travelling in a series of jolting hired vehicles, Temper's carriage halted in front of Fensworth House. With a solid central block flanked by two wings, all constructed of Elizabethan brick, it had a timeless quality…though the grey skies reflected in the thousand panes of the mullioned glass windows gave it a look of fatigue and sadness, too.

Small wonder, when it had lost both master and heir at a blow.

Wondering where the new master might be, Temper let the post boy hand her down and walked up the entry steps, her maid trailing behind.

She had to knock twice before the door was answered— by what looked to be a housemaid. Who froze, gazing awe-struck at Temper's fashionable cloak and bonnet, before hurriedly dropping a curtsy. 'Can I help you, ma'am?'

With the butler nowhere in sight, Temper concluded that Fensworth didn't often receive callers. 'I'm… Lady Fensworth,' she said, still finding it hard to identify herself by that name. 'Is Lord Fensworth at home?'

Her eyes widening, the girl took a step back. 'Oh!' she breathed, once again staring at Temper. 'You be the wild beauty Master Gifford up and married!'

So that was the staff's assessment of the younger son's bride. Suppressing a wry smile at that frank assessment, Temper realised that her first job would be to demonstrate to the staff that, however wild a bride they might think her, she meant to be the unquestioned mistress of the house.

A quick gaze around the hall solidified that intention. Knowing that the estate had been purse-pinched for years, she'd expected the furnishings might be somewhat shabby and they were—the aged window hangings needed replac-ing, the carpet was worn and the furniture dated from the last century. But poverty was no excuse for the layer of dust sitting atop the mahogany hall table, or the grit she felt under the soles of her travelling boots.

Either Giff's mother had been too absorbed in her own

concerns to bother about housekeeping—or the staff thought the 'wild beauty' who had unexpectedly become their mistress would be too ignorant to properly run a household.

Before she could decide how to proceed, a tall, stooped man in the garb of a butler approached from a door opening on to one of the wings. 'You may go, Maisie,' he said to the maid, who bobbed another curtsy and scurried off.

Turning to Temper, he bowed. 'You must be the new Lady Fensworth. Welcome to Fensworth House, your ladyship. I'm Mixton, the butler.'

'Thank you, Mixton. Is his lordship at home now?'

'No, your ladyship. He and the steward left early this morning to inspect the northern fields. He is usually gone most of the day, sometimes not returning until late evening, but I'll send a groom out to let his lordship know you're here.'

'Thank you—but tell him he need not change his plans. I'll see him whenever he gets home. Now, if you'd have a footman bring up my luggage and send a maid up with hot water, I'd like to be shown to my rooms and settle in. And I'd like you to send the housekeeper up to see me.'

'Of course, your ladyship. Had we known the time of your arrival, I should have mustered all of the staff to welcome you.'

'I'm sure you would have. But the circumstances have been…most unusual, haven't they? Please convey my sincere regrets to the whole staff on your loss. It must have been devastating for all of you.'

A wave of sadness briefly creased the butler's impassive countenance. 'It was…difficult. The late Earl was a good master, and we shall all miss him. Miss them both.'

Especially since they were now saddled with a mistress

about whom they knew nothing and a master they knew scarcely any better.

Which, however, was certainly not Giff's fault.

'You will find your new master to be a fine, capable, compassionate man, as well,' she said. 'How is the Dowager Countess?'

'Still laid up in her rooms, your ladyship.'

'Then you needn't notify her of my arrival. I shall have my husband introduce us when it is convenient for them both.'

'Very good. This way, your ladyship.'

Following the butler up the stairs, Temper noted that the head male servant, at least, seemed to know his job. Glancing around at the state of the stairs and the dusty hall furniture she passed on the way to her room, she wasn't sure about the housekeeper.

Her suspicions deepened after she'd been shown into a spacious bedchamber—whose dusty curtains were drawn, whose bed linens had obviously not been aired and which boasted an equally dusty hearth on which no fire had been laid.

The staff might not have known exactly when she would arrive, but there was no excuse for not having properly prepared a room for her. Temper frowned, girding herself for the confrontation to come.

The housekeeper was either too old to do her job properly, incompetent—or perhaps so loyal to Giff's mother, she fiercely resented her replacement? Or thought, with her former mistress prostrate with grief and the new mistress a 'wild beauty' with no knowledge of how to properly run a house, she might get away with neglecting her duties?

Whatever the cause, the slovenly condition of the house

must be rectified immediately. Giff had enough worries to deal with. At the very least, he deserved to return to a home that was clean, warmed and welcoming.

Half an hour later, a stout middle-aged woman knocked at her door. 'I'm Mrs Hobbs, the housekeeper, your ladyship,' she said, curtsying.

'Good day, Mrs Hobbs. First, let me extend condolences on your loss. I imagine the entire household has been at sixes and sevens, and I do sympathise. However, I must tell you candidly that what I have seen of the house thus far has been…disappointing. I may be young, but I assure you, I have been thoroughly trained in how to maintain a gentleman's establishment. And Fensworth is not just a gentleman's establishment—it is the home of an earl! There is no excuse for the state of neglect I have observed.'

The woman's face paled, then reddened. 'We… We've never had funds enough to properly staff—'

'Funding will be no problem now. Send to the village for extra staff, if you must. But before my husband returns today, I expect all the floors in the public areas to have been swept, all the furniture dusted and polished, and a fire laid in any room his lordship might be expected to occupy. By the end of the week, I expect every room in the house to have been thoroughly cleaned, the linens aired and pressed, the window hangings taken down and brushed, and all the windows themselves washed. I will add any additional requirements I notice when you give me a tour of the house. What have you planned to serve his lordship for dinner tonight?'

'We— Cook doesn't prepare a formal meal. As his lordship usually comes in so late, we just send up a tray of cold meats and cheeses.'

Incensed that they would treat Giff so shabbily, Temper shook her head. Obviously, his mother's slighting assessment of her younger son had been communicated—openly or subtly—to the staff. Temper meant to ensure that evaluation was changed forthwith.

'Henceforth,' she said in icy tones, pinning the woman with a glare, 'you will ensure that the cook prepares the Earl *of Fensworth* a proper meal every evening and have it ready to be served in the dining room. If he chooses to have a tray in his room, that will be his lordship's decision.'

'Y-yes, your ladyship,' the woman stuttered.

'My husband may not have been brought up to be the Earl—but Earl he is. I expect him to be served, and his home to be run, in a manner befitting his rank. If you and your staff are not capable of meeting that standard, I shall find staff who can. I trust I've made myself clear?'

'Y-yes, your ladyship,' Mrs Hobbs stammered again.

'Good. Later this afternoon, after I've rested, I would like that tour of the house. Also a list of the menus Cook proposes to serve for the next week. You may go now.'

Curtsying, the housekeeper turned and fled.

Temper went over to the window to pull open the curtains, coughing at the cloud of dust disturbed by their movement. At least the window had a pleasant view over the park. Sighing, she sank down on the sofa.

She might have made an enemy of the housekeeper, but there was no remedy for it. The woman needed to know that Temper was taking the reins and would hold them in a firm grip. If Mrs Hobbs resented the 'outsiders' who had arrived to take over from her beloved master and his heir, she would either get over it, or be replaced.

Besides, dealing with one recalcitrant English house-keeper would be good training for managing the coterie of foreign servants Giff would insist were necessary to protect her, once she began her foreign travels.

Chapter Eighteen

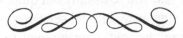

A few hours later, after recording on some stationary she'd found in the library desk the additional items she'd noted during her tour by the housekeeper earlier that afternoon, Temper set the list aside.

Fortunately, it appeared that, for the most part, Fensworth House was in sound condition. There wouldn't be a need for extensive repairs or renovations, and the furnishings, though outdated, were of a superior quality that would reveal itself after they'd been properly cleaned and polished.

To her surprise, once they completed the tour and Temper had gone over a summary of what needed to be done, Mrs Hobbs, who had been wooden-faced throughout the inspection, made her a deep curtsy—and thanked her!

'The Dowager was never much interested in Fensworth, your ladyship,' she confessed. 'We all knew she'd rather be in London. So I'm afraid…standards slipped. It will be a right pleasure to have the staff and funds to bring this old house back to what it should be.'

So it appeared she would not have to waste time wrangling with the housekeeper—or trying to replace her, Temper thought gratefully.

As she put away her pen, she heard a stirring at the doorway. Looking up, to her surprise, she saw her new husband striding into the library.

'Giff!' she said delightedly, genuinely glad to see him despite the disturbing sensual response he aroused, just by walking into the room. 'I didn't expect you to return this early. Mixton said you're usually out quite late.'

'I couldn't stay away and let servants welcome you to your new home,' he said, coming over to her, arms outstretched—before he lowered them and halted awkwardly a pace away. 'I'm so glad you're here,' he said simply.

Scanning his face, she thought with a shock that she'd never seen Giff so drawn and weary. 'You look so tired and thin!' she exclaimed, her heart flooded with such sadness and compassion for him that, abandoning the restraint she'd promised herself to exercise, she rose and walked into his arms.

As he hugged her tightly, she could almost feel his body vibrate with grief and sadness and a tension she understood only too well—a sense of being pulled out of his familiar world into a place and duties almost as foreign to him as it was to her. For long moments, she let him hold her, hoping to transfer to him her warmth, support and affection.

Finally, he let her go. 'I should go up and change. I'm still smelling of horse, although at least my boots aren't muddy this time. And you've already begun setting things to rights, I see. Such a flurry of sweeping and polishing and cleaning I passed as I walked in! I suppose Mama has been too...cast down to look after things and I've been so preoccupied with the estate, I simply haven't had time to deal with the house.'

'That, dear sir, is why you have a wife. Mama might have been infamous among the *ton*, but she was a capital house-keeper and she taught Pru and me well.'

'It will be a relief to come home and not find everything dark and grimy,' he confessed. 'Have you ordered dinner as well? Meals have been…haphazard of late.'

'You shall have a proper dinner tonight! And every night hereafter. Shall we invite your mama to share it?'

'I doubt she'll leave her room, but we shall ask her. Once I've washed and changed, I'll take you in to meet her.'

Temper blew out a breath. 'Oh, dear. I can only imagine what her friends in London have told her about me. About us.'

'She knows all about the scandal, that's for sure. Amid the flood of weeping that began the moment I walked in, the only thing she said was that she hoped I wouldn't create here any scandals as tawdry as the one in London.'

Though Giff gave her a rueful smile, she could tell by the hurt in his eyes how much that comment had stung. Furious on his behalf, she had a hard time restraining the acid comment that jumped to her lips. 'I allow your mother a great deal of latitude, given her loss,' she said after a moment, 'but even so, that was…unkind.'

'Probably, but about what I expected. The prodigal son come home to displace her beloved Robert? I couldn't hope to be greeted with open arms.' He sighed. 'I don't mind, really. I'm used to it by now. All I shall insist upon is that she treat you with respect.'

Oh, he minds, she thought, holding on to her temper with an effort. How could a mother be so oblivious to the worth of her son? Well, that was another thing Temper was determined to change.

'It's not your fault you had to replace her "beloved Robert",' Temper retorted. 'And if she and your father hadn't been so…short-sighted, you would have been far better prepared to step into his shoes. But enough of that. We shall have a good dinner, and I will do my best to amuse you.'

That drew a genuine smile. 'I could use some amusement. Although I'm not so sure how good the dinner will be.'

'It had better be excellent, or we'll be looking for a new cook.'

He chuckled. 'My little termagant. Have I told you yet how glad I am you are here?'

'You have,' she said, smiling at him fondly. 'We'll see if your "wild bride" can stir things up at Fensworth as effectively as she did in London. Let me change for dinner and then I'll be ready to meet your redoubtable mother.'

Giff tapped her nose with his finger. 'I'll see you shortly, then.'

Watching him walk out, Temper frowned. If the Dowager Countess thought grief over her losses would allow her to get away with abusing Giff any further, she was about to discover otherwise. And probably get an earful of plain speaking into the bargain.

A short time later, Giff walked Temper upstairs to his mother's rooms. 'She still occupies what should be the Countess's suite. I hadn't the heart to insist she vacate the rooms.'

'Are you occupying the Earl's suite?' she asked, more than a little nervous to know exactly where Giff intended to sleep.

'No, I've gone back to my old room—just down the hall from the one you have. Which is the prettiest of the guest bedchambers.'

Relieved to know he didn't sleep in a room adjacent to her own, she nodded. 'There will be time enough to change the living arrangements.'

Giff sighed. 'Yes. That's one battle I didn't want to have to fight yet.' Pausing before an imposing chamber door located at the centre of the bedchamber wing, he said, 'This is it. Are you ready?'

Her anger over his mother's shabby treatment of him still smouldering, Temper gave him an encouraging smile. 'Remember, you married a hoyden who possesses not a particle of conventional maidenly deference and lets no one intimidate her. I shall have no trouble dealing with your mama.'

He smiled down at her. 'I don't suppose you will. And for the first time, if I had to wager on the outcome, I wouldn't bet on my mother keeping the upper hand.'

They entered a room with shuttered windows and a mantel draped in black. As her eyes adjusted to the dimness, Temper made out the figure of a woman reclining against the pillows of a massive four-poster bed, a handkerchief clutched in her hand as she stared sightlessly ahead of her.

No matter how much Temper resented the woman for her treatment of Giff, she had to admit the Dowager had good cause to grieve.

'We won't disturb you for long, Mama,' Giff said, walking with Temper to his mother's bedside. 'But I wanted to present to you my wife, who arrived this afternoon from London. Mama, this is Temperance.'

The Dowager glanced over, her faintly contemptuous

gaze looking Temper up and down. 'So you're Felicia's daughter. You certainly have the look of her. And her propensity for scandal, apparently. If only Gifford had used his time in London more profitably.'

Squeezing Giff's hand to forestall his reply, Temper said pleasantly, 'Scandals have a way of being magnified out of all proportion. And Gifford has used his time in London most profitably, indeed. As I'm sure you know, he's a leading member of the group of Parliamentarians who are forging legislation that will make the most significant changes in the way the country has been governed since the Magna Carta. He's now turning that same intensity and attention to detail to mastering the requirements of managing Fensworth—after having received very little preparation for the task! You must be very proud of his achievements. I know Lady Sayleford is and so am I.'

The Dowager regarded Temper with some hostility. 'Impertinent chit, aren't you?'

'Forthright, certainly. I know you aren't feeling yourself yet, but we did want you to know we'd be delighted if you could join us for dinner.'

'Join you for—!' the Countess exclaimed, her eyes widening. 'I am by no means ready yet to leave my rooms!'

'I am sorry to hear it. You must let me know if there is anything I or the staff can do to make you more comfortable,' Temper replied.

'So eager to wrest control from my hands?' she said bitterly.

'Not at all, Countess. Only doing what must be done. We won't intrude upon you any further now, but I hope to visit you again soon.'

As the Dowager made no response to that, Temper dipped her a curtsy. 'Goodnight, Lady Fensworth.'

She could feel the anger vibrating in Giff as she took his arm. But he merely inclined his head and said, 'Goodnight, Mama.'

Giff blew out a breath as they walked back down the stairs. 'That didn't go too badly, I suppose. Though I wish you had let me tell her in no uncertain terms that I will not allow her to insult you.' Then he laughed. 'Not that she was able to intimidate you one little bit. Bravo, Temper!'

She chuckled. 'That was just the first round. I do sympathise with her loss, but whether your mama likes it or not, you are master here now. Sooner or later she will have to acknowledge that. Or maybe not,' Temper added thoughtfully, an alternative solution suddenly occurring to her.

'Enough about my mother,' Giff said as they walked into the dining room. 'Ah, what a delicious aroma! I'm ready to tuck into the best dinner that's been served me since I left London.'

'I certainly hope so,' Temper said as he held out the chair for her.

'Thank you again, Temper,' he said as he took his own seat. 'I'm sure the meal will taste as delicious as it smells. After dinner, though, I'm afraid I must study the estate books and then look over some agricultural journals I had sent out from London. Will you be too disappointed if I abandon you? I expect you are tired after your journey and will be longing for your bed. You…you needn't lock your bedchamber door. I intend to honour all the promises I made you.'

Her greatest worry alleviated—for the moment—Temper felt a swell of relief and gratitude. 'Thank *you*, Giff. I am tired. You don't need to entertain me, you know. Concentrate on your duties. And if there is anything I can do to help, please tell me.'

'You're already making a difference,' he said, motioning towards the gleaming silver, shining crystal and the array of dishes being brought in by the footmen. 'How could I ask you for anything more?'

So he wouldn't be asking for…that, Temper thought, unease stirring in her belly. In spite of this temporary reprieve, with her new husband no longer simply 'Mr Newell' but now 'the Earl of Fensworth', the terms of their marriage would inevitably have to change.

How much of a respite would she get before she must steel herself to perform *that* duty?

Deciding there was no time like the present to settle matters with the Dowager—who, if left to her own devices, would probably immure herself in her rooms in deepest mourning for years—after bidding Giff goodnight, Temper went up to knock on the door of the Countess's suite.

The door was answered by a dour-faced maid. Not waiting to give the Dowager time to refuse her, Temper walked past the woman and over to the bed.

Looking startled, Lady Fensworth turned to Temper and frowned. 'What are you doing here?'

'I wanted to see if there was anything I could bring you before I retire,' she said pleasantly.

'You could return me to my solitude.'

'And so I shall. Once we…understand each other a bit better.'

'Understand each other?' the Dowager repeated. 'All you need to understand is—'

'I imagine your London friends keep you updated on the latest gossip,' Temper broke in.

Exhaling an exasperated sigh, Lady Fensworth said, 'Of what interest to me is idle gossip?'

Declining to answer that comment, Temper said, 'You might want to leaven whatever you've heard about me—or my marriage to your son—with the knowledge that Lady Sayleford agreed to sponsor my debut, supported both of us through the fiasco at Lady's Arnold ball—I'm sure you've heard both sides of that story—and was present at our wedding. She loaned her own carriage and staff to bring me here. So I would weigh any...negative assessments of my character against the fact of her steadfast support and her blessing on our marriage.'

'Well, Gifford is her godchild. She would be bound to support him.'

'There isn't another high-ranking lady of the *ton* who knows more about what goes on in society than Lady Sayleford. You would agree?'

The Dowager nodded reluctantly.

'And Lady Sayleford has never given her backing to anyone who does not meet her exacting standards—has she?'

Lady Fensworth remained silent for a moment. 'Not to my knowledge,' she allowed at last.

'Exactly. In any event, what you think of me isn't of great concern. But I would ask you to remember that although Gifford wasn't your favoured son, he *is* still your son. The staff need to know that you support, rather than resent, his becoming the Earl. As head of this household, they take their cues from you.'

'That boy has been nothing but trouble since he was born!' she burst out. 'The birth itself was...difficult. I was recovering for months and, after that… I was never able to bear another child. Four babies I lost before their time, three precious daughters and another beautiful son.'

Shocked, Temper sat in silence. So that explained the Countess's animosity, she thought, compassion welling up for the woman. Her heartache and resentment of Giff were as deep as they were unreasonable.

'I've never lost a child,' Temper said softly. 'I can't imagine such devastation. But surely you recognise that it wasn't Gifford's fault?'

The Countess sighed. 'I suppose I do…in my head. But every time I looked at him as he was growing up, all I saw was the faces of those little dead babes.'

'Which is why you sent him away to school and left him there. Why it's so difficult for you to accept him here, now.'

'He represents everything that has been taken from me!' she cried. 'First the babies and now my beloved husband and s-son!'

'It must be hard,' Temper acknowledged, trying to summon up as much sympathy as she could—a difficult task, since this woman had cheated Giff out of the mother's love that should be a child's birthright, for tragedies over which he'd had no control. 'Giff tells me you love London. Your son may have married a woman your informers claimed is "infamous", but she is also very wealthy. If it is too painful for you to watch someone else take Robert's place, why don't you lease a house in London? Live there for as much of the year as you wish, visit friends, go to the theatre, shop for whatever you like. It may help to ease your grief, if you don't have to wake up every morning here, immediately remembering they are gone and feeling again that crushing loss.'

For a long time, the Countess remained silent. 'There might be something to what you propose,' she said at last. 'I do love London. Not that I could even contemplate going to balls or entertainments or the theatre.'

'Not yet, of course. But you would have friends to call on you and invite you to quiet dinners, walks or drives in the park, shopping and all the resources of a great city. Distractions only from your grief, I grant. But distractions have their uses.'

Lady Fensworth turned her head to gaze at Temper. 'Lady Sayleford approved of you, did she? Perhaps... I am beginning to see why. Very well, I will...consider what you've proposed.'

'That's all I ask. And now I will leave you in peace.'

Temper walked out, closing the door softly behind her, her heart grieving for the tragedies that had ruined an innocent little boy's youth and robbed his mother of loving a son who was so deserving of it.

Maybe, if the Dowager were able to get away and clear her mind, she would find it in her heart to love Giff now.

At the very least, Temper hoped she would take herself off where her contemptuous indifference wouldn't continue to unfairly wound the man Temper cared about so deeply.

Chapter Nineteen

Two weeks later, the bone-weary new Earl of Fensworth turned his spent horse over to a groom and walked back towards Fensworth House. The day he'd stood in the parlour in Vraux House and discovered that tragedy had overtaken his family seemed a lifetime ago, he thought as he trudged towards the entry. His only worry then, how to continue with his life and work with as little disturbance as possible after having taken an irresistible bride he must none the less resist. He laughed without humour. How much simpler life had been!

The last weeks had been a never-ending blur of packing, travelling, consultations with bankers, solicitors, estate agents, farm managers, housekeepers, tenants and the doctors who tended his still-ailing mother.

The one, unexpected bright spot in the long dark agony had been Temper. His new wife had proved herself tireless, industrious and surprisingly capable in doing all she could to assist him. Fortunately, by the time he took to his bed in the wee hours, he was so exhausted both mentally and physically that he fell asleep before he could be tempted by the knowledge that his beautiful wife reposed in a chamber just a short walk down the hall.

As he gradually gained mastery of the thousand estate details he had to learn, the merciful boon of those long hours of work would disappear. But for now, with everything else he had to deal with, he was heartily grateful not to have to wrestle with restraining his desire for her.

And then his heart leapt, pulling him from his tired reflections, as he spotted Temper approaching down the drive.

'Here,' she said, holding out a welcome mug of ale as she reached him. Craning her neck towards the stables, she continued, 'I hope the groom has something equally reviving for your horse, or I may have to charge you with animal neglect. The poor nag looks done up.'

'Yes, I told Hoarly to give him an extra ration. We rode the entire southern border today and, though the river level has gone down somewhat, it's pretty heavy going, with the sucking mud of the verges and the pools of standing water. I'd take you there, but the riding is still dangerous.'

'The two failed steam pumps haven't been repaired yet?'

The ones his father and brother had been going to investigate the morning they drowned. 'Not yet. After inspecting them, I agreed with Randolph that we should reinstall the windmill devices on top, so we may get some pumping use from them until we can bring in some steam mechanics from Lincoln. Our local wheelwright, wainwright, farrier and blacksmith have all had a go, trying to fix them, with no luck.'

'You trust Randolph's advice?'

He took a swig of ale before responding. 'I guess I have

to. He's been the estate agent here for twenty years and certainly knows the place far better than I do. I've not really lived here since I was sent away to school at age six.'

He brushed away the memory, still hurtful after all these years, that after a modicum of education at Eton, his elder brother had been summoned back home to be tutored by clerics, his father considering the education of his heir in the running of his estate more important than a stint at university. Even more important, Giff knew, he'd wanted his eldest son with him.

Unlike the second son, who languished alone at school, unless a classmate like Gregory invited him home for holidays and term breaks.

He resurfaced from those bitter memories to find Temper gazing at him. 'You are intelligent, grasp things quickly and have a strong sense of responsibility,' she said, gripping his hand. 'You will master the details you need to run the estate. You've already made a splendid beginning.'

He clutched her fingers, savouring the contact, inhaling the lovely spicy scent of her. 'I appreciate the encouragement.' He laughed ruefully. 'So many of the staff have been…sceptical of my abilities.'

'How could they not be, when you weren't brought up to run this place and have spent so much of your life away that they don't really know you? Once they see what a splendid job you are doing, they will come to admire and rely on you, as they did on your father and brother.'

'I certainly hope so.'

'I know so,' she said, gently withdrawing her fingers. 'Now that you're back, are you feeling the same attachment to Fensworth that your brother and father had?'

'I never felt it as a boy—I suppose I resented too much

being excluded. But it does grow on you, this sense of the land. Even more, the responsibility of knowing that how well you manage it will impact the lives of nearly a hundred souls. Though I still intend to continue my work in Parliament, I will spend much more time here in future than I have in recent years.'

'As the master, you must. Now, if Randolph is so competent, why hasn't he had the estate employ a mechanic who knows how to rebuild and maintain the steam engines? You have, what, fifteen of these pumping machines to prevent flooding and keep the fields dry and arable?'

'Oh, the usual answer—money. Not enough to hire permanent staff, Randolph said when I asked him.'

If the draining had been completed and successfully maintained, the tragedy that took his kinsmen's lives might have been avoided. And he would be back in Parliament, listening to testimony, crafting legislation, engaged in spirited discussions about things he knew well and about which he cared passionately—rather than in this remote area near the Wash, struggling to deal with agricultural issues about which he knew so little.

'Well, money will no longer be a problem, will it? I saw several pretty little cottages when I walked the perimeter of the high ground yesterday. With steady work and a nice thatched house, you might be able to lure one of the Lincoln mechanics to remain at Fensworth.'

'A good suggestion,' he said, once again grateful for the no-nonsense, practical advice she continued to dispense. 'How wise I was to marry a rich woman.'

She chuckled. 'Well, at least you derived one benefit from wedding a hoyden.'

As he looked down at her dancing eyes and lovely face,

despite his fatigue, the repressed desire came flooding back. Along with an unexpectedly strong surge of tenderness.

With his free hand, he caught hers again and brought it to his lips. 'I've received more benefits than I can count. For which I am more grateful than I can express.'

Sadness shadowed her eyes. 'Nothing can make up for the loss of your family. Whatever assistance I can offer, you know I'm happy to give.'

'And how useful it has been! Whipping the negligent housekeeper into shape, co-ordinating with the vicar to plan the funerals, organising the staff to receive condolences from the neighbours, keeping my mother supplied with doctors to tend her—even hiring your own post chaises to travel here, while I selfishly rode all the way from London.'

'Burdened with such worry and grief, I couldn't have stood being cooped up in a carriage either,' she said.

Although it wasn't just grief and worry that had compelled him to ride the long miles into Lincolnshire alone. With his emotions raw—grief, frustration at having to leave Parliament with his work undone, deep misgivings about the unknown duties awaiting him at Fensworth—and his strength at a low ebb, he wasn't sure he could have travelled for days with Temper in a closed carriage and still managed to resist his desire for her.

Just as he now worked himself to exhaustion, to make sure temptation didn't overwhelm him some lonely evening.

'No worried frowns,' she said, making him sigh as she smoothed her fingers along his forehead. 'See what a very capable explorer I shall make?'

'Capable indeed,' he had to admit, stifling a pang of protest. He didn't *want* her to head off for parts unknown. How quickly he'd grown accustomed to seeing her every day, to relying on the assistance she offered in a calm, capable manner he wouldn't have previously believed possible for impetuous Temperance Lattimar.

The impulsive child truly had grown into a competent manager, as well as desirable woman. And unlike his mother, who required the ministrations of various maids and dressers and a series of social engagements to keep her entertained, since their arrival, Temper had required almost no attention from him.

She cared for herself with the minimum help from a single maid. Rather than remain indoors to be waited on by the household staff when he was gone for long hours, riding about the estate, she rode out herself in all weathers to bring him a basket of meat and ale. When he did remain at the manor, occupied with the estate books, being tutored by Randolph about seeds, planting, crop rotation and harvests, or reading about the myriad agricultural topics of which he knew so little, not once had she interrupted him, demanding that he curtail his work to devote some time to her.

In the odd moments he'd found himself free and gone in search of her, he'd found her reading in the library. Or riding out, always with a groom he insisted accompany her—an impediment he'd worried the impatient Temper might try to evade. To which, at his apology for curtailing the speed at which he knew she preferred to ride, she'd replied simply, 'With all you have on your plate, you don't need to worry about me falling into a canal or being thrown into the mud.'

He didn't have much experience with women—other than with demi-reps in the bedroom—but he guessed that such independent self-reliance was rare among females.

He knew his mother had never exhibited a trace of it.

The more he was with her, the more she impressed him.

And the stronger grew the feeling that he didn't want her to leave and trek about the world for months at a time, without him.

'I hope you're not meaning to desert me for some exotic place quite yet,' he replied at last.

'Of course not! I won't leave Fensworth until you feel you have a firm handle on the duties you must perform here. Even after I return to London, it will be some time before I'm ready to travel.' She gave him a smile that didn't quite succeed. 'With Prudence and her soldier having taken over the mission that was to have framed my explorations, I must first decide where—and how—I wish to travel. And then there will be all that entourage-building you're so concerned about.'

'I've almost finished the essentials of what I need to do for the estate. Once the last pumps are working again, nothing else requires immediate attention. The crops are in, all the repairs and supplies needed by the tenants are being addressed and the household supplies not provided locally have been ordered from Lincoln or London.'

'You intend to go back to London soon, then?' she asked, looking surprised.

'Yes. In the last day or so, when I finally had enough time to think about something other than estate business, I realised that, though everyone has been addressing me as Earl, I don't legally hold that title yet. I won't until the Committee on Privileges reviews the documentation proving I am the legal heir and issues a writ of summons to the Lords. A process I expect will take some time. Until then, I'm plain Mr Newell and can legally remain in the House of Commons. If the summons is delayed long enough, I might actually see the factory bill to passage before I have to give up my seat and move to the Lords.'

'How satisfying that would be to see it through!' she exclaimed, looking delighted for him.

'The most satisfying thought I've had since I read that courier's message in London, another lifetime ago. Now,' he said, holding open for her the side door they'd just reached, 'I must go up and bathe before I drip mud all over the floors you just made the housekeeper polish. I think I can spare the time tonight to join you for dinner, if you'd like.'

'I would like that! Besides...' her smile faded and she looked suddenly...nervous and uncertain '... I, too, have something I've been putting off, that we really need to discuss.'

'That sounds ominous,' he said, watching her expression with concern.

She sighed. "I know. I'll see you at dinner.'

Whatever it was she wished to talk about, Temperance did not bring up anything serious at dinner. Instead, fortified by a bottle of his father's best claret she'd had the butler bring up from the cellars, she kept him chatting with a series of questions about the myriad details he'd been learning about the estate.

After dining, with Giff declining to remain and consume his port in solitary splendour, he accompanied Temper into the small sitting room, where a snug fire burned on the hearth.

He poured himself a glass of spirits and joined her on the sofa.

'I've been so busy, I've not had time to introduce you to the rest of the families in the county. When we return next, we'll need to give a ball, so everyone can meet the new Countess.'

Temper laughed and shook her head. 'Me—a countess!'

'No more incredible than me becoming the Earl. Who would have thought it?' He sighed. 'Certainly not my mother.'

'Is she feeling any better? I've had the doctor summoned whenever she calls for him and send in whatever her maid says she requires, but I haven't forced my company on her.'

'I looked in on her briefly tonight.' He gave a short laugh. 'She even seemed…rather happy to see me, although that would be such a novel occurrence, I might just have imagined it.'

'Perhaps she's beginning to realise that, though she may have lost a son, she has another just as competent—and worthy of her love.'

'I wouldn't go that far,' he said wryly. 'But you have been working your magic again, haven't you? She told me you'd suggested she might want to relocate to London, where she wouldn't be…surrounded by so many unhappy memories. She actually asked if there would be funds to support such a move.'

'I hope you assured her there would be!'

'I did. Fortunately, though the estate operated with barely a profit these last few years, Father was not forced to go into debt. There are no mortgages or loans to repay, so with the infusion of my rich wife's dowry, the Fensworth finances are finally on an even keel again.'

'I could visit her and encourage her intention of going to London. Perhaps add that if she cannot master her grief, her health will certainly suffer and neither her late husband nor her beloved elder son would have wanted that. That in

London, where she isn't daily reminded of their loss, she would have a better chance to heal.'

'So she wouldn't have to see me here, in Robert's place.'

'I could tactfully remind her of that, too,' Temper said drily.

He laughed. 'Temper, tactful? You may turn into a politician's wife yet!'

Her smile at that rejoinder was tentative and, from her suddenly tense and hesitant manner, he sensed that she was about to bring up whatever was concerning her. Tensing himself in apprehension, he waited.

'It's the matter of my becoming your wife that we need to discuss.'

'Thus far, I think you've done a marvellous job.'

'At part of it, I suppose.' She took a deep breath. 'With the shock of the news and the flurry of preparations to leave London, it wasn't until the long carriage ride to Fensworth that the full implications of your changed status occurred to me. No longer a private individual, a simple politician, but the holder of an ancient title and a vast property. Which must be handed down to an heir. Since my arrival, despite all the busyness, I've… I've thought of little else.'

Was she implying she might consider amending the terms of their *marriage blanc*? Tamping down a thrill of hope, he said, 'Naturally, the estate will be handed down to an heir. I have cousins.'

'Yes, but surely you would prefer to pass your inheritance down to…a son of your own.'

He swallowed hard against a rising tide of excitement and arousal. 'Does that mean…you are considering a change in our…intimate relationship?'

She nodded. 'I think I must.'

Hands trembling, he set down his glass. 'Are you sure you want to do this?'

She shrugged. 'You are responsible for the estate. As your wife, I am responsible, not just for the household, but for the succession. Try as I have to convince myself otherwise, that's a fact.'

With everything he desired almost within reach, Giff had to restrain himself from leaping up and dancing around the room. 'Are you *sure* you're sure?'

She nodded.

The fatigue of the last few weeks forgotten, Giff leaned towards her. As she angled her head up, he leaned down and kissed her.

Slow and easy, he cautioned himself, trying to hold back the rampaging desire. *She may now be willing, but she's still an innocent maid.* He shouldn't try to sweep her straight from a single chaste kiss to complete union, probably not even in a single night.

But the touch of her lips was so intoxicating, he had to have more. Slowly, he deepened the kiss, until, as he gently probed at her lips with his tongue, she parted them. He moved within, licking and sampling, drunk on the taste of her. And when, with a little sigh, she moved her tongue to meet his, thought was paralysed entirely and need seized control.

He kissed her with ever-increasing urgency, trailing his fingertips over the satin of her bare throat, her silken shoulders, tracing the edge of her low bodice. And then he had to touch her, cup the full, voluptuous roundness of her breasts.

One hand on her chin to hold her mouth to his, he skimmed the other down her arm and under her breast. Though she probably wore too thick a covering of chemise and stays to be able to feel the full effect, he had to rub his thumb over the nipple.

But at the first glancing touch, she stiffened and pulled away. 'S-sorry, Giff,' she gasped. 'But I—I am too tired to start anew tonight. Forgive me?'

Though he wanted to weep and snarl with frustration, there was only one answer. 'Of course, sweeting. It's been a long day. Go to bed and get some rest.'

She gave him a tremulous smile. 'Thank you, Giff.' Rising quickly, she practically ran out of the room.

Chapter Twenty

Back in the safely of her chamber, Temper closed the door and leaned against it, trembling as the panic slowly subsided.

It was her duty to give Giff an heir. She knew that. For the past few weeks, she'd been working up the courage to act upon that knowledge. And tonight, she had fully intended to allow him to claim all the rights of a husband.

But then he'd touched her *there*—and she just couldn't.

She stumbled over to the bed and sat on the edge. She was tired, just as she'd told Giff. Maybe tomorrow, after she'd rested, it would be easier.

But even as she whispered those comforting words, the sense of panic, of being barely able to breathe, descended again. *The dead weight of him crushing her, his harsh ragged breaths, the searing pain.*

Shuddering, she forced away the memories.

Despite all those weeks of trying to prepare herself, she didn't know if she could go through with it tomorrow, either. Or the next day or the next. No matter how competently she might be fulfilling the other duties of a wife, she couldn't *do* this.

Marrying Giff had been a dreadful mistake.

What was she to do about it?

All she knew was, after what had happened tonight, she couldn't remain at Fensworth and deal with him now. The ease of being with Giff, the satisfaction of helping him cope with the problems that had been dumped in his lap, the teasing, intoxicating, sensual thrill of his physical nearness—all of that had lured her into inviting him to begin something tonight that she hadn't been able to finish. She needed to get away from his disturbing, brain-numbing presence, so she could think clearly and decide what to do next.

She stood, waiting for her heartbeat to slow before she rang the bell to summon the maid who would help her prepare for bed.

Tomorrow she'd tell Giff she was returning to London.

And so, the next morning, after having barely slept, Temper rose early, needing to talk with Giff before he rode out with the estate agent. Sitting in the breakfast room, her ear perked for the sound of his footsteps, she toyed with a cup of coffee, her stomach too queasy to tolerate food.

Fortunately, a letter the maid brought to her last night, delivered to Fensworth by a servant returning late from the village, gave her a perfect excuse to implement the course of action she'd already decided upon.

Then the sound of bootsteps in the hallway reached her. She put a hand to her throat, conscious of the sudden acceleration of her pulse.

'Temper!' Giff said, halting in surprise when he saw her. 'What are you doing up so early?'

She curved her lips into a smile, hoping it didn't look as forced as it felt. 'I wanted to catch you before you rode out. I... I've had a letter from Pru. She and Johnnie are about to leave on their first voyage. Since I don't know when I might see them again, I want to return to London and bid them goodbye.'

'Of course,' Giff said, walking over to pour himself some coffee. 'It will be ten days or so before I can leave, but you needn't delay. When do you think you'll be ready to go?'

'Today.' At the surprise on his face, she added hastily, 'I must leave immediately, or I shall miss them. And I don't have much to pack. We departed London in such haste, only a few of the new mourning gowns I'd commissioned were completed. All the rest should be awaiting me in London.'

'Today!' he repeated, shaking his head. 'I wish you didn't have to leave so soon. But I wouldn't want you to miss saying goodbye to Pru.'

'Thank you for understanding, Giff. I'll leave you to your breakfast,' she said, rising from her chair, 'and go start my packing.'

He caught her hand as she walked by him, stopping her flight. 'The packing shouldn't take you long to do?'

When she continued to look away, not meeting his gaze, he sighed. 'I'm sorry about last night, Temper. I was...too hasty. I didn't mean to...frighten you. I promise, when I rejoin you in London, I'll do better.'

Ah, but could she? Or would it be better for her to repudiate her responsibilities, take a draft on her bank and begin provisioning a voyage—somewhere, anywhere—immediately, so there was no awkward reunion in London?

She'd figure that out after she got to back to Vraux House.

'You've nothing to apologise for,' she said. *This whole debacle is my fault, not his.* 'I'll…see you in London, then.' *Maybe.* 'Goodbye, Giff.'

Gently pulling her hand from his grip, she hurried out of the breakfast room.

A week later, Temper mounted the entry stairs at Vraux House, having just bid farewell to her sister and her new husband as they left on their maiden voyage. She couldn't help feeling an overwhelming envy of them for setting out on the adventure she'd always dreamed would be hers.

And for looking so happy in their marriage when she'd made such a hash of her own.

On the drive back to London, through the days and nights since, she'd done little but agonise over what to do about her dilemma. Insist on adhering to the original terms of their bargain, despite Giff's change in status? Flee to the West Indies? Force herself to do her duty, whatever the consequences?

The options kept going around and around in her head. Giff would be returning to London soon and she still had no idea which one she should choose.

As she crossed the second-floor landing, heading for the next flight up to her chamber, she noticed the library door was open, her father at his desk within. Acting on impulse, she checked in mid-stride and turned to enter his inner sanctum.

Unusually, he looked up as she walked in. 'Temperance?' he said, as if not sure he'd recognised her.

'Yes, it's me, Papa,' she said, coming over to stand by his desk.

'I gave you away to be married, didn't I? Where is your husband?'

'Gifford is still at Fensworth, settling matters at the estate. He'll be returning to London soon.'

Her father nodded. 'Good. He should be nearby, where he can protect you.'

Emboldened by her own desperation, she said, 'Is that why you married Mama? To protect her?'

At first she thought, as he had when she'd questioned him before, that he would simply not answer. Then, at length, he nodded. 'I knew her family would force her to marry money. Viscount Loxley wanted her. He was a bad man, he would have hurt her and she is so lovely—a treasure that must be safeguarded. Like you and Prudence. I couldn't give her—other things—she needed, but I could keep her safe and let her choose the men she wanted.'

'So...you loved her?'

He shrugged, as if the word didn't have any meaning for him. 'I could protect and support her.'

And wasn't that love, of a sort? Perhaps the only sort of which her father was capable? One couldn't expect of someone more than they had the resources to give.

'Did you ever tell her that?'

Lord Vraux shook his head. 'Why would I?'

Temper sighed, feeling a wave of sympathy for her father—and her mother. The world of emotion was foreign to him and trying to talk about it resulted in a conversation about as revealing as if she'd been questioning him in English and he responding in Urdu.

Before she could say anything else, he'd turned his attention back to the object on his desk—an illustrated medieval manuscript, its luminous blues, yellows and reds gleaming in the light.

Knowing he'd already forgotten her existence, Temper walked from the room.

Love came in many different shapes and varieties. The stilted, limited variety her father had given her mother hadn't been enough for her—yet it was probably all Vraux had to offer.

Would a limited marriage be enough for her—or for Giff?

Especially if, as Lady Sayleford claimed, he truly loved her? She'd not yet forced herself to fully examine how she felt about that possibility. How deeply her own feelings were engaged towards him.

She couldn't begin to consider those questions until she determined what she meant to do about the more immediate problem of whether, or how, she could live with him.

She told herself that he had agreed to her terms before they wed. He did have cousins to step into his shoes, safeguard the estate and carry on the family name, without needing heirs of his own body. The fact that he was now an earl shouldn't change anything.

But a small voice inside kept whispering that she, who prided herself on courage, was really just being a coward. That Giff was valiantly shouldering broad new responsibilities—while she was failing him in the only duty that counted for a peer's wife. Especially if he loved her, she owed him more.

She owed him an heir.

When he joined her in London, she would have to do better.

* * *

In the late afternoon a week later, with more than a little trepidation, Gifford Newell walked up the stairs to Vraux House.

'Lord Fensworth!' Overton said in surprise as he opened to door to him, a smile creasing his normally impassive face. 'Welcome back to London! Her ladyship is in the garden. Shall I tell her I'll bring tea to the front parlour? Or…would you prefer her to meet you in your rooms?'

As most newlyweds would? Giff thought, biting back an ironic smile at Overton's discreet phrasing. 'I'll need to wash off the dust of the road. You can tell my wife that I'll be in my rooms.'

Thus giving her the choice. Would she come up to him? Or send a footman to say she'd prefer to meet him downstairs for tea?

It probably depended on just how badly he had frightened her. For there was no escaping the conclusion that it had to have been his rather limited advances—and not so limited display of ardour—that had sent her fleeing back to the safety of London.

He sighed as he trotted up the stairs. If her sojourn back home had convinced her they must revert to the original restrictions she'd imposed on their marriage, he had no right to protest. He'd given his word, after all.

It wasn't fair, just because an earldom had fallen out of the sky to settle on his shoulders, to expect Temper to change something that, for reasons he hadn't yet been able to determine, she had felt so strongly about she'd hinged her whole acceptance of his proposal on them.

And so, if he had to, he must live with them. And hope that, in time, he might discover enough of the reasons behind her reluctance to help mitigate the constant state of frustrated arousal that bedevilled him.

Just in case, Giff dismissed his valet as soon as the man brought him hot water and towels, telling him he intended to rest after his long journey and would call him when he was ready to dress.

Unlike Overton, Miles permitted himself a grin before bowing himself out with a cheeky 'Enjoy your *rest*, sir.'

It appeared everyone in the household expected he would be disporting himself with his new wife. Except, probably, his new wife.

Resigning himself to the fact that he was going to feel rather foolish when he called Miles back, if she *didn't* come to his rooms, he had just wiped his dripping face when he heard a light footstep pause outside his door. Then a knock, and Temper's voice calling, 'Giff, may I come in?'

The half-arousal he'd been fighting for the last hour, knowing he would soon see her again, hardened instantly. Through a suddenly dry throat, he croaked out, 'Of course.'

He mustn't assume, just because she was joining him, that she was ready to give intimacy another chance. She would know as well as he what the whole household expected of a newlywed couple's reunion, and wouldn't want the staff speculating about the state of their marriage.

Patience, he urged himself, his hands trembling as he replaced the towel and turned to greet her.

She was walking towards him, looking so lovely and so welcoming that his chest tightened. With her golden hair and warm smile, she was like sunshine filling the cold and lonely void of a heart that had never received the affection it craved from the family that had been supposed to love him—and hadn't.

To his deep satisfaction, she allowed him to embrace her. *Thank you, Lord, that I didn't frighten her away completely*, he thought as he held her, breathing in the sorely missed jasmine scent of her. Whenever restraint was required, he would master it to keep her here, in his arms, where she belonged. Where he needed her. Even if this was all he would ever have of her.

When she pulled back, mastering the urge to hold on, he let her go. 'How stunning you look! I'd forgotten how beautiful you are.'

She laughed—seeming, to his infinite relief, to have regained the ease in his presence that had been so notably lacking their last morning at Fensworth. 'In ten days? And you're just being gallant. I look like a hag in black!'

'Nothing you wear in any colour could ever make you look remotely like a hag,' he retorted. 'Shall I have tea sent up? Or…would you rather take it in the parlour, after I've made myself decent?'

'I…thought we might remain here. And possibly become even more…indecent.'

His pulse rate accelerated so violently, he felt dizzy. 'You're giving me that chance…to do better?'

She nodded, looking nervous, but determined. 'I'd give us both that chance.'

Almost too afraid to breathe, Giff walked over to her, cradled her chin in his hands and leaned down to kiss her, hoping that first contact conveyed all the tenderness and respect and awe he felt for her, while muting the need.

To his great delight, she opened her mouth to him, inviting the invasion of his tongue. His arms went around her, pulling her closer, as his tongue played with hers, light strokes and parries that deepened and intensified.

Then, when she pulled his shirt from his trousers and ran her hands up the bare skin of his chest, he could wait no longer. Every sense exulting, he lifted her, carried her to the bed and laid her gently back against the pillows.

She settled back and, without any further preliminaries, started drawing her skirts up towards her waist. Startled out of his sensual haze, he stopped her hand—and looked into her face.

A face that was set, resolute—and devoid of any trace of desire.

Inwardly cursing, he sat down beside her and smoothed her skirts back down to her ankles.

'You look like one of those Christian martyrs, tied to the stake and waiting for the lions to be released. What sort of beast do you think I am?'

She attempted a smile. 'I know you won't…ravish me.'

He tried to contain the frustration, disappointment—and hurt. 'I have my pride, too. If my touch is so…repugnant, I certainly won't force it on you.'

'No, it's not that! Surely you can tell that I find you… attractive.'

'Then what is it?' he demanded. She flinched and he made himself soften his tone. 'I'm just a simple male, Temper. I don't understand and I want to.'

She shook her head, tears starting at the corner of her eyes. 'I should never have married you. If I'd known you were going to inherit…'

'What, unworthy me, becoming Earl?' he snapped, devastated that she might share his mother's opinion of his abilities after all.

Her eyes widened. 'You *unworthy*? How could you believe I think that? It's quite the opposite, really. You deserve
to have married a lady of impeccable reputation. Someone
better. Someone...whole.'

He stared at her. 'I have no idea what you're talking
about.'

With a deep sigh, she swiped at the tear that had started
to slide down her cheek. 'I suppose you deserve the truth.
So I will...tell you what I've never revealed to anyone. But
you must promise never to breathe a word of it to another
living soul. Absolutely *no one*. Do you promise?'

'Of course! Though I can't imagine any sin you could
confess worthy of the distress it's obviously causing you.'

'How about the fact that I'm not really a maid?' she spat
back bitterly. 'That I've been...used.'

Chapter Twenty-One

∞

As Giff stared, trying to take in that incomprehensible thought, Temper began, her voice almost expressionless. 'I was fifteen. We were staying at the country house of one of Mama's friends. Papa, as usual, remained in London. Pru had lingered in the parlour, playing charades with some other guests, but I wanted to walk through the gardens. They contained a grotto that was, for me, an enchanted space. I thought it must resemble the exotic landscapes of India or the Far East I'd read about and longed so much to visit.'

She paused and he waited, sick about what he knew must be coming, anxious to know the whole story, though knowing he mustn't rush her.

'I was sitting on a bench, listening to the splash of water in the fountain, when I suddenly realised I wasn't alone. A man stood at the grotto's entrance, watching me. I later learned that he'd attempted to force his attentions on Mama and been slapped for his efforts, dismissed and told never to return. So when he came upon me he was angry...and aroused.'

She blew out a breath. 'The short of it is, he...forced himself on me. Growing up as I did, I suppose I should have guessed what he intended, but I didn't. Not until he'd pinned me on the ground under him and dragged up my skirts. He was so heavy, I could hardly breathe! I fought him, but it was too late, I had no leverage and he was too strong. Afterwards, he went off and I just...lay there. Stunned. Horrified, disbelieving, that a perfect day under a sunny blue sky could have turned into such a nightmare.'

He could have howled with outrage at her anguished tone. 'And you never told anyone?'

'No,' She laughed shortly. 'Of course, he threatened me, saying if I said anything, he'd claim I'd invited his advances. That since, by then, I already looked so much like Mama, everyone would believe him.'

'The bastard!' Giff exploded. 'Surely you knew your family—'

She held up a hand. 'I did. Even at fifteen, I knew what he claimed was false. That I was *not* responsible and had done nothing to encourage him. But I felt so...soiled. I couldn't tell anyone. Pru would have been horrified. Gregory might have tried to call him out. And at learning that one of her rejected lovers had... Mama would have been devastated.'

She turned her face away from his gaze. 'I wanted to run away and hide for ever, but I knew I couldn't. So I tore my gown in several more places—he'd already ripped my bodice—and rubbed in more dirt. I went back and told them I'd fallen out of a tree. I could tell Pru thought it odd, because though I'd always loved climbing trees, I never lost my balance. The others just laughed—or scolded. Up in the chamber assigned to me, I stripped off the gown and soaked in a tub, made the maid bring me more and more hot water, but… I couldn't make myself feel clean. I've never really felt clean, ever since. Before my maid could attempt to repair the dress, I took it to the woods and burned it.' She turned her pained, devastated face to his. 'And now you know the whole of it.'

'Who was it?' Whoever he was, wherever he was, Giff would seek him out—and make him pay.

She shook her head. 'It doesn't matter. He's dead now, anyway—killed in a stupid wager, racing curricles at night. I actually felt cheated when I heard. For weeks after the… incident, I'd teased Christopher into helping me practise with a pistol, telling myself some day I'd shoot him and that would finally put an end to it. But…it has never truly ended.'

Giff swiped a hand over his face, furious, appalled and aching for her pain. He didn't know what to say. Words of comfort were meaningless in the face of the outrage perpetrated against her.

'If what I've just told you makes you feel…differently towards me, I'll understand.'

'Feel differently?' he echoed, uncomprehending.

'Because I'm not the pure maid you thought me. I'm… spoiled.'

Aghast, he said, 'You think I'd *turn away* from you, because—'

She nodded, scattering the tears now dripping down her cheeks. With a savage oath, he grabbed her and pulled her into his arms.

Where she clung to him and wept.

He whispered soothing noises into her hair and held her close while his heart ached and rage burned…because he knew there was nothing he could do to right the wrong done to her.

Finally, the flow of tears slowed and she pushed away from him. 'Sorry,' she muttered.

'You've nothing to be sorry for,' he replied, catching her chin and making her look at him, so she would see and believe the absolute truth of what he was about to say. 'But you're right—I do think differently about you now. I always knew you were strong and courageous, but I had no idea how strong and brave. That at fifteen, scarcely more than child, you bore the whole weight of this horrendous tragedy on your shoulders, alone. To protect those you loved. I don't know how you found the fortitude. I wish there were some way I could wipe the horror from your memory, but I can't. I will do whatever I can, however, anything I can, to make it more…bearable.'

'Thank you,' she whispered. 'I *do* find you attractive, which is why I've been so beastly, seeming to lead you on, then retreating. I was so afraid that if…if I let you go further, it would unleash all those ugly memories and… and I'd scream, or fight you, and I couldn't bear that. But I know now, I must risk it and become fully your wife. You have the responsibility of the Earldom and need to provide it with an heir. And… I've never known a better man, or one I trusted more.'

He smiled. 'I'm relieved to know you trust me. Do you also believe I would never hurt you?'

Again, that little nod.

'And I never will. There will never be anything between us that you don't want. *Want*—not just endure. There's nothing I crave more than to make you fully my wife, but I will only do so when—if—*you* desire it as much as I do.'

She looked troubled. 'I'm not sure I will ever truly desire...that.'

Holding up a hand to stay her from interrupting, he continued, 'Forget about the Earldom and its heirs. That's not important. What occurs between a man and a woman should be beautiful, not ugly. A mutual giving and taking only of pleasure. It will be that way between us, when you are ready. If you are ready. Not before. Never before.'

While she looked at him wonderingly, Giff managed a grin. 'I won't promise not to try to tempt you...but I will never take you. Now, dry your tears, my beautiful, strong, courageous wonder of a wife, and let's go down for tea. It was a long drive and I'm devilishly thirsty.'

Late that night, Giff tiptoed into the bedchamber adjoining his to look down at his sleeping wife. Who, God be praised, after they'd gone down to join the rest of her family, had seemed much lighter and freer than when she'd left Fensworth. As if an intolerable burden had been lifted.

Which, he supposed, it had. He couldn't imagine what it must have cost her, keeping her dreadful secret hidden for so many years.

He hadn't worked out her violator's identity until just a few moments ago, but the bastard who'd raped her must have been Ralph Petersmere. A man of dubious reputation, he'd chased after all the leading beauties of the day, Temper's mother included. Then burned through most of his hapless wife's fortune before dying in the wreck of his curricle during a mad dash across Hounslow Heath, his wager that he could do so in the pitch black of a cloudy, moonless night the talk of the clubs for weeks after the accident.

Had the man not already been dead, Giff would have arm-wrestled Temper to put a bullet through him.

Such sweet innocence, so brutally betrayed, he thought, gently brushing one burnished curl off her forehead. No wonder she reacted so bitterly to all the comments about how much she resembled her mother. His heart contracted again at the pain that miserable excuse for a man had made her endure.

Though he wanted with everything in him to help her heal, he hadn't the remotest idea how to start. Nor was there anyone whose advice he could seek, without risking revealing the secret she'd suffered so much anguish to conceal.

He also knew that unless she did heal, they would never be lovers. Would he be able to stand the frustration of wanting her, knowing he might never have her?

She'd given him permission to slake that frustration elsewhere, of course. But for weeks now, he'd found the idea of intimacy with any other woman…unappealing. He was more than his lusts. And the only woman he really wanted was the fierce, beautiful, unconventional woman he'd married.

As he smiled down at her, an emotion so powerful he could scarcely contain it welled up to immerse him. With sudden, stark clarity, he realised that sometime over the past days or weeks, he had fallen in love with his wife. Simply, completely and absolutely.

He loved Temperance Lattimar with all the fierceness of someone who'd never fully loved, or been loved, before. He would stand by her and protect her and do everything he could to ensure her happiness.

Even if it meant letting her travel abroad without him. Even if it meant never making love to her as he ached to.

But as for the latter, he thought, just barely brushing her lips with one gentle finger, he wasn't ready yet to abandon hope.

After all, she'd admitted she desired him. He would just have to move slowly, tempting her, teasing her, leading her one small step at a time deeper into intimacy. Until she was as ready and eager for that final step as he was.

He wouldn't stop believing that some day, she would be.

But in the meantime, he'd need some respite from the continuous sensual response she sparked in him. Thank heavens he would be spending the next few days with other members of the factory commission out of London, continuing their evidence-gathering at a mill just beyond the city.

While he would spend his evenings working to convince Temper just how complete, pure and perfect a woman she truly was.

The next afternoon, with her husband away at his Parliamentary duties, Temper was reading in her chamber when Overton came up to inform her that Lady Sayleford awaited her in the drawing room below.

Marvelling at the anomaly of that lady calling on her not once, but twice, she quickly put her book away and walked down.

Was she calling to see if Temper had followed her advice about treating her godson gently? Especially since his response to her shocking revelations, Temper couldn't imagine according him anything but gratitude, awe and reverence. In a world where gentlemen could conduct themselves as they chose, but women who didn't meet an inflexible standard for purity were condemned, she couldn't think of another man who would have treated her with such compassion.

Perhaps…perhaps he really did love her.

Certainly, there could be no greater love than attempting to understand the torment she'd suffered after the attack and pledging to do whatever he could to help her finally recover.

And though he'd said he didn't know how he *could* help—he already had. Just knowing she no longer carried alone the consequences of those terrible events eased the tightness that had sat like a boulder in her chest for the last seven years.

Perhaps some day, with Giff to lead her, she might even be able to contemplate the complete union between a man and a woman with something other than revulsion.

Right now, it was enough to know he *knew* and had comforted her, rather than rejected her.

Walking into the parlour, she made Lady Sayleford a deep curtsy. 'What's this, another visit? More deference to a lady who is your senior?' she teased. 'Although Giff tells me I shall not legally be Lady Fensworth until after he's summoned to appear before the Lords.'

'A mere formality,' Lady Sayleford replied.

'To what do I owe the honour of your visit?'

'I'd heard you had both returned to London and that Gifford meant to continue his work in the Commons for as long as he is permitted. I hear he's been learning all he needed to know about the running of the estate—a task for which, I understand, you provided considerable assistance. Thank you for that.'

'You are most welcome. I can't imagine why his father excluded him from the running of it for so many years. He's more than worthy and capable of his family's trust and admiration!'

She halted, near tears as she remembered his compassion and understanding yesterday. And thanked heaven that there was *one* secret in London Lady Sayleford didn't know.

'I'm glad to see you agree with my assessment of his worth. And perhaps are coming to believe you might be the right wife for him after all?'

'I don't know about that yet,' Temper replied with a rueful smile. 'But I am trying.'

Lady Sayleford nodded. 'Good. I imagine, with your sister's husband beginning a trading venture that rendered rather superfluous your plans to travel the world acquiring treasures for your father, you might be feeling as if you've... lost your purpose. I'd like to challenge you to become more involved and knowledgeable about your husband's. To that end, I've brought you a copy of the "Report of the Select Committee on Factory Children's Labour", based on testimony collected by Michael Sadler's Parliamentary committee last year. Though its publication this January was greeted by great public outcry, some in government argued the report was too one-sided and inflammatory. Which is why Gifford and his committee are now conducting further investigations. I thought you would find it...illuminating.'

She held out the heavy volume, which Temper accepted. 'Thank you! I'm sure I shall. Can I offer you tea?'

'No, thank you. I'll leave you to read the report—and think about ways you might help Gifford advance his cause in the short time he'll have before he must take his place in the Lords.'

'I will certainly do so.'

'That's all I ask. Well, I shall leave you to it.' As she walked out, Lady Sayleford paused, her surprisingly fond gaze fixed on Temper's face. 'I can't think of anything that would delight me more than seeing dear Gifford happy. I shall hope for you both to regain your rightful places—together.' After giving Temper's cheek a gentle pat, she walked out.

Temper watched her disappear, once again having to take a deep, shuddering breath to force back tears. Gaining Lady Sayleford's affection as well as her approval was a boon she'd never expected.

Now to follow her good advice. Hefting the heavy report, she headed back up to her bedchamber.

Hours later, Temper awakened from a light doze to see the candle on the table beside her had burned low—and to hear Giff's distinctive step in the hallway outside her bedchamber. When he walked past to his own door, she jumped up and went to open the one between their adjoining chambers.

'Temper!' he said in surprise, halting on the threshold. 'What are you doing up so late? Is something wrong?'

'Not with me, but certainly within our nation.'

He came to her and she held her breath. Contradictory as it seemed, given the way she had run from him in Fensworth, his nearness now seemed to spark a response in every nerve, more intense than ever—despite the fact that her reluctance to pursue that attraction to its logical end had not abated.

Perhaps it was knowing that *he* knew the truth about her, and would not press her into any intimacy she did not want, that made her so acutely conscious of him—and unafraid to be aroused by him.

Instead of the kiss she expected, however, he merely brushed his lips against her cheek. Conscious of an illogical disappointment, she held up the Factory Commission Report.

'Lady Sayleford lent me this, wanting me to understand more of the work you're doing. I've just finished reading the whole document, and am shocked and appalled! I know it's late and you must be tired, but could you take a few moments to tell me what your new committee is discovering? Are conditions truly as bad as those detailed in this report?'

'Too tired to discuss my great passion? Other than you, of course,' he added with a smile. 'Of course not.'

'Have you dined?' She followed him to the sofa in the small sitting area shared by the two rooms. 'I wouldn't rouse Overton, but I could rustle about in the kitchen and find you something.'

'Yes, we dined before we returned to London,' he confirmed, placing his lighted candle on the table. 'I'll just pour myself a whisky. Would you like one?'

'Not this time,' she replied, taking a seat. 'So, what has your committee found? I understand Sadler tried unsuccessfully to push through a bill in the last session, based on the evidence in this report. Do you think you will have any more success in this session?'

Bringing his drink with him to the sofa, he took a seat beside her, close enough to cause another delightful shiver to ripple through her. 'Although the current commission thinks some of the claims of the Sadler report to be exaggerated, there is plenty of evidence to confirm many of the abuses it detailed. We expect shortly to finish gathering testimony and a bill has already been drafted.'

'I'm so glad to hear it. Lady Sayleford seemed to think there might be something I could do to help, although I cannot imagine what.'

'If you truly are interested, Lady Maggie, Lyndlington's wife, has a Ladies' Committee that is working with us. Writing letters to newspapers, to owners of mills who are opposing legislation, calling upon their sense of compassion towards the weakest and most powerless among us, the children. Not to mention, pointing out the practical fact that undernourished and fatigued workers will produce an inferior product, the sale of which would eventually damage the factory's reputation and decrease demand for its products.'

'Yes, I can imagine that argument being more effective,' Temper said drily. 'I will send Lady Lyndlington a note tomorrow, asking if I might join her at their next meeting.'

'She would like that,' Giff said, downing the rest of his whisky. 'Did you wait up just to discuss this with me?' At her nod, he said, 'Then I'd better let you get some sleep.'

'I'll bid you goodnight, then.'

Before she could stand, she caught his eyes on her and froze. She felt his gaze, almost as palpable as a touch, travel slowly from her face down her neck to the swell of her breasts. Though he said nothing, she was intensely aware that she sat beside him clad just in a fine linen robe over an even thinner night rail.

She sucked in a breath, half-alarmed, half-eager, as he reached towards her. But he touched only her lips, slowly outlining them with a single fingertip, the pressure almost imperceptible. His gaze holding her mesmerised, he drew his hand back, kissed the fingertip, then brought it back once again to her lips, slightly moistened by its contact with his mouth.

Her breathing growing uneven, she remembered the softness of that mouth, the feel of his tongue against hers, licking, teasing. Heat began to spiral in her belly, while a skittering of sensation sparked below. Seemingly of their own accord, her lips parted.

She waited breathlessly, ready for him to place his mouth where his finger had been—tracing her lips, his tongue delving inside to suckle and caress.

Instead, he kissed her forehead and straightened. 'Goodnight, my sweet wife.'

With that, he walked back to his bedchamber and closed the adjoining door.

Leaving her sitting alone on the sofa, her pulse racing, *need* spiralling in her belly—and not sure whether to be indignant or relieved.

Chapter Twenty-Two

A week later, knowing the session would run late, Giff left Parliament in mid-afternoon, wanting to have tea with his lovely wife.

Better to see her during the day, in the near-public space of a parlour where at any time they might be interrupted, helping him keep a damper on his ardour.

Though Temper was responding to him more and more freely, he still tried not to return to his bedchamber until very late, when the promptings of conscience reined in his desire. It wasn't fair to try to lure her into the intimacy he craved when she was too drowsy to be fully aware of what she was doing.

For when—and he was increasingly confident it would be *when*—he finally made love to her, he wanted their union to be a conscious choice, made while she was in full possession of her faculties. Not something drifted into in a sleepy haze that she might regret in the cold light of dawn.

The hackney dropped him off and he ran up the steps,

telling Overton when the butler admitted him to ask Temper to join him in the small back sitting room and send in tea. He went there to wait for her, setting his gift on the table, filled with the delighted anticipation of seeing her.

A few minutes later, she rushed in, cheeks flushed. 'Giff!' she cried, coming over to give him her hands to kiss. 'What a delightful surprise! Did the session end early?'

'No, it's still going on. Since I doubt we'll break before midnight, I decided to sneak away for tea. And I wanted to give you this. I thought Lady Sayleford might have a copy and she did. She said you might keep this one, with her good wishes.'

'What is it?' she asked, picking up the package.

'Don't open it yet—let's have our tea. I only have time for one cup and then I'll leave you to it.'

So she put it back down and poured him the tea Overton brought in. While he quickly sipped his cup, she asked him about the progress being made in committee, adding in titbits of the responses they'd received from the letters she had been helping to write for the Ladies' Committee she'd recently joined.

A short time later, putting down his cup, Giff said, 'Having been a good little girl, waiting so patiently, you may now open your present.'

Giving him a look, she slapped his hand before picking up the package. Laughing, he watched expectantly as she removed the wrappings.

'*The Letters and Works of Lady Mary Wortley Montagu,*' Temper read from the title page of the leather-bound volume. 'You thought I would appreciate them?'

'Not the poetry, particularly, but the letters from Turkey. Her husband was the British ambassador to the Ottoman court in Istanbul. Lady Mary made extensive visits to Ottoman women, whose dress, habits and traditions are vividly described—even a trip to a *hammam*! When Lady Sayleford told me about the book, I immediately thought you would find it interesting.'

Her eyes shining with delight, she looked back up at him. 'I shall enjoy it indeed. Thank you, Giff! You are so good to me and I don't deserve it!'

'On the contrary, you deserve all the pampering in the world. And I mean to see you get it.'

And then as he waited hopefully, she set down the book and came over to embrace him. Catching his breath on a sigh, he held her close, drinking in the scent and feel of her, knowing if she wanted the moon, he would try to drag it out of the sky.

Then, surprising him, she tipped his chin down and kissed him.

Not just a quick brush of the lips, either. She licked and suckled his lips, then swept her tongue within and slowly, thoroughly, explored his mouth.

Sweat breaking out on his brow, he made himself pull away.

'It's not fair to kiss a man like that when he has to go back to work,' he chided.

'Just a taste to remind you why you should not arrive home quite so late,' she responded tartly.

Laughing, he walked away, stopping to blow her a kiss from the doorway. 'I hope that's a promise.'

'Come home early and you'll find out,' she shot back.

Ah, yes, he thought, as he took his hat and cane from Overton, more encouraged than ever. He just needed to be patient a little longer and everything he hoped for would be his.

Well, maybe not quite *everything*. But a man would have to be unreasonable to possess the fire and loveliness of Temper and feel himself lacking, because she had not pledged her love, as well.

Once all the barriers she'd erected to protect herself from hurt and shame finally came down, then there would be time enough to try to win her heart as well as her body.

Later that evening, Temper reclined on the sofa in their shared sitting room, fascinated by the accounts in the book Giff had brought her. He really was too good to her, she thought, closing the volume.

Several times over the past week he'd surprised her with small treats or presents he thought she'd enjoy. In the late evenings, when he finally returned from his Parliament sessions, he'd wake her, giving her the sweetest of goodnight kisses that always left her wanting more…though she'd not yet worked up the courage to press him for it.

And she didn't intend to, not until she was certain she would not suffer a recurrence of the panic that had sent her running from Fensworth.

Of course, she thought with a sigh, she couldn't decide she was ready for more if he persisted in coming to her so late she was only half-awake.

Opening her book again, she had turned to the next chapter when she heard footsteps approaching down the hall—Giff's.

Perhaps he was going to take her up on her challenge that he come home early—and see what happened.

She wasn't sure just how far she dared go, but she meant

to push herself to the limits. He'd been so patient with her and he'd waited long enough for his reward.

She heard his quick knock and smiled. Let the encounter begin!

'Hello, Giff,' she said as he entered.

He made her an elaborate bow. 'Here I am. Early, as requested.' Indicating the book on the table beside her, he said, 'Have you been reading all this time?'

'Yes, practically from the moment you left me.'

'Ah, then you must be in need of this.'

Stopping behind where she sat on the sofa, he reached down to rub her neck, then slowly massaged her shoulders, until she almost purred with pleasure. While his ministering fingers did effectively ease the ache in her neck, as they soothed, they also stirred back to glowing sparks the embers of the sensual awareness always glimmering between them.

Wanting, needing his kiss, she leaned back, pulling his head down. Finding the odd upside-down contact stimulating, but not nearly close enough, she broke the kiss and patted the sofa beside her. 'Sit here, please. So I may kiss you properly.'

Chuckling, he complied. 'I was hoping you might kiss me *improperly.*'

He took her in his arms and kissed her again. As his tongue probed at her lips, teasing, not demanding, she opened to him, the shock of sensation making her gasp as his tongue found hers and tangled with it.

Desire intensified as he stroked. Need spiralling through her, wanting to touch more of him, she tugged at his cravat and pulled it off, helped him shrug out of his jacket. She found the bare skin at the V of his shirt, rubbing him with her fingertips as he kissed her harder, deeper.

Slowly he moved his hands lower, from her shoulders down over to the swell of her breasts. This time, rather than stiffening, she moaned and leaned into him as he gently massaged and caressed. And then, as she gasped from the sheer mindless delight of it, he bent and took one rigid nipple in his mouth, suckling her through the thin linen of her night-rail.

She clutched his shoulders, pulling him closer, wanting more, so awash with desire that she whimpered in protest when he moved his mouth away, only to gasp with renewed delight as he moved his mouth to her other breast. Wanting to feel him against the length of her body, she pushed him back until he was half-reclining and slid quickly over him, not wanting to lose the delicious feel of his mouth at her breast—until she encountered the hardness of his erection at her belly.

Shock and a deep, primitive dread made her freeze, desire abruptly dissipating as she shifted away from him. Then, telling herself she *would* master this, she moved her hand down, determined to touch that which she most feared.

He caught her wrist. 'Enough for tonight,' he said, his voice strained.

'But you want me to touch you. Don't you?'

'I do. But *you* don't really want it. I could sense the change in you, from desire to…caution. I won't have you come to me because you think you should. Only when you are truly ready.'

Moving away from her, he kissed her forehead. 'Goodnight, my sweet wife.'

Once again, partly relieved, mostly frustrated, Temper watched her husband walk into his bedchamber, shutting the door behind him.

She rose and took a step towards that closed door. Then hesitated. How wonderful it would be to wake and find herself in his arms. And yet...

Recalling the feel of his hardness against her, she took a shaky breath. Much as she longed to give him everything he desired, she wasn't sure she was quite ready. Yet.

The thought of attempting, and failing, made her shudder. At some point, Giff would have to tire of being aroused, teased and ultimately refused. Swiping away tears of frustration and disappointment, she walked back to her solitary bed.

Two nights later, Temper sat up again, book on her lap, waiting to hear her husband's step approaching down the hallway. So nervous and undecided, she'd had the book open for hours, but read barely a page.

A remark made by Miss Henley when she'd brought her friend to meet the other members of the Ladies' Committee at Lady Maggie's house this morning had resonated in her brain all day. After discussing tentative plans for the group to continue after the anticipated passage of the Factory Act, Emma had gazed around at the group, a wistful envy in her eyes.

'How lucky you all are,' she'd said quietly. 'Each of you having found good men to protect and guard you, until that time women have enough legal rights to protect and guard themselves.'

Agreeing with her compliment, they had all assured her that a lady as intelligent and accomplished as she was would surely find such a man for herself, as they had—all through unlikely paths.

None quite so unlikely as hers, Temper thought. But she

certainly had found a man willing to guard and protect her. Whom she trusted absolutely never to hurt her.

Wasn't it time to trust that, with him, she might move past the fear that still bound her?

She'd almost managed it two nights ago. But then, the memory of that choking sense of suffocation, the pressure, the pain, had been vivid enough to cause the hesitation that had made Giff leave her.

It wouldn't be like that with her husband, she knew. 'A mutual giving and taking of pleasure,' he'd described it. How she wanted that!

Did she want it enough to brave breaking though the barrier?

She remembered how she'd felt after returning that afternoon long ago. How she'd soaked and soaked in the bath and never felt clean.

But Giff knew every degrading thing that had happened to her—and he hadn't looked at her that way. She'd braced herself for him to think less of her, to turn from her in disgust. Instead, he'd held her while she wept and told her he thought her brave and strong.

Maybe…if she were able to face the ugliness, with him to encourage her, she'd be able to let it all go, or most of it. The anguish, disgust and shame. Let it go and feel whole again, clean again, at last.

She'd been ready to face tigers, bandits and disease in pursuit of the exotic and extraordinary in faraway lands. How could she not have enough courage to cast off the shackles of the past and seize the extraordinary she'd found with Giff, right here and now?

As she sat there, considering that possibility, the dread slowly loosened its hold over her. As if the prison of horrific memories in which she'd been locked for so long was finally opening, she felt a sense of lightness emerging. Freeing her from fear. Freeing her to *feel*.

And not just to feel the physical and sensual. With the darkness that had overshadowed her life for so long lessening, she was at last able to see the truth that had been hidden in her heart. The depth and strength of the emotion Giff inspired in her.

The *love* he inspired in her.

She laughed, shaking her head in wonderment. She had probably been in love with Giff for years, blinded to that fact by her dread of physical intimacy and her determination to avoid any entanglement that might push her into it. Realising she didn't just like and admire and respect Giff, she *loved* him, filled her with renewed determination to brave the ugly memories and triumph over them.

Because she wanted to be his, body, heart and soul.

And so she would be, she vowed. Tonight.

So, late that night, abandoning her book, Temper went to her dressing table and dabbed a touch of her favourite jasmine perfume at her throat and wrists. Shrugging off her robe, she pulled the linen night rail over her head and tossed it aside, then slipped back into the robe alone.

Pouring herself a glass of wine for courage, she settled back on the sofa to wait.

Fortunately, before she went mad from the constant veering from anxiety to heated anticipation and back, she heard the footsteps she'd been waiting for. Her mouth going dry, as her husband walked into the bedroom, she gave him a tremulous smile.

'Waiting up for me again?' he asked. 'How fetching you

look,' After crossing the room, he bent down to kiss her forehead and halted.

'And how delicious you smell! I'd better give you a good-night kiss quickly and go, before I'm tempted to devour you.'

She caught his hand. 'Maybe I'm ready to be devoured.'

He froze, and she felt the pulse at his wrist jump.

'Let me show you,' she said.

Rising from the couch, she led him into her bedchamber and pushed him to sit on the bed.

She leaned over and kissed him, opening her mouth to him, then pursuing his tongue with her own. That giddy, now familiar heat began its slow spiral in her belly as he sucked and caressed her tongue.

Murmuring, she moved closer, wanting his hands on her—the hands that had created such wonderful eddies of feeling when he rubbed her back and neck and breasts the other night. But, to her frustration, he made no move to touch her or pull her against him.

Perhaps he wasn't yet sure she wouldn't end up denying him again. Well, time to be more convincing.

She stepped away and, while he watched, let the robe slide from her shoulders. Encouraged by his sharp inhale of breath, his hands clutching at the bed linens, she stood steadily under his gaze, letting him inspect her naked body in the candlelight.

Then, when he still made no move towards her, she stepped back to the bed, unknotted his cravat and pulled it off him. Tugged him out of jacket, then waistcoat, then stripped the shirt over his head. Sighing, she paused to admire his broad shoulders and strong chest.

After bending to pull off his boots, she urged him to

stand and plucked open his trouser buttons, the fabric pulled taut by his erection. He let her tug the garment down, stepping out of it once she got it to his ankles.

And then stood motionless as she sucked in a breath, getting her first good look at his arousal. He didn't try to cover himself, letting her stare at his fully erect manhood—while still making no attempt either to pull her against him or on to the bed.

'Don't you want to…do something?' she finally whispered.

'And wake myself from the most wonderful erotic dream I've ever had?' he said. 'Not a chance.'

'Then I suppose your erotic dream woman will have to take matters into her own hands.'

'Oh, I very much hope so.'

He let her urge him down against the pillows, but when she went to straddle him, he stopped her.

'Not yet,' he murmured. 'I've been waiting so very long, I won't last if you start that and I want so much to touch you. Will you let me?'

She nodded and he helped her to lie down in his place.

For an instant, the panic nibbled at her—could she bear it, to lie under him, crushed by his weight?

But she forced it out of mind. This was Giff, her darling Giff, and he would never hurt her.

Following his direction, she stretched out on the bed, acutely conscious of the heat of his body, so magnificently naked and so close to hers. But he didn't lie down atop her in that position of pain and domination she'd so long feared. Instead, he stretched out beside her.

Leaning over her, he kissed her, long and slow and sweet, until the last vestiges of resistance she hadn't quite been able to master dissolved in the liquid heat of his mouth. She arched her back, eager to feel the caress of his clever fingers over and around her breasts, and he responded, both hands going to circle and lift, both thumbs to tease at the nipples. And then, creating a sensation so intense it made her dizzy, he took one nipple in his mouth.

She could hardly bear the wonder of it, his warm wet tongue against aching hardness of her naked flesh. She could feel moisture gathering between her thighs, a pressure building there that had nothing to do with coercion or pain.

He moved down to explore her wetness, moving his fingers over the tender flesh, exerting only exquisite light pressure with his skilled touch, over, around and then, to her amazement, delving inside, sparking even more acute delight.

Only then did he raise himself over her. He withdrew his finger and she felt something thicker, blunter, nudging at the entrance of her body. But there was no unpleasantness, only a marvellous slow glide of his flesh into hers that instinctively made her arch to take him deeper.

It was incredible. It was marvellous. Quickly she learned his rhythm, arching up as he withdrew, feeling the wonderful liquid fullness as he pushed down again, driving himself deeper. The friction of it created a tension within her that seemed to build and build as they moved faster, her body straining to reach some release as the sensations grew more and more intense, until she felt she must shatter.

And then she did, one final thrust launching her into a starburst of pleasure so intense, it paralysed all thought and movement. She heard a cry and knew it must have been ripped from her own throat.

As she sank backwards, gasping for breath, the sensation slowly subsiding, she dimly noted that Giff, too, had gone rigid, crying out, filling her with one last thrust. She wrapped her legs around him, wanting to hold him there for ever in the centre of those powerful vibrations.

But she must have dozed, for when she came to herself, she discovered Giff lying against the pillows, one arm around her, snuggling her against his chest.

'That was marvellous,' she murmured and heard the rumble of his chuckle against her ear.

'I'm so glad to hear that, sweeting, for I'm afraid at the last, I lost any semblance of control.'

'You deserved to. I made you wait long enough for your pleasure.'

He leaned up on one elbow to look down at her, his expression grave.

'Was it long enough? You don't have any regrets?'

'Only that I waited so long. I've never felt so...cherished.'

'And I do cherish you, my darling wife. I admit, I wasn't initially enthusiastic about wedding you, but you turned out to be everything I needed. Everything I could possibly desire.' He laughed. 'I ought to send Miss Avery flowers. Without her ill-intentioned intervention, I might never have claimed the woman I love beyond everything.'

Her eyes widening, she looked up at him. 'You really do love me?' she asked delightedly. 'Lady Sayleford told me you did, but I hardly dared believe it.'

'Did she? When?'

'Oh, weeks ago, before we left for Fensworth. Though she said you didn't know it yet.'

'Wise lady,' he said ruefully. 'She truly does know everything—even before we do.'

'I must have loved you for years, but been too…compromised by what I'd gone through to be able see it.'

It was his turn to look surprised. 'Wait, now. What did you just say?'

'I love you, Gifford Newell.'

He stared down at her, the shock and surprise on his face gradually giving way to a huge grin. 'Say it again.'

'I love you.'

'Again.'

Laughing, she repeated, 'Love you…love you…love you', interspersing each avowal with a kiss. 'If I'm whole now, or almost whole, it's because you believed I was. You've replaced the fears I could not face with memories that are only joyous and beautiful.'

'And what of your dream to travel? Will you give me this bliss, and then leave me?'

'Reading the Sadler report convinced me there are places in England in need as foreign to me as anything beyond our shores. I would do all I could to help you make Fensworth the showplace it should be and bring progress to those needy areas. Now, while you work in the Commons, and after you take your seat in the Lords. I'll even try to become more… diplomatic, so I may preside over your dinner parties.'

'Temper, not saying what she thinks?' he teased.

'I can be discreet. Occasionally. I'll try to be whatever you need me to be.'

'Then be yourself. The child who once amused me, the woman who challenges me, the wife I love. Once the reform legislation passes and I take that seat in the Lords, I could apply to the Foreign Office for an appointment as an ambassador somewhere exotic. Give you chance to write your own "Turkish Letters". I'd like to give you everything you want.'

'Being with you *is* everything I want. Except…this loving business. All my life I've heard how it makes poets write rhapsodies and people do foolish things. But maybe they are mistaken. Maybe it wasn't quite as wonderful as I thought it was.'

Grinning at the sudden dismay on his face, she said demurely, 'I think you must show me again.'

'Devil,' he said, nibbling her shoulder. 'Now and for ever, gladly.'

* * * * *

Keep reading for an excerpt of
The Return Of Her Billionaire Husband
by Melanie Milburne.
Find it in the
Reunion In Marriage: Anniversary Collection anthology,
out now!

CHAPTER ONE

THERE WAS A weird kind of irony in arriving as maid of honour for your best friend's destination wedding with divorce papers in your hand luggage. But the one thing Juliette was determined *not* to do was spoil Lucy and Damon's wedding day. Well, not just a wedding day but a wedding weekend. On Corfu.

And her estranged husband was the best man.

Juliette sucked in a prickly breath and tried not to think of the last time she'd stood at an altar next to Joe Allegranza. Tried not to think of the blink-and-you'd-miss-it ceremony in the English village church in front of a handful of witnesses with her pregnancy not quite hidden by her mother's vintage wedding dress. The dress that scratched and itched the whole time she was wearing it. She tried not to think of the expression of disappointment on her parents' faces that their only daughter was marrying a virtual stranger after she got pregnant on a one-night stand.

Tried not to think of her baby—the baby girl who didn't even get to take a single breath…

Juliette stepped down out of the shuttle bus and walked into the foyer of the luxury private villa at Barbati Beach. The scarily efficient wedding planner, Celeste Petrakis, had organised for the wedding party to stay at the villa so the rehearsal and other activities planned would run as smoothly and seamlessly as possible. Juliette had thought about asking to stay at another hotel close by, as she didn't fancy running into Joe more than was strictly necessary. Socialising politely with her soon-to-be ex-husband over breakfast, lunch and dinner wasn't exactly in her skill set. But the thought of upsetting the drill sergeant wedding planner's meticulous arrangements was as intimidating as a cadet saying they weren't going to march in line on parade. Juliette had even at one point thought of declining the honour of being Lucy's maid of honour, but that would have made everyone think she wasn't over Joe.

She most definitely was over him—hence the divorce papers.

'Welcome.' The smartly dressed female attendant greeted her with a smile bright enough for an orthodontist's website homepage. 'May I have your name, please?'

'Bancroft…erm… I mean Allegranza.' Juliette wished now she had got around to officially changing back to her maiden name. Why hadn't she? She still didn't understand why she'd taken Joe's name in the first place. Their marriage hadn't come about the normal way. No dating, no courtship, no professions of love. No romantic proposal. Just one night of bed-wrecking sex and then goodbye and thanks for the memories. They hadn't even exchanged phone numbers. By the time she'd worked up the courage to track Joe down and tell him she was pregnant, he had insisted—not proposed, *insisted*—on marrying her soon after. They'd only lived together as man and wife for a total of three months. Three months of marriage and then it was over— just like her pregnancy.

But once Joe signed the papers and the divorce was finalised she would be free of his name. Free to move on with her life, because being stuck in limbo sucked. How would she ever be able to get through the grieving process without drawing a thick black line through her time with Joe?

She. Had. To. Move. On.

The receptionist click-clacked on the computer keyboard. 'Here it is. J Allegranza. And the J is for…?'

'Juliette.' She wondered if it would be pedantic to insist on being addressed by her maiden name while she was here but decided against saying anything. But why hadn't Lucy told the wedding planner she and Joe were separated? Or were Lucy and Damon still hoping she and Joe would somehow miraculously get back together?

Not flipping likely. They shouldn't have been together in the first place.

If her childhood sweetheart, Harvey, hadn't taken it upon himself to dump her instead of proposing to her, like she'd been expecting, none of this would have happened. Rebound sex with a handsome stranger. Who would have thought she had it in her? She wasn't the type of girl to talk to staggeringly gorgeous men in swanky London bars. She wasn't a one-night stand girl. But that night she had turned into someone else. Joe's touch had turned her into someone else.

Note to self. Do not think about Joe's touch. Do. Not. Go. There.

There was not going to be a fairy tale ending to their short-lived relationship. How could there be when the only reason for their marriage was now gone?

Dead. Buried. Lying, sleeping for ever, in a tiny white coffin in a graveyard in England.

'Your suite is ready for you now,' the receptionist said. 'Spiros will bring your luggage in from the shuttle.'

'Thank you.'

The receptionist handed her a swipe key and directed her to the lifts across the hectare of marble floor. 'Your suite is on the third floor. Celeste, the wedding planner, will meet with the bridal party for drinks on the terrace, to go through the rehearsal and wedding timetable, promptly at six this evening.'

'Got it.' Juliette gave a polite movement of her lips, which was about as close to a smile as she got to these days. She took the key, hitched her tote bag over her shoulder and made her way over to the lifts. The divorce papers were poking out of the top of her bag, a reminder of her two-birds-one-stone mission. In seven days, this chapter of her life would finally be over.

And she would never have to think about Joe Allegranza again.

There was only one thing Joe Allegranza hated more than weddings and that was funerals. Oh, and birthdays—his, in particular. But he could hardly turn down being his mate's best man, even if it meant coming face to face with his estranged wife, Juliette.

His wife…

Hard to believe how those two words still had the power to gouge a hole in his chest—a raw gaping hole that nothing could fill. He couldn't think of her without feeling he had failed in every way possible. How had he let his life spin out of control so badly? He, who had written the handbook on control.

Mostly, he could block her from his mind. Mostly. He binged on work like some people did on alcohol or food. He had built his global engineering career on his ability to fix structural failures. To forensically analyse broken bridges and buildings, and yet he was unable to do anything to repair his broken marriage. Fifteen months of separation and he hadn't moved forward with his life. *Couldn't* move on with his life. It was as if an invisible wall had sprung up in front of him, keeping him cordoned off, blocked, imprisoned.

He glanced at the wedding ring still on his finger. He could easily have taken it off and locked it in the safe, along with Juliette's rings that she had left behind.

But he hadn't.

He wasn't entirely sure why. Divorce was something he rigorously avoided thinking about. Reconciliation was equally as daunting. He was stuck in no man's land.

Joe walked into the reception area of the luxury villa where the wedding party were staying and was greeted by a smiling attendant. 'Welcome. May I have your name, please?'

'Joe Allegranza.' He removed his sunglasses and slipped them into his breast pocket. 'The wedding planner made the booking.'

The reception attendant peered a little closer at the screen, scrolling through the bookings with her computer mouse. 'Ah, yes, I see it now. I missed it because I thought the booking was only for one person.' She flashed him a smile so bright he wished he hadn't taken his sunglasses off. 'Your wife has already checked in. She arrived an hour ago.'

His wife. A weight pressed down on Joe's chest and his next breath was razor-edged. *His failure* could just as easily be substituted for those words. Hadn't the wedding planner got the memo about his and Juliette's separation?

The thought slipped through a crack in his mind like a fissure in bedrock, threatening to destabilise his determination to keep his distance.

A weekend sharing a suite with his estranged wife.

For a second or two he considered pointing out the booking error but he let his mind wander first... He could see Juliette again. In private. In person. He would be able to talk to her face to face instead of having her refuse to answer his calls or delete or block his texts or emails. She hadn't responded to a single missive. Not one. The last time he'd called her to tell her about the fundraising he'd organised for a stillbirth foundation on their behalf, the service provider informed him the number was no longer connected. Meaning Juliette was no longer connected *to him*.

His conscience woke up and prodded him with a jabbing finger.

What the hell are you thinking? Haven't you done enough damage?

It was crazy enough coming here for the wedding, much less spend time with Juliette—especially alone. He had ruined her life, just like he had done to his mother. Was there a curse on him when it came to his relationships? A curse that had been placed on him the day he was born. The same day his mother had died. His birthday: his mother's death day.

If that wasn't a curse, then what the freaking hell was?

Joe cleared his throat. 'There must be some mistake. My... er...wife and I are no longer together. We're...separated.' He hated saying the ugly word. Hated admitting his failure. Hated knowing it was largely his fault his wife had walked out on their marriage.

The receptionist's eyebrows drew together in a frown. 'Oh, no—I mean, that's terrible about your separation. Also, about the booking, because we don't have any other rooms and—'

'It's fine,' Joe said, pulling out his phone. 'I'll book in somewhere else.' He began to scroll through the options on his server. There had to be plenty of hotels available. He would sleep on a park bench or on the beach if he had to. No way was he sharing a room with his estranged wife. Too dangerous. Too tempting. Too everything.

'I don't think you'll find too much available,' the receptionist said. 'There's several weddings on this part of Corfu this weekend and, besides, Celeste really wanted everyone to stay close by to give the wedding a family feel. She'll be gutted to find out she's made a mistake with your booking. She's worked so hard to make her cousin's wedding truly special.'

Joe's memory snagged on something Damon had told him about his young cousin, Celeste. How this wedding planning gig for her older cousin was her first foray into the workforce after a long battle with some type of blood cancer. Leukaemia? Non-Hodgkin's? He couldn't remember which, but he didn't want to be the one to rain on Celeste's first parade.

'Okay, so don't tell Celeste until I make sure I can't find accommodation. I'll do a ring around and see what I find.'

He fixed problems, right? That was his speciality—fixing things that no one else could fix.

And he would fix this or die trying.

Joe stepped back out into the sunshine and spent close to an hour getting more and more frustrated when there was no vacancy anywhere. Beads of sweat poured down the back of his neck and between his shoulder blades. He even for a moment considered making an offer to *buy* a property rather than face the alternative of sharing a room with his estranged wife. He certainly had enough money to buy whatever he wanted.

Except happiness.

Except peace of mind.

Except life for his baby girl...

His phone was almost out of charge when he finally conceded defeat. There was nothing available close by or within a reasonable radius. Fate or destiny or a seriously manipulative deity had decided Joe was sharing a room with Juliette.

But maybe it was time to do something about his marriage. Keeping his distance hadn't solved anything. Maybe this was a chance to see if there was anything he could say or do to bring a resolution to their situation. Closure.

Joe walked back into Reception and the young receptionist gave him an I-told-you-so smile. 'No luck?' she said.

'Nope.' Luck and Joe were not close friends. Never had been. Enemies, more like.

'Here's your key.' The receptionist handed it over the counter. 'I hope you enjoy your stay.'

'Thank you.' Joe took the key and made his way to the lift. *Enjoy his stay?* Like that was going to happen. He'd been dreading seeing Juliette again, knowing he was largely responsible for her pain, her sorrow, her devastation. But at least this way, in the privacy of 'their' suite, he would be able to speak to her without an audience. He would say what needed to be said, work out the way forward—if there was a way forward—and then they could both move on with their lives.

BRAND NEW RELEASE

Don't miss the next instalment of the Powder River series by bestselling author B.J. Daniels! For lovers of sexy Western heroes, small-town settings and suspense with your romance.

RIVER JUSTICE

—R—

A POWDER RIVER NOVEL

PERFECT FOR FANS OF YELLOWSTONE!

Previous titles in the Powder River series

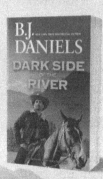

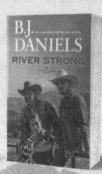

September 2023

January 2024

In-store and online August 2024

MILLS & BOON

millsandboon.com.au

Subscribe and fall in love with a Mills & Boon series today!

You'll be among the first to read stories delivered to your door monthly and enjoy great savings.

WE SIMPLY LOVE ROMANCE

MILLS & BOON